THE INCORRIGIBLES

THE
INCORRIGIBLES

A NOVEL

MEREDITH JAEGER

DUTTON

DUTTON

An imprint of Penguin Random House LLC
penguinrandomhouse.com

Copyright © 2024 by Meredith Jaeger

LIBRARY OF CONGRESS CATALOGING-IN-PUBLICATION DATA
Names: Jaeger, Meredith, author.
Title: The incorrigibles : a novel / Meredith Jaeger.
Description: New York : Dutton, 2024.
Identifiers: LCCN 2023040180 (print) |
LCCN 2023040181 (ebook) | ISBN 9780593473757 (paperback) |
ISBN 9780593473764 (ebook)
Subjects: LCSH: Women—Fiction. |
Resilience (Personality trait)—Fiction. | LCGFT: Novels.
Classification: LCC PS3610.A35697 I53 2024 (print) |
LCC PS3610.A35697 (ebook) | DDC 813/.6—dc23/eng/20230915
LC record available at https://lccn.loc.gov/2023040180
LC ebook record available at https://lccn.loc.gov/2023040181

Printed in the United States of America
1st Printing

For my husband, Will.

If it's a boring adventure, I don't want it!

—Monkey D. Luffy

THE INCORRIGIBLES

PART ONE

———◆·◆———

It may be that the bump of deviltry and the general inclination towards lawlessness is stronger in the female.
—*The San Francisco Examiner,* August 26, 1888

For every betrayed woman, there is always the betrayer, man. —Susan B. Anthony

1

Judy

San Francisco, 1972

I dress in corduroys and a collared blouse, pulling a crocheted sweater vest over my head, then I grab my résumé from the typewriter. A glint of gold on my ring finger catches the light, and a lump rises in my throat. I'm still not ready to take off my wedding band. Instead, I finish the dregs of my coffee and set the chipped mug down in the sink.

This dingy one-bedroom flat, south of Market Street, over-looking a row of weathered clapboard apartment buildings, doesn't feel like home. My real home is in Sacramento, a ranch house on a suburban tree-lined cul-de-sac. But if I think too much about it, I might cry. I try reminding myself that today is the first time in years I'm doing something for me.

After locking the apartment, I make my way down a flight of creaky, narrow stairs, wondering about the other tenants in my four-unit Edwardian building. I've barely introduced my-self, but I've seen a Black woman and her son, along with an old Filipino man. In the lobby, a lone bulb hangs overhead, illuminating a cork message board.

My eyes drift over the flyers offering discounts at a local supermarket, automotive repair, and social services. Bold words on yellow paper announce: TOOR: WE WON'T MOVE. I have no idea what the acronym means, another reminder that I'm an outsider, a young housewife masquerading as a city dweller, as if I belong here.

Walking down Natoma Street, I look up at laundry flapping on clotheslines strung along the rickety back stairs of the apartment buildings. The narrow street, more of an alley, really, is strewn with trash, but this was the cheapest rent I could find. Besides, it's sunny, flat, and centrally located. I turn right, walking past auto shops, a few greasy-spoon diners, and brick residential hotels, where old white men play dominoes outside.

The sound of a jackhammer pierces the air. There's a construction site a few blocks away, over on Fourth Street between Mission and Folsom, the empty lots cutting across blocks like a scar. I don't know what kind of new development the city is planning, but the demolished hotels give the area a postapocalyptic feeling, like Berlin after the Second World War. The only building left standing is a brick Gothic-style Roman Catholic church—Saint Patrick's.

When I reach Sixth and Howard, I pause in front of a black awning that reads GLASS PHOTO in white letters. For a week now, I've walked past the HELP WANTED sign in the window, trying to work up the courage to step inside. I hear Tony's voice in my head.

You don't need to work, Judy. You're my wife.

But Tony isn't here to stop me.

Taking a deep breath, I push open the door to the photography studio. A middle-aged man with a neat gray beard looks up from behind the counter. He wears wire-frame glasses and a small silver hoop in his left ear. He smiles, and his eyes crinkle at the corners.

"Can I help you?"

My mouth is dry and my palms are sweaty.

"Um, hi. I'm Judy. I'm here to ask about the open position?"

"Oh, wonderful!" He reaches across the counter for my résumé. "I'm Seth Glass, the owner. May I take a look?"

Reluctantly, I hand it to him, my skin prickling with self-doubt.

Seth's eyes narrow as he reads. "I see you worked at a color-processing lab in Berkeley. So you're familiar with developing C-prints?"

My shoulders relax a little. "Yes. I'm actually a photographer myself. I prefer chromogenic prints because I like to shoot in color."

But this statement rings false. I haven't shot anything I'm proud of in years—not since my days as an undergraduate at UC Berkeley. In Sacramento, I lost my focus. I tried photographing the manicured lawns and identical houses, the austere government buildings downtown, but my photographs weren't telling a story.

Seth nods. "We have a number of fine-art photographers as clients, and we hand process film in small batches. Are you familiar with developing black-and-white film?"

"Yes," I say.

I've never forgotten the magic of watching my first image

come slowly to life in the developing tray: an empty field, the golden grass beneath a blue California sky taking on an eerie quality in monochrome. From the moment I first set foot in my high school darkroom, I was captivated by the alchemy transpiring before my eyes.

"I pretty much arranged my life around having access to a darkroom when I was younger, and back then the only photos I processed were black and white."

It's sad to realize how quickly I lost myself. My identity as an aspiring photographer ebbed away, replaced with my identity as Tony's wife.

Seth sets down my résumé and leans against the counter. "Judy, you seem very passionate about photography. So, tell me this . . ." He frowns, his brows drawing together. "Why is there such a large gap on your résumé? No jobs, no local gallery shows of your work?"

My mouth feels dry. It's the question I've been dreading.

"I got married right after I graduated from UC Berkeley and my husband didn't want me to work."

I don't tell him how I fell into the same role as my mother, who smokes Pall Malls while doing the dishes, even though I thought I was a progressive young woman. How I spent my days cooking, cleaning, and ironing my husband's shirts.

"We're separated," I clarify.

As I say the words out loud, my throat tightens. I should be planning a romantic candlelit dinner with Tony for our third wedding anniversary later this month, not living alone in a derelict San Francisco apartment building.

Seth's eyes are kind. "Well, thank goodness for that."

"Right," I exhale.

But the relief is fleeting. Tony will never agree to a divorce. Besides, I'm not even sure that I want one. I'm still hoping he can change.

"Tell me." Seth gestures to the cameras in his display case. "What do you shoot with?"

I recognize a Japanese Olympus Pen-F and a rare Hasselblad 500C. Though they're beautiful instruments, I prefer my view camera.

"Don't laugh." I smile at Seth. "But I use a Gundlach Korona."

He whistles. "Like Ansel Adams used to?"

I nod. "An eight-by-ten."

Seth raises an eyebrow. "You're not one for modern technology?"

I fidget with a hangnail. "I also use a Rolleiflex 2.8 when I want to be able to take a photograph in less than twenty minutes."

He chuckles. "I like you. And I like the fact that you're not afraid to take your time to get the image right. Tell me, who inspires you?"

It's been so long since I've been asked about myself.

Who inspires me? What do I like?

"Dorothea Lange." The answer comes easily. "Her photographs of dust-bowl migrants are stunning. She tells a story while also raising awareness of social issues."

Seth hands my résumé back to me. "Great answer. So, are you ready for my spiel?"

"Sure." I'm desperate for work, but I don't want to seem too eager.

He clears his throat.

"At Glass Photo, we give film negatives the expert attention they deserve. And you seem like someone who pays attention. Do you have any experience with photo conservation?"

My stomach sinks. "No."

He gives me a reassuring look. "That's all right. We don't have many customers who come in for conservation work, but some do. I can teach you how to remove surface dust and correct planar distortion. It's a hobby of mine, collecting old photographs. Mug shots, especially."

"Mug shots?" I raise my eyebrows.

Seth nods. "Many surviving images from the past are of royalty or the very wealthy. I collect mug shots because they give a glimpse into the lives of ordinary people."

"Who happen to be criminals . . ."

He laughs. "Yes."

I nod. "I suppose a mug shot is a form of portrait photography."

"You'd be surprised how stunning some of them are. Here, look—" He reaches for an album, its black cover worn and frayed. "I bought this at a flea market."

I scoot closer to get a better view as he cracks open the old book. In cursive ink, the inside cover is inscribed: *D.A. Higgins, San Francisco, 1890. Property of San Francisco Police Station.* Seth turns the page, revealing a single card with two photos side by side—the first, a man's face in profile; the second, the same man staring straight at the camera, a prisoner number hanging around his neck, his dark eyes boring into mine.

"It's an old mug book," Seth says, turning the page again. "These images and their corresponding notes on the cards were used by police agencies and penal institutions in the late nineteenth and early twentieth centuries."

I look at the mug shots, the corners of the cards peeling, the paper water damaged. There are men of all ages and races, some as young as sixteen, others as old as sixty. There is something captivating about the rawness of these portraits. Reaching out, I brush the edge of the book. "Are these gelatin silver prints?"

"Right on the nose!" Seth winks. "You have a great eye." He nudges the mug book toward me. "Go ahead. Take a look."

I gently leaf through the yellowed pages.

"If you turn the Bertillon card over," Seth says, "the back has more identifying information, like the person's name, their scars, criminal history, aliases . . ."

"Bertillon card?"

"Alphonse Bertillon was a French police officer," Seth says. "His system of identifying criminals by their body measurements was an early form of biometrics."

I frown. "This was before fingerprinting?"

"That's right," Seth says. "He called them portrait parlé."

"A speaking portrait." I smile, my years of high school French coming back to me.

"Exactly."

I turn the page in the mug book again, expecting to find more men. And then I stop, my breath hitching. I'm staring into the haunting eyes of a frightened young woman.

2

Annie

San Francisco, 1890

Annie stood on the corner of Fourth Street and Mission, a block from Saint Patrick's Church. The bells pealed, and she smiled, feeling elegant in her Sunday best. The grueling year she'd spent in San Francisco, working in service for the horrid Mrs. Whittier, was soon to be worth something. Annie hated the word *service*. She came to this country to better herself, and it wasn't bettering to have her mistress ordering her around morning and night. Perhaps if there were such a thing as fixed hours, or more time to herself, she'd feel differently. But she only got time off every other Sunday, to attend morning Mass, and Thursday evenings.

Ellen looked her up and down. "Have ye spent all your wages on a dress?"

"Aye, she has." Nora tittered behind a gloved hand.

"Never mind them, ye look lovely." Kathleen smiled.

Annie adjusted the brim of her feathered hat.

"Right you are, Kathleen."

While Ellen Driscoll wore a simple shirtwaist, a straw hat with a black ribbon, and a woolen skirt, as she did most Sundays, Annie spent what money she didn't send home to her father on the finest clothing she could afford. Today she wore a muslin dress with a fitted bodice in a floral print, the cuffs and collar trimmed in lace. She'd purchased a velvet hat and suede gloves at the City of Paris department store and looked every bit a lady, as much as Mrs. Whittier.

Annie stood straighter, admiring the draping of her dress. Was this not the reason that she, Nora O'Donnell, Ellen Driscoll, Kathleen Kelly, and thousands of other Irish girls had come to this country? To better their stations in life?

Her cottage in Ballycroy, County Mayo, with its dirt floor and thatched roof, had no windows. Twice a year, she washed the walls with lime. After her mother passed away, God rest her soul, Annie took over cooking for her nine siblings, boiling potatoes and cabbage in a pot over a peat fire in the hearth. Several times a day, she hauled water from the well. At night, she read by candlelight. Now she had fine clothes, electricity, running water, and the chance to marry for love, not land. Girls who went away were the lucky ones.

"Tell us, then." Ellen smirked. "Who are ye trying to impress?"

"You don't know?" Nora's eyes widened.

Nora, Annie suspected, came to church more for gossip than for the good of her soul.

Nora smiled. "Annie has an American fellow. Albert, isn't it?"

Kathleen shaded her eyes from the sun, her fair, freckled skin turning pink. "Ach, Annie!" She lowered her voice. "A Yank? Is he a *Protestant*?"

A horse carriage went past, stirring up dust. Annie took a step back. Here, on the busy street corner, south of the Slot, grocers, boardinghouses, factories, boiler works, liquor stores, and furniture stores crowded against one another, dwarfed by the impressive Gothic spire of Saint Patrick's Church. Annie's cheeks warmed as she thought of Albert.

A fortnight ago, Mrs. Whittier's handsome nephew had arrived with his mother from Chicago to stay as a guest in the Whittier home. Though previous guests of the Whittiers' had refused to acknowledge Annie, despite the fact that she would faithfully serve them during their visit, Albert had looked at her kindly, pressing three silver dollars into her palm.

To compensate you for the extra work that our presence in the house entails.

His generous tip amounted to more than her week's wages. She'd been unable to hold her tongue, as she'd been instructed to by her mistress.

I'm not to smile under any circumstances, but you've left me no choice. If your aunt reprimands me today, 'tis your own fault!

He'd laughed, surprised. She loved the sound of his laugh—deep, like thunder.

"So what if he is Protestant?" Annie replied, thinking of the strong lines of Albert's jaw, the warmth of his hands. "I'd still attend morning Mass."

"Jesus, Mary, and Joseph!" Kathleen winced, making the sign of the cross.

Nora shook her head. "If you were to marry him, no one

would attend your wedding. Cissy Callahan married an Italian, and no one came, I tell ye. Not a soul."

"Albert is studying medicine to become a doctor," Annie said, annoyed with Nora. "And if he does propose marriage, I'll have a fine home where you'll all be welcome."

Ellen shook her head. "Be careful, Annie. Nothin' is more important than your virtue."

"Ye think I don't know that?" Annie straightened. "Albert is a gentleman."

Kathleen frowned. "Doctor or not, there's plenty of suitable Irish fellows right here at church. You ought to join us for a dance."

Annie had been to the Irish dances on Thursday nights, every maid's night off, and enjoyed the sounds of home—the fiddles, accordions, and singing. But if she were to do what she intended, to bring all of her siblings to America, and to become lace curtain Irish, not shanty Irish, she would need to marry well. The other girls were content to settle for butchers and factory workers. But not Annie. She had her sights set on Albert.

"Perhaps another time, Kathleen."

"Have you heard from Rosie O'Brien?" Nora asked. "Her sister Katie married one of the Sullivan boys. Do ye remember Patrick? The big rogue, always huggin' on all the girls."

Annie and her church friends had come from rural parishes in Ireland—Ballycroy, Kilkeedy, Drinagh, Kilgarvan—and they often spoke of their cousins and of the people they knew back home. Nora and Kathleen were domestics, like Annie, with Nora minding two small children and Kathleen a maid of all work, a position no one envied. Ellen had a factory job making hatboxes, with better hours than theirs but worse wages.

Secretly, Annie thought domestics made for better wives. She knew how to recognize fine linen and the lines of good furniture. She could set a beautiful table, something a factory girl would never learn to do.

As Nora, Kathleen, and Ellen chatted away, Annie thought of Albert, how they'd snuck glances at each other across the dining table while she served the Whittier family their meals. He'd found her after supper and led her to a dark alcove beside Mr. Whittier's Turkish smoking parlor, where they could speak in private. *You're not like other girls*, he said. *You aren't afraid to speak your mind.*

She smiled at the memory, then sighed, dreading her afternoon chores.

"I best be gettin' back."

It would take her more than half an hour to walk the nearly two miles back to Mrs. Whittier's mansion, north of the Slot, an iron opening on Market Street that housed the cables that pulled the streetcars to and fro. On the other side of the Slot were fine theaters and hotels, respectable businesses, banks, and large, beautiful houses.

"I ought to go as well." Nora rolled her eyes. "My mistress will want her morning nap."

Annie scowled. "God forbid we take a day of rest."

"Aye," Kathleen replied. "But me da is twice the man he was since he got my last letter. I sent home two dollars."

The other girls nodded, murmuring affirmation. Their sisters and cousins had brought them here—more daughters than sons left Ireland every day. Annie's cousin Eileen had been the first in their family to make the steamship voyage to America.

Annie had been shocked when her cousin rejected an arranged marriage with a farmer twice her age.

I'll take me chances in the New World, Eileen had said. *I won't be a farmer's wife digging in a little garden.*

Until then, Annie hadn't seen much choice in the matter. Only one son would inherit the family farm, and her father hadn't the fortune to pay his daughters' dowries. An Irishwoman's lot in life wasn't easy. She who didn't marry could become a servant in her brother's home or a nun. Even those who did marry might become wet nurses or take in boarders, to help their husbands pay the rent. And yet, Eileen had chosen a different life for herself.

When she sent Annie a letter from Boston with both money and her photograph enclosed, Eileen wrote to say she'd found work as a cook for a wealthy family. In her photograph, she wore a feathered hat and a fine dress, the likes of which Annie had never seen. In their village, girls walked barefoot and wore dresses made of bleached flour sacks, saving shoes and secondhand clothes for Sunday Mass.

By the time Eileen had moved from Boston to San Francisco, she had saved enough for Annie's steerage-class ticket across the ocean. Six months ago, Eileen had married a shopkeeper and moved to Colorado. Now Annie would take her cousin's place and send money home to Ireland, until she herself was married. She'd nearly saved enough for her da to slate the roof of their cottage.

"There's no bad penny in our money," Annie said, turning to her friends. "We ought to be proud, even when these Yanks look down their noses at us."

———◆———

ANNIE ENTERED THROUGH the back-door servants' entrance of the Whittier mansion. When she first arrived in San Francisco, she'd walked right up the grand staircase to the front of the house, believing she could enter through the stained-glass double doors like any other guest—*mercy on her!* Annie walked through the back parlor, past the laundry room, where Greta was elbow-deep in soapsuds, and into the kitchen, where Mary was stirring a pot of soup.

"Dia duit." Annie smiled at the plump middle-aged woman, whose curls had come loose from her topknot, her face flushed from the heat of the stove.

"Ach, Annie." Mary wiped a bead of sweat from her forehead with the back of her hand. "You know we aren't to speak Irish belowstairs."

"Fine." Annie smiled. "God be with you."

"God be with you too." Mary pursed her lips, looking at Annie's dress. "And don't let the mistress catch ye lookin' above your station. You best be changin' into your uniform."

Mrs. Whittier believed the Irish to be lowborn, impertinent, and lacking in social graces, and she told them as much. Annie had seen the cruel caricatures of Irish domestics in the local papers—namely, a large, brutish woman named Bridget, drawn with a simian face—but Annie would prove to these Americans that she was not lazy, dimwitted, or insolent.

Annie's father, like many Irish peasants, had understood the link between education and success. Thanks to him, she could read and write in English. She even knew some Latin. Her years walking barefoot to the national school had prepared her for meeting a man like Albert, with whom she could converse about Dickens and Shakespeare. If Mrs. Whittier resented her for dressing like a middle-class woman, then so be it.

Her mistress's voice carried from the parlor.

". . . and she demands to attend Mass. Naturally, I'd prefer a native-born girl."

Annie rolled her eyes. "Well, good luck finding the likes of *her*. I'd like to see an American girl tolerate the nonsense we do."

Mary chuckled.

Annie nodded toward the doorway. "Have ye served them lunch?"

"Not yet," Mary said. "The mistress will be askin' after ye soon enough."

"That she will."

Annie sighed. She didn't have any idle time now, like she had in Ballycroy. But she reminded herself that in spite of the many NO IRISH NEED APPLY signs posted in shop windows and newspaper advertisements, she had secured herself a position as a domestic in Mrs. Whittier's home. She'd watched. She'd used her head. Quickly, she had understood how to make beds and to dust *their* way, how to arrange fruit and flowers and to properly place a salad fork.

Every day, Annie woke at half six, lit fires in the fireplaces, opened the windows in the front parlor, swept the front hall and the steps, and straightened and dusted the furniture, all before serving Mr. and Mrs. Whittier their breakfast. Then she aired out linens, made the beds, used the carpet sweeper on the bedroom floors, cleaned the bathrooms, and returned to the kitchen to wash the breakfast dishes and to prepare for lunch. After serving lunch, she washed the windows, polished silver, cleaned woodwork, and prepared to serve dinner. When she fell into bed, late at night, she wondered if her soul was her own, so much did her mistress demand of her.

". . . fish on Fridays?"

Annie recognized the nasal voice as belonging to Mrs. Hughes, Albert's mother, a pinched little woman with a sour face.

"Whatever for?"

Did these American women not observe Lent? They ate meat on Fridays like heathens? The gulf between Annie and her mistress felt as wide as the ocean. Mrs. Whittier never touched a drop of alcohol, whereas in County Mayo, it wasn't improper for young women to drink at weddings and wakes. Annie's mistress picked at foods Annie had never tasted— bananas, celery, iceberg lettuce—with the appetite of a bird. Meanwhile, Annie enjoyed hearty stews and roast beef, which tasted so much better than salt pork.

In her garret at the top of the Whittier mansion, Annie looked around at her uncarpeted, hardly furnished room, with a sloping ceiling, a single bed, a chest of drawers, and a wash-stand. There was no running water on the third floor, so she had to carry a bucket up from the kitchen to bathe. Her attic room was stifling hot in the summer and bitter cold in the winter. But it was preferable to the dark hole off the kitchen where Mary and Greta slept.

Annie changed out of her Sunday dress and into her ser-vant's uniform—a simple black dress with a white apron. A knock rapped on her door.

Startled, she paused. No one came up here, not even the staff. When she opened the door, Albert stood in the hall, his blue eyes sparkling like sunlight on the water.

He smiled. "May I come in?"

"You gave me a fright."

Though warmth spread through her at the sight of him, a prickle of fear followed. To be alone with him in her room was not only improper but dangerous as well.

Albert smoothed a hand over his short golden curls. Then he took a step forward, grasping her hands in his. They were soft and warm.

"I had to see you."

Biting her cheek, Annie ushered him inside and shut the door. It was folly to be standing around in the hall, where anyone could see them together. She felt ashamed as Albert took in the sparseness of her room—the cobwebs in the corners, the sagging bed. But he turned his magnetic blue gaze to her, touching a strand of her hair. "You look beautiful."

Then he pressed his lips against hers, and she nearly swooned, lightheaded, her heart hammering in her chest and Ellen's warning ringing in her ears.

Annie pulled back, her lips tingling.

"Albert," she whispered. "We can't."

He brushed her cheek gently with his thumb.

"I have something for you."

Reaching into his coat pocket, Albert smiled, retrieving an object. In his fingers, he held a gold ring. Three opals glittered, luminous, like the waters of Cuan Mó. Surrounding the opals, tiny diamonds glittered like stars.

Annie gasped. Never had she dared to imagine she would

wear such a priceless piece of jewelry. Did this mean . . . ?
Would he . . . ?

"Albert . . ."

He touched her lips, silencing her. Then he slid the ring
onto her finger, sending a shiver down her spine. Albert kissed
her again, his mouth hot and insistent. This time, she let him,
her hands finding his curls. Soon she would no longer be Miss
Annie Gilmurray, Mrs. Whittier's maid. She would become
Mrs. Annie Hughes, Albert's wife.

3

Judy

San Francisco, 1972

The woman in the mug shot is younger than I am now. Her dark hair is parted down the middle and twisted into a bun, a few strands hanging loose by her face. Her chin is lifted and her cheekbones are high, but her lips are set in a thin line, like she's trying not to cry.

Her piercing stare is striking, her eyes a light shade of blue or green, but it's the urgency in her gaze that unsettles me. I feel a tinge of excitement as I take in her mug shot—a life awaiting rediscovery. Reading aloud, I look at her Bertillon card.

"Age, twenty. Occupation, servant. Nativity, Ireland."

"See?" Seth smiles. "I knew you'd like the mug book. It's fascinating, isn't it?" He pushes it toward me. "Here, take it home with you."

"No, it's yours." I shake my head. "I couldn't."

He winks. "Consider it a loan."

"Are you sure?" I bite my lip.

I look at the Bertillon card again, at the woman's measurements: her height, her head width, cheek width, the length of her ears and feet. I see the date of her arrest, April 13, 1890. But I want to know more—her name, what crime she committed, and why.

"Absolutely." Seth nods. "Take it."

"Thank you," I say, slipping the mug book into my large leather satchel.

Seth extends his hand for a handshake. "I'd like to offer you the job."

I release the breath I didn't realize I was holding. "Really?"

He nods. "You're bright. I think you'll do well with the customers. Can you start tomorrow at nine?"

"Y-yes," I stammer. "I would love to. Thank you so much."

I shake Seth's hand and then leave Glass Photo, walking past pawnshops, diners, hotels, and automotive garages along Sixth Street. I want to call someone, to tell them the good news. But my friends from UC Berkeley have all moved on with their lives—starting graduate school, becoming mothers, or getting promotions.

The thought deflates me. Tony made me feel like I didn't need friends—after all, I had him. In Sacramento, I tried photographing the landscaped yards and homogenous homes, but the banal beauty of the suburbs didn't inspire me. I waited for a baby that never came. With every heartbreak, I slipped deeper into inertia.

I try not to think about Tony as I cross Sixth Street, focusing instead on how I'll be able to use a darkroom again. It's been so long since I've watched my images taking shape in the developing tray, slowly revealing their final forms.

Back inside my flat, I set down my bag and look out the kitchen window. Two versions of San Francisco are juxtaposed—the old and the new. I'm drawn to the rows of brick and clapboard buildings, the shabby Victorian apartments, their bay windows jutting over the sidewalk. Behind them, skyscrapers in the Financial District appear like a swelling wave. This grid of narrow streets has hidden layers embedded with years of history.

Without warning, my mind flashes to the young woman in Seth's mug book, her eyes imploring me to . . . to what? To know her? Is this a neighborhood she might have lived in, back in the last century, when San Francisco was made up of immigrants? I imagine the alleys south of Market Street filled with horse-drawn carriages, lined with stables and boardinghouses.

What is it about her photograph that has captured my attention? I think of the early photographers I admire: Julia Margaret Cameron, Gustave Le Gray, Charles Marville, and Lewis Carroll. I've seen countless powerful and harrowing images in library books, bodies of dead soldiers on the battlefield of Gettysburg, children working in cotton mills, migrants unable to feed their families. And yet this prison portrait, a mug shot of an unknown immigrant woman, is as stunning as those of the greats—a portrait parlé.

Suddenly, clarity sparks like a lightning strike. I need to take a photograph that *speaks*. I feel a tingling sensation in my fingertips. This prisoner, impoverished and dehumanized, was disregarded by society. But who was she really? A sister? A daughter? A friend? I think about the overlooked people I pass every day on the street. The elderly pensioners, the laborers, the homeless. They have humanity too, and I want to capture it.

Taking my Rolleiflex camera with me, I leave my apartment and head out into the neighborhood. Street photography has never been my specialty but that doesn't mean I can't start now. I head back toward Sixth Street, where I see an old woman standing outside the Hotel Rex. She's wearing a dirty striped housedress and holding a fat black-and-white cat in her arms. She looks confused and afraid, the cat clawing her as it tries to break free.

"Hi," I say, approaching her. "Can I help you?"

"He tried to get out." She gives me a wary look, her wild gray hair coming loose from her bun. "But I caught him before he could run into traffic."

I look up at the residential hotel behind me, a narrow brick building with laundry flapping from the metal fire escapes. "Do you live here?"

She nods. "I been here for twenty years."

"Let me open the door for you."

Pulling the heavy door open, I stand against it, holding it with my body so she and the cat can get back inside. Then I shut it behind us, and she relaxes.

"Thanks. That was a close one."

Her dress is stained and frayed, the material thin. I can see how she might be perceived as unkempt or undesirable. She looks like she's had a hard life. But she clearly cares about her pet, which she probably isn't supposed to have in this building.

"Can I buy you a coffee?" I ask. "After you take your cat inside?"

She narrows her eyes at me. "Why?"

"I'm new to the city." I shrug. "I don't have any friends."

Her face softens. "Okay, then. My name's Hope, by the way." She looks down at her cat. "And this here is Meaty."

I smile. "It's nice to meet you both. I'm Judy."

———◆◆———

BACK AT MY apartment, I set my camera down. Even though I haven't developed Hope's portrait yet, I feel like it's going to be one of those magical captures. After coffee, she invited me up to her room in the Hotel Rex. It was narrow and small, furnished only with a twin bed and a battered chest of drawers. Hope told me how she moved to San Francisco, left an abusive marriage, and then ended up on the streets before finding a job as a cleaning woman.

Now she scrapes by on social security payments, her room at the Rex only thirty dollars a month. I'm inspired by her resilience. When I took her portrait, I got up close, so I could see every wrinkle, every hair, and the sadness in her eyes. I hope my photograph captures both Hope's beauty and her humanity, offering a glimpse into her life story. By allowing me to photograph her today, she's put her trust in me. And now I feel a little less alone.

Guilt pulls at my stomach as I think about how I still haven't told my mother where I am. I've been in San Francisco for a week now. Tentatively, I pick up the phone, holding my breath as I dial her number. The line continues ringing, and I hope she won't answer.

"Hello?"

She sounds harried, flustered.

I let out my breath. "Mom, it's me."

"Judy, thank *God.*"

Her tone turns shrill. "Where are you calling from? What's going on?"

My insides clench.

"I'm safe. I just . . . I had to get away."

"Tony called and said you up and left in the middle of the night. Is that true? I've been worried sick!"

My eyes prick. Of course Tony called her already.

"You don't need to worry. I'm fine."

"Well, why the hell did you leave?"

My lip trembles. I want to tell her the truth.

"His drinking has been really bad." My voice cracks. "And I caught him cheating again. This time with the barmaid at the Trap."

My mom sighs, softening her tone. "Judy, every man needs to let off steam once in a while. Tony works hard. He loves you. You know that."

I blink back tears. Even though I expect this kind of response from my mother, I still feel the sting of betrayal. "If he really loved me, he wouldn't hurt me like this."

"Hurt you?" My mom sounds puzzled. "He's never laid a hand on you, sweetheart."

I pinch the bridge of my nose. It's true. Tony has never physically harmed me. I almost wish he had, because it would make my decision to leave easier. He's screamed in my face and thrown things in my direction. But he's never laid a hand on me.

My voice shakes. "It's not working. I need to figure things out on my own."

"On your own?" My mother sounds incredulous. "Judy. *Where* are you?"

I don't have the energy to resist. "San Francisco."

She swears under her breath. "With all those homosexuals and all that crime? Now, listen, Judy, you go right back to that husband of yours before it's too late."

I know she's been watching Phyllis Schlafly on television again. My mother adores her, the conservative lawyer from Illinois who believes the Equal Rights Amendment shouldn't be ratified because "American women never had it so good." I can still hear Phyllis and her smug voice arguing with Barbara Walters on the *Today* show.

She said most women would rather cuddle a baby than a typewriter. She said it's easier to get along with a husband than an office manager. She believes it's God's will for a woman to stay home. Well, excuse me, Phyllis, but some of us can't have the babies we so desperately want, and some of us don't have a great situation with our husbands at home.

A lump rises in my throat. "Mom, I can't go back to Tony."

"Judy." She sounds both furious and desperate. "Don't listen to those women's libbers. You'll break the Ten Commandments and the sanctity of family."

My free hand clenches into a fist, my nails digging into my palm.

"I just wanted to let you know I'm okay. But I should go."

"How will I reach you?"

I give her my new phone number, which is taped to the receiver of the kitchen phone. Then panic hits me.

"Wait, Mom? Don't tell Tony where I am. And don't give him this number."

My mom sighs. "Fine. But I think you're making a mistake."

I hang up, hoping she'll stay true to her word. Then I wipe away a tear; I've never felt so lonely. My mother is a woman of her generation, who believes my duty is to serve my husband, no matter his faults, and his duty is to protect me. But Tony, the man I gave up everything for, made me feel insignificant and small. And yet I can't help reaching for him at night, feeling surprised to find his side of the bed cold and empty.

My throat tightens when I think of Tony's hearty laugh, the strength of his hugs, and the smell of his skin. He was my college sweetheart, my only serious boyfriend. When we met, I was still searching for my place in the world, but Tony seemed so assured of his. He was a working carpenter, a real man—so different from the boys on the UC Berkeley campus, aspiring philosophers who liked to spend afternoons arguing the merits of Hume versus Descartes.

Walking home from my art history class my senior year, past the shingled Craftsman bungalows on College Avenue, I spotted Tony, high up on some scaffolding, his tanned, muscular arms sheened with sweat. He caught me looking at him and he smiled. I was a skinny thing, all long, tangled hair and frayed corduroys, not yet possessing much confidence in my sexuality. But watching him I felt a rush of desire that emboldened me. Tony climbed down and stood so close, I could smell the scent of his sweat mixed with Old Spice.

"Need a hand, Freckles?"

My skin tingled. As a child, I'd been teased for the spray of freckles across my nose and cheeks, but as I got older, I came to appreciate them. And from the look in Tony's eyes, it seemed he did too. He took my heavy book bag from my shoulder before

I could protest, but when he reached for my Rolleiflex, I pulled my camera away.

"What's wrong?" He gave me a teasing look. "Are you afraid I'm going to steal it?"

"No." I smirked. "I'm afraid you're going to drop it."

He threw back his head and laughed.

"Freckles, I don't drop things. I'm *very* good with my hands."

I blushed at the innuendo, shaking my head.

"I can't let you carry it. I don't even know your name."

He extended his palm. "Tony Morelli."

I liked the way his dark hair hung in his warm brown eyes, his thick eyebrows, his strong jaw, and his easy demeanor. When his hand enveloped mine, our connection was electric, like a lightning strike. I knew right then he was the man I was going to marry.

"My name's not Freckles," I said without letting go. "It's Judy."

I dab at my eyes, wishing things hadn't gone so wrong. I was swept up in our romance, and I refused to see the warning signs. My History of Photography professor, an intimidating academic named Carol Roberts, gave me a pointed look when I returned to her class with an engagement ring on my finger. Two weeks later, she pulled me aside to tell me my grades were slipping. *Are you sure about getting married so young?*

I found her concern offensive. What did she know? Plenty of girls married at twenty-two. My degree was nice to have, but Tony would take care of me for the rest of our lives. And we *were* happy. At first at least. We left the Bay Area, buying a home in Sacramento, in a tree-lined suburban neighborhood, an hour's drive from where I'd grown up in Chico. We painted one of the bedrooms a cheerful yellow in the hope that it would soon become a nursery. Then we made love on the floor, gallons of lemon-colored paint anchoring the canvas beneath us.

I wipe my eyes with the back of my sleeve, tears now falling in earnest. I have to stop reminiscing about the good times, back when I was filled with hope for my future. I still love my husband, but I don't love his yelling, his drinking, or his possessiveness. Then I see the corner of Seth's mug book poking out of my bag, reminding me I took it home.

Removing the old leather tome, I open it, carefully turning the pages until I've reached the Irishwoman's haunting portrait. Then I run my finger lightly over the edges of her Bertillon card. As I do, I notice it doesn't lie flat against the page—two corners have come loose. My heart beats faster as I slide my nail beneath the card, dislodging it. I feel guilty tampering with Seth's mug book, but I need to know her name.

There, pressed flat and tucked beneath the card, is an old piece of paper that has been folded into quarters. I pull it out, setting it down on the table. Then I turn over the Bertillon card, reading the information on the back.

Name: Annie Gilmurray
Alias: none
Residence: 824 Grove Street
Date of Arrest: April 13, 1890
Crime: Grand Larceny
Arresting Officer: Branson & Lowell

I turn the Bertillon card over again, looking at Annie's mug shot. She meets my gaze with a look of shock and fright, as if she's saying, *Help me*. It's uncanny, the feeling that I'm communicating with someone over the span of nearly a century. Carefully, I unfold the piece of paper I found tucked behind her card. It's thin and yellowed with age—an affidavit from 1890. Intrigued, I read the mixture of text and cursive. This is a written statement to be used as evidence in a court case, the witness a girl named Greta Nilsson.

GENERAL AFFIDAVIT
State of *California*
County of *San Francisco*
In the matter of *Annie Gilmurray vs. Whittier Family*,
    case no. 6033

Greta's words, translated from Swedish, leap off the page as if they've been spoken aloud. I feel a pang of indignation so strong, it exerts physical pressure around my chest. Annie Gilmurray was no thief. She was betrayed by someone she loved.

4

Annie

San Francisco, 1890

Annie trembled as Albert moved his hand to her breast, his fingers groping her through the fabric of her dress. She gasped. Then his mouth was against her neck, his tongue wet. Suddenly, a knock sounded at the door. Albert stepped back, panting. Annie stood frozen, staring at him in stunned silence. The knock rapped again.

"Hide," she whispered.

Albert's eyes darted around the room. She pointed at her bed, then smoothed her hair. But Albert hesitated; he couldn't bear to get on the dusty ground, to crawl beneath her sagging mattress. Instead, he flattened his body against the wall.

Annie let out her breath, then opened the door, only a crack.

Greta, the sullen Swedish laundress, stood in the hallway.

"What is it?" Annie hissed the words.

A stocky, pale-haired girl of not more than eighteen, Greta

stood there holding a bundle of unwashed bedclothes. Her bottom lip poked out, and her ruddy cheeks flushed.

"Madam want . . . you."

Annie gripped the wood tightly with her left hand. "The mistress is calling for me? Is that what you're trying to say?"

Greta nodded. Then her mouth fell open, and Annie watched in horror as the girl's eyes moved from the opal ring on Annie's finger—which she'd forgotten to take off—to the gap beneath the door behind which Albert stood, breathing heavily.

"I'll be there shortly," Annie said, slamming the door in Greta's face. She pressed her back against the wood, her perspiration wet beneath her arms.

Then she tugged the precious ring from her finger and opened her top drawer, shaking as she placed it inside her nightdress, along with the money she'd saved to send home. Annie folded her nightdress around her belongings and gnawed her lip. Dread pooled in her stomach. Had Greta seen Albert enter her room? He too appeared flustered, smoothing his golden curls back into place. "I must go."

"Of course," Annie said, though her heart clenched.

Greta had ruined everything. Albert hadn't time to speak the words she longed to hear, to properly ask for her hand in marriage. But he'd given her the ring, hadn't he?

His eyes met hers, sober and blue.

"Tell no one of this."

"But Greta—"

He stroked Annie's cheek. "She didn't see me. And even if she had, the girl can hardly speak English."

That much was true. Albert kissed her hand. And then he was gone.

———•◆•———

In the lull of activity after the midday meal, Annie looked around achingly for Albert. She stiffened whenever she passed Greta, who skulked about the laundry room. Annie swallowed, her mouth dry. Would Greta tell the mistress what she had seen? Could she form the words? Mere hours had passed since Albert had kissed Annie with such passion. And yet he hadn't met her eyes while she served his lunch. Now it was nearly time for dinner, and she couldn't find him anywhere.

The pain of his apparent indifference seared like a burn, but she understood he didn't wish to arouse suspicion. However, Albert was to return to his medical college in Chicago within the week. Would Annie travel with him? Would she stand beside him when he announced to his mother that they were engaged to be married?

Her youngest sister, Maggie, had sent a letter last month, a lovely shamrock enclosed, for the celebration of Saint Patrick. *I am so lonesome without you.* Annie longed to write her sister back with the good news—she was to be married to a wealthy American man. Maggie could soon join them in Chicago, closer to the point of entry at Castle Garden.

"Yer away with the fairies." Mary scowled, pulling a roast chicken from the stove. "What's gotten into ye?"

Annie wiped her palms on her apron. She chose her words carefully.

"Have you seen Mrs. Hughes?"

"Aye." Mary began cutting into the bird. "She and the young Mr. Hughes are taking a stroll in the gardens."

Annie swallowed. "And where is the mistress?"

"Upstairs." Mary gave her a sharp look. "Been in an awful state about somethin' valuable gone missin'. I 'eard her on the telephone."

Annie's arms prickled with gooseflesh. There were many things she'd learned since her arrival in this country. Once, she'd been tempted by an untouched tartlet left on a plate in the parlor, but Mary gave her such a crack on the back of her hand with a spoon, she gasped in pain. Mary had pulled Annie into the kitchen that day and sat her down.

"Ye dimwit. Never eat what ain't yours."

From that moment onward, Annie learned she was constantly being tested. She only ate with the other servants in the kitchen, and she never took what wasn't hers.

She shuddered. "What was taken?"

Mary shrugged. "Don't know."

The doorbell rang.

Annie's pulse jumped at her throat. She walked from the kitchen to the front of the house and answered the door, expecting Albert and his mother.

Before her stood two uniformed police officers.

"Good afternoon." The taller one eyed her warily. "Is your mistress at home?"

Annie's stomach felt oily with fear. "Aye."

"May we come in?"

Annie led the officers inside the entryway. As she took them to wait in the front parlor, panic fluttered inside her.

Barely breathing, she went to fetch her mistress. But Mrs. Whittier was already standing at the foot of the staircase as if she were expecting them. She gave the policemen a simpering smile, her waist cinched tight in her silk dress.

"Thank you for arriving so quickly."

Annie lowered her head and then made her way toward the kitchen, where Mary was lingering in the doorway.

"Gilmurray." Her mistress's tone was sharp. "You may stay."

An icy feeling of trepidation came over her.

Annie, Mrs. Whittier, and the two policemen stood silently in the parlor, as if they were actors in a play, waiting to speak their lines. The shorter policeman looked down at the velvet chaise lounge, while the tall one surveyed Mr. Whittier's bookcases, statuettes, and lamps. Annie stared at the shiny gold buttons on their black uniforms. Her heart hammered.

"This is the thief." Mrs. Whittier sniffed.

Opening her palm, she produced the ring that Albert had given Annie only hours earlier, its brilliant opals and diamonds sparkling in the sunlight. Annie felt sick to her stomach, watching as Mrs. Whittier passed the delicate ring to one of the officers.

"As you can see, this piece of jewelry is *quite* valuable."

"I am no thief," Annie said, her heart pounding. That ring belonged on her finger. Not in this policeman's meaty palm.

Mrs. Whittier narrowed her eyes. "Do not speak out of turn, girl." Then she pursed her lips. "Like many of her kind, Gilmurray has an Irish temper. She is both impudent and a liar."

Annie's eyes stung. It was degrading to be called by her surname and infuriating to be falsely accused. She met the taller officer's dark eyes.

"Albert gave me that ring."

Mrs. Whittier blanched. "What a preposterous suggestion. He is Mr. Hughes to you."

The officer tugged at his mustache.

"And who is this Mr. Hughes?"

"My nephew. He is a guest here."

The officer turned to Annie and frowned. "Your mistress tells me this ring and also twenty dollars was found in your possession?"

"Yes, but—"

"This ring is my sister's property," Mrs. Whittier said in a high-handed tone.

"Albert gave it to me," Annie blurted, unable to stop herself. "And that money is my wages, all of me earnings I've saved."

The two policemen exchanged a dubious look. The short, stout officer raised a bushy eyebrow. "Your earnings?"

"Every cent," Annie replied, trembling.

"Lies." Mrs. Whittier folded her hands. "I found three silver dollars in the girl's drawer that cannot be accounted for."

Annie blinked back tears. "Albert gave me that money. As a tip, you see—"

Mrs. Whittier gave a scornful little chuckle. "Officer Lowell, Officer Branson, surely you cannot believe a word she says."

Officer Lowell, the taller one, turned to Annie.

"Did anyone see Mr. Hughes give you this *tip*?"

Annie's stomach clenched. They had been alone when

Albert pressed the silver dollars into her palm. They had laughed together. Until now, it had been a cherished memory.

She hung her head. "No."

Just then, as if by divine intervention, Albert and his mother entered the parlor, their cheeks flushed from the warm weather. Seeing her beloved's face, Annie felt relief spread through her. Albert had arrived in time to clear up this misunderstanding. Though he'd requested their courtship remain secret for the time being, circumstances required otherwise.

"Albert!" Annie cried out. "Please. They think I've stolen the ring."

Albert flinched, his eyes darting from Officer Lowell to Officer Branson to Mrs. Whittier and then back to his mother.

"So, this is the young Mr. Hughes," said Officer Lowell. "Tell me, did you give Miss Gilmurray this ring?"

He held the delicate gold band between his thick fingers. Annie held her breath, waiting.

Albert stood in stunned silence. His mother lifted her pointed chin. "He most certainly did not. The ring went missing from my jewelry box this morning."

Annie looked at Albert, her gaze imploring him to tell his mother she was wrong. Had he taken the ring? Either way, Annie hadn't taken it.

She wet her lips. "Tell them, Albert."

Albert's cheeks bloomed with color.

"I—" he stammered.

Annie's heart beat faster. He would tell the truth, wouldn't he? She gazed into his blue eyes, as deep as the Atlantic, the planes of his face as if chiseled by an artist.

"Albert, tell them we are to be engaged."

His mother laughed. "That's impossible. Albert is already engaged to be married to Miss Geneva Palmer, of the Lake Forest, Chicago, Palmers."

The room begin to spin. Annie thought she might vomit.

"I'm sorry," Albert whispered, refusing to meet her eyes. Then he spoke in an assured cut-glass voice, addressing the officers.

"I didn't give Miss Gilmurray my mother's ring."

Blood rushed in Annie's ears, drowning out all other sound. With the full weight of heartbreak and betrayal bearing down on her, she lunged at him.

"Ye feckin' bastard! How could you?"

Tears blinded her eyes, and the policemen pinned her arms behind her back. As she keened and wailed while they led her away, Annie knew she had become what they already believed her to be—crass, immoral, a dirty little Bridget.

5

Judy
San Francisco, 1972

Pigeons scatter, flapping their wings as I walk up the San Francisco Public Library steps. The Beaux-Arts building is made of Italian marble, and it looks like a palace that belongs somewhere in France, not in the midst of San Francisco's grime. At the reference desk, a middle-aged woman sits waiting, wearing cat-eye glasses and a paisley dress.

I can't stop thinking about the affidavit I found tucked behind Annie's mug shot. The statement was given by an eighteen-year-old girl named Greta Nilsson, also a resident of 824 Grove Street. A deputy officer transcribed Greta's words, and under "signature of affiant" she'd shakily written her name, like a child.

Removing the affidavit from my purse—though it probably shouldn't be traveling around the city with me—I read it again.

GENERAL AFFIDAVIT

State of *California*

County of *San Francisco*

In the matter of *Annie Gilmurray vs. Whittier Family*, *case no. 6033*

On this *3rd* day of *June* 1890, *Greta Nilsson* personally appeared before me, *a deputy officer of the San Francisco Police Department*, and who is being duly sworn according to law, deposes and says, in relation to the aforementioned case as follows:

I carried soiled bedclothes when I saw young Mr. Hughes emerge from the bedroom of his mother, Mrs. Hughes. I saw him put something in his coat pocket. He did not see me. I followed him as he went to the attic room of Annie Gilmurray. I knew he should not be in there. I waited, and then I heard my mistress calling. I knocked on Annie's door to give her a warning. After a pause, she opened the door and asked me what I wanted. I told her the mistress was calling for her. Then I saw a gold and diamond ring on her finger. It had three lovely stones, opals. I had never seen her wear this ring before. Mr. Albert Hughes was inside her room. I saw his feet beneath the door before she slammed the door in my face. I do not believe she stole this ring. I believe Mr. Hughes gave it to her as a token of his love.

NOTES:

* *Trial of defendant concluded in April. Verdict: guilty.*
* *Witness cannot speak English.*
* *Affidavit translated from her native Swedish by a cousin, Astrid Nilsson.*

   * *Unofficial until notarized and a formal police interpreter
      is present.*

I fold the affidavit and return it to my bag. The document
has left me with more questions than answers. Was Greta's
testimony used as evidence? According to her Bertillon card,
Annie was arrested on April 13. Yet Greta didn't come forward
until June. Was Annie given a new trial? Or did Greta's affidavit languish in a drawer at the police station? I don't know
where Annie was sent to prison, or how long she remained
there, but I am determined to find out.

The librarian looks up from her desk and smiles.

"Can I help you?"

I clear my throat. "I'm trying to find information about
someone who was arrested in 1890. An Irish immigrant."

The librarian taps her lips. "Now, that's an interesting query.
Is he a famous person?"

I shake my head. "No, she's not. She was a servant."

"Well," the librarian says, "you can try upstairs, where we
have the microform readers. It's possible that this woman's arrest was mentioned in the newspapers at the time. We keep
hundreds of old newspapers on reels of microfilm."

"Thanks," I say, feeling hopeful.

She smiles. "If you don't have any luck upstairs, try the San
Francisco courthouse a few blocks over on McAllister Street.
They keep court records that go back decades."

"I appreciate that information."

"Ask for Mark," she says. "Turn right and continue down the
hall until you reach Magazines and Newspapers."

I cross the marble lobby, the heels of my clogs echoing as I walk through the main library's vast interior. When I find my way upstairs to Magazines and Newspapers, I notice an Asian guy around my age sitting behind the counter. He looks up, his dark eyes shining behind his shaggy mop of hair. He's handsome, like Bruce Lee.

I force a smile, even though all I can think about is how Tony would be furious if he saw me talking to another man. The hypocrisy is not lost on me.

"Are you Mark?"

He nods. "That's me. Can I help you?"

"The woman downstairs sent me?"

I hate the uncertainty in my voice.

Mark's face softens. "Maureen."

I swallow. "I'm searching for an Irish maid who was arrested eighty-two years ago. Maybe there's a mention of her arrest in the newspaper?"

Mark's smile lights up his eyes. "Searching the archives is my specialty. We've got loads of source documents stored on microfilm and microfiche. What information do you have about the person you're looking for?"

"Can I write it down for you?"

Mark nods, giving me a library pencil and a slip of paper. "Sure."

I write down what I know:

Annie Gilmurray
Arrested April 13th 1890
Employer: Whittier Family

Address: 824 Grove Street, San Francisco
Arresting officers: Branson and Lowell
Charge: Grand Larceny

"Sorry for my handwriting," I say, giving the paper to Mark. He takes the sheet and then looks at me.

"Are you a historian? Or a researcher?"

The question catches me off guard. I'm used to being defined as Tony's wife.

"No, I'm . . . a photographer."

"Oh, really?" He raises his eyebrows.

"I just got hired at a photography studio, and the owner collects mug shots. I saw Annie's photograph in an antique mug book of his and got curious. The note on the back says she was arrested for theft."

Heat flushes my cheeks. I'm rambling, and I need to stop.

Mark smiles. "Cool. Sounds like an interesting story."

"Thanks. It is, actually. I think she's innocent."

"You do?"

I lick my lips. "Yeah. There was an affidavit tucked behind her photo, from a girl who might have been another maid in the home, saying she doesn't think Annie stole what she was accused of stealing."

Mark clears his throat.

"Well, the good news is we have 1890s newspapers stored on microfilm, like the *Daily Alta California* and *The San Francisco Call*." He turns to the metal drawers behind him and pulls one open. It's filled with tiny blue boxes. "But the bad news is it'll take me some time to search through these reels."

"Oh," I say, deflating.

"Give me a few days," Mark replies, turning to face me again. "I'll do my best to find Annie."

"You'll look through the microfilm for me?" I shake my head. "You don't have to do that. I've used microfilm readers before."

Mark laughs. "I'm afraid you'd be here until closing. Besides, it's my job."

I smile. "Well, thank you. I appreciate it. When should I come back?"

"If you give me your name and number," Mark says, passing me a new slip of paper, "I'll contact you when I find something."

"Thanks," I say, writing my number down. "I'm Judy."

"Nice to meet you, Judy."

His warmth feels genuine. I'm so out of practice talking to strangers—talking to anyone, really—but I surprised myself today. I've managed to get a new job with Seth, and now I have Mark helping me with my research. If I'm being honest, digging into Annie's past is a distraction from my own problems. But in a way I can't explain, I feel connected to her. Maybe it's that she led me to my first great photograph, or my gut feeling that she was also betrayed by a man she loved.

Either way, I want to know more about the family she worked for. Suddenly, a thought occurs to me. Grove Street is two blocks away from the library, and it would be a straight walk uphill, maybe fifteen minutes, toward Alamo Square to see the Whittier mansion, at 824 Grove, if it's still standing. With nothing on my schedule for the day, I decide to check it out.

———◆◆———

STANDING OUTSIDE THE aging Victorian between Webster and Fillmore, I look up at the stately stick-style Italianate, number 824 Grove. Its paint is flaking, and the old dame has certainly seen better days. Though the facade is dilapidated, petunias burst from ceramic pots on the porch, and the window curtains look new. Someone lives here.

Summoning my courage, I push aside the iron gate and climb up the steep steps leading to the portico. Impressive double doors with full-length stained-glass windows greet me, and I'm nervous to knock, but I do. A few moments later, a bald man, maybe in his forties, opens the door. He's wearing a white turtleneck underneath a corduroy jacket.

He frowns at me behind his glasses.

"Can I help you?"

I lick my dry lips, my heart thumping. "Sorry to bother you, but I'm researching the history of this house. Are you the owner?"

He opens the door a little wider, though he still appears dubious. "I am. May I ask what your research is regarding?"

"I discovered a mug shot of an Irish servant who used to live here in the year 1890. She was arrested for stealing. However, another resident of the home, a Swede, provided an affidavit to say she thought the Irish servant was innocent."

The man looks at me like he still isn't convinced I'm telling the truth.

"I have the affidavit in my purse," I say, rummaging in my

bag. "I just came from the library, and I wanted to know if the house where she lived was still here."

I hand the affidavit over. The man's eyes widen as he reads.

"Incredible," he says, returning the paper to me. Then he pulls the door open. "My name is Michael, and I've spent the last seven years working to restore this splendid home to its former glory. I'm afraid it will take me a few decades more."

I laugh. "It's a big house."

He gestures toward the interior. "Would you like to come in?"

Normally I don't make a habit of entering strangers' homes, but Michael has a calming presence, and I highly doubt he's going to hold me hostage. Besides, it's why I'm here.

"Thank you. I'm Judy."

I step over the threshold and find myself in a formal entryway attached to a darkened hallway that connects to a front parlor. It's carpeted in crimson, with ruby wallpaper, and two antique velvet chairs sit on either side of a marble-topped credenza beneath a gilded mirror. The interior of Michael's Victorian home, complete with crystal chandeliers and antique lamps, looks just as it might have looked one hundred years ago, full of sumptuous reds and golds. Michael leads me over to a red velvet settee embroidered with flowers.

He smiles when I hesitate to sit down. "It's okay, sit."

Carefully, I take a seat on the firm settee.

Michael sits in a Victorian rosewood chair across from me and nods at the settee. "I tracked this piece for ten years as it traveled to different antiques shops, never able to afford it. Finally, last year, I found it at a warehouse sale and snapped it up."

"It's beautiful."

Michael gestures around the room. "I've been collecting Victoriana for fifteen years. Finally, this house is beginning to take shape. I need to repaint the exterior, but that's a big job, which I'm still saving up for. You should have seen it when I first moved in."

"Was it bad?"

Michael nods. "The house was decaying, in a total state of disrepair."

I gaze up at a grand carpeted staircase with an intricate printed metallic panel that lines the wall alongside it, and I imagine Annie climbing those stairs, more than eighty years ago. The mansion is impressive, with high ceilings and bay windows, but its restoration seems like a huge undertaking.

"What made you want to save this house?"

"I fell in love," Michael says, laughing. "It's a stunning Italianate mansion. And you simply can't find interiors like this anymore. Also, nobody else wanted it."

"Really?"

His shakes his head. "The city is demolishing hundreds of these beautiful old homes here in my neighborhood. It's a travesty."

I frown. "Demolishing them? Why?"

Michael grimaces. "Urban renewal."

I'm vaguely familiar with the term, but not really. Michael seems to sense my confusion. He leans forward in his chair.

"Twenty years ago, President Truman authorized the demolition of urban neighborhoods that were considered slums."

I think of the desolate area around Saint Patrick's Church

that's also been cleared. But I would hardly consider my neighborhood a slum.

As if reading my thoughts, Michael says, "To the Redevelopment Agency, a *slum* means a place that's low-income and not white, with land they deem valuable." He gestures out the window. "Black families have lived in these Victorian homes for generations. Now the city is forcing them out."

I press my lips together. "That's awful."

He nods. "Up until the sixties, the Fillmore was a famous jazz corridor. There were Black-owned bars, restaurants, and clubs all up and down the street. Miles Davis played here; so did Duke Ellington and Ella Fitzgerald. Music was everywhere."

"Wow," I say. "I didn't know that."

Michael frowns. "Many people don't. But the Fillmore was called the 'Harlem of the West.' After the 1906 earthquake, Fillmore Street became the main drag while Market Street was being rebuilt. Back then, the Western Addition was filled with Jewish and Japanese families. But when the Japanese were forced into internment camps during World War II, Black families moved in. That's when industrial workers flocked to the area."

I bite my lip, thinking of the Black men who might have come here from the South in search of jobs during the war. This place had been their home for more than thirty years.

"It sounds like it was a thriving neighborhood."

"It was," Michael says, sighing. "I'm lucky my home wasn't taken. The Redevelopment Agency has cleared seventy city blocks already, displacing thousands."

My jaw drops. "Seventy?"

He meets my eyes. "Actually, this block of Grove Street was originally included in the city's redevelopment plans. But my neighbors are white, like me."

"You think that's why they spared this block?"

"The white part, yes. As for the fact that we're all gay, I'm pretty sure the city thinks we're just a bunch of lonely bachelors."

I think of the countless Black homeowners who weren't as lucky as Michael.

"But that's racist and wrong. I don't understand. How can the Redevelopment Agency just take people's homes?"

Michael looks at me like I'm naïve. And maybe I am. I've been living in the Sacramento suburbs for the last three years, unaware of what's going on.

"By eminent domain. The government can take away a person's home or business for public use. Then the land is sold to private developers."

I shake my head. "But to destroy a historic jazz corridor?"

I always thought San Francisco was a tolerant city, a place for flower children and free love. But now its Black families will have no access to generational wealth. There are miles of empty lots where their homes and jazz clubs and businesses used to be.

"Did the people who lost their homes get paid?"

Michael shakes his head. "Not nearly enough. Some, not at all."

I'm too shocked to say anything.

He shrugs. "You may think San Francisco a progressive place, but the power players only care about money." Then he smiles. "At least the straight homeowners fled to the suburbs, leaving the spoils for us. Not to toot my own horn, but I think I have an eye for historic preservation. I know beauty when I see it."

Michael lovingly pats the wall of his home.

I clear my throat, hoping to steer the conversation back to Annie.

"You know a lot about the history of your neighborhood. What can you tell me about the history of this house, specifically?"

He smiles.

"Well, it was a Baptist church when I bought it back in 1965. The ground floor was used as a ballroom and the upstairs rooms were rented to parishioners."

"That's fascinating." I chew my lip. "And before that?"

"It was built in 1886 for Clarence Whittier, by an esteemed architect named Henry Geilfuss. The Whittiers moved out after the 1906 earthquake, and then the house was sold to a family called the Mortons. They maintained it as a single-family home until 1952."

My stomach flutters with excitement.

"The Whittiers are who I'm researching."

"You're in luck." He stands up, smoothing his jeans. "I did some digging and I have copies of the original deed to the house, along with an early census record."

I follow Michael through the high-ceilinged rooms, past a formal dining room, and then into a kitchen with an antique stove, then through the kitchen and into a back parlor. Holding on to hope, I watch as he opens a drawer in an armoire and pulls out a faded green folder.

"Here you go."

I open the folder and suck in my breath. Beneath an original handwritten deed to the house is a 1910 federal census. My hope deflates. Annie Gilmurray's name won't be listed among the occupants of 824 Grove Street. This census was taken twenty years after her arrest.

I'm no closer to knowing who Mr. Albert Hughes was, or if he once lived in the Whittier mansion. Did he break Annie's heart? With my own heart just as broken, I'm curious to learn more. If Annie spent time in prison for a crime she didn't commit, because her lover was a liar, then maybe I'm meant to vindicate her.

6

Annie

San Francisco, 1890

Annie opened her swollen eyes, struggling to remember where she was. She felt the damp seeping through the jail walls and gagged at the stench of the piss bucket in the corner, a sharp pain piercing her shoulder, reminding her she'd spent the night on the cold, hard ground. Annie whimpered, gathering her skirt, the hem soiled with dirt.

Bile rose in her throat. A week ago, she'd lain in her own bed, dreaming of a future with Albert. But it was her doomed love for Albert, the lying bastard, that had brought her here, to a cramped cell in the San Francisco county jail. She stifled a sob. Her mouth tasted sour; her limbs felt shaky and as heavy as lead. In the cell next door, a woman moaned.

"Shut yer mouth, you old hag!" Annie's cellmate, a skinny prostitute with sores around her mouth, pounded her fist against the cement wall. "You're doing my head in."

The woman had been moaning in pain all night. Others,

whose voices carried down the corridor, hollered and banged their fists against the iron bars. Wishing to block out the noise, Annie hugged her knees tightly to her chest. She clenched her eyes shut, hoping to find herself in her attic room in the Whittier house. But she knew she wouldn't.

Up until the moment of her trial yesterday morning, Annie harbored hope that Albert would testify in court. Though he'd lied to the police, it wasn't too late for him to admit that he, not she, had taken the ring. With his word, her good name would be restored. And so she sat in the stuffy courtroom, praying for him to arrive. But when she realized he wasn't coming, her heart broke all over again.

There, in front of a sea of curious onlookers, Mrs. Whittier appeared on the witness stand, in her impeccably tailored dress, the epitome of a lady. She dabbed her eyes as she spoke, explaining how her sister's precious opal and diamond ring had been taken from a jewelry box in the guest bedroom where she was staying. Mrs. Whittier told the jury how she had searched for the ring, then discovered it folded inside Annie's nightgown.

Annie remained expressionless, though inside she wanted to scream. The jury was made up entirely of men, and they nodded sympathetically as her mistress spoke. She had no witnesses to vouch for her good character. Father Peter at Saint Patrick's Church, whom she took Communion from every Sunday, couldn't help her now. And though she hadn't stolen, she had sinned. She'd invited Albert into her room, and her immoral thoughts had led them both into temptation. Burning with shame, she remembered the feel of his hand on her breast.

Neither Greta nor Mary appeared in court. Annie hadn't

expected them to—they would risk losing their jobs if they contradicted their mistress—but their absence upset Annie all the same. When she was called to the stand, her hands trembled. She had no legal counsel, only a police officer to accompany her. She had requested her mother's rosary so she could rub the smooth beads between her fingers, but the officer had refused to provide it.

"And how do you plead?"

The judge looked at her with distaste.

"Not guilty." Annie's pulse thudded. "I didn't steal the ring. It was given to me, as a gift, by Mr. Albert Hughes. We are . . . we were to be married."

Whispers rose from the courtroom.

Mrs. Whittier's lawyer, a skinny, hawkish man, cleared his throat. "May it please the court, my client, Mrs. Elizabeth Whittier, can attest that her nephew, Mr. Albert Hughes, is already engaged to be married to a Miss Geneva Palmer of Chicago."

Annie hung her head as the gallery erupted in snickers. Hot tears pooled behind her eyelids. Who would believe her now?

The jury took only an hour to deliberate.

Holding her breath, she looked at the judge, his sagging jowls like a basset hound's, his mouth turned down, as she waited for the verdict.

He glared at her.

"The defendant, Miss Annie Gilmurray, is found guilty of grand larceny. I hereby sentence her to one year in San Quentin State Prison."

Annie gasped, crying out as he sounded his gavel. "No!"

The officer grabbed her by the arms so she couldn't fall to

her knees. And then he brought her, handcuffed, back to her cell in the county jail.

Opening her eyes, Annie wiped her runny nose with the hem of her sleeve. Any sense of decorum she once had was long gone. Was it only yesterday that her prison sentence, a fate worse than death, had been handed down to her? Hazy light filtered through the barred window overhead, and she wondered what time of day it was. Suddenly, a key turned in the iron lock, and the bolt was pulled aside. Annie flinched.

The door swung open and a stout officer appeared before her.

He wrinkled his nose. "Christ, it stinks in here."

"Fuck off!" Annie's cellmate yelled, waving her hand. "I ain't scared of you, copper."

He took a step closer.

"Shut your sauce box, whore, or I'll give you a reason to be afraid of me."

Annie recognized him now. It was the shorter officer from the afternoon of her arrest—Officer Branson. His eyes were the color of dirty dishwater.

He pointed at her. "You. Get up."

She struggled to stand, using only her legs, her hands cuffed in front of her.

"Move!"

Her bones felt leaden as she placed one foot in front of the other. Then her heart began to beat too fast, her breath coming in shallow gulps. She felt lightheaded. Annie had read about men taken to San Quentin State Prison, the "Castle up the Bay," but they were real criminals, murderers. She hadn't felt an ounce of sympathy for them.

Now she thought she would faint as she followed Branson down a dimly lit hallway, past a block of cells, and then down a narrow flight of stairs. She'd vomited yesterday afternoon after the verdict, and the stench clung to her hair. Would she be able to bathe in prison? Prison . . .

Annie wanted to tell Officer Branson there'd been a terrible mistake. But she'd already said as much on the afternoon of her arrest, and he hadn't listened. She looked down at her dirt-encrusted hands, the very same hands that had once touched Albert's face.

On the first floor of the jail, a broad-shouldered officer sat behind a large oak desk, shuffling through a stack of papers. Branson cleared his throat.

"Officer Murphy. This one is bound for San Quentin."

The officer nodded, his limbs as sturdy as tree trunks. "Aye. Take her. Next ferry ought to arrive at Meiggs' Wharf within the hour."

Hearing a familiarity to his brogue, Annie pressed her tongue to the roof of her mouth. Was he a recent immigrant like herself? She wanted to tell him she was nothing like the dirty, heavily rouged trollop upstairs. Couldn't he see she was a respectable, churchgoing young woman? But he didn't give her a second glance.

When her battered carpetbag emerged from beneath Officer Murphy's desk, Annie heaved a sigh of relief. Her good dresses, her books, her sister's letters, her mother's rosary— they were all she had left. And they were inside. Murphy shoved the bag at Branson.

"Her belongings. Take them to be sorted."

Branson pushed her roughly through the door and outside,

onto Pinkney Place. The stink of piss and liquor hit her immediately. This was the Barbary Coast, the roughest neighborhood in San Francisco, with saloons, melodeons, deadfalls, and opium dens crowded up against one another like rotten teeth. Vagrants whistled and leered, while working girls stumbled down narrow alleys back to their houses of ill repute. Annie avoided this part of the city, only passing through on the trolley, and this was the first time she had ever seen it up close.

Branson grabbed her by the elbow, shoving her into a waiting buggy. Then he climbed in beside her, smelling faintly of aftershave. She felt dirty, disgusting, and disheveled, and she inched away from him, hoping he wouldn't smell her. Sweat had pooled beneath her arms, and she itched under the tight collar of her servant's uniform. The horses whinnied, and the carriage bumped along Broadway, past groggeries, theaters, and dance halls.

As they approached the wharf, a briny scent filled the air, and Annie heard the caws of seagulls. Branson led her down from the carriage and through the throng of people waiting for the ferry to Marin. Never in her life had she felt so humiliated. A man with a pet monkey on a chain played an accordion, and he gave her a sympathetic look, but a group of stevedores with tattooed forearms whistled and made obscene gestures in her direction.

"Look at the kettle drums on that one!"

Annie's cheeks burned. No man would ever comment on her breasts if she weren't in handcuffs. Did they think her a common prostitute? She remembered how Albert had courted her—a private wink, the brush of his fingertips against hers. He had treated her with respect, and she'd been captivated by his charm, his erudite conversation. Now he'd left her so degraded, she could barely breathe. Their entire courtship was a lie.

When she boarded the ferry, Annie kept her eyes trained on the ground so she wouldn't see the disapproving looks of the other passengers. She remembered the night of her American wake. Back in County Mayo, in the midst of the dancing, the drinking, and the fiddle playing, neighbors pressed coins into her hands. Many of them cried, for going to America was the same to them as going to the grave. A deep chill ran through her.

Ellen, Nora, and Kathleen would wonder where she had gone. Would news of her arrest reach them? She hoped not; she couldn't bear for her friends to think poorly of her, to think her a thief and a sinner. Because of Albert, she would never spend another Sunday with her friends, riding Ellen's bicycle— a boneshaker, they called it—on the cobbled streets of South of the Slot or going for ice cream after church. Annie replayed Albert's last words.

I'm sorry. I didn't give Miss Gilmurray my mother's ring.

The coward. Her lip trembled when she thought of him, even now. How foolish she was for thinking she could do better than marrying a butler or a butcher. She would have done well to have settled for living south of the Slot with a lad she met at a dance. Annie ought to have listened to Kathleen. The choppy motion of the waves made her feel sick with fear. Casting her eyes to the horizon, she watched the outline of San Francisco slip away.

On the train ride from Tiburon to Greenbrae, well-dressed women on their way to picnic in the hills of Marin County whispered behind gloved hands as they stared at her. She wished she could tell them that she too was a woman who picnicked, who had shared lemonade and sandwiches with Nora and Ellen beneath the shady trees in Golden Gate Park.

Departing the train at Greenbrae station, Annie felt unsteady on her feet. Panic swelled within her, her heart pounding. Officer Branson grabbed her elbow, righting her.

"Please," Annie whispered, licking her dry lips. "I'm innocent."

He smirked. "That's what they all say."

Annie stumbled as he pulled her toward a horse-drawn omnibus, which sat waiting for what she assumed would be the final stretch of her journey. She shuddered, her stomach knotting as she approached a group of prison guards lounging about the bus, laughing. They fell silent as she climbed aboard, eyeing her like dogs salivating over a piece of meat.

"Look at her," said one. "Now, she's a bit o' raspberry."

"Branson!" shouted another, his eyes red. "You missed all the fun last night."

Officer Branson shook his head. "Don't let me catch you at the bordellos."

The guards laughed. "But where else would we spend our nights off?"

A lone horse stood, tied to a post, saddled and bridled. Annie wished she could pet its soft nose and press close against its flank for comfort. He was a beautiful beast, black with a starburst of white on his forehead. She would ride him away from here, as far as she could.

One of the prison guards caught her looking.

"Horse Point. Last stop on the edge of the prison grounds.

We keep Scout here ready to catch any of you convicts trying to escape."

Annie swallowed and looked away. She didn't dare speak. The longer she stayed silent, the longer she could pretend none of this was happening. The bus lurched forward, a bearded man in a bowler hat tugging at the horses' reins.

For about a mile, as the wheels rattled and bumped over the rutted road, Annie looked at the landscape outside the window. It was the middle of April. The rolling green hills were aflame with wildflowers, orange poppies and yellow buttercups. The bay shimmered blue beneath the California sky. What cruel irony, the beauty of this place.

As the omnibus clattered along, Annie's breath grew shallow. *Murderers. Thieves. Cutthroats.* She would be locked behind bars with these criminals. She would have to be careful, and alert. More so than she had ever been. Then she saw the prison up ahead, its walls looming over her, terrifyingly large. The omnibus slowed to a stop in front of iron gates, a three-story brick tower built into the wall. A guard approached.

"How many?"

"One," Officer Branson said.

The guard's dark eyes appraised Annie, though not unkindly. He wore a military-style uniform, blue with brass buttons down the center.

"I'll take her for processing."

He led Annie by her shackled hands through a narrow door in the gate, and the other guards disembarked, making lewd jokes as they elbowed one another. Annie shivered. She'd never been in the company of so many strange men. Looking up, she saw more prison guards, perched in the watchtowers above her, their Gatling guns at the ready. For a brief, wild moment, she considered breaking free and running for her life.

In the prison yard, a red-haired guard approached, twisting the end of his waxed mustache. He reeked of liquor. Annie didn't like his glassy blue eyes or his cruel smile.

He leered at her.

"And what have we here? Fresh meat?"

Annie's cheeks burned.

He licked his lips. "Cat got your tongue?"

The dark-eyed guard stepped in. "Corcoran, Gilcrest is waiting." He gave Annie a sympathetic look. "Pay him no mind."

Annie did as she was told, walking along the gravel path toward a rectangular two-story building painted white, with a covered porch. Blinking, she took in the garden, where calla lilies and roses bloomed in carefully tended plots surrounded by a low, white-picket fence. A water fountain with a sculpted swan burbled in front of the barred windows. Nothing about San Quentin made any sense. Perhaps she had already gone mad.

"I'll find you later," Corcoran whispered, winking at her.

Inside the building, it was dark. The guard led her down the hall to an office, which looked much like Mr. Whittier's, aside from the barred windows. A white-haired man with a bushy beard and mustache sat beside a fireplace. Pictures of men in uniform hung overhead, and oddities graced the table—handmade checkerboards, a box made of matchsticks, leather bridles, wooden picture frames, an embroidered handkerchief.

"Thank you, Reddy. You may go now." The older man turned to Annie. "I'm Officer Gilcrest, captain of the yard."

Taking a seat behind his desk, he opened a leather-bound book.

"State your name."

Annie swallowed. "Annie Gilmurray, sir."

"Age?" He asked, pen at the ready.

"Twenty."

"Country of origin?"

"Ireland."

Captain Gilcrest nodded. "You're a long way from home." Then he frowned. "Can you read and write?"

"Yes, sir."

Annie felt a lump form in her throat. What would her sisters think when their letters sent to Mrs. Whittier's house went unanswered?

He pointed his pen at her. "I've started a school for the boys here. Some are as young as thirteen. They haven't been given a chance." He gave her a hard look. "You've had some education, and yet you succumbed to vice."

His pale eyes bored into hers, and she felt cold with shame. She opened her mouth to object and then decided against it. She was so lost in her pain, so stunned by Albert's betrayal, she had lost her will to speak. The edge of an Irishwoman's tongue was well-known, but hers was thick with the effort of swallowing her tears.

Gilcrest stood. "Come, this way to our Bertillon Room. Your photograph will be taken for our rogues' gallery."

Annie trembled. "My photograph?"

He nodded. "We distribute them to every police station in the state. Makes it far easier for us to catch escapees."

Escaped prisoners. A rogues' gallery.

Months ago, Annie's middle sister, Kate, had written, asking for her photograph. *My darling Annie, as lonesome as ye are, we are more lonesome. I would like to have your likeness, so I may see that sweet face of yours. It would do me lots of good.*

She'd intended to have her picture taken at the photography studio on Mission Street, so she could mail a tintype home to her family. Never could she have imagined that her first photograph would be taken here, in San Quentin State Prison. Her stomach roiled. Captain Gilcrest continued speaking as he led her down a dank hallway. Annie thought she heard a rat scurrying by in the darkness, and she flinched.

"We use the Bertillon system of record by taking each criminal's measurements. It's proven quite effective."

Annie turned a corner and found herself in a small brick room with no windows, the feeling of being constricted sucking the air from her lungs. Her heart started beating so fast, she wondered if Captain Gilcrest could hear it. A scale stood against a brick wall, while a low wooden table on the wall opposite held boxes of strange instruments.

Her breath came hard and fast.

Captain Gilcrest nodded at a man in a white coat.

"Dr. Stanley will have you measured and weighed, then you must stand very still for your photograph. Understood?"

The doctor's hands were cold against her skin as he measured the length of her head, her left foot, her middle finger, and the distance from her elbow to her fingertips. Annie pulled up the sleeve of her dress to show him the burn scar on her right wrist, where she'd been careless with a pot of boiling water. She shivered as he inspected the small mole on her left cheek. When he fixed his beady eyes on her, she wanted desperately to pull away.

"Eyes, blue," he said. "Hair, brown. Her teeth are good."

When a gaunt-eyed man in prison stripes entered the room, Annie gasped.

"No need for alarm." The captain gestured at the prisoner. "This is our resident photographer. Inmate 12876."

But Annie was afraid. This man was a convicted criminal. Captain Gilcrest took the paper with her measurements from Dr. Stanley and then he looked her in the eye.

"Your prison number is 13475. You will respond to it from this day forward."

If she had found it degrading to be called by her surname, to be known as a number was far worse. Annie felt like a rabbit caught in a snare. She didn't belong here; she didn't want her photograph taken by this man. Every instinct implored her to run.

Annie thought of Father Peter's sermons and wondered if the devil himself was waiting to see how far she could descend before her soul became irredeemable. She wanted to cry, but she forced herself to look at the camera, her body stiff with terror. The male convict took two photographs of her—one straight on, and one in profile.

God, help me, she begged silently. *Please*.

When Captain Gilcrest handed her over to the prison matron, a woman named Mrs. Kane, Annie tried to listen to the rules—first bell at six o'clock in the morning and no visitors except on Sundays. No speaking after lockup. The matron described the prison grounds: the hospital, the mess hall, the jute factory, the tailor shop . . . but it was as if Annie were floating above her body, watching the whole experience happen to someone else.

Her neighbors in County Mayo had been right to cry at her American wake. She had failed them all, failed her family. How would she send them money now? She wasn't the intrepid first-born daughter who would bring her siblings to California—she was as good as dead. When the iron door to her cell was shut and locked behind her, Annie let out a sob. America was no land of promise. Its soil was rotten to the core.

7

Judy
San Francisco, 1972

The metallic smell of the darkroom is exactly what I have been missing. I go by feel, making sure the film rolls are perfectly aligned before I dip them into the chemicals. First comes developer, then the bleach, then the wash, then the fixer. It's important for me to get these photo prints exactly right—I want to show Seth I'm capable and competent. After carrying the rack of film from the developing tank to the drying shelf, I reemerge into the light.

Seth smiles back at me, a nest of lines framing his bright-blue eyes.

"You look happy."

I smile. "I love being back in a darkroom again."

"Would you like to use it after hours for your personal photography?"

I think of my street photography, which Annie's mug shot inspired. In addition to the picture of Hope I took in her hotel room, I've also photographed two old men playing dominoes;

a butcher unloading meat from his truck; a homeless man smoking a cigarette, the marquee of the Hotel Rex glowing neon bright behind him; and a woman sweeping the sidewalk. These are the people living south of Market Street, who go by unnoticed.

I can't wait to see how these photos turn out.

"Yes. Thank you so much."

Seth nods. "Great. I'd love to see your work sometime."

I shake my head. "Oh, I'm just an amateur."

Seth gives me a look. "Only if you treat yourself like one. If you're serious about photography, then you *are* a photographer. Believe it."

Once again, I leave Glass Photo feeling lighter than I have in a long time. I'm rediscovering my interests and remembering the person I was before Tony turned me into a shell of myself. On my way home, every street scene becomes a photograph— the brick buildings with ghostly signs from businesses long gone, the narrow Victorian apartments, the children sitting on stoops. I have my Rolleiflex with me, in case inspiration strikes.

Walking down Natoma Street, I recognize a woman with her small son exiting my apartment building. I think she's one of my neighbors.

"Hi," I say, waving. "I'm Judy. I just moved in upstairs."

The woman smiles, her natural hair framing her face in an Afro. She's beautiful, like Pam Grier. "Nice to meet you, Judy. I'm Vanessa, and this is Eddie."

"Hi there," I say, waving at the little boy. My heart constricts—it always will when I see children—but it's a pain I have to live with.

She shifts him on her hip. "What brings you to the neighborhood?"

"Oh," I say, unprepared. "I'm, um . . . I'm in the process of separating from my husband."

My cheeks grow hot, and my eyes prick with tears.

"Hey," she says softly. "It's okay. I've been there."

I'm so grateful for her kindness. "Sorry," I say, wiping away a tear. "I don't know what's wrong with me."

"Listen," she says, setting Eddie down. "I'm in 2B. If you need anything at all, knock on my door. I mean it."

"Thank you," I say.

She nods at my camera. "You a photographer?"

I nod. "I work at Glass Photo, over on Howard."

A jackhammer pierces the air, the sound interrupting our conversation.

"Hey." I raise my voice. "Do you know what the city is planning to build over at Fourth and Mission? Construction has been going on day and night."

Vanessa frowns. "They're calling it the Yerba Buena Center. A sports center, I think. Or a convention center. All I know is the Redevelopment Agency has wiped out half the neighborhood already. They want to bring in tourists."

I press my lips together. "Do you think our rents will go up? I mean, after the convention center is completed?"

"I do. And this is one of the last places folks can get by."

"How long have you lived in the building?"

She strokes her son's head. "Three years now, since I split from Eddie's dad."

"Sorry to hear that."

Vanessa shrugs. "Honestly, it was for the best. Besides, I love it here. People look out for one another. You'll see."

"I'm still getting to know the neighborhood," I say, thinking of how I'm scared to walk around at night. "Is it safe? I mean, as a single woman?"

"Safe enough." Vanessa shrugs again. "Most of the people without homes, they don't bother nobody. And once you get to know folks, you'll feel at ease."

"Mom!" Eddie says, tugging on Vanessa's hand. "Let's *go*."

She smiles apologetically. "I've got to run. But it was nice meeting you."

"It was nice meeting you too," I say, watching her walk away. And then I smile to myself. Now there's someone I can talk to in my building.

———◆———

WALKING UP THE stairs of San Francisco's main library, I'm eager to see what Mark has discovered. He called right after I got back to my apartment, to let me know he looked through several reels of microfilm and found what could be Annie's arrest record. When I reach the Magazines and Newspapers department, Mark stands up from his desk.

"Hi, Judy." He pushes his shaggy dark hair out of his eyes. "Follow me. I've got the microfilm set up already."

"Thanks." I walk behind him down the hall until we've reached a dimly lit room humming with microfilm machines. One is already turned on, with a newspaper article filling the screen. I sit down on a plastic chair and adjust the blue dial, making the newspaper font a little larger. Then I twist the brown dial, bringing it into focus.

"This is *The San Francisco Call*," Mark says. "Eighteen ninety."

My eyes read over the text.

CHARGED WITH THEFT

A Society Woman Charges
Her Maid with Stealing a Ring

Annie Gilmurray, a young Irish maid, is locked up in county jail on a charge of grand larceny, preferred by Clarence M. Whittier of San Francisco. The accused girl will be taken tomorrow for trial. Last year, the girl was hired as a maid by Mrs. Elizabeth Whittier. Five days ago, a valuable opal and diamond ring was found in the maid's possession, which had gone missing from the jewelry box of Mrs. Whittier's sister, Mrs. Hughes, of Chicago, a guest in the home. According to the girl's story, she placed the ring in a bureau in her room after it was given to her by Mr. Albert Hughes, Mrs. Whittier's nephew, a medical student. Mrs. Whittier charged the girl with dishonesty and discharged her immediately.

"This is it," I say, my pulse thrumming.

Now I know who Albert is—the nephew of Annie's employer, a guest visiting from Chicago. I wonder if he was around Annie's age, or perhaps slightly older. I can picture how he appeared to Annie, educated and refined, charming, and perhaps worldly.

"There's one more," Mark says, discharging the microfilm reel and loading another one. I wait anxiously as he scrolls through the pages.

"Here. This is the *Daily Alta California*, April 1890."

My eyes jump to the text on the screen.

MAID UNDER FIRE

Larceny Trial Concludes After Short Deliberation

The trial of Annie Gilmurray, the young Irish girl who is charged with stealing a valuable opal and diamond ring from the sister of Mrs. Elizabeth Whittier while employed as the latter's maid, concluded yesterday before Judge Davis in San Francisco.

"I didn't steal the ring," said the maid. "It was given to me, as a gift, by Mr. Albert Hughes. We are . . . we were to be married." The maid's statement drew whispers from the court, but then she was given over to Mr. Jones for questioning, special counsel for the prosecution. Mr. Jones commenced his cross-examination by stating, "My client, Mrs. Elizabeth Whittier, can attest that her nephew, Mr. Albert Hughes, is already engaged to be married to a Miss Geneva Palmer of Chicago."

Snickers erupted, and the defendant hung her head as she was subjected to further questioning. After only an hour of deliberation, the jury found Miss Gilmurray to be guilty of the crime. Judge Davis has sentenced her to one year behind the walls of San Quentin Prison. She swells the ranks of the women convicts to the number of sixteen.

I gasp, feeling Annie's sentence like a gut punch. *One year in San Quentin?* The prison complex across the bay is notorious for housing cold-blooded killers. It's a men's prison for death row inmates. Not a place for a naïve young maid. I had no idea women prisoners were even sent there. Annie's punishment seems unbelievably harsh.

And the man who promised to marry her was already engaged to someone else. Looking down at my gold wedding band, I think of Tony and how he promised me his love and fidelity. My throat tightens. He lied to me, just like Albert lied to Annie. How cruel Albert was, giving her his mother's ring. Maybe he wanted sex, knowing the promise of marriage was the only way she would ever consider it.

Mark looks at me. "Are you okay? You look angry."

"I am," I say. "But not at you."

He laughs. "At who, then?"

I point at the screen. "At Mr. Albert Hughes, the man who betrayed Annie and had her sent to prison after he promised to marry her."

Mark's eyes widen. He gives me a sheepish smile.

"I'm pretty sure he's dead."

"You're probably right, but still."

If Annie were alive today, she would be more than a hundred years old. Even though this happened eighty-two years ago, I want justice for Annie. I need to know if she served her entire sentence for a crime she didn't commit. Did she get a new trial? Was she released early?

"Thank you so much for your help," I say to Mark. "I'm going to head downstairs and see if I can find any information about the female prisoners of San Quentin."

"No problem," he says. "You know where to find me."

Downstairs, I locate a few books in the nonfiction section on the topic of San Quentin State Prison. I skim through them, but there's no mention of any female prisoners. One, written by a warden in the 1940s, doesn't even bring up the women's ward. Frustrated, I approach a reference librarian sitting behind her desk.

"Hi." I set down the books. "I've been combing through these, but I can't find any information on San Quentin's women's ward, or the female prisoners kept there." I bite my lip. "Do you have any suggestions?"

"Well," she says, tapping her chin. "For San Quentin Prison records, you can try the Bancroft Library at the University of California, Berkeley."

"Oh really?" I feel hopeful. "That's my alma mater. I had no idea they kept San Quentin Prison records at the Bancroft Library."

She smiles. "You ought to give them a call."

I don't have time to drive across the Bay Bridge to Berkeley today. But I do have something the librarian can help me with—researching the history of my South of Market neighborhood. Michael learned so much history about his home—Annie's former home. If I'm going to live south of Market Street, then I ought to know who lived here before me.

"Do you have any maps of San Francisco from before the 1906 earthquake?"

"You're in luck," she says, her eyes brightening. "We have a rare Sanborn Fire Insurance Map from 1905. But it's for library reference only."

"I understand. I won't take it out of this room."

"One moment," she says. "I'll go get it."

While I'm waiting for her to return with the map, I think about what a shame it is that the Fillmore district survived the 1906 earthquake, only for the whole historic neighborhood to be razed by redevelopment. I wonder if any buildings south of Market Street from before 1906 are still standing. The librarian returns, holding a dusty leather volume.

"Be careful," she says, setting it in my arms. "This map is very delicate. Some of the pages have water damage."

"Thanks," I reply, carrying the book to an empty table.

Flipping through the yellowed and torn pages, I look at the grid of streets, all laid out in color. I recognize downtown San Francisco, and the curve of the city's edge with its many wharves, where the Financial District meets North Beach. There are pencil markings everywhere, indicating the different types of buildings and even their materials. There's a color-coded key: pink for brick, blue for iron, and yellow for wood frame.

A shiver runs down my spine—only six months after this map was created, the majority of the city burned to the ground. It's fascinating to see what it looked like in 1905. Downtown, near where the newly completed Transamerica Pyramid is now, are grocers, a ship's blacksmith, saloons, tenements, and stables. In North Beach, on Broadway between Columbus and

Kearny, on a small alley called Pinkney Place, I find the San Francisco County Jail.

I think that alley is called Romolo Place now. I haven't been to San Francisco's Little Italy in quite some time, not since Tony and I first started dating. My throat tightens at the memory of eating dinner at Fior d'Italia and laughing together at Vesuvio Cafe, a quirky little bar frequented by Jack Kerouac. Gritting my teeth, I push away memories of Tony.

Instead, I turn the page and find my neighborhood. Bingo. The blocks between Mission and Folsom, designated for the Yerba Buena Center project, are made up of flats, saloons, hotels, breweries, and coal yards. I recognize Saint Patrick's, the Catholic church that still stands. Then I find my flat on Natoma Street, between Russ and Sixth. There's a stable at number 14, a Chinese laundry, a drugstore, a saloon, a cabinet shop, and a cereal mill. Written in pencil are the words *South of the Slot, Workingman's Quarter.* Nearly seventy years later, the neighborhood retains much of its original character, an old-fashioned blue-collar charm.

Returning the map to the librarian, I make a mental note to call the Bancroft Library, to see if I can look at the San Quentin Prison records from 1890.

"Thank you. I loved looking through these."

She smiles. "It's nice to see a young person like you interested in history."

"Do you know if many structures south of Market Street survived the 1906 earthquake and fire?" I bite my cheek.

The librarian shakes her head. "Very few, I'm afraid. Before the quake, South of Market was a largely Irish neighborhood made up of wood-frame boardinghouses, factories, and small businesses. Sadly, it was the site of the most death and devastation."

"Oh." I draw in my breath.

"Sixth Street was completely destroyed. Everything was rebuilt afterward," she says. "By 1910, it was a new neighborhood, full of hope."

I remember what Michael said about President Truman authorizing the demolition of urban neighborhoods considered slums. But South of Market is no slum. Based on what the librarian is telling me, the buildings designated as "blighted" are at most sixty years old. It seems unnecessary to knock them down when they're structurally sound. These buildings are much newer than the Victorian homes in the Fillmore. How did the project get approved?

I leave the nonfiction section and make my way back upstairs, looking for Mark. When I approach the reference desk, he grins.

"Back already?"

I laugh. "Yes, I am."

He cocks an eyebrow. "Looking for more information on Annie?"

"Well," I say. "On South of Market, an old Irish neighborhood. Do you know when demolition began in that area next to Saint Patrick's Church?"

Mark frowns. "For the Yerba Buena Center? Demolition began in 1966."

"Okay, thanks. I'm looking for any articles mentioning redevelopment plans for that site. So, newspapers from the last decade."

He gives me a curious look. Then he nods, turning around

to retrieve some boxes of microfilm from the metal filing cabinet behind him.

"Try these," he says, handing me two reels.

Settling in at a microfilm machine in the reading room, I load the first roll of film into the reader. It doesn't take too many adjustments before the newspaper is centered, filling the screen. Turning the dial on the right clockwise, I turn the newspaper pages, one by one. My eyes skim the text, but I don't see anything interesting. Then an article in the September 1966 edition of *The San Francisco Examiner* catches my attention.

REDEVELOPMENT AGENCY RUMORS: TURMOIL SOUTH OF MARKET

The actions of the Redevelopment Agency have caused some confusion and discontent among property owners. In 1961, the agency asked supervisors to designate the South of Market neighborhood a "redevelopment area" and listed its major aims as "spot clearance" with "extensive conservation techniques." However, during the years 1962 to 1965, the project retained only 15 percent of the buildings originally on the site, and the Central Blocks portion was totally cleared, except for St. Patrick's Church.

I pause, thinking about how this aligns with what I've seen. The desolate area between Mission and Folsom must be the "Central Blocks." And it sounds like the agency promised to conserve most of the buildings, but then they didn't. I continue reading.

In 1966, the Department of Housing and Urban Development gave final approval to the Yerba Buena Center Redevelopment Project. Acquisition of properties for this 87-acre downtown redevelopment project has started, and relocation assistance services are being offered to residents and businesses within the area. The redevelopment of the Yerba Buena Center area will free 87 acres of San Francisco's downtown blight and will stimulate new economic growth in the entire South of Market area.

My shoulders tense. It angers me to see my neighborhood described as blighted. Sure, some of the apartment buildings need a new paint job, and there's some trash in the alleyways, but crime in the area is low, and the community is strong. I see the same elderly men sitting in the lobby of their hotel, playing dominoes, laughing, and drinking coffee. Every morning, I wave to Helen, the Chinese woman who owns Helen's Diner, an affordable place to eat.

I load the second reel of film into the machine, this time a newspaper from 1969. Once again, I skim through the pages until a headline stops me.

RESIDENTS OUT OF LUCK SOUTH OF MARKET STREET

South of Market Street's remaining residents are finding it tough to get along in their once-familiar neighborhood. Gone are the grocery stores where they bought their produce. The laundromat where they took their clothes is all boarded up, and the hotel next door is nothing but a divot in the ground. This isn't the same place it was before demolition began in earnest. It is soon to become the Yerba Buena Center, which is frightening and upsetting to the people who remain. They don't want to leave the only home they have ever known.

A lump rises in my throat as I picture my elderly neighbors, like Hope, who live in residential hotels. What kind of relocation assistance have they been offered? Some of the men I see sitting with their newspapers look like they could be ninety years old. South of Market is familiar to them, and probably the only place in San Francisco where they can afford to eat and sleep, and where they have a community. *Where will they go?*

Returning to the front desk, I find Mark.

"Thanks for the microfilm," I say.

He takes the film rolls, holding them in his palm. Then he looks at me.

"You know, I'm involved in a movement that's working to preserve the neighborhood south of Market Street." He points to a pin affixed to his jean jacket.

It's a white button with the words TOOR: WE WON'T MOVE! The same phrase I've seen on the flyer tacked on the bulletin board in the lobby of my building.

"TOOR," I say. "I've seen that on a flyer before. What does it mean?"

Mark looks surprised, then pleased.

"I'm a member of the Tenants and Owners in Opposition to Redevelopment. We're an organization that meets once a month in the lobby of the Milner Hotel to inform South of Market residents of their rights. We're organized around one goal— decent relocation housing."

I scrunch my brow. "But it says you won't move."

He laughs. "It's more of a metaphor at this point. We won't move residents out of the neighborhood they know, into housing that's substandard."

Then he lowers his voice. "If you're interested, you should come to our next meeting. It's this Friday at six o'clock."

I consider the idea. A TOOR meeting could be a great opportunity to talk with my South of Market neighbors, to listen to their stories, and, possibly, to take their photographs. Ever since Annie's mug shot led me to Michael's house, I can't stop thinking about all the people today who are being displaced.

"I'll think about it. How did you get involved?"

"Well," Mark says, "I'm getting my master's degree in urban studies at San Francisco State. But also, I feel an emotional connection to the cause. Some of the elderly people around here remind me of my parents, who immigrated from China. I want to help them keep their homes and businesses."

I'm moved by Mark's dedication to help, especially when he's already busy with graduate school and working at the library.

"I'll come," I say, and I mean it. "See you on Friday at the Milner."

When I return to my apartment, I notice the answering machine light is blinking. I've only given this phone number to two people: my mother and Mark.

Hitting the playback button, I flinch when Tony's voice fills the room.

"Judy, you're breaking my heart. I am so, so sorry. Please call me. We can fix this. I promise we can. Don't give up on us. You're still my wife."

I sink to my knees, shaking. My mother gave my number to Tony.

8

---◆◆---

Annie

San Quentin, 1890

Annie awoke to the sound of clanging metal doors. Dim light filtered through her barred window overlooking the garden below. She rubbed her eyes, disoriented. Then she remembered: she was locked in a prison cell above the captain of the yard's office, one of twenty female prisoners kept inside "the Porch." Annie shivered in the damp, her skin cold and clammy. Her throat was parched, but there was no glass of water for her to drink. She pressed her palm against her chest, trying to still her rapidly beating heart.

With a screech, the iron bolt to her cell door slid aside. Matron Kane stood in the corridor, her expression blank.

"Inmate 13475, you have a quarter of an hour to wash and dress in uniform."

Stumbling from bed, she felt exposed in her flimsy night-dress. The matron, a slight woman, perhaps a decade older than Annie, wore a white shirtwaist with a band collar and a dark skirt, her hair swept up in a neat topknot. Undressed, her hair disheveled, her name taken from her, Annie felt stripped of her dignity. She cowered in the corner of her cell.

"Quickly, now," the matron said.

Stepping into the dimly lit corridor, Annie clutched the rough towel she'd been given and watched as figures emerged from the cellblock like specters in a ghost story, pallid and thin, their eyes ringed and sunken. With her gaze lowered, Annie joined the queue of women convicts, her breath rapid and shallow. Gas lamps hissed as she walked the dark corridor.

Some women laughed, drawing reprimands from the guard, while others scowled. Annie felt their eyes boring into her back, marking her as a target. She was not like them. These criminals could beat her to a pulp—a thought that brought on a swell of panic. Annie had never come to blows with another woman before. The damp washroom at the end of the hall smelled sharply of brine, the stones slippery beneath Annie's feet.

Annie waited for her turn at the sink. She noticed a bathtub sitting beneath a rusted metal pipe, but perhaps baths were only permitted at certain times. There were also flush toilets. Though she'd used an outhouse in County Mayo, Annie had grown accustomed to modern plumbing and she hadn't gotten up to squat over the bucket in her cell last night. Now her bladder was painfully full. When it was her turn for the toilet, someone violently yanked her hair from behind. Annie cried out, breaking free to see a ruddy-faced woman, her large body like a pugilist's, her eyes full of menace.

"Shove off, you tart!"

Annie feared she would wet herself. Her legs began to

shake. The aggressor laughed, revealing stumps of blackened teeth and a jowly face lined with years of hardship. Her gums were the color of rot.

"It's me turn, not yours."

The middle-aged woman pushed Annie aside, then slammed the door to the toilet. Trembling, Annie wrapped her arms around her midsection. She wanted to cry. If she'd been an easy target before, she'd only made it more obvious. Taking a shaking breath, Annie tried to steady herself. She could not cry. Not now.

A young, dark-haired girl touched her shoulder.

"That was Mary Von," she whispered. "She's in for murder."

Annie felt like she might vomit.

The girl smirked. "She's nasty as a rattlesnake and has a mouth like a sailor. Don't let her bully you none. Stand tall."

Annie looked into the girl's large, soulful eyes. *What could she have possibly done to end up in here?*

"All right," Annie whispered.

Her body tensed like a spring. She'd never met a murderer before. When Mary emerged from the toilet, Annie gritted her teeth, refusing to be cowed before this frightening woman. She clenched her legs together, breathing slowly. She would not piss herself from fear. Mary snarled at Annie, then shoved past her, shuffling down the hall.

"Her bark is worse than her bite," the dark-haired girl murmured. "Go on."

Darting into the toilet stall, Annie gasped when she saw a dead fish floating in the bowl. Shutting her eyes, the need to relieve herself too great, she tried not to think of its small corpse floating below her as she let go. The smell of brine was overpowering—this wasn't fresh water; it was seawater pumping through the pipes.

After leaving the stall, Annie washed her hands and face, then she turned to her fellow inmate, who'd shown her a glimmer of kindness.

"Thank you. What's your name?"

"Bessie," she said. "And yours?"

"Annie."

"You ain't from around here, are you?"

Annie shook her head. She thought of Mayo—the green hillsides, the rugged cliffs, the purple heather, the smell of a peat fire burning in the hearth. Her longing was so strong, she nearly doubled over. But there was no going back.

"Best hurry," Bessie said. "We report to the mess hall in five."

In her prison cell, Annie donned her striped uniform. The thick material felt scratchy against her skin. She had been given a shift to sleep in and a towel, but her own clothing had not been returned. She wanted to ask for her bag so that she could have her mother's rosary, her books, and her stack of letters from home. Bringing a finger to her trembling mouth, she shut her eyes. She did not belong in this place.

In the mess hall, breakfast was gruel made from watery oats. Annie's eyelids felt heavy, her limbs stiff. Last night she had barely slept, instead finding herself in a state between wakefulness and dreaming. In the dream she could remember, her opal ring had turned into a manacle, tightening around her finger until it severed the digit, exposing the bone beneath. She'd awoken in a sweat, tangled beneath her bedsheet, a scream caught in her throat.

Outside, Annie followed the female prisoners as they

crossed the prison yard, the matron in front, a guard behind. She took in the other buildings—a four-story brick warehouse, decrepit old cellblocks made of stone, a hospital, a barbershop, a laundry, a commissary, a belfry beyond the gate. In the distance, dozens of male convicts milled about.

Annie sucked in her breath as they jeered and whistled. Goose bumps prickled her neck. Though the men were kept separate, she didn't like their proximity.

"Attention!" the matron shouted. "Those of you reporting to laundry duty today, you are dismissed."

A group of seven women, led by a guard, broke off from the rest. The matron looked at her. "Inmate 13475 . . ."

Annie shivered, realizing she'd been called, her number an unlucky one. There were thirteen people around the table at the last supper of Jesus, and Judas, who betrayed him, had the thirteenth seat. Albert had betrayed her. What had she done to deserve such a fate?

"You're assigned to the tailor shop."

The matron folded her arms and narrowed her eyes.

With a prison guard behind her, Annie climbed the stairs inside the brick manufactory, following the convict women. In the dark interior, she saw a carpenter shop and several other rooms filled with machines, workbenches, and tools. By the time she reached the fourth floor, her legs ached. Male prisoners began to file in on the ground floor below, and Annie gasped, meeting the hungry eyes of a man in stripes on the stairwell. He leered at her, and she stumbled on the top step, hitting her knee. Pain shot through, throbbing beneath the bone.

"Move!" the guard called, grabbing her elbow.

The top floor was dusty, with low ceilings and wooden

rafters. Annie's knee smarted as she entered a room with workbenches lining the walls. Articles of clothing hung from a line stretched between two beams. Each convict took her place at a workbench with a sewing machine. Rivulets of sweat ran down Annie's back. She looked to the other women for guidance, but no one spoke. Spotting an empty seat, she sat down next to a woman with hair the color of flax, her features as delicate as a Gibson Girl's.

The guard, a man older than Annie's father, walked up and down the aisles, inspecting each station. He grunted.

"You know the rules. Keep quiet until the lunch signal."

The room hummed to life with the rattle of treadles and the whir of balance wheels. No one asked Annie if she knew how to use the sewing machine, though she'd mended some clothes on Mrs. Whittier's new Singer model. Her bones felt sharp inside her baggy prison stripes. When had she last eaten more than a few bites of food? Feeling dizzy, she gripped the table.

The girl next to her spoke, her voice like a song.

"Ye all right?"

Tears welled behind Annie's eyes. "Are ye from Mayo?"

"Ach, don't cry. Ye can't be doin' that in 'ere."

Annie looked up at the ceiling and blinked hard.

The girl nodded. "That's better. And right you are. I'm Emma, from Sonnagh."

For the first time in days, Annie smiled. It was a town to the east, an eight-hour journey from Ballycroy by horse carriage. She'd never been, but she knew where it was, another rural parish much like her own. Though there were many Irish in America, for Annie to meet Emma, a girl from Mayo, in *here* felt like a hand pulling her from the darkness.

"I'm Annie. From Baile Chruaich."

The guard approached and they both fell silent. After he walked away, Emma hummed as she worked, the same tune Annie knew from the women herding sheep and cattle in the fields back home. She thought of country fairs, the tinkers and merchants, the children running barefoot, travelers and ballad singers. Emma's voice transported her.

When the guard wasn't looking, Annie whispered.

"What are we sewing?"

"Underclothes," Emma said. "For the male prisoners. They used to do it themselves until the warden seen we can do it faster."

Annie flushed. "Their unmentionables?"

An old lady missing a tooth howled with laughter, pointing a knobby finger at Annie's pile of fabric. "That'll soon be touchin' a pair o' bollocks!"

"Quiet!"

The guard smacked his truncheon against the table, and the room fell silent. Annie threaded the bobbin on her machine, and then the needle. Though she had no pattern to work from, she would copy Emma. At first, her thread only moved back and forth, rather than going in a single direction. She cursed under her breath and gave it another go. Finally, she got the machine working, its gentle clicking a familiar accompaniment.

Emma leaned toward Annie.

"What are ye in for?"

Annie's heart clenched, thinking of Albert. "A man, who I thought loved me, gave me a ring. It belonged to his mother. My mistress said I stole it."

Emma clucked her tongue. "Oh, ye poor lass. You're green, aren't you?"

It had been more than a year now since she had arrived at the port of entry in Castle Garden, where a priest had counseled her and set her up in a lodging house. A year since she'd taken a steam train across the country from New York to San Francisco, to stay with her cousin Eileen. A year since she'd been employed in Mrs. Whittier's home. Six months since Eileen had married and moved to Colorado, leaving Annie on her own. And yet she'd learned nothing.

She'd been a fool.

Emma gave her a sympathetic look.

"If you're goin' to lay with a man, make sure ye get paid."

Annie gasped. "I didn't lie with him. I—"

Emma laughed. "It's all right, love. I'm a sportin' woman. A soiled dove. I don't care what ye done."

Behind Emma's eyes, there was a hint of weariness. Annie couldn't believe this country girl had sold herself for money. Did she work in one of the Barbary Coast bordellos, rouged and dressed in silk? Annie realized she owed a debt of gratitude to Greta. If the girl hadn't knocked on her door when she did, Annie might have lost her virtue along with her freedom. She shivered at the thought, to be so defiled by a man. Annie bit her bottom lip.

"Been here long?"

"Nearly two years." Emma sighed. "I've been sentenced to three."

"For . . . the trade?" Annie asked delicately.

Emma shook her head. "Stealing. On account of the trade and a cad named Lawrence who took me earnings, and so I took me money back."

"But that's not stealing," Annie whispered.

Emma glowered. "Tell a judge that. How many years have you got?"

"One," Annie replied.

Emma folded a pair of men's undergarments and placed them in her basket. Her eyes darted across the room. "You see that woman there?"

Annie looked at a grim-faced lady with a long gray braid and sad eyes.

Lowering her voice, Emma leaned in closer.

"That's Julia Ryan, mother of three sons, all of them criminals. They broke her heart, they did. When her youngest was arrested, she gave a false alibi and got twelve years for perjury."

"Twelve years?" Annie swallowed.

Emma shook her head. "And she can't see them on visiting day. Because they're all in 'ere."

"Here in San Quentin?" The thought of an entire family behind bars broke her heart. And Julia wasn't a violent criminal. She had lied to protect her sons.

Emma pointed out the others. "That Mexican woman, Margarita, she shot and killed her lover. And those four are pickpockets, all of them. Bridget, Maud, Minnie, and Nellie. Maud's the youngest. She's been stealing since she was a child."

The red-haired girl bent over her sewing machine looked no more than seventeen. Her face had the shifty appearance of the street urchins Annie had seen south of the Slot.

Annie winced. "How long does she have?"

"Four years." Emma pushed a fresh piece of fabric through her sewing machine. "But she's served two already."

Bridget, the older woman who'd laughed at her, had hair that was completely white and light-blue eyes framed by deep wrinkles. Nellie was perhaps in her late twenties. So was Minnie. They both had dark hair and olive skin, like the immigrants Annie had seen from Southern Europe. She remembered the boat journey to America, how the Italians and Greeks had come with their large families. Only the Irish girls traveled alone.

Emma nodded at the pickpockets. "Minnie and Nellie lured a drunken sailor into their den on El Dorado Street. He was an Irishman, all set to return home. But they drugged him and took his purse of two hundred dollars."

With a clatter, a garment basket fell to the floor and a woman burst out laughing. She kicked aside her folded pieces and shrieked, then buried her face in her hands. Annie tried not to gawk, but she noticed the woman's shiny hair and pale skin. Aside from her prison uniform, she looked like Mrs. Whittier—a woman who'd never worked a day in her life.

"That one's a crank," Emma said, shaking her head. "Margaret Kerrigan. She's the wife of a well-to-do gentleman, but mad as a hatter."

Annie dropped her voice to a whisper. "Why wasn't she sent to an asylum?"

"Perhaps she isn't truly mad." Emma's forehead tightened. "She had a fit of jealousy and slashed another woman's face with a razor. A little blond widow named Mrs. Fanny Lanthrop. Margaret thought her husband had taken a shine to her."

"How do you know all this?"

Emma winked. "Gossip. It travels like wildfire round here."

———◆◆———

At the dinner bell, the soup was thick with gristle, and the bread was stale. Only last week, Annie had eaten Mary's buttered rolls, hearty stews, and braised chicken. Her throat tightened when she thought of sitting in the kitchen with Mary and Greta at the end of the workday in companionable silence, sipping tea. She looked around for Emma.

Bessie slurped her soup and wiped her mouth with the back of her hand. Annie had never seen an American woman eat a meal in such an unrefined way, like a man in a saloon. Though Annie and her siblings had eaten potatoes with their hands around the hearth, the shock must have shown on her face. Bessie laughed.

"Ain't no reason to mind your manners here, Annie."

"Right."

Annie thought of the countless hours she'd spent learning the proper placement of silverware, arranging flowers, bowls, and porcelain plates, practicing for the day when she'd set a table for her own husband. *Who would marry her now?* She looked at Bessie, a petite girl with large, soulful eyes. She didn't act like any type of woman Annie had ever met. Unlike some of the other convicts, who frightened her, Bessie did not appear vindictive or violent.

"Bessie," Annie said. "What did you do, before this?"

Bessie grinned. "Oh, I've been a cowpuncher, an elevator

boy, an errand boy, and a sailor. It's a boy's life and a boy's opportunities that I want."

Annie had never heard of such a thing. She was at a loss for words.

"My mother named me Jean," Bessie said, stirring her soup. "But when I was fourteen, I found out my parents weren't my real parents. It did my head in. And so I ran away."

"I'm sorry," Annie whispered.

Bessie shrugged. "I put on boys' clothing and stayed gone for two weeks. My father, adoptive father, he's a big hot-shot attorney. He had me detained at the train station in San Luis Obispo. But then I escaped, ran for miles down the railroad tracks."

"Weren't you afraid?"

Annie couldn't imagine the courage it took to run away from home at such a tender age, to be out in the elements, alone.

Bessie shook her head. "Not at all. I ran away again at sixteen and joined a road crew, dressed as a boy. I wore overalls, plied a shovel, and got paid well, all for smoothing out rough spots on the new boulevard."

"You were paid men's wages?"

Bessie nodded. "Yes, ma'am. After I was caught, the matron of the city prison released me to my parents. But I ran away again, this time finding work on an ocean steamer in San Diego. I lived in a cheap lodging house on the waterfront. I also worked as a ranch hand in Arizona. Then, when I found out the cops were after me, I fled to Tijuana."

Annie gasped. "Mexico?"

Bessie laughed. "Yes, Mexico. When I tired of it, I got caught back in San Diego." Her face fell. "My parents placed me in a detention home."

Annie could hardly believe Bessie's life story, so very different from her own. "How long were you in there?"

"Until I came of age." Bessie wiped her mouth. "When I left, I stole boys' clothing again and found work in San Jose. When the police arrested me, they called my penchant for dressing as a boy a *mania*." She turned to Annie. "But it is no mania."

Annie bit her lip. "Isn't it dangerous?"

Bessie shrugged again. "It can be. I was shot in the arm in Arizona, when I was riding the range. I didn't want to lay up sick for very long, for fear I'd be discovered as a girl. But it's easy to travel as a boy. No one gives you any trouble."

It had never occurred to Annie to pretend to be anyone other than who she was. If she'd been smarter, braver, more like Bessie, then perhaps she would have left Mrs. Whittier's house to find a better position elsewhere. As she thought of Albert, Annie's shoulders slumped, the sounds of the mess hall fading as she sank deeper into herself. She was unlovable. Unmarriageable. Green as the day she arrived. The shock of his betrayal took her breath away.

Suddenly gasps and whispers filled the room. Annie stiffened, a prickle of fear running down her back. The women convicts were talking to one another behind their hands.

"Maud." Bessie elbowed the young pickpocket, a girl Annie recognized from the tailor shop. Red tendrils framed her heart-shaped face. "What's the word?"

"It's Crawford," Maud said, her sharp, dark eyes meeting Annie's. "He killed himself. Gilcrest found him hanging by a rope in the Bertillon Room."

Annie stiffened. Was Crawford the prison photographer—the man who had taken her mug shot—dead?

"Damn." Bessie shook her head. "He had less than a year left."

Maud nodded. "Another one gone to an early grave."

Annie sat in shocked silence. The prison walls felt oppressive, like they were closing in. Though Bessie and Maud were still talking, their words seemed to come from very far away. She didn't feel right, as if she weren't really here. She imagined her own body swinging from the noose, then lying crumpled in a heap on the ground.

Annie had the distinct feeling she was headed toward something terrible and that there was nothing she could do to stop it.

9

Judy

San Francisco, 1972

My hands shake as I dial Tony's number. He should be off work by now, and if he's not out at the bar getting drunk, then he'll be at home. If he doesn't pick up, that tells me everything I need to know. But if he does . . . then maybe there's a chance he can change. I swallow the hard lump in my throat and ignore the voice in my head telling me I'm making a mistake.

"Hello?" he says, picking up on the second ring.

The sound of his voice makes my eyes well with tears. "Tony . . . it's me."

"Judy, babe." He sounds remorseful. "Where are you?"

"My mom didn't already tell you?"

He sighs. "Look, I had to call her. I was out of my mind with worry when I woke up and you were gone. What was I supposed to do?"

I take a deep breath. "You know why I left."

His voice breaks. "Judy, I am so sorry. That girl from the Trap means nothing."

Anger bubbles inside me, the sting of my husband's infidelity cutting me afresh. I pinch the bridge of my nose. "It's not just the cheating. I don't like who you become when you drink."

There's a long pause, and my muscles begin to tense. In the past, when I've confronted him, Tony has called me every horrible name under the sun. He doesn't take criticism well.

"I know . . . my drinking is a problem." He sounds clear-headed and focused. "And I'm going to go to one of those meetings."

"Really?" Hope swells inside me. "Alcoholics Anonymous?"

"Yeah. I met a guy at work who's sober. He said he'd bring me."

I think of all the times I begged Tony to attend an AA meeting, or to go with me to see a marriage counselor. He always said it was a stupid idea. Maybe it's taken me leaving for him to realize he needs to change.

"That's great," I say. "I'm proud of you."

"Judy," Tony says. "I'm a wreck without you. Your parents and I are so worried. Come home. Please?"

I shut my eyes, wishing I could drive back to Sacramento—it would take me less than two hours. But then I remember my job at Glass Photo, how I promised Seth I wouldn't let him down. Also, I've been through this cycle with Tony before. He gets drunk, he has an outburst, yelling and accusing me of disrespecting him. Then he feels remorse, apologizes, and promises it won't happen again. Just because Tony is saying he'll stay sober doesn't mean he can do it.

"I'm sorry," I say, opening my eyes. "I'm not ready to come home yet."

Tony grows aggravated.

"Judy, you're my *wife*. You're not safe in San Francisco. I'm sorry you're so upset with me, but *you're* the one who chose to leave. I'm putting my heart on the line for you. What more do you want from me?"

I can feel myself disassociating, the sounds of the city becoming muted.

"I don't know," I say in a small voice. "I need to think."

"What's there to think about? Tell me where you are."

"No, Tony. I'm not ready yet."

With tears streaming down my cheeks, I hang up the phone. Then I sink to the floor, my body wracked with sobs. I don't want to walk away, to be the partner who's unwilling to fight for our love. But Tony is controlling about money, about whom he lets me see, and about the kind of woman he expects me to be. I never measure up.

———— ◆ ————

FRIDAY NIGHT ARRIVES, and I approach the Milner Hotel on the corner of Fourth and Mission, one of the few brick buildings still standing in the empty footprint of the Yerba Buena Center. It looks as good as new, with elegant, clean lines and a welcoming neon sign. I'm nervous about attending tonight's TOOR meeting, but my camera gives me a sense of purpose.

Entering the lobby, I look around for Mark. I'm surprised to see a crowd of nearly eighty people sitting on folding chairs, most of them elderly white men. I didn't expect such a large turnout at the meeting. But these are the South of Market residents in danger of losing their homes. The hotel exudes a cozy warmth with its leather armchairs, white tiled floor, and fancy wainscoting. I spot Mark in the corner wearing a plaid flannel and his TOOR pin, and I walk over to him.

He smiles at me. "Judy, I'm so glad you could make it."

"Me too," I say, looking around. "This is a big turnout."

A hush falls over the room as an old white man with a bushy gray beard strides over to a table at the front. He's dressed in a checkered flannel and a black woolen coat with a TOOR pin fixed to the lapel, his eyes serious behind his clear-framed glasses.

"That's George Woolf," Mark says. "He's TOOR's elected chair and the former president of the Ship Scalers Union."

"How old is he?" I ask.

"Eighty," Mark says. "But there's still plenty of fight in him. His front teeth were knocked out in the 1934 general strike. He's not somebody to bully."

Another man enters the room, about fifteen years younger, bespectacled and balding, also wearing a TOOR pin on his black jacket. He walks over to stand beside George, waiting as a few more people take vacant seats. Then he speaks.

"My name is Peter Mendelsohn. I'm co-chairman of Tenants and Owners in Opposition to Redevelopment. We call it TOOR, a tenant's organization formed in order to fight the injustice of redevelopment in our neighborhood."

Applause fills the air, and I take a good look around at the people in the audience. The men are in their eighties, some possibly in their nineties, and dressed in old-fashioned derby hats and well-worn suits, like they have someplace fancy to be.

They've shined their shoes and shaved. They may be working-class pensioners, but they have dressed up for the meeting.

Peter continues. "I've lived south of Market for over forty years. I live down here because it's close to the docks and for forty years I worked as a seaman. Other people in our organization worked as longshoremen or in the machine shops, factories, and warehouses. We have families. We live here because rent is cheap."

Murmurs of agreement float through the room.

"There are a lot of people like me," Peter says, looking around, "who have lived here their whole lives and who have settled down in hotels now that we're retired. We're living on our union pensions, and around here, there are plenty of small restaurants and stores that we can afford. Now the Redevelopment Agency wants us out."

"Boo!" cries an old man next to me.

Peter grins. "But they weren't counting on us to fight back." He claps his hands, sitting down as George Woolf stands up.

George looks formidable, taller and stronger than most men his age. He clears his throat and his voice booms, deep and powerful.

"The late Justin Herman called us nothing but a bunch of skid row bums. But I am not a bum and I resent being discredited and discounted!"

The old men around me appear infused with new life, on their feet, applauding. Shivers run down my spine as I watch George speak.

He yells into the microphone.

"The Redevelopment Agency has been using dirty tactics

to push us out. Heat and water are being shut off in our hotels. Garbage is piling up in our hallways. They won't give us clean sheets. Toilets are locked. The friendly staff we've come to know are being fired and replaced with incompetent personnel who harass us. We won't stand for it!"

I'm shocked by what I'm hearing. What George Woolf is describing is inhumane. Would the Redevelopment Agency really stoop so low?

George paces as he talks, gesturing.

"They're letting our buildings deteriorate. They're creating blight where there was none. And they're trying to intimidate us into leaving. But we're here to secure our legal rights to relocation housing and to keep them from chasing people out."

When George sits down, the applause is thunderous. Peter Mendelsohn stands up again. His voice is clear and determined.

"When I returned from my final voyage in 1970, I discovered the Redevelopment Agency had taken over my hotel. My room had been broken into and I'd been robbed of all my valuables. This never would have happened under the original management."

His eyes blaze with intensity as he looks at the crowd.

"When the Redevelopment Agency told me to move, I told them I've lived on this block for forty years. I know everyone here and they know me. To move me even five blocks away would be the same as moving me to another city. It'll take years for me to build up new relationships and take years off my life in the process."

George stands beside Peter, placing a hand on his friend's shoulder.

"We are a power and a force; don't you forget it! We went to the federal courts to fight against the corruption that's taking place here. If you feel attacked by the Redevelopment Agency, then come forward and speak now!"

A large bald white man wearing a gray woolen sweater and dark woolen pants held up by suspenders comes forward.

"My name is William Colvin," he says, his voice trembling. "I'm a retired painting contractor. For years, I've lived in my room at the Hotel Albany on Third Street. It's clean and it's warm." He pauses, and when he looks up, his eyes are filled with tears.

"Most people don't understand, but let me tell you something. A man can enjoy freedom here. We have friends here. This has been our home for years. If you're ill or hungry, your neighbors will help. I don't think you'll find any finer people in the world. We're good citizens. We have something that couldn't be replaced by all the money the federal government could put in here. We like it the way it is. We want to stay."

The roar of the crowd is deafening. My eyes tear up—I'm so moved by this man's speech. These people don't need a sports center, a massive parking garage, and luxury hotels. They need their community that already exists.

When the meeting concludes, I linger near Mark as he talks with TOOR volunteers and South of Market residents, handing out flyers. But then I remind myself why I'm here: to meet the people in attendance, to listen to their stories, and to take their photographs.

I approach an elderly Black man who's sitting in a chair with his hands clasped in his lap. "Hello," I say, smiling. "My name is Judy. I live in the neighborhood, and I'm interviewing people displaced by redevelopment. Would it be all right if I talked to you?"

The man smiles. "Sure, sugar. My name's Charlie."

I sit down beside him, taking a notepad and pencil out of my purse.

Charlie shakes his head. "This's the second time I've lost my home to redevelopment."

My eyes widen. "The second time?"

Charlie's eyes are cloudy with cataracts, but they light up when he speaks. "I used to live in a nice flat on Sutter Street in the Fillmore. You see, I came here in 'forty-three from Louisiana, to work the shipyards at Hunters Point."

"The naval shipyard?"

"That's right." Charlie rubs his jaw. "I could've lived over there, but I heard the Fillmore was the closest thing to Harlem, outside of New York."

I think of what Michael told me, about Black residents losing their homes in the Fillmore back in the sixties, and how it used to be a thriving jazz corridor.

Charlie smiles sadly, revealing a missing incisor. "You should've seen the Fillmore back then. It was the place to be! I lived around the corner from the Flamingo, which was a jumping club. Ladies dressed to kill. I'm talking furs, hats, heels . . ."

I smile at Charlie's memory. "How long did you live there?"

"Twenty years," he says solemnly. "That was before the men from the Redevelopment Agency came. Back when music was everywhere. We had church suppers, fish fries, jazz joints on every corner. Bop City. The Champagne Supper Club. The New Orleans Swing Club. I knew every neighbor on my block. We looked out for each other."

I'm scribbling down what Charlie is telling me. "And then what happened?"

"The men from the Redevelopment Agency bought us out. I don't have no family here, so I found a room at the Knox Hotel. Now the same people want to tear the whole place down."

Charlie shakes his head. "When I lost my job in the ship-yard, I couldn't find work. I was a welder. And none of us Black workers got promoted. White members made sure we didn't become foremen, and they blocked us from joining the union."

I press my lips together. Charlie came to San Francisco as a young man full of hope, and then he ended up facing the same discrimination he had in the South.

"I'm sorry to hear that," I say.

His eyes get a faraway look. "That's how it is. But let me tell you something. In the Fillmore, after the jazz musicians played the whites-only clubs downtown, they came back home to per-form for family and friends. And those were beautiful times."

I swallow hard. Charlie established a home here in San Francisco, twice—first in the Fillmore, and then in South of Market. And each time the Redevelopment Agency decided to destroy not only buildings but a thriving community as well.

When I've finished talking to Charlie, I approach William Colvin, the painter who spoke so eloquently, and he agrees to let me photograph him in his hotel. Several others agree as well, eager to tell me about their lives and their connection to the neighborhood. Feeling hopeful, I write down each person's name and address in my notebook, making appointments to visit.

After snapping a few candid shots and milling about the

room, I feel like I'm capturing an important moment in history. Mark introduces me to a few other young people like us, a lawyer named Sandra who works for the San Francisco Neighborhood Legal Assistance Foundation, and some students from the UC Berkeley School of Law.

"We asked the local branch of Housing and Urban Development for a relocation plan four years ago," Sandra says, looking at me. "But HUD falsely claimed that relocation hadn't begun yet." She shakes her head. "These tenants need affordable housing."

I'm struck by Sandra's confidence and authority when she speaks. She is the kind of woman I aspire to be, intelligent and independent. She smiles at me, her dimples indenting, her long wavy brown hair framing her face.

"I'm here to give a voice to clients in our underserved communities. They deserve to influence the powerful organizations that hold so much sway over their well-being."

"You're doing important work," I say, looking around the room at the frail and elderly. I think of Hope, and how maybe she could use Sandra's help. I've been meaning to visit her again, to bring by some groceries or some cat food.

"Can I have your business card?"

"Sure," Sandra says, handing it to me.

"Thanks. I know a woman who lives at the Hotel Rex named Hope. She may need help accessing whatever social services are available to her."

"Have her call me," Sandra says.

Like Hope and the low-income residents here today, Annie was seen as expendable. She could have used a lawyer like

Sandra, but instead she wasn't given a fair trial—I feel sure of it—and she ended up in San Quentin.

Though I'm armed only with my camera, I am going to fight for Annie and for all the people in this room today. I've already made an appointment with the UC Berkeley Bancroft Library, like Mark's colleague at the San Francisco Library suggested. I hope their collection of 1890s San Quentin Prison records will reveal more details about the female inmates. I'm glad that Mark invited me here. I feel stronger, surrounded by these passionate activists, like maybe I'll gain the courage to fight for myself too.

10

Annie

San Quentin, 1890

Annie's world felt muted and colorless. The days passed in a fog—she had no appetite and she barely slept. There was nothing to bring her solace; her belongings still had not been returned. Perhaps they were lost somewhere in the bowels of the prison. Though she tried to ignore the brutish guards, the foul smells, the rats, the cold, and the damp, and to dim the sounds of the iron doors and the women fighting, she couldn't.

She had nightmares of hellfire consuming her. She awoke sweaty and shaking, the air pungent with hot tallow. Ada Werner, the woman in the cell next to hers, often left her candle burning at night. She had sad eyes and a long face. A murderer, she had killed her husband in his sleep. But Annie wondered if she had done it in self-defense. Ada never spoke. She was frightened and skittish, like a mistreated horse.

As the days passed, Annie began to feel less than human. Her only emotions were sadness, fear, emptiness, and hopelessness. The guards looked at her with disdain, if they looked at her at all. She had no interest in eating her meals or joining the women convicts in the courtyard on Sundays. Her mind felt as though it were made of jelly, her thoughts slow and sluggish.

Sometimes, while dreaming, she was back home in Ireland, her sisters and brothers laughing as they did their morning chores. *Safe. She was safe.* But then the walls of her prison cell slid back into focus. A headache persisted behind her temples. She chewed her fingernails down to the quick. She was worthless. To Albert. To her family. To everyone.

She could sit in her chair, or lie on her stained mattress, staring at the moldy ceiling. Annie could stretch her arm through her window bars. There was no glass, for it could be broken and used as a weapon. She understood the urge to end it all. A piece of glass pressed into the soft flesh of her wrists, her blood spilling out crimson red. Time here was measured by bells. Bells at lockup, bells at mealtimes, bells in the morning.

Annie remained assigned to a work crew in the tailor shop. Sometimes she sewed undergarments for the male convicts, other times socks and buttonholes. Margaret Kerrigan, the woman who'd slashed the widow's face with a razor out of jealousy, was taken off sewing duty and sent to "Crazy Alley," a corridor with a high picket fence in the exercise yard, where the mentally unstable were made to do scavenger work during the day.

Annie learned the names of the other convicts and their crimes—Lizzie Ross, larceny; Rosanna Core, robbery; Fannie Thompson, a gang member from Oroville who'd been part of a ring of burglars who stole chickens. They ranged in age from seventeen-year-old Maud to fifty-year-old Bridget Smith. Some were quiet, some loud, some mean-spirited, others kind, like Bessie and Emma. But Annie didn't feel like speaking to them.

She forced herself to eat a few mouthfuls of prison food in the mess hall, but she had no appetite, and she grew accustomed to the proximity of the women sitting at the long tables beside her, pungent with body odor. Annie learned the layout of the prison—the upper yard, where men in stripes huddled like cattle; the hospital building, where prisoners went to die; and the jute mill, where male convicts were forced to work long hours among the clattering machinery and heavy dust, making bags used for grain.

The women knew things, passing news from cell to cell. Annie learned of the morphine and opium smuggled into the prison through relatives, prison guards, and trustees—male prisoners given special treatment due to their "trustworthy" nature. Trustees could drive a commissary wagon, clean the officers' quarters, or tend to the garden outside, working alone and unsupervised. She learned of successful escape attempts made by male trustees, but never by the women, for they didn't have the freedom to roam the prison grounds. She learned of "the appliance"—a straitjacket used to bind and torture male prisoners.

Entombed in her cell, she thought of her mother cooking supper in a big pot, and smelled the burned turf, distinctive, rich, and earthy. Her mother had died in childbirth years ago, leaving the world along with Annie's youngest sister, Aoife, born still. Would her mother be ashamed of her now?

She didn't belong here, and yet here she was, amid the hair pulling, the feuds, the tears, and the love affairs. Some women took comfort in one another's touch. But Annie did not see the point in romance, or even friendship.

"Yer skin and bones," Emma said. "Ye need to eat."

Annie shrugged. "I have no appetite."

Gently, Emma took her by the shoulders and looked into her eyes. "Annie. Ye can't let this place break you."

She'd been here now for forty days. Jesus had fasted for forty days in the wilderness, but Annie didn't have his strength. She hadn't even prayed. Annie and Emma were sitting together in the women's courtyard, a rectangular enclosure where they were permitted outside for exercise, away from the prying eyes of the men. But she looked up at the surrounding walls with their barred windows, the cells at the back of the Porch, the hospital. A guard tower overlooked the walls, the guard holding his rifle.

"Have ye anything to bring you comfort?" Emma asked.

"No." Annie shook her head. "They took my mother's rosary."

"Who took it?"

Annie shrugged. "The matron, or the captain perhaps. It's in my bag. It came with me to prison, but I haven't seen any of my belongings since."

Emma patted Annie's hand. "Give me a few days."

⸻

THE NEXT SUNDAY, music carried from the hillside, a band playing for the men and women who had stepped off the ferry at Minturn's Wharf. Prisoners were permitted to wear civilian clothes, and in the reception room they could speak to visitors for a quarter of an hour through a mesh screen. In spite of the music, Annie's spirit felt heavy.

Two newspaper reporters from *The Examiner* had come for a story. Supposedly, a female journalist intended to write about the women of San Quentin Prison. Bessie had agreed to talk to her about life behind bars, but Annie and Emma chose to remain behind in the women's courtyard. Annie looked warily at the male reporter who'd joined them, watching as he sketched in his notepad. She felt like a caged animal in a zoo.

"Here," Emma said, pressing something into Annie's palm.

Annie clasped her hand around the smooth wooden beads. She looked down at her mother's rosary, tears welling in her eyes. "How did you get this?"

Emma smiled. "I know the right people."

A tear slipped down her cheek, a ray of light piercing the darkness. Every night at ten o'clock, Annie's brothers and sisters would come home from wherever they were to kneel together and say the rosary. She felt them now, their warm bodies pressed against hers in their settle bed, where they slept together in a heap like kittens, the fire still burning in the hearth. Emma had given her a piece of home.

"Thank you," Annie whispered.

"Is giorra cabhair Dé ná an doras," Emma said, patting her hand.

Annie let out a sob. She hadn't heard Irish spoken in so long, but Emma was here to remind her of the saying *God's help is nearer than the door.* In many ways, Emma was the only person who could understand who she had been before. A daughter. A sister. A girl who wore her one fine dress to church. A girl who laughed while trying to ride a bicycle. A girl who dearly loved her family and felt deeply ashamed of how she had failed them.

Emma rubbed her back. "Hush now, Annie. Never forget ye did nothin' wrong. Ye trusted a man ye loved, same as meself."

Annie wiped away her tears. Emma had called her green, that first day in the tailor shop. But had this man, this Lawrence, been someone Emma loved? She watched as Emma pulled a lace collar from the folds of her dress, along with a spool of thread. Using a slender crochet hook, Emma created a rose as if from thin air, her stitches fine and delicate.

"Where'd ye learn to do that?"

"Ma taught me," Emma said. "She learned from the nuns. They had a lace-making school in Monaghan, where she's from. This is Clones lace."

Annie knew of a few women back home who'd learned lace making. Even in the poorest parts of Ireland, women, men, and children could make lace by the light of a peat fire, laundering the dirty thread until it shone anew. But she'd never seen it done like this before, with only a needle. Each of Emma's motifs, the roses, grapevines, and shamrocks, were connected together by knots, little balls dotting the tight mesh webbing. Annie knew of bone-and-pillow lace, named for the bone bobbins and the pillow that supported the work in progress. She frowned.

"You don't have any bobbins."

"I don't need them." Emma laughed. "Watch."

Emma tugged her thread, carefully adjusting the tightness. She finished a shamrock, tied her thread, then cut it with her teeth and set it aside to begin something new. She smiled at Annie. "When this piece is finished, it's meant to look like Venetian point lace. I crochet each motif separately, see? Once all of the pieces are stitched together, the flowers and the shamrocks, you wouldn't know it was made here in prison."

"It's beautiful," Annie said.

Emma slid the ring off her hook. "Would you like to learn?"

Annie nodded. "Aye. I would."

Though her hands had become rough and chapped, she longed for something to occupy her mind. She had once enjoyed embroidering and needlepoint. As a child, she'd sewn all her own dresses from bleached flour sacks. Her fingers had been nimble once.

"All right," Emma said. "This is a buttonhole loop. I'll start you off easy."

Emma's ring resembled a puffy button. Annie attempted to make her own, though the hole in the middle of hers was far too large. Then Emma showed Annie how to form a padding cord, taking a piece of thread one yard long and folding it into four strings.

"How we use padding cord is we do crochet over it," Emma said, crocheting slip stitches around it. "To give it a raised effect."

Annie took a turn with Emma's crochet hook, working with the padding cord Emma had started.

"Look at the state of my stitches." Annie sighed. "They're not evenly spaced."

Emma patted her knee. "Ye can fix that later."

Annie learned that once she'd already completed a few stitches, she could slide them by hand down the cord so they were spaced closer together. She returned the crochet hook to Emma and watched as the padding cord took shape under Emma's expert hands, becoming a pretty flower with a defined edge. When Emma gave the hook back so that Annie could work on the part of the cord that would become the flower stem, Annie fell into a rhythm, enjoying the sensation of the thread between her fingers. The clouds parted and the sun shone down on her face, warming her. After some time, Bessie approached, wearing baggy trousers.

Emma looked up. "Did you speak with Winifred Sweet?"

Bessie nodded. "She's working on a story about us."

Emma pursed her lips. "What rubbish, I tell ye."

Annie set her thread down. "What did she ask you, Bessie?"

"About us gals, forgotten and left to rot behind these prison walls. Our crimes, our regrets, our feelings."

"Did you tell her about that man who hanged himself?" Annie's voice dropped to a whisper. "Or the drugs smuggled in here?"

Bessie kicked at the dirt.

"No. The guards are listening, breathing down our necks. And the warden wants that covered up." She plopped down on the ground, sitting cross-legged. "Besides, Winifred Sweet wants to sell papers. She'd rather portray us as sad fallen women than real people."

"Then why talk to her at all?"

Bessie shrugged. "I like having someone to talk to on the outside. We ain't allowed to read newspapers in here, and no one's sending me letters."

Annie swallowed the hard lump in her throat. She still hadn't written to her sisters. What would they think when their letters went unanswered? Perhaps they'd wonder if she'd changed employers, taking work with a new family, or if she'd injured herself. Once, when Ellen hurt her hand in the factory, she hadn't been able to write home for weeks.

"What's wrong?" Emma asked.

Annie hung her head. "My family. They don't know I'm here."

She thought of her sisters: Lizzie, Mary, Kate, and Maggie. And her brothers: Patrick, Thomas, Joseph, Peter, and James. Eileen would also wonder why she hadn't written. Annie's eldest siblings had taken work, boarding with families who had farms. But her younger siblings were at home alone with their father, barefoot and hungry, waiting for her to send money. American letters with no money enclosed were known as "empty ones."

Emma's eyes held empathy, but sadness too. "Patience, Annie. Perhaps that's for the best."

The male journalist approached them, sketchpad in hand.

"Pardon me." He cleared his throat, gesturing at Emma and Annie. "I noticed the two of you making lace. May I have your names?"

Bessie grinned. "Can we see your drawings first?"

Annie worried he had sketched them like the caricatures she'd seen in the newspapers, their faces like "Irish Bridget," as ugly as apes.

He paused, then nodded. Annie looked at his paper, surprised by the realistic pencil sketch of her and Emma, sitting in the shade of the tree. She smiled.

"That rather looks like us."

Emma nodded. "Aye. It does."

"Annie Gilmurray," she volunteered, glad to identify herself by something other than a number.

The journalist nodded. "Thank you."

"Emma O'Sullivan. I like your picture."

Then Bessie's eyes traveled to the stairs leading down to the courtyard, where a gaunt woman was accompanied by Matron Kane. "Well, I'll be damned. She's back."

"Who's back?" Annie looked at the new convict.

"Mary Martin." Bessie frowned. "She came here on a stretcher, and she's been in the prison hospital ever since. This is the first I've seen her in months."

"Why was she in the hospital?" Annie grimaced, taking in the new convict's pallid complexion, her skin nearly translucent.

"She has a tumor," Bessie said. But her eyes didn't hold sympathy.

Emma nodded. "I heard it's in her stomach. But she's nasty, she is. She swindled a woman in Alameda out of fourteen thousand dollars. A fortune."

Annie couldn't fathom such a sum. "How did she do it?"

"Hypnosis."

Annie looked at Emma. "You must be joking."

"I'm not," Emma said, rubbing her arms. "Mary gives me a bad feelin', like me skin is crawlin'."

Annie turned to Bessie. "Do *you* believe she's a hypnotist?"

Bessie shrugged.

"She got ten years in here for obtaining money under false pretenses, so she's cunning all right. Tumor or not, she gives me the willies."

The journalist picked up his sketchpad, his interest piqued

by the mention of a hypnotist. "Excuse me, but I must take my leave."

Annie considered the frail, middle-aged convict. "She seems harmless."

Emma frowned. "I heard her tumor has gotten so big, she needs an operation."

Bessie shook her head. "Don't let her appearance fool you. She's vindictive, nasty, and just plain mean. I don't like her one bit. Neither does anyone here."

A group formed beneath the tree where Annie sat—Maud Manner, Nellie Osborne, and Lizzie Ross. Margarita Grinilla, the Mexican woman who shot her lover, idled against the wall while Ada Werner, the convict in the cell next to Annie's, found a spot to stand in the shade, like Mary Martin was drawing them into her orbit. "The hypnotist is back." Maud grimaced, her heart-shaped face flushed from the heat. "I heard Mary Martin bewitched Mrs. Murray, her nurse."

Margarita stepped forward to glare at Maud. "That bitch don't scare me."

Maud squared her shoulders. "She don't scare me neither and I ain't said as much."

Margarita spat on the ground. "Puta."

Maud's hands balled into fists.

"What'd you call me?"

Annie's skin felt clammy. She'd seen plenty of fights break out among the women convicts, but she'd never been in the middle of one before. So far, her only allegiance had been to Bessie and Emma, who hadn't crossed any of the other female convicts. Ada Werner flinched as the shouting began.

Mary Von sidled up to the group, snorted, cussed, then spat a lump of green mucus on the ground.

Her lumbering presence silenced the women convicts, reminding them she was still the reigning terror of San Quentin Prison, no matter the rumors about Mary Martin. Margarita and Maud both looked away from Mary Von's sneering face, like chastised schoolchildren. Mary's lips curved into something resembling a smile, revealing her blackened stumps of teeth. Then she spat again, wiping her mouth with the back of her sleeve.

The matron approached, glaring.

"Disgusting. Have you no shame?"

For a moment, something like hurt crossed Mary Von's face. But then her features contorted into a mask of hatred.

"Ain't got nothin' to be ashamed of."

Annie shivered all the way to her core, recognizing the furious look in Mary Von's dark eyes. It was the same look she'd seen in the eyes of her Irish neighbors when their English landlords had come to seize their homes. Mary Von wasn't going to let the matron's comment slide . . . Annie would bet a silver dollar Mary would have her vengeance.

———◆———

THAT NIGHT, ANNIE held her mother's rosary. She rubbed the first bead between her fingers, praying the Our Father. Then she held the next three, praying the Hail Mary. Emma's kindness today had brought her a great measure of comfort.

Closing her eyes, she drifted away until she could see the blue Atlantic and the dramatic sea cliffs of Oileán Acla. She felt the wind in her hair and smelled the briny scent of the ocean.

And then she was home, in her lime-washed cottage. Her mother smiled, lighting turf for the fire. But the smell was no longer peaty and subtle. It was smoky and strong, like tallow.

Annie coughed. "Ma, you've put in too much."

Her mother looked at her. "Wake up, Annie."

Annie startled awake, gasping for breath. Her eyes and throat burned, and smoke filled her cell. Next door, Ada screamed.

"Help! My room is on fire!"

Dread filled Annie's veins, her heart pounding as her narrow cell grew unbearably hot. She grabbed the hem of her night-dress to cover her mouth.

"My candle!" Ada screamed. "It fell. My bedding is on fire!"

Annie got out of bed, smoke burning her lungs. She pounded her fists against the iron door to her cell.

"Let us out!"

But the guards on night watch were nowhere to be found. Annie shook the bars of her window, but the iron wouldn't give way. Her heart thudded as the room grew smokier. Soon, the other female prisoners were screaming and pounding on their doors too.

"They're leaving us to die!"

"Help us!"

Annie coughed until her throat felt raw. Panic rose inside her as she envisioned flames engulfing Ada. Through her door's barred window, she could see black smoke filling the hallway. Sinking to her knees, she felt dizzy. She closed her eyes, coughing, praying this was nothing more than a night-mare. But she had already woken up, and no one was coming to the rescue. She would die here in prison, just as Emma had given her the will to live.

PART TWO

———◆◆———

This land is too valuable to permit poor people to
park on it.
> —Justin Herman, Executive Director, San
> Francisco Redevelopment Agency, 1970

Every boy in our civilization knows that society will
excuse in him, the superior, what it will relentlessly
condemn in her, his inferior.
> —Ellen Battelle Dietrick

11

———◆———

Judy
San Francisco, 1972

I'm in room 402 of the Knox Hotel on Sixth Street, a block away from the Salvation Army, interviewing two men— Nathan Desmond and his friend Ken Roth, both white SRO residents. The room is small, eight by ten, and sparsely furnished with an iron-frame twin bed, a sink, a wooden dresser, a coffee table, a chair, and a little cabinet full of teacups. Shared toilets and showers are down the hall, and a few towels hang haphazardly around the room.

Nathan is eighty-eight years old, and he wears a derby hat and a herringbone suit, complete with a vest and watch chain attached to a pocket watch. He sits on his bed with his hands folded in his lap, wearing a silk tie. I wonder if he dressed up for me and for our photographs today. His friend Ken sits in a wooden chair beside the bed, looking less formal in woolen pants and suspenders. On the cracked wall hangs an American flag, a small painting of Jesus, a wooden cross, and a tattered calendar. Adjusting my camera bag, I hope I can put both men at ease before I start taking pictures.

"Thank you so much for having me."

Nathan chuckles. "Well, it's not every day a nice young lady like you comes over to visit." He gestures around the room. "It ain't much, but it's home."

"So," I begin. "Tell me about yourselves and your neighborhood."

Nathan looks at Ken. "Well, here at the Knox, we're mostly single retired men living on small fixed incomes. Rent here is only thirty-five dollars a month. We like it here."

"That's right," Ken says. "We get clothes and shoes from the Salvation Army. We've got a great little café run by a Chinese family downstairs, with decent food and decent prices. We get free haircuts at the barber colleges, and—"

Nathan laughs. "You ain't got hair anymore!"

Ken smiles, rubbing his bald head. "I suppose you're right. But I *used* to have a nice head of thick, dark hair. That was back in the thirties, of course."

"What did you do for work?" I ask Nathan, taking my twin-lens Rolleiflex out of my camera bag.

He rubs his chin. "During the forties, I was a ship's steward for the troops going to war. After World War II ended, I kept sailing on Liberty ships."

"What about you?" I turn to look at Ken.

Ken seems wistful as he stares out the window. "I was a longshoreman. There used to be a big maritime industry here."

I wind the arm on my camera, making sure my film is in place, and then I look through my viewfinder at the photo I want to compose, with Nathan sitting on his faded floral bed-spread. His wooden cane is propped against it, leaning at an angle.

"What was this neighborhood like when you were young?" I ask.

"It was great," Nathan says. "Full of little coffee shops, bar-bershops, saloons. The Greeks came in the twenties and thir-ties and opened restaurants. I love Greek people!"

"He loves Greek food," Ken says, smiling. "And South of Market was a bustling place during and after the war—people were everywhere. We lived with our buddies. We talked, we went out, we played dominoes. This neighborhood is our home."

I imagine the residential hotels during World War II, filled with war-industry workers, sailors, seamen, soldiers, and other military. They must have frequented the bars and restaurants nearby, giving the area an economic boost. Even though the neighborhood is sleepier now, it still retains a lot of its original charm.

Nathan nods. "Seasonal workers came in the thirties through the fifties. Fruit pickers. Lots of Filipinos brought their families. Real nice folks."

"Friendly people," Ken says. "And we love having kids around here."

I think of my neighbor Vanessa, and of the Black and Fili-pino families I've seen in the neighborhood, their kids roller-skating down the street or playing at the nearby park, bringing a smile to the faces of the elderly SRO tenants who live alone. More than any other neighborhood in the city, South of

Market captures the diversity of San Francisco. It's awful that this community is in danger of erasure. I turn to Nathan.

"What happened after the Redevelopment Agency started buying properties?"

Nathan's face falls. "They put up NO VACANCY signs and they tried to get us to leave. When we refused, they kicked down doors."

My stomach drops. "Seriously?"

Ken nods. "Plenty of our friends are scared to leave their rooms. They took away the comfy chairs in the lobby and replaced them with hard benches. They fired all the friendly staff and hired security who don't give a damn, men who drink on the job."

"Two years ago," Nathan says, grimacing, "our friend James Gregory was robbed, beaten, and murdered in his room. He lived at the Westchester Hotel, owned by the Redevelopment Agency."

I suck in my breath. "He was murdered?"

"He signed a petition," Nathan says, shaking his head, "asking for better security. But the Redevelopment Agency rejected it, ignoring all the signatures. Then they covered up his murder—said it had nothing to do with them. But they have blood on their hands."

I shudder, thinking of the cruel intimidation tactics the Redevelopment Agency is using to force evictions. These men are elderly and frail. They literally have no family and nowhere else to go. I hope that TOOR is successful in their legal fight and able to secure decent, safe, and clean relocation housing for Nathan, Ken, and others like them.

Looking through my viewfinder, I have both men sit solemnly in the frame, and I take my photograph. Though I usually shoot in color, for these residential hotel portraits I'm choosing to shoot in black and white, to give a timeless quality to the images. I want people to think about how long these men have lived here—some for more than forty years.

"Thank you so much," I say. "For sharing your stories with me. I'm going to do what I can to amplify your voices. You're part of a powerful movement."

Both Nathan and Ken take a moment to clasp my hand in theirs.

"Thank you," Nathan says. "For speaking up for us."

———◆———

I TALK TO and photograph more elderly residents at other low-income hotels. I visit the Hotel Rex, the Rock Hotel, the Joyce Hotel, and the Milner Hotel. Each person tells me stories about their life, the South of Market neighborhood, and the strong connection they have to the community. I hear horror stories of clean bed linens being taken away, garbage piling up in hallways, mail being thrown out, toilets being locked, or the heat and water being shut off. Of the four thousand residents who lived in the Yerba Buena Center project area, only about a quarter still remain. The intimidation tactics of the Redevelopment Agency are working.

Next I take my Gundlach Korona camera to the locally owned cafés to take color photographs. I order a meal and talk with the owners, mostly Chinese and Greek immigrants, and by the time I'm finished eating, it no longer feels strange to have my bulky, Ansel Adams–style rig set up to shoot. I photograph more local businesses—the blacksmith, the barbershop, the grocer. Then I photograph the faces of people who would otherwise be passed without a glance on the street. In black and white, I capture a homeless man in profile, the smoke from his cigarette curling up into the air. His name is Anthony, and I buy him a meal.

When I develop my photographs in the darkroom of Glass Photo, my heart thrums with anticipation. Slowly, I see my images come to life, ghostly as they appear in the tray of developer. Hope's portrait turns out just as exquisitely as I thought it would. Her light eyes are haunting in black and white, like Annie's eyes. It's as if Hope is saying, *See me.*

In my portraits of the hotel residents, there's a sense of loneliness and despair, but many display spirited independence and dignity. In contrast, my photographs of local businesses are vibrant and colorful. They show a neighborhood still thriving, in spite of all the forces working against it. As I hang each image to dry, my heart swells with pride. I've lacked a sense of purpose for so long—and now I have one. Emerging from the drying room, I smile.

Seth smiles back at me. "Do you mind if I take a look at your photos?"

He's been wiping down the glass counter with a rag and a spray bottle of Windex, fastidious in how he cleans his photography studio. Though I've offered my help, he doesn't expect me to do all the cleaning. We share duties, even though he's my boss. It's a big shift from living with Tony, who expected me to do everything around the house.

"Okay," I say, feeling shy.

We enter the drying room together, and Seth takes his time silently appreciating each photograph. I wonder what he's thinking. Though I'm happy with how they turned out, I value his opinion as a professional and my boss. Seth gives me a serious look.

"Judy, these are incredible."

My skin warms at the compliment. "Really? You think so?"

He nods. "They tell a powerful story. What inspired them?"

"Actually," I say, smiling, "I was inspired by a mug shot in the book you lent me. A portrait of a young Irishwoman named Annie."

Seth laughs. "I love it! Art begets art."

"It was the look in her eyes," I say. "It haunted me. Then I remembered what you said about portrait parlé. I wanted to take a photo that speaks, just as hers did."

"Wow." Seth smiles. "You just gave me goose bumps."

He points at the black-and-white photo of Hope's face. "This image is especially good. It's evocative. I can't stop staring at her eyes."

"Thank you," I say. "That was the first one I took."

"What do you plan to do with this series? Does it have a name?"

"I haven't thought about a name yet." I take a deep breath, ready to admit my long-held ambition aloud. "As for the series, I want to use it as my portfolio to apply for a master of fine arts degree in photography."

I exhale. Going to graduate school has long been a dream of mine. I wanted to apply when Tony and I were first married, but he discouraged me from doing it. Now that I've spoken this desire aloud, I feel like it could actually come true.

"Wonderful," Seth says. "Where will you apply?"

"The San Francisco Art Institute, California College of the Arts, and Academy of Art University." I bite my lip. "Maybe San Francisco State as well."

"That's great." Seth's eyebrows draw together. "But you could dream even bigger. Have you ever thought of applying for an arts grant?"

I shake my head. "I don't think I'd have a shot at anything like that."

Seth gives me a stern look. "You'll never know until you try." He gestures at my photographs. "What I see here is the story of a city in transition. The bigger an audience this project has, the bigger the impact."

He's right, of course. Many of my photographs document how redevelopment will affect the neighborhood, its low-income residents on the verge of being displaced. Tony has made me feel small and insecure for so long, it's hard for me to build up confidence about my work. But I try to imagine my photographs in a gallery and people coming to see them, then thinking about the impact urban renewal is having on this neighborhood. Maybe I could even do the show in collaboration with TOOR, to bring awareness to the cause.

"Thanks, Seth," I say. "For having faith in me."

"Sometimes we need to be reminded of our power," Seth says, giving me a knowing look. "People will try to take it away from you by breaking you down. Especially when you don't fit the norm of what they expect you to be."

I nod, listening.

"When I came out," he says, "I discovered that a lot of my fears were unfounded. I really had more friends than I thought."

"That's great," I say.

He smiles. "What other people think about you isn't your problem, Judy. Don't let anyone stop you from being the most authentic version of yourself."

In his vulnerability, Seth is encouraging me to be strong. Gay men are more feared in society today than divorced women—and yet Seth is living his truth. But I can't ignore my mother's admiration for Phyllis Schlafly, or the fervent wave of anti-feminist sentiment that Schlafly has created. How many women believe divorce is destroying the American family? How many men fear the agency of a single woman?

I think of all the advertisements I've seen in magazines—women happily shining their husbands' shoes or standing in front of ovens, their breasts spilling out of their tops.

After failing to convince Tony why I needed a job outside the home, I'd open the newspaper and see an advertisement for a Kenwood Chef mixer: *The Chef does everything but cook—that's what wives are for!* Or a Hotpoint washer and dryer: *My wife Jean is happy, pretty & pregnant. Boy, am I glad I bought her a new Hotpoint washer & dryer!*

I failed at being happy, pretty, and pregnant. And for years, it broke my heart. But here, working for my own money and pursuing my own interests, I'm beginning to think there's more to life than being a wife and mother. Yes, that was my dream, but sometimes dreams don't turn out as planned. There will be people who feel discomfort, even rage, at my newfound autonomy outside of marriage. Even I find it terrifying to think about what could be on the other side of leaving Tony. But I'll never find out if I don't take the leap.

———◆———

AT THE SAN FRANCISCO courthouse on McAllister Street, I wait for my number to be called. The clerks behind the glass look tired and bored. I gnaw my bottom lip. It's toward the end of the workday, and I hope they can locate Annie's court records. I need to know if Greta's affidavit was included as evidence in Annie's case, and if she was given a new trial.

"Number one seventy-five," a court clerk calls out.

Jumping up from my seat, I clutch my purse containing the original affidavit. I smile as I approach the glass. "Hi. Thank you for seeing me."

The woman doesn't smile back.

"Did you fill out your form?"

"Yes," I say, sliding the piece of paper under the glass. "I filled out everything I could. Sorry if it's incomplete."

She looks it over, frowning. "Docket number?"

"Well, it's an old case. Could the docket number be the same as the case number?"

The woman looks at me like I'm an imbecile. Her fingernails clack against her keyboard. She shakes her head.

"Is this a civil case?"

I swallow. "A criminal case?"

She adjusts her tortoiseshell glasses, looking down at the form, then back at me. "You want a case file from *1890*?"

I keep a polite smile on my face. "Yes."

"Sorry." She shakes her head, pushing the form away. "All courthouse records were destroyed in the earthquake and fire of 1906."

My stomach sinks. "All of them?"

"Yep," she says, turning back to her IBM 3270, a modern green-screen computer. "Some records were reregistered, but not many."

"Do you think there's any way this case was reregistered?"

She doesn't look at me. "Unlikely."

I press my lips together. "I need to know if an affidavit was included as evidence in a trial that took place back then. I have the original in my—"

The woman frowns. "We don't do research here, honey."

"Oh," I say, my cheeks coloring. "No, of course not. I was just hoping you could assist me in finding the original case materials."

I sense a man standing in line behind me, tapping his foot and loudly clearing his throat. The court clerk looks over at him and then back at me.

"Some early court records were sent to the California State Archives. Wills, deeds, marriage bonds, estate inventories."

"Okay," I say, deflated. "Thanks."

The clerk shuffles some papers at her desk, signaling that she is done with our conversation. The man behind me steps forward, and I move aside, frustrated at having reached a dead end. Annie was punished for a crime she didn't commit, and now I have no way of knowing whether she was given a new trial. I was optimistic I would find her court records, that the clerk would be able to tell me if Greta's affidavit was ever submitted as evidence.

After my disappointing visit, I leave the courthouse, thinking of the elderly hotel tenants I interviewed earlier today, and how their friend James Gregory was murdered in a building owned by the Redevelopment Agency. Powerful institutions are skilled at concealing their corruption. And though I'd like to have faith in our state court system, I'm starting to lose hope that Annie was given the justice she deserved.

12

Annie

San Quentin, 1890

Annie drew in a painful breath, choking and coughing as a guard dragged her from her cell. The hallway was filled with smoke, and her eyes stung with tears. Matron Kane stood beside the night watchman, covering her mouth with a kerchief.

"I've got the keys!" a guard shouted. "Take the women to the courtyard until we get the blaze under control."

She watched in a daze as cell doors were unlocked one by one. The prisoners coughed, some crying as they made their way toward the stairs down to the courtyard. An alarm sounded, and prison firemen arrived in uniform, shouting commands at one another. Ada Werner's cell was empty, the iron door bent and battered, ripped away from its hinges. Feeling a tug at her elbow, Annie rose to her feet, her head spinning. It was Emma.

"Don't worry. I've got you."

Emma wrapped her arm around Annie's shoulders,

supporting her weight. Together, they stumbled through the smoke, toward the door at the end of the hall. When it opened, Annie gulped fresh air, her lungs burning. The moon shone overhead, and the trees cast eerie shadows, shrouded in fog. She shivered in her nightdress, looking around at the groups of frightened women, their faces smudged with soot.

"Are ye all right?" Emma asked.

Annie nodded. "I thought they had left us to die." Her throat burned as she spoke, and her voice was low and scratchy.

Emma rubbed her arms. "I heard such terrible banging and screaming."

Bessie approached them, coughing. "Shit. That was frightening."

Annie shuddered. "Have you seen Ada? The fire was in her room."

"They dragged her out." Bessie coughed into her elbow. "The night watchmen battered Ada's door down because there was no time to go downstairs for the keys."

Annie coughed. "There wasn't?"

Bessie shook her head. "One more minute, maybe two, and Ada would have suffocated from the smoke. They took her to the hospital."

Shaking, Annie realized how close she'd come to dying. In prison, she was vulnerable in ways she'd never been before. The guards mercilessly tortured the men with straitjackets, and the prisoners in Crazy Alley were in no mental state to make their own decisions. Annie had watched them behind the fence during the day, as they dug in the dirt. Here, she had no rights and no one to advocate for her. She was forced to work for no wages, day after day, bent over a sewing machine.

Hot tears slid down her cheeks.

"I thought I'd never see my family again."

"Shh," Emma said, wrapping her in a hug. "You've only got one year. Soon you'll be out of here and you can send for them."

Annie rested her head on Emma's shoulder, grateful for the comfort of her arms. It had been so long since anyone had held her like this. "I miss home." She sniveled into the cotton sleeve of her nightdress. "I shouldn't have left Mayo."

Emma pulled away, holding Annie by the shoulders. "You can still go home to old Ireland. But ye can't give up."

Drawing in a deep breath, Annie considered this. She didn't have a dowry, and neither did her sisters. She didn't want to be married off to an old farmer, to spend her life sweeping the dirt floor of his hut, pulling potatoes from the ground. She had to survive for Lizzie, Mary, Kate, and Maggie, and for her brothers, Patrick, Peter, Joseph, Thomas, and James. She was the next link in the chain; Eileen had gone first, bringing her here. Now it was Annie's turn.

Bessie nodded. "Emma is right. We'll be free of this place soon enough. They can try to break our spirits, but they won't succeed."

Annie looked around at the women convicts. Maud huddled between Nellie Osborne and the crew of pickpockets, her small frame trembling. Bridget's white hair had come loose from her braid, and when she pushed the long strands away from her face, Annie saw Bridget had tears in her eyes. Yes, they were criminals, but they deserved to be treated with dignity.

"We won't let them break us." Annie squared her shoulders. "When we leave this place, we'll be free as birds."

"And we'll go dancing," Emma said.

"And drink whiskey!" Bessie winked.

The three women laughed, and Annie was no longer shaking. Somehow, in this brutal place, she'd managed to find solace.

———◆◆———

LEAVING THE BRICK workshop building with Emma walking beside her, Annie cracked her knuckles. Her back hurt from hunching over her sewing machine, but she supposed it was no worse than working in the prison laundry. Annie would've preferred to be on kitchen duty, but only one female prisoner worked there, May Johnson, a kind Black woman who had a sweetheart named George. He'd been given the job of driving the commissary wagon on account of his good behavior, and he fell for May while making kitchen deliveries.

"Well, if it isn't two soiled doves out for a stroll."

Annie gasped as a guard stepped in front of her. She recognized him. It was the red-haired man who reeked of liquor, who'd threatened to find her on her first day in prison. She could tell from his glassy eyes he was drunk.

"Feck off, Corcoran." Emma glared at him.

He licked his lips. "I could put you in the dungeon for speaking to me like that."

"Leave us be," Emma said. "Besides, she ain't no soiled dove."

Annie's heart pounded. Though it was brave of Emma to speak up for her, the last thing she wanted was the attention of this menace. They weren't far from the Porch, but with Corcoran delaying them, they'd been separated from the women in their work crew. Corcoran leaned in so close, Annie could smell him, his alcohol and perspiration.

"You're all sportin' women. And I can take any one of you."

Annie looked around for help. But the other guards were unmoved by the fate of two female convicts. She glared at him.

"Let us go."

Corcoran narrowed his eyes and spit on the ground. Then his lips twisted into a smile. "You're a fiery little Bridget, aren't you?"

Annie felt his eyes tracing her body like worms crawling up her skin.

He stroked his jaw. "I like your shape."

Even though her prison uniform with its vertical black and white stripes was buttoned up to her neck, Annie felt naked.

He laughed and grabbed Emma's arm. "I like her shape too."

Emma yanked her elbow, but Corcoran tightened his grip. Emma winced in pain.

Annie took a step forward. "Let go of her or I'll scream."

Corcoran dropped Emma's arm. "If you scream, I'll send you to Crazy Alley." He licked his lips. "Never forget who's in charge."

He took a wobbling step forward, then a Gatling gun erupted overhead, shots ringing out over the prison wall. Annie froze, while officers and guards began sprinting across the yard. Within a minute, the escape bell sounded, loud and shrill.

"Corcoran!" a guard yelled. "Move to position, now!"

Corcoran took another long, lascivious look at Annie, swaying from side to side, while his comrade's face hardened.

"If you're drunk on the job, Captain Gilcrest will hear about it." He motioned to Annie. "Hurry now, get back to the females' ward."

Annie grabbed Emma's hand and ran toward the Porch. But she could still feel Corcoran's eyes and smell his breath. In the mess hall, her hands shook. A cacophony of conversations and banging plates filled the room while Matron Kane called for order, but no one paid her any mind. Everyone wanted to know who had escaped and how. Annie made her way toward the front of the line, where May stood stirring a pot. At twenty-eight, May Johnson was older than Annie, but her soft, round face looked young. She was the only woman in a kitchen full of men, and the only Black woman in the prison.

May gave Annie a concerned frown.

"What's troubling you?"

Looking into May's kind, dark eyes, Annie sighed. "It's Corcoran."

May sucked her teeth. "Watch out for him." She looked over at Matron Kane to make sure she wasn't eavesdropping. "My George says Corcoran smuggles whiskey and opium in here. He don't play by the rules."

Annie gritted her teeth. "We ought to have him fired."

May gave her a sympathetic look. "You know it ain't that easy." She ladled stew into Annie's bowl. "Brooks and Cramer are in on it too. They've been lowering packages of drugs down to the prison yard from their guard tower."

Annie could picture the two guards, dark-haired Joseph Brooks and skinny John Cramer, conspiring with trustees to keep San Quentin's opium ring running. She wasn't surprised Corcoran was involved. It was a lucrative business for the guards and for the prisoners who sold their wares. Money could get you whatever you wanted—an oil lamp and matches for your cell, two bits of whiskey in a soda bottle, tobacco, opium, morphine, a better job.

Convicts paid double for opium in here what they'd pay outside—and spent time smoking it, chewing it, and then shaking violently when they went without. Annie didn't want to touch the stuff. She'd seen the way it sent men to the hospital, glassy-eyed and broken.

"I wish the warden would do something," Annie mumbled.

May nodded. "Me too. But he won't."

Emma pushed her bowl toward May.

"Can your fella George get me a crochet needle?"

May frowned. "Another one?"

"For Annie. I'm teaching her to make lace."

May smiled. "I'll see what I can do."

"Number 22966," Matron Kane called out. "Cease speaking with number 13475."

Annie felt a stab of guilt. "Sorry," she mouthed.

Carrying a bowl of stew and hunk of bread to the table, Annie caught snippets of conversation as the women in the mess hall speculated about who had escaped.

"Gould's the type to make a run for it. He's wily, he is."

"What d'you reckon it's one of Julia's sons? Should we ask her?"

Male murderers were afforded more freedoms than the best-behaved female prisoners. Annie thought bitterly about how many jobs trustees were allowed outside the prison: looking after the gardens lining the road to San Quentin, bringing meals to the guards at their posts, repairing old buildings, driving wagons. She didn't doubt today's escape attempt had been made by a male convict entrusted with the freedom to wander beyond the prison walls. Meanwhile, her only sense of freedom came from sitting in the courtyard with Emma and Bessie, breathing the fresh air and practicing her crochet lace.

In her dank prison cell, Annie stared at the ceiling. With the fugitive still at large, the women had been locked up so they could be counted. Without a needle, Annie practiced the lace making Emma had taught her in her mind: she made a slip stitch, then a single crochet, bringing the needle and thread over the padding cord and then under—then on the twentieth single crochet, she hooked into the back, made a slip stitch, and formed a ring. Annie pictured the design, simple yet complex. She worked back around, with one double crochet in each stitch, until she'd completed the scroll.

"Psst! Annie!"

Annie got up and looked through the bars of her cell to see who was calling her name. Across the hall, Maud waved. "I have news."

Annie glanced down the empty corridor. "What is it?"

"The guards nabbed 'em."

"Who are they?"

"Two stagecoach robbers and a murderer. Baker, Manning, and Turcott."

Annie didn't know the men. She shifted her weight, her bare feet cold.

"How'd they do it?"

"They were working outside the prison and hid in a brick building. One of 'em had a cousin who stashed three rifles near the windmill. They carried their tools like they were going to work and then picked up the rifles and ran."

Annie shook her head. Earlier this year, a trustee who'd

worked in the guards' quarters donned a guard's uniform and walked out the prison gates. No one even blinked an eye.

"Were they trustees?"

Maud scoffed. "Of course. By the time we heard guns firing, they were already hiding in the hills. One of 'em shot a guard in the arm."

"And they were taken back alive?"

"Not a scratch on any one of 'em. They'll have bread and water in the dungeons, then they'll be released back to work duty soon enough."

Annie wished Corcoran had been the guard shot in the arm, but he was likely too drunk to be found anywhere near the skirmish.

"Do ye think we'll be allowed out now that they've been caught?" Annie asked.

Maud sighed. "I hope so. I'm bored as shit in here."

Matron Kane's shrill voice carried down the hallway. "Silence! The next one of you to speak out of turn will eat your evening meal in your cell."

"Shut up, you fuckin' cunt!"

There were gasps and peals of laughter as Mary Von's gruff voice echoed throughout the women's ward. Annie suppressed a smile. Mary Von was as nasty as they came.

"Order!" Matron Kane called. "Prisoner 12705, you'll eat supper in your cell."

"And I'll pick my teeth with your skinny bones," Mary muttered.

Though the inmates liked to insult one another, none of them were brave enough to point out that Mary didn't *have* any teeth left. At forty, her mouth was nothing but a gaping hole of blackened stumps. Perhaps the pain in her gums was part of the reason she was so vile. Annie waited quietly, hoping the door to her cell would be unlocked soon. But as much as she wanted to be let out of this suffocating room, it meant she would be back in Corcoran's path. Here in San Quentin, she wasn't only a prisoner, but also prey.

13

Judy

San Francisco, 1972

I check my purse one last time to make sure I have everything I need for my research trip to UC Berkeley. The employee at the Bancroft Library informed me that only a pencil will be permitted inside—no ink in the reading room. I won't be allowed to bring in my purse either, but I can store it in a locker. My notebook will be inspected before I leave, and if I take any photographs, they're for personal use only; I can't exhibit them anywhere.

In spite of the strict rules, my skin tingles with excitement. I'm eager to look through the San Quentin Prison records from 1890, to see when Annie was released from prison. The Bancroft Library also holds scrapbooks with photographs, mug shots, and newspaper clippings kept by a police sergeant during his career in the late 1800s.

A knock at the door startles me. I press my lips together, my heart racing. *Is it the landlord?* He's a grumpy old man, concerned about me living alone, but he hasn't bothered me so far. Besides, I've already paid my rent this month. Maybe it's Vanessa.

I pull the door open and gasp when I see Tony. My body isn't prepared for the reaction—I want to embrace him as much as I want to slam the door in his face.

My heart thuds. "What are you doing here?"

He stands across the threshold, and it feels like there's an ocean between us, even though he's only an arm's length away.

He looks tired. "Can I come inside?"

Tony isn't one to ask for permission. I'm so taken aback that I nod. He steps through the doorway, closing the distance between us, and I breathe in the familiar scent of his Old Spice cologne. He's wearing a clean flannel shirt and faded Levi's, and his strong, tanned arms hang at his sides. When he looks at me, his deep brown eyes are full of remorse.

"So, this is where you've been staying, huh?"

I see the apartment through his eyes—lonely and sparsely furnished. It doesn't look like much of a home, especially compared to our ranch house back in Sacramento. But then I remember—I didn't give him my address. My stomach knots.

"How did you find me?"

He scowls, giving me a hurt look. "I looked up the phone number your mother gave me in the San Francisco White Pages. Do you know how long it took me to find an address that matched? You should have just told me where you were."

My hands shake, I'm so angry at him. Now that he's here, I steel myself for a confrontation.

"There's a reason I didn't tell you where I am, Tony."

He sighs, then he rubs his face. "I know, Judy. And I'm sorry."

My eyes well with tears. "Why did you do it? Did you *want* me to catch you?"

My heart breaks from his infidelity, but Tony cheating on me with the barmaid at the Trap is only one problem. I haven't forgotten the shame of waiting for him to come home, and then getting fed up, driving to the bar, and seeing my husband kissing her, a bottle blonde, in a dark corner next to the jukebox. He groped her ass and laughed. And when he turned and saw me, instead of looking horrified, he looked confused, as if he couldn't fathom why I was there. His wife belonged at home, not out at a bar after midnight.

"I don't know," Tony says, his voice breaking. "You deserve better. I don't think sometimes. I drink too much and then I make bad choices."

I nod, blinking back tears.

"But she means nothing." He takes a step closer to me, his eyes pleading. "I promise it will never happen again. I'll do anything you want. Hell, I'll even go see a shrink."

I'm shocked to hear this. Tony has been vehemently against couples counseling for years. He thinks all therapists are quacks and a waste of money.

He smiles sadly. "I've been sober, Judy. I went to my first AA meeting."

Looking into his eyes, I believe him. Tony is more clear-headed than I've seen him in months. He reaches for my hand and squeezes it.

"You wanted me sober. This is me sober. I'm doing this for you."

Suddenly, I'm overcome by resentment. *Why is Tony making the effort now?* I've fought with him about his behavior for years, and I'm supposed to be on my way to the Bancroft Library for my research appointment. How many times have I pleaded with my husband to get help, offering my support? And now that I've finally gotten some time and space to think, he's demanding my attention. But I am happy for him. This is a good sign.

"Tony," I say, pulling my hand away. "I'm proud of you, I really am."

His face clouds. "But?"

"But I'm on my way to the library in Berkeley, and—"

"And?" He throws up his hands. "I'll come with you. Judy, I *need* you. I can't do this without you."

I shake my head. "The appointment is for me only. You can't come in."

"Then I'll drive you there and wait outside." Tony's eyes glisten with tears. "Judy, I've missed you. I've been so worried about you—you have no idea."

I've only seen Tony cry once—when his beloved grandmother, his nonna, died. Sighing, I shut the door to my apartment so we can have some privacy. Maybe I can still make my appointment in Berkeley if I leave in ten minutes and traffic isn't too bad on the Bay Bridge. In the kitchen, I pour a glass of water from the tap, then turn to face my husband.

"You don't need to worry about me. I'm fine."

He laughs. "Are you kidding me? Living alone in a big city with pickpockets and creeps? A pretty girl like you?" He shakes his head. "No. It's not safe."

Swallowing the lump in my throat, I think about all the times I didn't feel safe with him at our home in Sacramento. My body tenses as I remember Tony screaming in my face, whiskey on his breath, pounding the wall next to me with his fist. My lips tremble.

"Tony, you *know* why I left."

My voice is hoarse, and I brace for him to become defensive, but instead he looks wounded. Tony hangs his head.

"I'm so sorry. I know I fucked up. But I'm going to change. I promise. Please, you're my wife. I need you."

He reaches up and strokes my cheek. Even though I want to stay impassive, I can't help leaning into his caress. Tears wet my lashes, then slip from my eyes. I don't want to fall back into the same cycle I've been stuck in, of Tony apologizing and then hurting me.

"How do I know it won't happen again?"

"It won't," he whispers, wiping my tears away. "I never want to scare you, Judy. I have trouble controlling my anger, but I'm working on it."

I reach up and cover his hand with mine. It's so warm and familiar, his calluses rough against my cheek, his hands weathered from working with wood. When I look into Tony's deep brown eyes, I'm overcome with emotion. These eyes held mine at the altar as he promised to love me and to cherish me until death do us part. And today I see something new in them— vulnerability. Tony is afraid of losing me, and he's willing to change. Maybe his first Alcoholics Anonymous meeting truly got through to him.

"Judy," he whispers, standing so close I can feel his warm breath on my cheek. "I can't do this without you. I love you. We're family."

For what feels like an eternity, I stand there, my face cradled in his palm, my lips a hair's breadth from his. And then I close the distance between us. I'm tired of running, I'm tired of spending my nights alone, and in spite of everything, I still love this man. He kisses me hard, and I moan softly as I breathe in his scent. I've missed the feel of his strong arms around me and his stubble against my mouth. Tony pulls me close, caressing my skin. We fit together so perfectly, like we always have. When he picks me up and carries me to the bedroom, I don't resist. We undress quickly, throwing our clothes in a pile next to the bed. Nothing matters anymore, only the feel of Tony's bare skin against mine and the sound of his heart beating steadily in his chest. I lose myself to his touch, letting my mind go blissfully blank.

— ◆ —

When I wake up, it's late in the afternoon, and Tony is snoring beside me. I press my lips together, feeling sick with regret. Just because Tony told me all the things I want to hear doesn't mean anything has changed or that our problems will simply disappear. As much as it hurts to acknowledge, distance from Tony has given me clarity. I've fallen into this cycle before, reveling in the high of makeup sex after the low of a bad fight.

Careful not to wake him, I slip from the bed, pulling on my underpants and jeans. I button up my shirt and pad barefoot to the kitchen, where I drink the glass of water I poured earlier. When my eyes land on my spiral notebook and pencil, my stomach sinks, reminding me I missed my appointment at the UC Berkeley Library.

I was looking forward to it, and once again, I dropped everything for Tony, as if my own desires don't even matter. But in researching Annie's story, I've begun to unbury something dormant inside myself. And as much as I want to blame Tony for keeping me from reaching my potential, I'm the one who has been holding myself back.

Setting my water glass on the counter, I feel restless. I don't want to get back into bed with Tony. Instead, I grab my camera and a jacket. I think about leaving Tony a note, but I decide not to. He's a sound sleeper, and it's not my job to tell him where I'm going anymore. One of the things I hate most about our marriage is his constant surveillance. I felt suffocated, always reporting to him about every small errand, like a person on parole. After closing the door softly behind me, I make my way down the creaky stairs to the lobby. When I walk outside, the sun is low in the sky and the street is empty.

Head down, I decide to walk through the neighborhood, even though I don't have any particular destination in mind. I tighten the strap on my camera bag and walk down Natoma toward Ninth, passing worn brick warehouses and weathered wood-frame apartments lining the alleyways. I make a left on Ninth toward Folsom, then walk Folsom for a few more blocks until I've reached Eleventh Street. I keep going; disco music carries from the doorway of a gay bar called the Stud, an old Victorian building next to Norfolk Street, a narrow alley.

There's a man sitting out front, straddling his motorcycle, a red Honda. He's wearing a leather vest and a leather cap, but he doesn't have on a shirt—his bare chest is adorned with a silver necklace. He wears black leather chaps over his blue jeans. I smile at him. Someday soon, the people on the edges of the Yerba Buena project site will be priced out, and I want to capture my South of Market neighborhood as it is now.

"I like your outfit," I say, nodding at his leather ensemble. "Would it be all right if I took your picture?"

The man smiles, revealing a gap in his front teeth. "Sure," he says.

"What's your name?" I ask, adjusting my focus.

"Kevin." He leans forward on his motorcycle. "Do you want me to smile?"

I shake my head. "No. Try to look natural. I like your hand on the throttle, like that. You can leave the other hand hanging by your side."

Kevin does what I say, relaxing his face for the camera. I love the pop of color from his cherry-red motorcycle, the contrast of his pale skin against the black leather, and the neon sign for Hamburger Mary's in the background, across the street.

"Thank you," I say, taking the photograph. "You look great."

He tips his cap. "You're welcome. Have a good one!"

Leaving the bar, I continue meandering around the neighborhood, snapping pictures of graffiti and interesting street corners. When I return to my apartment, I've nearly forgotten Tony is inside. I set down my keys and camera bag when he emerges from the bedroom, wearing nothing but his Jockey briefs. Even though I've seen him naked a hundred times, I avoid looking at the dark trail of hair running from his stomach down to his pelvis. It feels too intimate.

"Where were you?" Tony narrows his eyes.

"Out." I straighten my shoulders. "Taking photographs."

He scoffs. "You didn't think to tell me where you were going?"

I take a deep breath in and let it out. "You were asleep. Besides, this is *my* apartment. You showed up here uninvited."

He throws up his hands. "Uninvited, huh? Why are you looking at me like I'm some kind of creep or something? I'm your husband."

My hands feel clammy and my heart begins to race. It was a mistake to sleep with Tony. In the moment, the pull of our sexual chemistry was so strong, but now I've given him the wrong idea. Our marriage isn't working, and something needs to change.

I pinch the bridge of my nose. "Tony, I need more time to think."

He stands there, half naked, looking confused. "About what? I'll pack your bags."

"No." I take a step back. "I have work in the morning."

His dark eyebrows draw together. "*Work?*"

I swallow. "That's right. I got a job in a photography studio." I look him square in the eyes. "I need to work so I can make my own money, so I can be independent."

Tony laughs. "Judy, you don't need to work. We have a nice house. I pay the mortgage."

I can feel myself growing smaller.

"I know. But, Tony, I need this for me. I've been unhappy these last few years. I need you to listen to me, okay?"

Tony sighs. "Fine. You want to take pictures? Take pictures. I've never stopped you."

"I want to earn money from my photographs," I say, my voice shaking. "And in order to do that, I need to build my portfolio. I need to—"

He stares at me. "Do you know how many women would kill to be in your position? To stay at home all day, with a husband who loves them?"

My heart beats faster. "Yes," I say. "*Some* women dream of staying at home. But I'm not one of them. I want something for myself, Tony."

Tony's face changes, his eyes growing hard.

"So you don't appreciate everything I do for you?"

I can feel my body going into fight-or-flight mode.

"Tony, I do. I—"

He takes a step closer. "Do you know how hard I work so you can have a roof over your head? Food in the refrigerator? So you can buy the things you want?"

My hands are shaking now, and I want to curl up into a ball. I should apologize, should tell him how grateful I am, and silently watch as he packs up my clothes. But when I think about Annie, I can't do it. She endured time in San Quentin for a crime she didn't commit. I refuse to imprison myself in this marriage any longer. I can show resilience too.

I square my shoulders. "I think you should leave."

Tony blanches. "What?"

Focusing on my breath, I count the seconds in my mind. "This is my apartment. I am on the lease. I pay the rent. And I am asking you to go."

He laughs. "Are you crazy? A few hours ago, you jumped into bed with me. Judy, I'm taking you home."

I force myself to meet Tony's eyes. "I am home."

Before he can stop me, I charge to the front door of my apartment and swing it open. If he starts yelling or tries to restrain me, I want every person in this building to hear. I stand in the doorway, shaking and defiant, challenging him to do something.

"I'm sorry, Tony."

Tony scowls, gesturing at the open door. "Do you mind giving me some privacy?"

I swallow. "You can dress in the bedroom. I'll be right here."

Tony cusses under his breath, glares at me, and then stomps off toward the bedroom. When he returns, his eyes burn with resentment.

"You're making a mistake." He buttons up his flannel shirt. "Do you know how hard it is to not *fucking* drink? You're the person I'm doing this for!"

I blink back tears. "Do it for yourself, Tony. Not for me."

He shakes his finger in my face.

"I don't know what game you're playing, but you'll come crawling back to me."

"I'm sorry," I whisper. "Now, please go."

Tony gives me one last look, a mixture of rage and sorrow, then pounds down the stairs. My ears are ringing and my hands are still shaking. Shutting the door behind me, I bolt the lock. Then I sink to the floor. But I don't cry.

"You did it," I whisper.

I slept with Tony in a moment of vulnerability, but I don't want to be married to him anymore. And if I'm not coming back, then I need to move forward, which means I have to let go of the life I envisioned. There will be no more ranch home with garden beds full of ripe tomatoes. No more kisses on the forehead. No more anniversaries celebrating our love. I don't know what's on the other side of this. I'm afraid. And I wish facing the truth didn't hurt so much. But I'm proud of standing up for myself.

—◆—

14

Annie

San Quentin, 1890

In the courtyard, Annie practiced her Clones lace. May had managed to smuggle her a crochet needle, thanks to her beau, George, a trustee who had procured one from a contact on the outside. Beside her, May smiled as she wrote, sitting next to a pile of small stones stacked on the bench. When George couldn't come up with excuses to visit the women's kitchen, he and May exchanged letters. In her second-story cell overlooking the prison garden, May tied her love notes to rocks and dropped them out the window. George had a friend, another trustee who worked as the prison gardener. He picked up May's notes and brought them to George.

Though Annie didn't desire a beau, she had to admit that exchanging love letters was romantic. But she worried for May—if her friend was caught, punishment would be swift. And May was far too kind to face solitary confinement in the dungeon. Admiring a rose she'd crocheted, Annie smiled. Her fingers weren't as nimble as Emma's, but she was getting better, and she felt grateful for a way to pass the time.

Watching May write her letter, Annie thought of her sister Maggie. With every passing day, her heart ached. Her siblings were wondering what had become of her. And what *had* become of her? In prison, she'd changed. The gloves and hats she'd once coveted were ridiculous frivolities. Her calico day dress, finally returned to her for good behavior, was lovely and soft. Yet once, she'd deemed it too plain for church.

Annie had wanted a better life for herself, yes. But she'd also wanted to reach above her station and believed marrying a wealthy man was the answer. That thought was shameful now. She was no better than any of these convict women. May, Bessie, and Emma had become people she felt she could trust. Even Maud, with her tough exterior, was only seventeen, still a girl with a love of gossip. Despite their faults, these women were not below her.

May shook her head, her natural curls pinned beneath a straw hat.

"The strangest thing happened this morning at breakfast."

"Oh?" Annie looked up from her crochet lace.

May set down her letter, turning to Annie.

"My stove lifter went missing. I damn near burned my hand trying to get the lid off a pot of beans."

Annie winced. "Are ye all right?"

May shrugged. "I suppose. Hazard of the job."

Annie thought of how she'd been burned, carrying hot plates to the table for Mrs. Whittier, and of her friend Ellen, who'd injured her hand at the hatbox factory where she worked.

They were paid meager wages, but the convicts in the jute factory, the men ordered to turn out one hundred yards of cloth a day, didn't see a cent from their own labor. Only in prison could human beings be treated worse than dogs.

Bessie approached, suspenders holding up her trousers, while Emma walked beside her in a long blue cotton dress. Bessie looked like a vagrant, but perhaps she feared if she took her trousers to be laundered, the matron would confiscate them. It was nice, Annie thought, to wear their own clothes on Sundays, to be reminded of who they were beneath their stripes.

May frowned. "You're a pretty girl, Bessie. Why do you dress like that?"

Bessie squared her shoulders.

"I've hated girls' clothing with its fuss and muss since I was a child. My mama let me romp around in boys' overalls and I would cry every time she put me in a dress."

"Not me," Emma said. "I dreamed of owning a new dress and a pair of shiny shoes. I was barefoot and wearin' a dress made from flour sacks."

"You had no shoes?" May gave Emma a sympathetic look.

Emma shook her head. "Too many children. Too many growing feet."

"In the first letter I sent home," Annie said, smiling, "I told my sisters to tell everyone I wear shoes now, every day."

Bessie and May laughed. But when Matron Kane appeared with a stern look on her face, they fell silent. The matron frowned.

"The time for socializing is over. Report to the mess hall."

Annie picked up her lace-making supplies while May

tucked her letter to George into the bosom of her dress. The matron began her ascent of the stairs leading from the courtyard to the cellblocks above the Porch. When the matron was out of sight, Mary Von sidled up behind Annie, her dark eyes glittering in her ruddy face.

"Nasty little bootlicker."

Annie stiffened. Mary Von gave her a hard poke in the back. "You do whatever the matron tells you, eh?"

Remaining silent, Annie held her breath, hoping Mary would leave her alone. But then she felt a hard shove from behind and stumbled, knocking into Bessie.

Mary laughed.

"Clumsy little strumpet. Watch where you're going."

Bessie's hands balled into fists. Annie tensed. She didn't want to come to blows with Mary Von, who had shot her lover in cold blood while he was boarding a boat back to his native Australia. Annie didn't doubt that Mary was capable of murder—the foulmouthed woman didn't seem to possess an ounce of remorse.

Annie stood as still as a statue and stared at the ground, waiting for the queue of women in front of her to move. No one else spoke, but Mary continued to talk, stumps of teeth protruding from rotten, swollen gums.

"I don't listen to no one. Especially not that skinny old cunt. Mark my words, the matron is a dead woman walking."

———◆◆———

AMID THE WHIR and clack of the sewing machines, Annie fell into a rhythm, producing each garment as quickly as she could.

The top floor of the workshop building trapped heat, and Annie wiped a hand against her sweaty forehead. She looked up at the guard, a quiet man named Davis, who sat in the corner with his eyes closed. Then she looked out the window at Mount Tamalpais and the shimmering blue bay.

Turning to Emma, she sighed. "The weather is fine today."

Emma nodded. "Aye. I envy the guards' children who can take a dip at the beach. We could walk there, if only we were allowed. Or we could picnic in the hills."

Annie closed her eyes, imagining she could smell the grass and wildflowers. Spring had turned into summer. Opening them, she looked at Emma. "What will you do when you're free of this place?"

Emma hunched her shoulders. "I've got more than a year left."

"But time will pass." Annie smiled. "Isn't that what you tell me?"

Emma pushed a strand of her fair hair behind her ear. "I suppose. I don't want to go back to the sportin' life. I'd love to open a shop of me own."

Annie glanced at the guard, who was still sleeping.

"A shop? What kind of shop?"

Emma's cheeks flushed. "Oh, it's rawmaish. But I'd sell my lace to the fine ladies of San Francisco. I'd make christening gowns, veils, collars, cuffs."

"It's not foolish." Annie touched her friend's hand. "Your lace is lovely."

A smile lit up Emma's face like sunlight. "I'd call it Emma's Lace. It would be a respectable little shop."

"I could be your assistant," Annie said, pushing fabric

beneath the needle. "You'd make fine blouses and dresses, and I'd help with a flower or two."

Emma smirked. "Your grapevines need work."

Annie laughed. "Isn't the joy of crochet lace that no two women make it the same? My vines are just how I like them."

Emma shook her head. "You're usin' me own words against me."

"But you did say them." Annie nudged her.

They fell into a fit of giggles, earning glares from the other convicts. But in that moment, Annie didn't feel the heat of the room or hear the deafening clack of the sewing machines. Sharing laughter with a friend on a summer afternoon, she felt as though she were free.

LEAVING THE WORKSHOP, Annie and Emma walked across the dusty prison yard. Hearing the crunch of heavy boots behind them, Annie tensed. She could smell the scent of cheap whiskey—coffin varnish—much like the poitín brewed by men at home in Ireland. Corcoran's scent, it made her feel sick to her stomach.

"In a rush, are we?"

Corcoran stepped in front of them, then stood there in his blue uniform, glassy-eyed, twisting the end of his red mustache. Annie looked at the brick building up ahead, which housed the warden's office. She felt the impulse to grab Emma's hand and run. A bit farther, the Porch contained the offices of both the turnkey and the captain of the yard. All three men were superior to Corcoran and wouldn't look fondly upon his drinking or his harassment of Annie and Emma. Could she make a run for it? But Annie and Emma were convicts, while Corcoran was a guard—albeit not a very competent one. Running from him would only cause trouble.

"Leave us be," Emma said, trying to shoulder her way past him.

Corcoran blocked their path, a grotesque grin on his face.

"Are you asking to be sent to the hole? Because I can arrange that."

Annie looked around for anyone to help—but the nearby guards either sneered or looked the other way. Steeling herself, Annie glared at Corcoran.

"We must report to Matron Kane."

Corcoran rolled his eyes. "What an ugly old cocksucker she is."

Annie gasped at his foul language, and Corcoran laughed. "Have I offended you, prisoner? I'd think you girls have seen your fair share of cocks."

"But none as small as yours," Emma hissed, grabbing Annie by the hand.

Corcoran's eyes narrowed to slits.

Without hesitating, Annie broke into a run, Emma beside her, their shoes stirring up dust as they sprinted toward the Porch. Inside the building, Annie gasped for breath.

"We ought to report him to the warden."

Emma clenched her jaw. "No. Nothin' will come of it."

But Annie didn't have so little faith. Captain Gilcrest seemed like a man of morals. Surely if she went to him, he would reprimand Corcoran for drinking on the job—perhaps even have him fired? He could report to the warden on her behalf.

In the mess hall, Emma's face clouded, and she fell into a dark silence. Annie decided not to push the matter any further, at least not for now. She waited in the queue while May served each female inmate her supper. Cutlery clattered and the women laughed. May ladled pork and beans onto Annie's plate, which smelled good, thoroughly seasoned.

"May," Annie said, her heart pounding. "Can your George prove Corcoran is smuggling opium in here? Because if he can—"

Behind Annie, Nellie Osborne grunted.

"Move! I ain't got all day."

Annie gritted her teeth. She couldn't muster the energy to fight with Nellie. Not today. Instead, she thanked May and carried her plate to the long communal table, sitting between Bessie and Maud. Maud grunted in greeting, her dark eyes flashing before she turned back to her food. Annie hated to see Emma, who sat across from them, looking so defeated. She would find a way to prove Corcoran's corruption. She readily believed Corcoran was involved in the opium-smuggling ring; she knew he was the type to sell drugs to the prisoners for a profit. Corcoran had no sympathy for the desperate men—he was a man without a conscience.

———◆———

WITH THE DOOR to her cell locked and bolted, Annie stared through her barred window across the courtyard at the hard outline of the Stones. The male convicts in the decrepit stone cellblocks were housed four to a room. Sometimes at night, she could hear them yelling—a terrible sound, a reminder that they too were treated as less than human.

In these summer months, the sun hadn't yet set behind Mount Tamalpais, which looked like a woman sleeping, her face in profile, nose turned toward the sky. Annie used the remaining light to work on her newest crochet-lace motif, a large rose with layers of petals. Pulling her thread and moving the needle, her fingers found a comfortable rhythm.

Matron Kane walked from cell door to cell door, her keys jingling. It was an awful feeling, being locked in—something Annie would never grow accustomed to. She heard the matron descend the stairs to her room, having done her job. Every female prisoner was accounted for. Suddenly, a terrible crack sounded, like metal on bone. A shrill scream pierced the air and Annie froze, her heart pounding.

"Help me! *Please!*"

The strangled voice belonged to the matron. Annie's whole body went cold. Again, she heard a thwack—the sickening sound of flesh being pounded like meat. And then the unmistakable gruff voice of Mary Von.

"You had it coming, you bitch."

The corridor came alive with shouts and whispers.

"What's going on?"

"Someone help the matron!"

"Where are the guards, for feck's sake!"

Mary Von hadn't been in her cell at lockup. Somehow she had hidden, deceiving both the matron and the guards. A bead of sweat ran down Annie's back, her mouth dry as she realized the matron had stopped screaming. The silence was deafening.

15

Judy

San Francisco, 1972

Taking a deep breath, I walk through the imposing marble doorway of the San Francisco Art Institute. Three years ago, I dreamed of earning a master of fine arts degree in photography, but then that dream was derailed when Tony slipped a ring on my finger. Today, for the first time, my wedding band is gone. And though my finger feels naked without it, I feel free. There's no need anymore to pretend to be someone I'm not.

I find myself in a tranquil courtyard, surrounded by a covered corridor. A fountain burbles in the center, and students sit on benches, sketching and reading. The Spanish Revival building has red clay roof tiles and a bell tower, like a real Spanish monastery. Imagining myself as a student on this historic campus brings a smile to my face.

In the arcade on the way to the admissions office, I admire the greenery in the courtyard—fruit trees and hanging vines. It's as if I've stepped out of the city and into another world.

The admissions office is modern, like a stylish Bohemian living room, with a cobalt-blue wall, gold-framed abstract paintings, a gilded mirror, and a brown leather sofa.

Taking a seat on the sofa, I check my watch. I'm a few minutes early. A woman wearing jacquard-pattern pants and a collared blouse peeks her head around the doorway, smiling at me from behind her octagon-shaped glasses.

"Are you Judy?"

I smooth my corduroy slacks. "Yes, I am."

She enters the room and extends her hand. "I'm Linda. We spoke on the phone."

"Nice to meet you, Linda." Her hand is soft and warm.

"Follow me," she says, leading me down the hall to her office, where I take a seat. Linda settles behind her desk and meets my eyes.

"So, Judy. You're interested in applying for your MFA in photography. Why do you want to study at the San Francisco Art Institute?"

My stomach flutters, but I'm prepared.

"The photographers I admire most have roots here. Ansel Adams started the fine-art photography department in 1946. Dorothea Lange was an instructor. Annie Leibovitz was a student here, and her photographs of the Rolling Stones on tour are dynamic."

Linda nods. "You're familiar with our school." She shuffles a stack of papers, then sets them aside. "Admission to SFAI's graduate program is highly selective."

I sit up straighter. "I understand."

She adjusts her glasses. "You'll have to fill out the graduate school application and pay the application fee. In addition, you'll write an artist statement, in which you'll describe the techniques, concepts, and process of the work presented in your portfolio."

The street photography Annie's mug shot inspired feels different from anything I've done before. I hope the series of photos will be good enough.

Linda pauses. "A little advice. In your artist statement, be honest and sincere in your intentions, and explain a goal you plan to reach with your graduate education."

I nod. I want to improve my craft, to make a living as a photographer, and to work on projects that shed light on social issues.

"You'll need two letters of recommendation, at least one from an undergraduate professor," Linda says, tapping her pen. "And also, your official transcripts from the institution where you earned your degree. Finally, you'll need to include your portfolio."

My shoulders tense, remembering my art history professor who didn't hide her disappointment in me when I told her I was marrying Tony.

I look at Linda.

"Can you tell me more about the portfolio submission?"

Linda nods. "Your portfolio should demonstrate personal vision, with photographs completed within the last two years. We want to see twelve to twenty images, each demonstrating an exceptional command of materials, ideas, and space."

Thinking of the photographs I've taken so far, I want to take even more, to show how redevelopment is affecting the lives of my South of Market neighbors—to give them a voice with my camera. "When is the graduate application due?"

"July tenth." Linda smiles, handing me a thick packet. "Good luck."

Leaving the San Francisco Art Institute, I decide to visit the nearby California Historical Society. Although the Sanborn maps I found at the San Francisco library were helpful in learning more about the history of South of Market, I want to dig even deeper. To make people care about this neighborhood, I need to peel back the layers, to show the strength of a community that has existed here for generations.

My Volkswagen Beetle sputters as it climbs San Francisco's steep hills, forcing me to accelerate every time I change gears. I grit my teeth when I get stuck at a red light, terrified of my car rolling backward.

The California Historical Society is housed within an 1896 mansion—a colossal thirty-room residence in Pacific Heights. When I reach the corner of Jackson and Laguna, I park my car. Stepping outside, I stare up at the Romanesque Revival building with its sandstone edifice and curved twin towers, looking vaguely medieval and a little bit haunted. I heard a rumor the mansion was sold to the Third Reich in 1941, which turned it into a Nazi consulate. Supposedly, one of Adolf Hitler's top aides, Fritz Wiedemann, lived here but was forced to leave after the bombing of Pearl Harbor, when the US government seized the mansion.

I shiver when I enter the building, surprised at how cold it is inside. This storied mansion survived the 1906 earthquake and is the oldest structure on the block. The entry hall is all dark redwood, with a high arched doorway and a parquet floor covered with a Persian rug. A chandelier hangs above a statue of a cherub. Climbing the stairs to the reception room, I pass my reflection in a floor-to-ceiling mirror—its ostentatious frame looks heavy.

In the reception room, I'm struck by the marble fireplace, framed on either side by lions. When I look closer, I notice the details: women in flowing dresses, seashells with pearls, masks from a Greek tragedy. Like Michael's Victorian home, this mansion is decorated in the style of its time—opulent and busy, with antique lamps and heavy velvet curtains.

A docent sees me and stands up. "Welcome to the California Historical Society."

"Hi," I say, admiring the paneling on the ceiling. "I'm researching the history of South of Market. I'd like to know if you have any historical records."

She nods. "You've come to the right place. Follow me."

The docent leads me through the mansion, past parlors and dining rooms that put Michael's Western Addition home to shame, filled with palm fronds, antiques, mirrors, and crystal chandeliers. In the north parlor on the east wall, a glass case houses books and documents. The docent gestures for me to take a seat at a long wooden table.

"My name is Bonnie," she says.

"I'm Judy," I reply.

Bonnie smiles. "It's nice to meet you, Judy. Let me tell you about some of the materials we have here. Have you heard of the South of Market Boys?"

I shake my head. "No. Who are they?"

"They were a group of men who grew up south of Market Street prior to 1906. In the Depression era, they formed an organization. They held charity balls and picnics, dedicated to the spirit of the old South of Market."

I nod. "I heard the neighborhood was completely rebuilt after the earthquake and fire, but it used to be an Irish working-class neighborhood."

"That's right," Bonnie says. "The founder of the South of Market Boys, Peter Maloney, was born to Irish parents who owned a bar, but he became a respected police inspector. Other members became judges, supervisors, and fire chiefs. But the majority were working-class people, longshoremen, tailors, railroad workers."

"Did they publish anything?" Reading an oral history of people who lived during Annie's era would be extremely helpful.

Bonnie beams. "They published a monthly journal called the *South of Market Journal.* I have a copy here from 1926. Would you like to see it?"

"I'd love to."

It's not the right time frame, but I'd still like to know more about my neighborhood back then. There's always the other side of something—railroad tracks, a river—that divides a city along class lines. Here in San Francisco, it was the cable car slot along Market Street.

Bonnie gestures toward a room. "Give me a moment, and I'll be right back."

A few minutes later, Bonnie returns with a pair of latex gloves and an old journal. *South of Market Journal, Picnic Edition,* is written in red letters. It's illustrated with people gathered in a park, children participating in a sack race while men and women picnic on the grass.

"Please wear these gloves while handling the journal,"

Bonnie says. "We don't want the paper to be damaged with oils from your hands."

"I understand," I say, tugging on the gloves. "Thank you."

I turn the journal's pages, learning what I can. One hundred twenty-seven men attended the initial South of Market Boys meeting at the new Call Building, and only ten years later, the organization boasted more than thirty-five hundred men. They were dedicated to the "perpetuation of the spirit of the old South of Market" and established the long-standing tradition of placing a wreath on Lotta's Fountain on the anniversary of the great earthquake.

Men who grew up in the rough-and-tumble neighborhood South of the Slot went on to pay for groceries for struggling families, to fund a homeless shelter called Saint Patrick's on Minna Street, to pay for schooling and medical care for anyone who couldn't afford it. The balls, sporting events, and picnics they hosted raised money for charity.

I think of William Colvin and the words he spoke at the TOOR meeting: *If you're ill or hungry, your neighbors will help. I don't think you'll find any finer people in the world.* Nearly a century later, the spirit of the old neighborhood lives on, just like these men intended. My eyes land on a section in the journal with the heading "Where I Met Her."

Beneath it is a list of addresses:

St. Joseph's, Tenth and Howard
Archery, 1155 Mission Street
Barra's, corner of First and Minna
Irish-American, 818 Howard Street

Tammany, Folsom and Eighth
Armory, 134 Fourth Street

I imagine these men meeting their wives or sweethearts at Irish organizations, on street corners in my neighborhood, places lost to time. Thinking back on the Sanborn map, I can picture the streets as they once were, narrow alleyways packed with flats, saloons, barns, factories, and small businesses. Immediately, Annie Gilmurray's face comes to me. Did she ever attend Irish dances at these places? Meet friends?

Turning the page again, I see advertisements for local businesses—ironworks, caterers, millineries, tailors—and political advertisements for justices of the Supreme Court of California. The Irish who moved up in society kept ties with those who remained working-class, giving them political power. Another heading stops me: "Memories of the Past."

I read the text on the page.

As each month rolls around and we assemble in large numbers to meet and greet those friends of old, you recognize among the new faces some dear old crony you knew well in the days of your youth. And what a joy that is. In this alliance of the old South of Market, we renew friendships of the past with increased warmth.

You may remember the old Albany Brewery at 75 Everett Street, whose special brew was known as the Superior Cream Ale. The celebrated Vermicelli factory was run by J.P. Tenthorey and Co. at 558 Mission Street between 1st and 2nd. Going back to Fremont Street, the Globe Iron Works looms up in our vision. Coming back to Langton, between Harrison and Folsom, we remember old man Cunningham, a carpenter who owned several houses in the neighborhood, had no children and was very much a grouch—God rest his soul.

I laugh out loud. Then I cover my mouth, remembering I'm supposed to be researching quietly. I continue reading, touched by the fact that the author knew every single person on the block. Next door to old man Cunningham was a family named Ross, with "three fine sons," Jack, Jim, and Alex, and a daughter named Mary who married a wealthy man and became the mother of a fine family herself.

There was Mrs. McDonough, a short, quiet little woman who was a widow and owned several flats on Natoma Street. She went to Mass every morning at the old Saint Joseph's Church on Tenth and Howard. Farther down Natoma were the Dougherty family, with Ellen Dougherty, the "best dresser in San Francisco," who worked in a big department store. Mike Welsh of the Welsh family became a well-known architect. The Hallahan family had two sons and four daughters. But Hughey Hallahan passed away as a young man, beloved by all.

There were longshoremen and machinists whose children went on to become policemen and vaudeville performers. The Reilly family, the McGees, the McFarland girls, and the Meade family lived on the corner of Drury Lane, now Decker Alley, and Langton. Old Drury Lane was where boys learned to play marbles, run footraces, and start amateur prize fights. At Butler's Distillery on Ninth and Bryant, children would catch minnows with bent pins and go swimming on Sunday mornings when old man Butler was at church.

I close the book. These are ordinary people who lived in my neighborhood, and I've been given an extraordinary glimpse into their everyday lives. South of Market was leveled once in the 1906 earthquake and fire. It can't be lost again to redevelopment.

Bonnie approaches. "Would you like to see anything else?"

"Yes, please." I close the journal. "Do you have any photographs or newspaper articles about San Quentin Prison in the 1890s?"

"Most historical items pertaining to San Quentin are at the Marin History Museum in San Rafael. But, I have a marvelous 1910 photo album of the prison."

"I'd love to see it," I say.

Ten minutes later, Bonnie returns with an album, its black cover embossed with gold. I marvel at the faded script. *Views of San Quentin Prison, July 1910, Dan Sullivan, Turnkey.*

"Let me see if we have any newspaper articles," she says.

Thanking Bonnie, I turn my attention to the album, opening its cloth binding. Inside, there are black-and-white photographs with descriptions typed on strips of paper. It's funny, how we expect a photograph to tell us the truth. But a photograph is reality filtered through the lens of the photographer, in this case, the San Quentin turnkey, a prison employee.

Still, I am grateful for this window into the past. There's a photo of the interior of the warden's office, furnished with a fireplace and a wooden desk. I wonder if Annie might have been taken there for processing when she arrived.

Next, I find a photograph of the women's ward, a two-story brick building with prison cells above the offices of the captain of the yard and the turnkey. Underneath the photo, a description reads, *The Porch*. In front of the Porch, roses grow in a well-tended garden. I try to picture Annie here, looking out from behind her barred window.

There are photographs of the Bertillon Room, where mug shots were taken, a barbershop for prison guards, and a barren hospital ward that sends a shiver down my spine. In the tailor shop, rows of sewing machines sit side by side. Laundry, or perhaps finished pieces of clothing, is strung on a clothesline hung between two wooden ceiling beams.

The jute mill looks cluttered and dangerous, with dust floating in the air amid rows of machinery, whereas the commissary department is organized, canned food lining the shelves. There's a photo of San Quentin Village, quaint Victorian homes nestled behind a stone wall, where the prison guards lived. There's even a little wooden schoolhouse and a photograph of the guards' children playing at the local beach. How hard it must have been for Annie to be surrounded by Marin's natural beauty but unable to access it.

Turning the pages, I see a mess hall with long tables set with cups and bowls. Then I come upon a photo of the women's courtyard. Two sets of staircases on opposite sides of the hospital building lead to the grounds below. There are benches and a tree growing from the concrete. Maybe Annie found solace here, with space to walk and think. Did she miss her family back home in Ireland, or plot revenge against the man who wronged her?

Bonnie returns with a yellowed newspaper. "You're in luck. This 1890 issue has an article you might find interesting."

"Thank you," I say, closing the photo album.

"Would you like me to take those?" Bonnie gestures to the

South of Market Boys journal and the San Quentin photo album.

"Please." I smile at Bonnie. "They were both so helpful. Thank you."

Smoothing the newspaper, my hands sweat inside my latex gloves. Before me is an issue of *The Examiner*. My eyes scan the faded text, landing on a shocking headline.

SAN QUENTIN PRISON SCANDAL: CORRUPTION, VICE, AND OPIUM

It is now known that the prison is on the verge of the greatest opium scandal in history and that the discharge of guards Cramer and Brooks is simply the beginning of the investigation into the corruption and impropriety within the prison. More guards will follow, and it is believed that several will be implicated before the investigation is over.

Last Sunday, Warden McComb remained sequestered in his office, a stenographer taking testimonies from a dozen guards. The tip came from a convict named Miller, who assisted in the tower gate, and informed Gatekeeper Gillardin that Joseph Brooks and John Cramer were smuggling the drug into the prison. Gillardin saw Cramer walk down the wall between the tower gate and the jute mill and hand Brooks a package, which the latter lowered to a convict by means of a string. Gillardin waited until the convict was out of sight of the two guards, then made him give up the package. It contained half a pound of opium.

To one who has even a remote idea of the inside of Warden McComb's methods of management, the only surprise is that periodical prison scandals are not more frequent. Though they come to the surface to torment him, he is a shrewd diplomat with more pulls than any other man in public life on this coast. He should have been kicked out years ago, but whenever a charge is placed against him, witnesses become dumb and men of influence arise to declare him immaculate. However, San Quentin will not be free from troubles, curses, and scandals so long as the present management remains.

The Warden is already under scrutiny due to an attack on the prison matron, Mrs. Mary Kane, which sent her to the hospital. Mary Von, who is serving a life sentence in San Quentin for the murder of George Bishop, attempted in June to murder the matron of the department for female prisoners. Mary Kane, the matron, had closed the female ward, locking the women inside, and was descending the stairway that leads to the washrooms when Mary Von, who had concealed herself there, assaulted her with an iron stove lifter.

Pushing the paper away, I feel sick to my stomach. Annie was not safe in that place. Without a responsible warden, something could go terribly wrong.

16

Annie

San Quentin, 1890

S he ain't dead."

Maud fell into step beside Annie as they trudged up the creaky flight of stairs leading to the fourth floor of the workshops building. Annie's eyes darted to the guard, a mean old bugger named Vinegar Face Bailey, who never parted with his wooden truncheon.

She lowered her voice. "The matron?"

Maud nodded. "She's in the hospital, looking like she lost a prize fight. I heard Mary Von cracked her skull."

Annie winced. The matron was lucky to have survived Mary Von's vicious attack. And the mystery of what happened to May's iron stove lifter had been solved.

"How long do ye think she'll be in the hospital?"

Maud shrugged as they entered the tailor shop, taking a seat at her sewing machine. Annie did the same, feeling Vinegar Face Bailey's eyes on her. He licked his lips. Meanwhile,

Emma's sewing machine sat empty. Annie worried for her friend, who'd been feverish this morning, too weak to report for work duty. Emma had been sent back to her cell for the remainder of the day. Others who feigned sickness were taken to the Loafer's Elysium, a room with no chairs, where they were fed only bread and water.

Looking out the north windows, Annie saw the gray water of the San Francisco Bay churning with whitecaps. The dismal weather felt ominous. She shivered in the cold air, though it was June, fog swirling thick and wet outside. Taking her cloth from her basket, Annie ran it through her sewing machine, listening to the clack of the needle.

Eventually, old Vinegar Face stepped into the hallway to sneak a swig of whiskey from his flask, and chatter among the female prisoners resumed. Glancing at the doorway, Maud stood up. Then she made her way between the rows of sewing machines toward Annie, her frizzy red hair framing her face like a halo. She bent down to whisper.

"I heard they're building gallows up here."

A shiver ran down Annie's spine. "Gallows?"

Maud jerked her head toward the doorway. "It'll be across the hall in the old sash and blind factory. Haven't you noticed? The machinery is gone."

Annie swallowed. Hangings took place in county jails. She'd been lucky to never witness one, though plenty of folk in prison had, eager to explain the gruesome experience in detail. Sometimes the hangings were botched and the prisoner's head was snapped off from the fall. Other times the noose came untied during the drop, and the proceedings had to be staged again. She'd heard about the clamor for execution invitations and about executions with more than two hundred people in attendance. It sounded like a sick spectacle.

"There'll be hangings at San Quentin now," Maud said, her dark eyes wide. "In that room where the men used to build doors, instead they'll get the rope."

Annie shuddered, imagining a hanging taking place mere yards away from where she sat at her sewing machine. She could imagine the grisly scene—the witnesses and guards standing outside the execution room along with reporters and busybodies, a wooden coffin in the corner, waiting to be filled. She'd heard about the leather strap that bound the prisoner's legs, and the black cap to be pulled over their head, the sound of hard breathing, the tripping of the trap, the figure hurtling into space, the snap of the broken neck.

"You're shivering." Maud frowned at Annie.

"I'm cold."

Annie looked out the window at Mount Tamalpais, peaceful in the distance. It would be the last sight for many before they died. For most of these convicts, there would be no one to mourn them, only to judge. *What of the men and women who died alone in their cells, no announcement made in the local paper?* They'd be buried in the prison graveyard, given a wooden marker with their prison number, lives extinguished, no mourners.

Annie refused to be remembered as a number. She would serve her time and then leave this dreadful place. Emma and Bessie would too, and eventually they could put San Quentin behind them. Annie had some skills—lace making, needle-point, the ability to read and write, housekeeping. She wasn't too old to begin a new life. She'd be twenty-one upon her release, though she felt as if she'd already aged a hundred years.

Remembering the fine ladies on the train to Greenbrae, whispering behind their gloved hands as they stared, Annie no longer envied them. She'd once desperately wanted to be accepted by these society women, but now she realized she was more resilient than they ever would be. *What did they know of life?* The naïve maid with ambitions of bettering herself through marriage was disappearing. It would not be Albert, or any man, who raised Annie's station in life. That was up to her alone.

———◆·—◆———

"Did you hear? Winifred Sweet is back."

May filled Annie's bowl with a mixture of beef, carrots, and potatoes. Today, the meat looked decent, and for that she was grateful.

"No." Annie surveyed the mess hall as if the journalist might be sitting there among them with her notepad. "The woman from *The Examiner*?"

May nodded. "Remember what I told you about Brooks and Cramer, smuggling drugs in here?" She dropped her voice to a whisper. "A trustee named Miller, I heard he's gonna squeal. The whole thing will come to light eventually."

"How many guards are involved?" Annie asked.

"At least ten." May leaned forward, holding her ladle aloft. "If word gets into the papers, Warden McComb will have to let them go."

Annie held her breath. If Corcoran, who was visibly drunk nearly all the time, were let go, she'd be free of him. Annie carried her bowl to the long wooden table and ate her meal, feeling more at ease than she had been in days. After dinner, with the matron gone, a guard accompanied the women while they prepared for lockup.

Waiting for the washroom, Annie whispered through the bars of Emma's cell.

"Emma. Are you well?"

Emma answered in a scratchy voice.

"Aye. I'm not too poorly. I think me fever's broken."

"Good." Annie shivered in her nightdress. "It's been awfully cold and damp today."

Emma coughed. "It's Baltic out there."

Only in San Francisco were summers as cold as winters.

"Get some rest," Annie said, dropping her eyes as the guard shot her a menacing look. She didn't make a sound as she passed Mary Von's cell. Rather than being sent to the dungeons, Mary had been allowed to remain in place—she ate her meals in her cell and was no longer permitted in the courtyard.

In the quiet of her prison cell, Annie worked on her crochet lace, admiring her finished motifs, joined together with chain netting. Though the floral design was rudimentary, she'd improved. She was still learning how to perfect the tight buds falling from stems, but her picots had gotten much better. Her little sister Maggie would love a fine lace collar for one of her dresses. She was fifteen and always trying to emulate the latest fashions. Annie's heart clenched, thinking of sweet Maggie. Still, no one in her family knew where she was.

If she hoped to make a life for herself after her release, they could never find out she had been imprisoned. Part of her would always be a stranger to them now, a buried secret, a dark truth. The only way she would ever be able to start again in America as a respectable woman would be to erase any trace of a criminal past from her history. She'd been a fool not to see Albert for what he was—a coward unwilling to defend her good name for fear of spoiling his own. But her hatred for him didn't change anything. She remained locked in here while he was out there, free to do as he pleased.

The twilight faded to black, and Annie set her padding cord aside. Candles were no longer permitted at night, after the incident with Ada Werner. Annie would continue to work on her flower motif in the morning. Her stitches had become much neater now, and she had learned how to hold the threads of her padding cord together in her left hand, while using a finger on her right hand to secure her loops. She heard Emma's voice in her head: *Hook under, yarn over, pull it through.* Drifting off to sleep, her body sank into the lumpy mattress.

Annie awoke in the darkness, aware of a strange noise. A cry. But it wasn't an animal outside in the garden—it sounded human. She sat up, alert, straining to hear, while a pale moon shone through her barred window. First, there was a beat of silence. But then she heard a man's voice, low and gruff, right outside her door. Her blood ran cold.

"I'll take this one. The little one."

A key turned in the brass lock, and then the cell door across the hall from hers creaked open. Annie's body froze. It was past midnight. *What is happening?*

A scream pierced the silence. Maud.

"Get the hell out!"

Annie's heart began to pound—there were sounds of a struggle. She jumped out of bed and ran to her door, pressing her face against the bars. Two figures materialized in the grainy darkness—a male convict in prison stripes, as large as a prize pig, and Maud, pushed up against the wall, her nightdress hiked around her hips.

"Stop it!" Annie yelled. "Guard! We need a guard."

The man turned and sneered, his hand clamped over Maud's mouth, muffling her cries. "Shut your trap or I'll kill you."

Annie trembled, her mouth dry. "How did ye get the keys?"

The convict grinned. "I got friends in high places."

The strange cry rang out again—loud, pained. Annie's eyes adjusted to the darkness, and she turned toward the sound. Another cell door stood open at the end of the hall.

Then she heard Emma's voice. "Stop! Get off me!"

Her heart dropped into her stomach. "Emma!"

Annie shook the cell door, even though the iron wouldn't budge. She was powerless, locked inside and unable to help her friend. She screamed until her throat was raw, then watched in horror as a figure emerged from Emma's cell—a man in uniform. He strode toward her, bare-chested in the grainy darkness, the brass buttons on his coat glinting. In the dim light she could see his copper hair and the sharp angle of his jaw. It was Corcoran. He licked his lips.

"Where are you, little Bridget?"

Annie backed away from the door, her heart pounding. He was coming for her. She looked around desperately for anything she could use as a weapon. Spotting her crochet hook, still attached to the length of cord, Annie grabbed it. She waited, holding the fine needle tight in her trembling hand. She felt sick, listening to a key turn in her lock. The iron door swung open and Corcoran stood before her, his pants unfastened.

Gritting her teeth, she tightened her grip around the metal hook.

"Don't!"

"Or what?" he sneered, taking another step closer. "I'm going to have my way with you, just like I did with the Irish whore."

Then he was on her, his hands on her shoulders, shoving her hard against the brick wall. Annie gasped, the air squeezed from her lungs, but she didn't drop her crochet hook. She smelled him, alcohol and perspiration, and felt his breath on her neck. Then she stabbed blindly in the darkness at the hand that pinned her shoulder. Feeling the fine tip of the crochet hook lodge into the webbing between Corcoran's thumb and forefinger, she drove it in deep.

He screamed in pain. "You bitch!"

Annie yanked the hook out and Corcoran hunched over, grabbing his bleeding hand. Seizing her moment, Annie looped her length of padding cord around his neck and pulled. Corcoran thrashed as he gasped for breath, and the cord cut into Annie's hands as she yanked it, but it didn't break. And yet, she couldn't hold the threads for much longer. The iron doors banged and shook, the whole women's ward awake now, screaming for help.

Suddenly, a kerosene lamp illuminated Annie's dark cell.

"What's going on in here?"

Corcoran broke free from her grasp, and Annie fell backward, her hands smarting. In the dim light, Captain Gilcrest emerged, and behind him, Captain Reddy, the turnkey. Shaking with adrenaline-fueled rage, Annie pointed at Corcoran.

"He attacked me. He . . . has the keys."

"She stabbed me," Corcoran said, holding up his bleeding hand. "And then the bitch tried to choke me."

Captain Gilcrest's eyes were hard. He grabbed Corcoran's elbow, hauling him to his feet. Then he turned to Reddy. "Search the cells."

When Reddy reappeared, he had Maud's assailant in handcuffs.

"It's Fat Jack Kiley, sir."

Annie felt disgust, looking at his flappy jowls and beady eyes, his unrepentant expression. Maud was crying quietly in her cell.

Gilcrest glared at Corcoran.

"You let *him* in?"

Corcoran shrugged. "Come on, Captain, we were just having a bit of fun."

Annie held up a shaking finger, pointing it at Fat Jack. "He raped Maud. And Corcoran . . . he raped Emma."

She looked at Captain Gilcrest, her eyes pleading. This white-haired man believed in justice, in morals. He'd started the San Quentin Prison school so the young male convicts could educate themselves, so they wouldn't end up like these *animals.* Annie believed he would do the right thing. But the captain's face remained impassive.

"Lock them up," Gilcrest said, nodding at Reddy.

Annie's skin burned with rage—her faith shattered. The captain didn't mean Fat Jack and Corcoran. He meant the women who'd just been raped, the victims of the crime.

17

Judy

San Francisco, 1972

I love your photographs," Mark says, walking beside me. "They humanize the cause in a powerful way. You have talent, you know that?"

I cringe at the compliment, ready to deflect it. But I'm tired of diminishing myself to make people—Tony—feel better. Instead, I smile at Mark. "Thank you."

After meeting me at Helen's Diner for a cup of coffee, Mark looked through my portfolio. I wouldn't have taken pictures of the TOOR meeting at the Milner Hotel or photographed the single-room-occupancy hotel tenants if it weren't for him. He's encouraged me to approach local galleries with my work, for a showcase. If more people can see whom redevelopment is impacting, they may feel differently about it.

"Mark," I ask, trying to keep up, "is there any hope for the future of South of Market? Is TOOR making progress?"

We're headed to an anti-eviction demonstration, and we

pass beneath a string of Chinese lanterns, past storefronts selling dumplings, ginseng tea, and souvenirs.

Mark nods. "TOOR provided evidence of harassment and violence against the remaining tenants by the Redevelopment Agency." He smiles. "Judge Weigel ordered them to stop, halting all demolition and relocation. He cut off funds to the Yerba Buena Center."

I raise my eyebrows. "That sounds like a huge win."

"It was." Mark nods. "The Redevelopment Agency was ordered to build replacement housing concurrent with demolition. Nearly four thousand SRO units have been removed, so the agency has to build at least fifteen hundred new ones."

That's two thousand five hundred units fewer than there were before. I think of the furnished single-room units in the residential hotels I've visited. Each one has a twin bed, a chair, a sink, a closet, and a cupboard, while the tenants share the kitchen, bathrooms, and laundry facilities in the building. Though their units are small, about eight by ten feet, the men living in the residential hotels seem to be happy there.

"When will the new housing be built?"

"Judge Weigel ordered a deadline of November 9, 1973."

"That's a year and a half from now," I say, feeling hopeful.

Mark smirks. "The executive director of the Redevelopment Agency, Justin Herman, was damned if he was going to build those units."

My stomach knots. "How many have been built so far?"

"Eleven." Mark shakes his head.

My mouth falls open. "You're kidding me."

Four thousand single rooms have been destroyed, and since then, only eleven new ones have been built? I think of Nathan and Ken, the old men who live at the Knox Hotel. Where will they go? SRO housing is the last affordable option for many in this city.

Mark grits his teeth. "The Redevelopment Agency has made living south of Market Street lonely and hostile. Over the years of this fight, between demolition and the elderly dying, now only eight hundred people are left."

I swallow. How scary it must have been for the people who once lived south of Market Street to have their lights and water shut off, to have their friendly security guards fired and replaced by guards who drank on the job. With trash piling up in their hallways and their neighborhood being torn down, it's no wonder they were intimidated into leaving.

"But the Redevelopment Agency still has to build new units, right?"

Mark nods. "They do, but only because Judge Weigel ordered them to. The agency thinks it's absurd they should have to build housing for people who are no longer here."

My shoulders tense.

"But lack of affordable housing is a citywide problem," I say, thinking of all the Black families evicted from the Western Addition and the Fillmore.

"Exactly," Mark says. "The Redevelopment Agency can't get rid of their obligation to provide a minimum of fifteen hundred new single-room units."

I want to keep talking to Mark about this, but we've come to a stop at the edge of Chinatown, where Kearny Street meets Jackson.

"We're here," Mark says. "There's the I-Hotel."

I look up at the International Hotel, a three-story redbrick structure, the Transamerica Pyramid jutting into the sky behind it. The hotel is home to 150 elderly Chinese and Filipinos, and a crowd has gathered out front, a mix of hotel tenants, staff, and volunteers—students wearing UC Berkeley sweatshirts, church leaders, and grassroots activists. There are people of all races, all holding signs that say WE WON'T MOVE!

Mark told me this neighborhood was once Manilatown, ten blocks of Kearny Street between Market and Jackson, a thriving Filipino American enclave. It was home to migrant farmworkers, merchant marines, and service workers before the area was cleared for "blight." Now only one block of the old neighborhood remains. But the International Hotel is the next building to fall victim to redevelopment.

"A few years ago," Mark says, "the corporate owner, Walter Shorenstein, sent everyone an eviction notice. But the tenants, represented by the United Filipino Association, marched to the company offices and negotiated signing a new lease agreement."

"That's good. Right?"

"Well." Mark licks his lips. "The morning Shorenstein was supposed to sign the lease, a suspicious fire swept through the top floor of the hotel, killing three tenants."

I shudder, thinking of the story Nathan told me about his friend James's murder at the Westchester Hotel, owned by the Redevelopment Agency.

"That's unconscionable."

Mark nods. "The owner backed out of the lease agreement, using the fire as justification for the demolition of the building. He said it was unsafe."

I raise my voice, incredulous. "Because he made it unsafe. And 'blighted.'"

"Exactly." Mark gestures to the growing crowd in front of us. "But this time, grassroots organizers fought back. Community volunteers renovated the hotel rooms, fixing everything that was burned. And public pressure convinced Shorenstein to sign a three-year lease."

He points to the storefronts on the bottom floor of the hotel.

"Now there's an Asian Community Center, Asian Legal Services, Everybody's Bookstore, the Chinatown–North Beach Youth Council."

I bite my lip. "When does the lease expire?"

Mark gives me a pointed look. "A week from today. And there's nothing to stop Shorenstein from selling. Everyone will be evicted."

A young Filipino man wearing glasses and a red windbreaker takes a step forward. He lifts a bullhorn and speaks into it. I look around at the faces of the frail, white-haired men and women in the crowd, their eyes filled with pain and worry. It makes me feel equal parts heartbroken and angry that the city has no plan for relocation housing.

"My name is Emil, and I'm a tenant of the I-Hotel. We're here today because we are fighting to claim what little space we have left in a city that's trying to erase us."

Cheers rise. I ready my camera, focusing on the speaker's face.

He gestures at the elderly tenants.

"The manongs who live here, they've been working hard in this country for over fifty years. They deserve to live the rest of their lives here in peace."

I take Emil's photograph and look around at the swelling

crowd. There must be about a hundred people here in total, and a chant breaks out:

"We won't move! We won't move!"

Emil raises his voice.

"Walter Shorenstein, the chairman of Milton Meyer and Company, who owns this hotel, says he's getting rid of a slum. But we are no slum. We are a community!"

I take pictures of pastors, students, and tenants—their protest signs and their faces. A short, white-haired old man in an orange cardigan comes to the forefront, aided by a student volunteer, and Emil hands him the bullhorn. The old man smiles.

"My name is Freddy De Los Reyes. I am eighty-five years old." He gestures down Kearny Street. "I remember when this sidewalk was all wood. The milkman delivered milk by horse and wagon. And the fare for the cable car was five cents."

Freddy continues speaking.

"We had Filipino-owned barbershops, pool halls, and cigar stores." He shakes his head. "Now many businesses are gone. But we still eat at Bataan Lunch, or cook together downstairs in our kitchen—chicken adobo, fish, pork chops. We all know each other. We come from the same place and we feel at home here."

He places his hand gently on the arm of an old woman in a flower-print dress. "This is my wife, Evelyn. We have been married for sixty years. Every day, she waters the plants in our rooftop garden. We like it here. We don't want to move."

I'm making a mental note to ask Freddy to show me the rooftop garden when a police siren wails nearby. Suddenly, a cruiser pulls up to the curb and two officers with batons step out of the car, wearing riot gear. My stomach knots. A third officer clops toward us on horseback, wearing a helmet and wielding a baton. He glares down at the gathered crowd.

"This is an illegal gathering. Disperse, now!"

My heart thumps. *Some of the men and women here are in their eighties.* Many of them don't speak English, and they look confused. He's scaring them. What about his duty to protect and serve this community?

"This is a peaceful protest," Emil says, remaining calm. "We have a right to be here."

The policeman stares him down. People band together, linking arms.

"Are you the leader of this riot?"

"It's not a riot," Mark yells. "We are protesting the failure of a system that prioritizes property rights over human rights."

I look at Mark, unarmed, standing there facing this power-hungry cop on horseback. My mouth is dry. But Mark is unafraid.

"This is a peaceful and lawful protest."

I'm shaking with adrenaline, but I lift my camera and take a photo, capturing the sneer on the policeman's face, his aggressive posture as he looks down from his horse at the group of peaceful protestors, their arms locked, and Mark, standing up to him.

The cop nods at the other two policemen, and then he blows a whistle and charges into the crowd, swinging his baton. Screams erupt, and I'm frozen in place, watching the melee. The horse rears and stamps its hooves. Protestors cover their heads while the police hit them with truncheons—students run to escort the elderly back inside the hotel.

Mark grabs my hand, tugging me away from the stampede.

I turn to look back, watching as activists are grabbed and shoved to the ground. We run from the scene, my camera bag slamming against my hip. We don't stop until we've crossed Broadway and reached North Beach. Mark looks at me, his dark brown eyes filled with concern.

"Are you okay?"

I nod, breathing heavily. "Are you?"

He wipes sweat from his brow. "Yeah." Then he shakes his head. "I'm so sorry about that. I never meant to put you in danger."

I think of Freddy De Los Reyes with his arm around his wife, telling me how the I-Hotel is his home, his community. I frown.

"It's not your fault. The gathering was peaceful until the cops showed up."

Mark scowls. "That's why folks call them pigs. We're lucky we didn't get hurt."

I swallow, thinking of how sheltered I've been. I've never put myself on the front lines of a protest before. "I'm not brave like you."

"Hey," he says. "You're documenting all of this, aren't you? And turning it into art. That's not only brave, but pretty radical too."

I look down at my feet. Tony never said anything positive to me about my passion for photography. Tony . . . *whom I just slept with.* Slowly, I look up again.

Mark smiles. "Do you want to grab some lunch?"

I shake my head. "I'm heading over to Berkeley. I have a research appointment at the Bancroft Library."

"To find out more about Annie?" He raises his eyebrows.

"That's right." I smile. "To look through the San Quentin Prison registers."

"Cool." He grins, pushing his shaggy hair out of his eyes. "Tell me about it when you get back. I'd love to hear what you find."

"I will." I wave goodbye. "See you later."

After Mark leaves, I'm taken aback by how different his reaction was compared to Tony's. He seemed *excited* for me to go and visit the Bancroft Library, not disappointed that I couldn't join him for lunch. Suddenly, I feel angry with myself all over again for sleeping with Tony and missing my original research appointment.

But then I pause, realizing I'm at Broadway and Romolo Place, a seedy part of North Beach. This steep, narrow street was once Pinkney Place, which housed the county jail. I picture Annie, sitting in a cramped cell, waiting to be transferred to San Quentin. Maybe she was overcome with shame too, for trusting the wrong man. If I can have sympathy for Annie and her situation, I can work on being kinder to myself.

———◆———

IN THE QUIET of the Bancroft Library's reading room, I look out the window at the UC Berkeley campus with its aged stone buildings and London plane trees, their gnarled branches heavily pruned and barren. They line Campanile Way all the way to Sather Tower, where the campanile's bells chime twice, announcing the time. Nostalgia hits me hard—suddenly I'm young again, full of hope and possibility, earning my degree and falling in love with Tony.

The research librarian approaches, carrying a cardboard box, and I turn away from the window and my memories.

She adjusts her glasses. "I'm glad you could make your appointment this time. I have the materials you've requested."

Guilt spreads through me. I never should have missed my last appointment. Going forward, I will not allow Tony to derail my plans.

"Sorry about that." I smile apologetically. "And thank you for the materials."

Once again, I put on latex gloves so I won't damage the fragile pages, and I remove two volumes with frayed cloth bindings. The first is a scrapbook kept by a policeman named Jesse Brown Cook, a member of the San Francisco Police Department from the 1890s to the 1930s. The second is a compilation of San Quentin Prison records from the year 1890.

I open the volume of San Quentin Prison records. The yellowed paper is water-stained and as thin as onion skin, the ink so faded it's hardly legible. I squint, trying to read the slanted handwriting. It takes a while to figure out what I'm looking at—letters addressed to the district attorney and to the State Board of Examiners. Where are the inmate intake forms and discharge notes? I need to know if and when Annie was discharged from prison.

Disappointed, I turn the yellowed pages, reading about the prison budget and exports from the jute mill. I see a letter addressed to "His Excellency" the governor, Robert Waterman, sent from the clerk's office.

Dear Sir,

I have the honor to inform you that the state board of prison directors met at San Quentin, October 15th, 1890, to recommend the pardon and commutations of the following prisoners:

Convict #11536 David Waite, pardon recommended.
Convict #10337 Joseph Divine, pardon recommended.
Convict #10687 James "Fat Jack" Kiley, commutation
*   to 15 years.*
Convict #11260 Julia Ryan, commutation denied.

Seeing the name of a female convict, I perk up. As I trail my finger down the page, my mouth falls open. "Fat Jack" was sentenced to fifty years for rape, while Julia Ryan was sentenced to twelve years for perjury. Why was a dangerous criminal—a rapist—given a reduced sentence, while a woman who hadn't physically harmed anyone was denied the same privilege?

On the next page, fifteen Chinese American convicts are listed by name. Below their names, I read a letter written to the governor.

When released from prison, to be turned over to the Chief of Police of San Francisco, and then to be sent back to China, never to return to the United States. Each shall waive his legal right to a "release certificate" for the following reasons: Doctor Stanley—a San Quentin doctor who has examined each inmate—declares every Chinese so afflicted

with some incurable form of mental and physical disease, they
are rendered utterly incapable of being of service to the state.

A white rapist had his fifty-year sentence commuted but
fifteen Chinese prisoners were declared mentally ill by an ob-
viously racist prison doctor and sent back to China? Heat
washes over me. Today's events at the International Hotel
resurface—the cop on his horse, the city trying to rid the area
of its Chinese residents—and it feels eerily like past wrongs
are being repeated.

Setting aside the album of San Quentin Prison records, I
pick up the police officer's scrapbook. I'm not sure what I'll find
in here, but I'm hopeful it will contain something useful. Turning the pages, I look through a hodgepodge of yellowed newspaper clippings, playbills, and photographs. There's a picture
of a horse and carriage in the partially built belly of a ship and
a photograph of a monkey on a chain, both dated 1885, Meiggs'
Wharf. There are more photos of North Beach in the 1880s,
and a program from the Bella Union Theater, featuring acts by
Billee Taylor and Harry Montague.

Then my breath hitches. Stuck between two of the thin
pages is a yellowing piece of newsprint. It's an 1890 article
clipped from *The San Francisco Examiner*, written by a journalist named Winifred Sweet. The article, DEAD TO THE WORLD:
WOMEN BURIED BEHIND THE BARS OF SAN QUENTIN PENITENTIARY,
includes thumbnail sketches of each female inmate. I bring my
fingers to my lips. These women were imprisoned with Annie.

Below each inmate's illustration is her name, prisoner number, and crime. I look at a woman named Ada Werner. She has
a long, thin face with a slender nose and sad, light eyes. Her

black dress is buttoned up to her neck, and I can't tell if she's wearing a black feathered hat, or if her hair is feathered and short. She's only twenty-four, charged with shooting her husband in the head while he slept. Looking at her young face, it's difficult to imagine this sad woman as a murderer.

My eyes jump to Mary Von, whose name I recognize; she was the woman who attempted to murder the prison matron. Though her age is written as thirty-nine, she appears much older. Her light eyes are grooved by deep wrinkles and her mouth has heavy jowls. She is described as a "hideous old crone" who shows no signs of ever reforming. After a romantic liaison with an Australian tourist, Mary robbed him of all his savings and then shot him dead.

Next I see May Johnson, a twenty-eight-year-old Black woman with a friendly face, though in her mug shot, her dark eyes look sorrowful. Around her neck she wears a placard announcing her prison sentence—four years for grand larceny. There are more women: pickpockets, arsonists, and murderers. A pickpocket named Maud Manner is drawn with a sly smile. At seventeen, she is the youngest woman in the penitentiary.

Seventeen. A teenager. I shudder, wondering what life was like for Annie, locked up among these women when she herself was innocent. Did she befriend them? Or were they her enemies? The newspaper article has been cut off, leaving the rest of the female population of San Quentin a mystery. Taking out my notebook, I scribble down as much information as I can, hoping I might be able to find the full newspaper issue somewhere else.

Leaving the library, I feel frustrated. Every female convict was punished, but nothing was done to treat the social circumstances at the root of their crimes. How many of these women had access to an education or to childcare, or the ability to earn a living wage? A few lines from the newspaper article come to mind, and I can hear the scorn dripping from the journalist's voice.

There is hardly a chance of these prisoners ever reforming. They are dead to the world, no longer capable of reentering respectful society. They are incorrigible.

18

"Corcoran and Fat Jack should be hanged," Bessie muttered, spitting on the ground.

Annie's arms pricked with goose bumps at the mention of his name. She looped her needle through the cord of her crochet lace, her hands trembling.

"Aye. But they won't be."

Her eyes traveled to Emma, sitting alone under a tree, unable to hide her black eye and split lip. Emma hadn't picked up her Irish lace since the attack—a pretty collar she'd planned to trade for a pot of beeswax cold cream. Maud, whose constant chatter had become as regular as birdsong, had gone silent as well. Even the choicest pieces of gossip didn't interest her.

"I wish I had my gun." Bessie scowled. "I would've shot them both." She kicked the toe of her boot into the dirt.

Annie's chest clenched like a fist at the memory of Corcoran pinning her against the wall. She turned to Bessie, her mouth dry.

"Teach me how to shoot?"

Bessie gave a sad smile. "I can't teach you how to shoot if I ain't got a gun."

Annie looked up at the south tower, at the guards with their Gatling guns. To think she'd once practiced words like *credenza* and *chintz* and learned the difference between a cruet spoon and a basting spoon. She'd polished silver, gold, mahogany, oak, and walnut, using different oils and cloths for each surface. Her head was filled with useless knowledge, when what she needed to know was how to defend herself against a man.

Fat Jack was locked in the dungeon, but this fact brought Annie no solace. He would be released soon enough. Corcoran hadn't received any punishment. He'd been reassigned to the guard tower near the Stones. But Annie had seen the deep purple line of a bruise on his neck and the dried blood on his bandaged hand. It gave her a small swell of pride to know she'd caused him pain. But she also knew that Corcoran was more dangerous now than ever—hungry for revenge like a rabid dog. She felt his eyes on her, even from across the prison yard.

"If I ever got the chance," Annie said, looking into Bessie's blue eyes, "I'd like to see Corcoran meet his maker."

Bessie let out a low whistle. "What would Mrs. Whitmeyer say if she heard you talking like that?"

Once a month, members of the Woman's Christian Temperance Union visited San Quentin to hold Sunday services at the prison chapel. Mrs. Whitmeyer was a volunteer. At first, Annie had listened to the sermons in earnest. But she no longer felt an unwavering connection to her faith. In the prison chapel, the convict women were scorned, judged, and reminded they had failed to resist the cohorts of Satan.

Annie glowered. "She'd quote the Gospel of Matthew."

Bessie raised her eyebrows. "Enlighten me."

"'For if you forgive men their trespasses, your heavenly Father will also forgive you.'"

"Horseshit." Bessie shook her head. "They don't deserve forgiveness."

Annie clenched her teeth. She could never forgive Corcoran for what he had done to Emma. She wanted retribution, even if it went against God. Looking over at Emma and Maud, pale, scarred, and withdrawn, Annie took a deep breath.

"Promise me we'll leave this place before it breaks us."

Bessie reached for her hand. "We will. I promise."

───◆─◆───

THE WET SUMMER fog burned away, and September blew in hot and dry. In the months that had passed, not only had Fat Jack been released from the dungeon for good behavior, but he'd also saved the warden from a knife attack. Now he'd applied for a commutation from the governor.

"Do you think his sentence will be commuted?" Annie bit her knuckle.

Fat Jack had brutally assaulted and killed a woman returning home from visiting her children at an orphanage. She'd been so destitute, she had to give them up. She was a widow, in poor health, who died from her injuries after the attack. Annie couldn't imagine her heartbreak, and she seethed at the thought of Fat Jack preying on the weak.

Emma pushed her garment aggressively through her sewing machine.

"Captain Gilcrest and Warden McComb are calling him a hero."

Annie grimaced. "He's a monster."

"And yet here we are," Emma said, her voice bitter. "Locked up with him."

"Not for much longer," Annie said, looking over at Bridget, Julia, and Minnie, hunched over their sewing machines, three older women who weren't as fortunate. Julia had applied for a commutation as well, but she feared her request would be denied.

"I've got seven months more. Once I'm out, I'll be waiting for you."

Emma gave Annie a pitying look. "Do ye think anyone will hire a housemaid who was sent to prison for stealing?"

Annie's stomach tightened. "Someone will."

But Emma was right. Annie couldn't find work as a maid with no reference. And she'd stopped sending money, along with letters, home to her family in Ireland. She felt hot shame spreading through her. There had to be another way to fulfill her promise.

"I can find other work besides service."

Emma's brows drew together. "Working your fingers to the bone in a factory? You won't earn enough to eat."

"I could work in a department store," Annie said, thinking of her Sunday dresses, unworn since she began her prison sentence. She could look the part.

"And still have nothing to eat," Emma retorted. "Shop girls spend their wages on clothes and barely get by."

"What are you implying?" Annie said, her anger rising like bile. "That I should become a *sporting* woman?"

Emma glared at Annie. "There's no shame in it."

Annie bit her lip, heat rushing to her cheeks.

"I'm sorry, Em. You're right. It's a job, like any other."

Pushing her straw-colored hair out of her face, Emma gave Annie a hard look.

"When I first arrived in America, I worked in a laundry. I earned five dollars a week, standing on my feet ten hours a day, feeding clothing through that awful mangle in the steam and heat. I lived in a dark little flat with me aunt, uncle, and cousins."

Annie's hands stilled. "You have family here?"

"Aye." Emma pressed her foot against the treadle. "My cousin Fiona was like a sister. But we were too many in that little flat on Minna Street."

Annie had seen the slums of South of the Slot, rats running through the narrow alleys between cramped apartments. She winced.

"Did your aunt ask you to leave?"

Emma nodded. "I rented a room in a boardinghouse for two dollars a week. That left three dollars a week for food. I figured I'd not buy new clothes or shoes." She frowned. "I had ten cents for breakfast, fifteen for lunch, twenty for supper."

Annie had loathed her job as a domestic, but she had both enough to eat and a safe place to sleep at night. In some ways, her life in service was easier than that of a factory girl or a shopgirl. But Emma had freedom—a room of her own and no mistress to scold her.

"What was it like, to live alone?"

Emma smiled. "At first, it was grand. Whenever lads invited me to the theater or to a restaurant, I'd bring Fiona along. We had such a laugh."

Remembering the neighborhood dances and church

gatherings she'd attended with Ellen, Nora, and Kathleen, Annie felt a pang of sadness. Her social life, Saint Patrick's Church, her friends—it all felt as intangible as a dream, impossible to reclaim.

"I'm lonesome for those happy days."

"Me too," Emma said sadly. "But it wasn't all cheerful. Like you, I wanted to marry a man of my choice in America. I'd met a customer at the laundry, Lawrence."

Annie froze, meeting her friend's blue eyes.

Emma grimaced.

"One night I met Lawrence before we were meant to go to the theater. He told me he'd forgotten something at his apartment and he invited me up. Then he said he was too tired for the theater. He poured red wine, which I didn't much like. But I wanted to appear sophisticated. One thing led to another and he told me it was only human nature . . ."

Swallowing hard, Annie thought of Albert. With only three servants in the house—herself, Greta, and Mary—she and Albert never had more than a few stolen moments alone before she was needed by her mistress. Yet, she could have easily been in Emma's position. If it weren't for Greta knocking on her door, she might have lain with him.

"How old were you when you met Lawrence?" Annie frowned.

"Eighteen. He asked me to move in with him, to his flat downtown. I was pleased, thinking I'd become his wife."

Emma laughed, but it was a bitter sound.

"I was so green. I thought Lawrence would provide for me. But he told me I should keep my laundry job and also earn money on the side."

Annie sucked her teeth. "Oh, Emma . . ."

"Aye." Emma wiped away a tear. "He said I was a pretty girl with her own room downtown, and he had friends with money."

"What did ye say to him?"

"I told him I wasn't that kind of girl."

Emma straightened her shoulders. "But one day, outside the laundry, an old man approached me. He said, 'Pardon me, but don't you room near here?' At first, I didn't understand. But then I saw the ten-dollar gold coin in his hand."

Annie nodded. She'd earned two dollars a week working her hands to the bone in Mrs. Whittier's home: cleaning bathrooms and bedrooms, washing dishes, scrubbing floors, and serving meals. She been desperate to marry Albert for money and social status, so she could leave her job as a domestic. Who's to say she wouldn't have done the same?

"I don't want ye pitying me." Emma lifted her chin.

"I don't." Annie shook her head. "There's no bad penny in that money."

The prison guard, Vinegar Face, snorted awake, and Annie quickly turned away from Emma and resumed her sewing. But then he dozed off again, his head lolling to the side. His whiskey flask was empty by now, no doubt.

"I bought new clothes," Emma whispered.

She rubbed the rough cloth of her prison uniform between her fingers as if she could remember them. "Fine silks, petticoats, and feathered hats. I quit my job in the laundry and saw more clients. At that point, I didn't mind the life."

Annie remembered her own penchant for fine clothing.

"You had your own coin."

Emma nodded. "I had enough to take Fiona to the theater, to a fancy dinner, to buy her pretty gloves." Her face fell. "But

when Fiona asked me where I was working and I didn't answer, she looked at me differently. Then she said she couldn't
speak to me anymore."

"No." Annie's heart broke for Emma.

Emma's lip trembled. "My new clothes . . . I hated them.
They were better than Fiona's, but they revealed to everyone
what I was." She took a deep breath in and let it out. "When I
lost my family, I lost everything. And then Lawrence stole all
the money I'd saved."

Annie clenched her jaw. "How much?"

"Two hundred dollars." Emma blinked back tears. "While I
was sleepin'."

They were both in prison because of men they had loved,
had trusted. Emma was disowned and branded a fallen woman.
Annie was branded a thief. And yet there was no word for
fallen men like Lawrence, like Albert.

"You don't have to go back to that life," Annie said softly.
"You've got your lace."

Emma nodded, a spark of hope in her eye. "That I do."

Annie reached for her friend's hand. "And you've got me.
You'll open your shop, Em. I'll help you do it."

"It's a beautiful dream, Annie," Emma said. "But that's all
it is."

———◆◆———

Sweat ran down Annie's back in rivulets while she walked
with Emma across the dusty prison yard to the toll of the
dinner bell. The roses in the garden had lost their petals,

withering on their thorny stems, and the hillside shimmered golden in the heat. She felt hopeful—heartened Emma had taken up lace making again. Annie would be discharged, find employment, save enough to rent a little shop, and wait for Emma to be released. Together, they would start over.

"Did you hear?" Maud panted as she ran up beside them. "Brooks and Cramer have gotten the sack."

Annie spun around. "The two guards smuggling in opium?"

"The warden called them into his office." Maud grinned. "I heard they were dragged out by Captain Reddy like criminals. Tompkins, McBride, Ellis—them too."

Emma placed her hands on her hips. "Never thought I'd see the day."

Maud giggled. "I reckon Winifred Sweet's already got word of the scandal."

Annie smiled. "Good. She ought to write the truth."

A gust of wind blew across the yard, stirring up dust and fallen leaves. Suddenly, shouts erupted in the distance.

"You have no right, you fuckin' bastard."

Annie froze at the sound of Corcoran's voice. Across the prison yard, he materialized through the dust, his red hair disheveled. Emma stiffened beside Annie. The three women stood paralyzed, watching as Corcoran stumbled. A gasp arose from the female inmates gathered around the Porch. The dinner bell continued to ring, but everyone ignored it.

"Your employment is terminated," Reddy's voice boomed. "Now, get out."

"Like hell!" Spittle flew from Corcoran's mouth.

He swung at Captain Reddy and missed. Then Reddy, a

tall, strong man, pulled back his fist and punched Corcoran square in the face. Annie watched Corcoran fall to the ground, where he landed with a dull thud.

Corcoran grabbed his bleeding nose. "I'll kill you!"

Reddy smirked. "Leave the prison grounds now if you value your life. On account of smuggling both whiskey and opium, you're finished here."

Stumbling to his feet, Corcoran sneered, wild-eyed.

"Is that a threat, Captain?"

Reddy stepped aside, making way for Captain Gilcrest. The older man stood tall in his freshly pressed uniform, his brass buttons gleaming.

"It's an order."

Gilcrest gave a quick nod, and Reddy yanked Corcoran by the elbow through the main prison gate. He gave Corcoran a shove, then he slammed the gate behind him.

"If you're looking for fisticuffs," Reddy called through the bars, "by all means, return. I'll happily best you again."

Annie let out a laugh, giddy with relief. Corcoran had gotten the sack for his involvement in the opium-smuggling ring. The women gathered—Nellie, Bridget, Minnie, Ada, Rosanna, and Julia—hollered and cheered. Emma and Maud looked stunned. Their tormentor was gone. But the feeling was bittersweet. Corcoran was a free man.

"Order! Order!"

Matron Kane shouted at the female inmates, her cheeks flushed from the heat. She wiped sweat from her brow, glaring at the group.

"Report to the mess hall at once. There's nothing to see here."

"Nothing to see, my arse."

"Bloody Corcoran got the sack!"

"The sack? He got a knuckle sandwich, he did!"

Rosanna, Nellie, and several others were too lively to be subdued by Matron Kane's reprimands. Annie smiled, a weight lifted from her shoulders. Bessie would be inside the mess hall, eager to hear the details of Reddy punching Corcoran. And Annie would be glad to describe the look on his face when he fell to the ground, holding his bloody nose.

She touched Emma's hand.

"He's gone, Emma."

Emma pressed her lips together. "Aye."

But Emma's eyes shone with fear.

Dread pooled in Annie's stomach. "What's wrong?"

Emma brought her trembling fingers to her lips. She shook her head.

Annie hated to see her friend so distraught. Emma was resilient, like a rose pushing through concrete. In spite of all the ugliness surrounding them, Emma had found beauty and solace in her lace. She had protected Annie, encouraged her. She'd taught Annie her most valuable skill, pulling her from the darkness when she needed it most. Annie couldn't bear to see Emma this way, when Emma was the strongest person she knew.

"Please," Annie whispered. "You can tell me."

Emma's face crumpled.

"Oh, Annie. My troubles have only just begun."

19

Judy

San Francisco, 1972

My heart thumps as I stand outside Doe Library. When I first set foot on this campus as a freshman, I loved the old buildings the most: South Hall with its worn red bricks and European architectural style from a century ago, and Doe Library, home to the art history department, with its large windows and marble columns like a temple in ancient Greece. Walking beneath the old oaks, the laurel and eucalyptus trees, I felt so grateful to be a student, to be inspired, and to be exactly where I wanted to be in that moment.

Now I'm on the verge of a divorce, I've lost touch with my college friends, and I have no support from my family. But I still have a memory of that feeling—the privilege of getting a higher education. And though I could leave the UC Berkeley campus now, having already finished my research at the Bancroft Library, I know what I need to do, to reach for my goal of a graduate degree. Taking a deep breath, I enter through the main doors to Doe Library, the smell of books and leather flooding my mind with memories of senior year.

At twenty-two, I couldn't imagine the heartbreak that lay ahead. I had a ring on my finger and a handsome husband by my side. A husband who I thought would respect me and respect my desire to work. Our young love acted like a bubble, protecting me from the realities of what our marriage would become—full of bitter disagreements, resentment, misunderstandings, Tony's drinking, his constant criticism.

As I ride the elevator to the fourth floor, I hear my mother's voice. *You're Tony's wife, Judy. Your role is in the home. Don't let a good man go.* But if I'm ever going to become the woman I want to be, I need to choose myself. The elevator doors open, and I step out into the hall, a place that used to be familiar to me but feels like another life.

In the art history department offices, Faith, my undergraduate student advisor, looks up from her desk. She's a heavyset older woman, her hair held in place with a pencil. I haven't been up here to her office in years. But it smells the same, like her rose perfume.

"Hi, Faith. How are you?"

Her face breaks into a smile. "Judy! How are *you*, honey?"

"I'm good," I lie, my heart beating faster. "Listen, I don't have an appointment, but is Professor Roberts available for office hours?"

Faith nods. "I can check."

"Thank you."

When Faith leaves the room, I wipe my sweaty palms on my corduroys. Maybe Carol Roberts is busy and I'll need to come back another time. The thought brings me relief. I don't have to do this now. But then Faith pops her head around the corner.

"Come on back, she's waiting for you."

My stomach tenses. But I won't be admitted to graduate school if I don't face my past. Stepping into my former professor's office, I force myself to smile.

"Hello, Professor Roberts."

Carol Roberts looks up from behind her tortoiseshell glasses, her mouth a thin line.

"Judy. It's been a long time."

"Three years," I say, my mouth dry. "Thank you for seeing me."

She clasps her hands. "What can I do for you?"

I resist the urge to bounce my leg beneath her desk as I sit down. "I don't know if I ever told you, but your art history class History of Photography was one of my favorites."

She smirks. "Flattery will get you nowhere. Get to the point."

I swallow. Professor Roberts has always been blunt. "I'm applying for my master of fine arts degree in photography."

Her lips curl. "And you want me to write you a letter of recommendation."

"Yes."

"Tell me. Why would I do that?"

Humiliation washes over me. But this is Carol's style. She needs me to prove myself, to argue my case. I remember her messy handwriting on all my papers, urging the importance of a strong thesis statement. I take a deep breath.

"Because your class is the reason I became captivated by

twentieth-century photography. The work of Alfred Stieglitz and Dorothea Lange inspired me to look differently at the world around me. Out of all my professors, you know me the best. I came to you often, during office hours, so I could improve, until I consistently earned top marks."

Professor Roberts fixes her gray eyes on mine. "You were a bright and passionate student, Judy. But then your work suffered in your final semester. You were distracted."

My cheeks burn.

"I know." I lick my chapped lips. "I've made mistakes. One of them being putting my husband's desires ahead of my own. We're separating."

Carol raises an eyebrow.

"I'm sorry to hear that."

I'm surprised at the compassion in her eyes. I half expected her to say, *I told you so.*

"Thank you."

"So." She smiles. "Tell me about your portfolio project."

"I've been photographing my San Francisco neighborhood, South of Market, and documenting the changes taking place."

"Oh?" Carol leans forward.

She's interested now. This is my chance.

"You taught me photographic images are shaped by culture, politics, and social life. You gave me the tools to critique the work of Julia Margaret Cameron, Alice Seeley Harris, and Henri Cartier-Bresson."

"Those critiques were some of your best papers."

I'm reminded of how much time I've lost by setting my education to the side. I used to be a great student, but I failed to keep my mind sharp, to stay engaged in the art world. I left academia to become a housewife because Tony wanted me to. Now I have a chance to write new papers, to take new photographs, and to reclaim who I am.

"I want to show the devastation urban renewal is causing among marginalized communities. I want to effect social change."

Carol's lips curve into a smile again. "You're passionate about this."

"I am."

I think of Annie's frightened eyes in her mug shot, of my desire to seek justice for her. She was naïve to the danger of being a poor young immigrant woman, and both of us were betrayed by men we loved. She inspired me to see the humanity in people who are overlooked and to see the beauty in my neighborhood, a place the Redevelopment Agency has declared inconsequential and blighted. Annie was resilient in the face of adversity, and I will be too.

"Look, I've learned a lot in the years since I graduated. I don't want my past mistakes to hold me back from being the woman I want to become."

Carol straightens. "And what kind of woman is that?"

I pause for a moment. A woman who is divorced but unashamed. A woman who lives life on her own terms. I think of Annie, her fellow female inmates, and what the newspaper reporter called them in her condescending article.

Incorrigible.

"One who doesn't give a damn what other people think," I say. "Because she already knows who she is and what she stands for."

———◆———

WALKING UPHILL ON B Street in San Rafael, I smile to myself. Not only did Professor Roberts agree to write me a letter of recommendation, but Seth did as well. I'm learning so much as his employee, and I've noticed my photography techniques improving. Once I finish writing my artist's statement, I'll choose my very best photographs to include in my portfolio, and then I can mail in my graduate school application, which is due in July.

I check my watch, frustrated with myself for arriving late to my appointment at the Marin History Museum. There was a car accident on the Golden Gate Bridge blocking two of the outbound lanes, and I was stuck in traffic for nearly an hour. Now I'll have far less time than I wanted for my research appointment. I approach the Gothic Revival building that houses the museum, its gables adorned with gingerbread trim.

"Welcome to the Boyd Gate House." The docent smiles. "Are you Judy?"

"I am." I take off my jacket. "Sorry I'm late. There was an accident on the bridge."

"I'm Miriam, a research librarian." She frowns. "Unfortunately, someone else has reserved the next hour, so I can't allow you to go over your allotted time."

"I understand," I say, mentally kicking myself for not leaving earlier.

Miriam smiles. "You're here now. Follow me."

She leads me down the hallway of the Victorian home, past a curving wooden staircase with a beautifully carved balustrade. We enter what must have been a bedroom, a narrow room with a bookshelf crowded with binders and a cozy fireplace painted black. In the center of the room, a long wooden table is surrounded by six chairs.

"Take a seat." Miriam gestures to a chair. "First, a bit about the property. This home is nearly a hundred years old, built in 1879 for Ira Cook as a guest house for the family mansion next door, known as Maple Lawn. Ira's granddaughter, Louise, was given both buildings and the surrounding property when she married."

"It's a beautiful building."

I don't want to be rude, but I'm eager to get to my research.

Miriam points to a black-and-white framed photograph of a woman in Victorian dress surrounded by her three children, a girl and two boys.

"John and Louise Boyd raised their three children at Maple Lawn, but their two boys died within months of each other from heart failure."

My stomach clenches, the pain of my miscarriages fresh in my mind. It's the hardest thing I've ever gone through, and I can't imagine anything worse than losing a child.

"That's heartbreaking."

"Rheumatic fever," Miriam says. "In their memory, the Boyds donated the gatehouse and the gardens to the city of San Rafael in 1905. Since 1959, the Boyd Gate House has been home to the Marin History Museum."

"I'm so glad to visit," I say. "I've been to the California Historical Society and the Bancroft Library at UC Berkeley, but I'm especially interested in the San Quentin Prison materials in your collection."

Miriam nods. "Let me bring you the materials you requested. But first, would you like to see some objects made by the prisoners?"

I shouldn't waste any more time. But I feel like I can't pass up this opportunity.

"Absolutely."

"Come this way," Miriam says.

I stand up and follow her to another room, filled with glass display cases. Some hold Native American artifacts—obsidian arrowheads, mortars and pestles for grinding acorns, and abalone shells—while other cases hold antique glass bottles. Miriam leads me to a display case on the right side of the room, and I peer into it. Inside are wooden boxes made from matchsticks, a chessboard, carved figurines, and a leather bridle. Then I notice something else, a swatch of lace so fine, it looks as intricate as a spider's web.

"These objects were made by San Quentin prisoners and given as gifts to the warden. You can see some of the inmates were very skilled."

I admire the details on the lace.

"Incredible. How did they access these materials?"

"The men were permitted to work in the San Quentin furniture shop and they learned both wood carving and leatherwork."

"And the women?"

"They worked in the tailor shop, sewing the men's uniforms, or in the prison laundry. There were also a few women over the years who worked in the women's ward kitchen."

"But this lace . . ."

Miriam nodded. "It's beautiful, isn't it? That's Irish crochet lace. One of the female inmates must have made it in her spare time, using a crochet needle." She looks at her watch. "We better get you started on your research."

I want to spend more time with the lace, but I don't have much time remaining. Instead, I return to my seat at the table and pull on a pair of latex gloves, which I've become used to, even though I still don't like the sweaty, powdery sensation. Miriam brings over a thick book, its burgundy cloth binding fraying at the corners.

"Here's the register of San Quentin Prison inmates that you requested, beginning in January 1890."

"Thank you."

I open the register. There, clear as day, is the list of prison inmates I had hoped to find at the Bancroft Library.

No. 14247, Glover, John, embezzling, 2 years.
No. 14794, Han, Ah, murder, 10 years.
No. 15605, McKee, George, rape, 5 years.

My stomach sinks when I realize there are only male prisoners listed for several pages. I flip through the remainder of the register, but even when I reach the year 1891, I don't see the names of any women.

My shoulders sag. The register ends in December 1891. I close the volume and bite my lip. Then Miriam returns with a sturdy leather book, bigger than a photo album, and sets it down on the table beside me. It has a black leather cover embossed with gold writing.

"This is the turnkey's log. It describes daily changes at the prison and the daily weather conditions at San Quentin from the years 1890 to 1892."

"Thank you so much. But I believe you brought me the wrong register. I asked to see the female prisoners who were received from 1889 onward."

Miriam smacks her forehead. "I'm so sorry about that! And here I brought you a register full of men."

"Yes." I laugh, handing the book back to her.

Then I remember the newspaper clipping I found pasted in the Jesse Brown Cook scrapbook at the UC Berkeley Bancroft Library.

"Oh!" I say, turning toward Miriam. "I'd like to know if you have any May 1890 issues of *The San Francisco Examiner* here. I'm looking for an article written by a female journalist named Winifred Sweet."

Miriam scrunches her brow. "What's the headline?"

"'Dead to the World: Women Buried Behind the Bars of San Quentin Penitentiary.'" I lick my lips. "It has thumbnail sketches of the female inmates. I saw a clipping in a scrapbook at the Bancroft Library, but I'd love to read the whole thing."

Miriam smiles. "Winifred Sweet was famous for her stunt reporting. She pretended to faint on the streets of San Francisco to expose the poor emergency services."

I raise my eyebrows. "Really?"

Miriam nods. "She scored a number of exposés and scoops. Let me search our newspaper collection to see if we have that article for you."

"Thanks. I appreciate it."

Miriam makes her way into the back and then returns with a yellowed newspaper.

"This isn't the issue you're looking for, but I thought you'd find it interesting. It's about the release of one of the female inmates."

"Wonderful," I say. "If you happen to find any mention of a prisoner named Annie Gilmurray, that's who I'm researching specifically."

"Good to know," Miriam says, nodding. "Let me find our 1889 female prisoner intake register, and I'll keep looking for that Winifred Sweet article in *The Examiner.*"

She disappears again into a back room. Carefully smoothing the yellowed newspaper before me, I read through the text of an 1898 article in *The Marin Journal.*

MRS. MARTIN PARDONED

Governor Budd today issued a commutation of the sentence of Mrs. Mary E. Martin, sent from Oakland for having defrauded a woman in that city out of her property, whom she got under her hypnotic control. The case excited much attention at the time. Recently Mrs. Martin became very seriously ill from a tumor that was developing within her and she was a constant inmate of the prison hospital. Finally, her condition became so bad that it was deemed necessary to remove her from prison. Her tumor must be operated on without delay, if her life is to be saved. Such an operation, to be successful, demands the services of skilled surgeons and subsequent care that this institution cannot provide for female patients.

I'm glad to see a female inmate had her sentence commuted by the governor so that she could receive the medical attention she needed. Unfortunately, learning about the fate of Mary Martin brings me no closer to finding Annie.

I set aside the newspaper and open the turnkey's log, where I discover the most beautiful handwriting I've ever seen, like the work of a master calligrapher.

> New Year's Morning, January 1890.
> Rained until ten o'clock last night. Cleared up and wind went down. Beautiful sunlit morning, calm and pleasant. Prisoners are locked up. No work in shops today.

I'm captivated by the simple yet lovely description. Turning the pages, I skim through the entries in the year 1890.

> Penal search at all the cells in the prison made today. Cold, sharp morning. Wind changeable from N to W. threatens to rain and dark. Commenced heavy raining at 9:30 AM. Two prisoners discharged by expiration of sentence. Louis Booth and Joseph Francis.

The log goes on to describe the minutiae of each day—prison cell changes, weather conditions, visitors, chapel services, prisoners sent to the dungeon, prisoners arriving by steamer, prison breaks . . . I can't stop reading, I'm so absorbed in the details. This original source document is proving invaluable to my research.

Bell rung this morning at fifteen minutes before eleven o'clock AM . . . Beautiful morning, soft and clear . . . Cold night with some frost . . . Very heavy fog this morning . . . Divine service in the chapel this morning . . . Has been a charming day . . . Gloomy morning, disagreeable wind . . . Raining occasionally at night. Hot and dry morning . . . Beautiful sunset tonight.

Before I know it, I've read through most of the log. An inmate who worked as a photographer in the Bertillon Room hanged himself. Ada Werner nearly burned down the women's ward, after her candle fell over, catching her bedding on fire. Mary Von attempted to murder the prison matron, beating her with a piece of iron. I picture Annie, locked up among these dangerous women, and I shudder.

The shocking portrait of life behind San Quentin's walls recounts guards fired for smuggling opium into the prison, along with prisoners tortured with straitjackets and hoses. I'll never have certainty about what Annie's life in San Quentin was like, but the turnkey's log gives me a much clearer picture of how frightening it must have been.

Miriam returns, a sympathetic smile on her face.

"I'm sorry, but your appointment time is almost up. Unfortunately, I couldn't locate the 1889 female prisoner's register or the Winifred Sweet article you mentioned. I'll need more time."

Dismay fills me. "That's okay, I understand."

"Would you like to make an appointment to come back?" Miriam asks.

"Yes, please," I say.

She smiles. "Let me see when I can pencil you in. I'll be right back."

I turn a few more pages of the turnkey's log, hoping for more glimpses of Annie's life behind bars. My breath catches in my throat.

Tuesday, November 11th.

Gloomy morning, heavy rain. A female inmate, serving a term for grand larceny, died in hospital at eleven o'clock last night. She was too far gone to be saved.

Annie

San Quentin, 1890

W hat is it?" Annie asked, her pulse racing.

Emma looked to her left and then to her right, making sure they were alone, standing outside the Porch after the other female inmates had gone in. "My monthly. It hasn't come since . . ."

Annie sucked in her breath. "Surely it could be something else?"

Wiping away a tear, Emma shook her head. "Annie, I know the signs. In my line of work, this isn't the first time . . ."

"Oh." Annie's mind raced. *Did Emma have a child?* But then she remembered advertisements she'd seen in the papers for "diseases peculiar to females," promising the removal of an "obstruction." Turpentine, tansy, and pennyroyal, a madam's best friend. Though some unfortunate women might poison themselves in the process, it kept unwanted infants out of baby farms, where they were neglected and starved to death. Poor wee souls.

Emma blinked back tears. "What am I to do?"

Annie brought a shaking hand to her mouth. "Oh, Emma."

Emma trembled. "I'm doomed."

Suddenly the matron appeared, her nostrils flaring. "Inmate 14055 and inmate 13475, what are you doing still standing here?"

Emma flushed, a sheen of sweat on her upper lip. She covered her mouth.

"I'm going to be sick."

And then she vomited across the wooden slats of the Porch, right at the matron's feet. Matron Kane jumped back, disgusted.

"Inmate 14055. You shall return to your cell." She glared at Annie. "Inmate 13475, report to the mess hall at once."

Annie watched as Matron Kane escorted Emma toward her cell. She felt sick with dread. Emma was pregnant with Corcoran's child, a fate worse than her prison sentence. The outlook was bleak, for both herself and the baby. Working as a domestic, Annie heard whispers of desperate girls who turned to baby "farms" for help. Farms in the countryside they were not, but foul San Francisco establishments hidden on cramped floors in dark alleyways.

Some girls paid monthly in the hopes of getting their babies back. They were the fortunate ones, their wee babes sick with rickets and crowded twenty to a room. The infants paid for in full were never adopted out as promised. Why keep them alive with cash already in hand? Such cruelty and greed brought Annie to tears. It was no wonder some women made the choice for a child never to be born at all.

—◆—

THE SEASON TURNED along with the leaves, and the whispers among the prison inmates grew. By the wet, cold days of October, Emma could no longer hide her condition. She vomited in the tailor shop nearly every morning, earning shouts from the prisoners and the guards alike for spraying the garments with her sick. As her stomach swelled gently beneath her prison uniform, everyone knew what Corcoran had done. Emma had already served two years of her three-year sentence. And yet, here she was, in prison and with child.

On the first day when there was a break in the rain, Annie sat in the courtyard with Bessie, Emma, and May, working on her lace.

Bessie shook her head, frowning at Emma. "It's wrong to keep you locked up when you're in the family way."

May nodded. "You ought to be put up in one of the guard's houses."

Emma set down the lace cuffs she'd been working on.

"The warden wants to be rid of me and the problem inside me, for feck's sake! Why would he help me?" She wiped a tear from her cheek.

Annie, Bessie, and May had rallied around Emma in her time of need, forming a surprising sisterhood. May patted Emma's shoulder. "Deep breaths, sugar. We got you." But May's dark eyes shone with concern.

Anger seethed like hot coals in Annie's chest. She couldn't bear to see her friend suffer. Emma ought to put her feet up, to sit with a cup of tea. Annie remembered her mother, her ankles swollen with each pregnancy, complaining of backaches. She'd made sure her mother was comfortable, warmed by a peat fire in the hearth. She brought her sprigs of mint and lavender from the garden to ease her morning sickness. Now, she couldn't do the same for Emma.

"Warden McComb is responsible." Annie gritted her teeth.

Bessie nodded. "He's crooked as a fishhook."

Annie stilled, suddenly struck by an idea. She looked over at her friend, Emma's face pale and blotchy from crying. "What if I were to write to that reporter at *The Examiner*, Winifred Sweet? What if I told her to expose the scandal?"

Emma wiped away her tears. "So that everyone may know I'm a fallen woman? So that I may never claw my way back to a respectable life?"

Annie shook her head. "Corcoran forced himself on you. We're meant to be kept safe in here. You did nothing wrong."

Emma's silence spoke volumes. It didn't matter what had actually happened. A woman would be judged for her sins more harshly than a man.

Bessie cleared her throat, looking at them.

"The women's charities will take an interest. Some Christian do-gooders will insist you get proper treatment."

"And a female doctor," Annie said. "Or a midwife. We'll demand it."

She set down her lace and took Emma's hand. "Think of it. Winifred has already exposed the opium-smuggling ring. This is far worse. It could cost Warden McComb his job."

Emma sniffed, then wiped her nose. "Who would believe us?"

Bessie furrowed her brow. "Any journalist worth their salt."

Maud, who'd been watching them from across the courtyard, bid goodbye to Nellie and Minnie, then approached, her cheeks flushed from the cold. She blew on her chapped hands and rubbed them together. "I heard you talking." She looked at Emma, her eyes dark and serious. "And I think you ought to tell Winifred the truth."

Emma blinked. "Why?"

Maud set her jaw. "Because I don't have proof of what Fat Jack did to me."

"And for that you should be grateful!"

"I am." Maud softened. "But you can make them pay. Please, Emma."

A cold wind blew through the courtyard, stirring up the last of the dry autumn leaves. Annie bit her lip. She used to be afraid of these women, even young Maud, because they were convicts and she considered them dangerous. But in this moment, she understood they were the ones in danger. It was up to her to fight for them.

"Maud's right. With the truth out, Fat Jack's commutation will be denied. Corcoran will be arrested. We may be prisoners, but we deserve human dignity and protection."

Emma looked at Maud, Bessie, and May. Then she looked at Annie and sighed.

"Fine. I'll do it."

Maud smiled, giving Annie a glimpse of the girl Maud would have been if not robbed of her childhood. "And Warden McComb will go down. He's a right bastard, he is."

"Do you have Winifred's address at *The Examiner*?" Annie turned to Bessie.

Bessie nodded. "I do. But who will sign the letter?"

Annie looked at her friends. "We'll sign it anonymously, on behalf of us all. The women of San Quentin Penitentiary."

Maud scowled, kicking her boot in the dirt. "Captain Gilcrest will open it. He doesn't want no one to know the truth. Especially after that drug scandal made the papers."

May's brown eyes widened.

"My George can help. Food and supplies are brought to the prison weekly on a steamer called the *Caroline*. He can drive the letter on the commissary wagon down to the dock, then ask a deckhand on the boat to mail it for him when they reach the city. Captain Leale hires mostly ex-cons, so George already knows these men."

The women looked at one another, weighing the risk of getting caught.

Annie spoke first. "It's a grand idea. I'll slip you the letter beneath my bowl when I come to the mess hall for breakfast."

———— ◆ ————

ANNIE TOOK OUT a pen, paper, and pot of ink. She and her friends had combined their prison credits to purchase them. Her heart pounded as she dipped the quill into the ink. If they were caught, what would happen? Would she, May, Bessie, Maud, and Emma be locked in the dungeon? Annie pushed the thought away and began to write.

Dear Miss Sweet,

I am an inmate of San Quentin Penitentiary. And I speak on behalf of every woman imprisoned behind these walls. A great scandal has taken place under Warden McComb's watch. No matter what you may hear, these allegations are not unfounded.

In late June, the women's ward was without its guardian, Matron Kane, for she was in hospital after the attack by Mary Von. After lockup, David Corcoran, a prison guard, and a prisoner, "Fat Jack" Kiley, entered the women's ward under the cover of darkness.

They unlocked the cells of prisoners Emma O'Sullivan and Maud Manner with stolen keys. They forced themselves upon both women. When Corcoran unlocked my cell, I fought his advances and stabbed him with my crochet needle. You may interview other guards to verify his hand was bandaged at this time.

Captain Gilcrest arrived on the scene and witnessed what had come to pass. But he did nothing to protect us. And now Emma O'Sullivan is with child. And the father is Corcoran, a former guard. This is the truth. I invite you to visit San Quentin to confirm her condition. We are not safe under the management of Warden McComb. We ask that the public be made aware of this scandal. We request a female doctor to attend to Emma, and for her to be moved outside the prison, to comfortable accommodations. You may not look upon us favorably, but we are women, the same as you. We deserve dignity and protection. Please, do not ignore our cries for help.

Sincerely,

The Women of San Quentin Penitentiary

Annie waited for the ink to dry and then she blew out her candle. The truth would come to light in the morning.

———◆◆———

ANNIE GREW MORE anxious with each passing day. It had been two weeks since she had slipped her letter to May and since George had confirmed he'd given it to a crew member for delivery. There was no way to know if Winifred had received their letter or if she even believed them. Emma and Maud remained stoic, but guilt gnawed at Annie's insides, knowing she had brought them hope, perhaps under false pretenses.

"These things take time," Bessie said, walking beside Annie in the courtyard.

Annie frowned. "Do you think Gilcrest suspects anything?"

"I hope not." Bessie's shoulders tensed. "He's got ears everywhere."

Since the incident with the candle, the prison authorities decided Ada Werner ought to be at the end of the hall, closer to Matron Kane. Emma and Ada had switched cells, so Emma was now in the cell next to Annie's. At night, they spoke through the wall, sometimes singing Irish ballads until one of the women told them to bugger off. Though San Quentin remained a brutal and lonely place, having Emma near made it easier to endure.

Still, Emma belonged in the comfort of a home, in one of the officers' buildings in San Quentin Village, or somewhere else outside the prison walls. At night, Annie dreamed of Mayo, of the plain thatched-mud hut in which her village held chapel, of the pilgrimage she made with her mother to visit the shrine of Our Lady of Knock. Sometimes she dreamed of Emma's baby, who she thought was a girl, and watched her playing among the fields of orchids, heather, foxgloves, buttercups, and thistle. But when she awoke, she remembered what a cruel fate the child had been dealt—to be born behind bars.

On the third week of waiting, Annie stood behind Emma in the mess hall queue. Bessie approached them from the opposite direction, a plate of food in hand. "She's gotten it."

Annie's heart fluttered. "The letter?"

"That's right," Bessie said, keeping her voice low. "May has the details."

Emma's eyes widened.

Matron Kane gave them a sharp look and they fell silent. But when the matron turned her gaze, Bessie whispered, "She's bringing a doctor, like we asked."

Emma looked pale. Annie wanted to reach for her friend's hand and squeeze it, to remind her she wouldn't be alone. But under the matron's watchful eye, she kept her distance. Bessie cast her eyes at the ground, then took a seat at one of the mess hall tables, next to Nellie.

"You heard?" May said as she ladled a portion of fish onto Annie's plate.

Annie nodded, too nervous to speak.

May's fingers brushed Annie's, and she could feel the flicker of paper, a note, being slipped beneath her plate, hiding seamlessly under the edge. Annie stiffened but then forced herself to relax. She nodded at May, then carried her food through the mess hall as if nothing had changed. But she could feel the paper burning her fingertips, waiting to be unfolded.

———◆—◆———

SUNDAY MORNING ARRIVED, and with it, heavy rain. Annie's stomach knotted in anticipation of Winifred Sweet's arrival. May's note had contained few words: *Sunday. Bridget O'Brien. Cousin. Patrick Donohue. Uncle.* But Annie had understood. The journalist would be in the visitors' log as Annie's cousin, while the doctor would be logged as Emma's uncle.

"What if the weather delays the ferry?" Annie turned to Bessie, shivering in the courtyard.

"Don't fret," Bessie said, pulling her woolen cap low over her eyes. "It won't."

Annie nodded. "Is the reception crowded?"

"Usually." Bessie blew on her hands. "There's an omnibus for visitors to and from the railway station. Ten to twenty people inside the room at a time."

Annie licked her dry lips. "What if Miss Sweet is recognized?"

Bessie frowned. "Let's hope not. At least not before the doctor has a chance to see Emma. Is she ready?"

Annie smoothed her calico dress. She felt sick to her stomach with nerves.

"I hope so."

That morning, at the breakfast bell, Annie and Emma had exchanged glances but no words. She'd given Emma's hand a squeeze before they parted ways. Now Emma had chosen to remain indoors due to the rain, but Annie needed the fresh air to clear her head.

A guard, Bottle Face Buckley, appeared at the top of the

stairs to the enclosed courtyard. He leered at the women, his belly straining against the buttons of his uniform.

"Inmates 13475, 12879, 11691, and 12765, come with me."

"Good luck." Bessie punched Annie's arm.

Annie's heart thumped as she followed Minnie, Bridget Smith, and Lizzie Ross up the stairs. When she reached the top, the guard stared at her, rubbing his pockmarked face. "Ain't like you to have visitors."

Annie remained silent. She didn't owe him an explanation. The female inmates followed Bottle Face through the dark corridor, the gas lamps hissing, past the rows of cells and the matron's quarters. Then they descended the stairs and waited outside the captain of the yard's office. Annie looked through the barred windows into the office of the turnkey. She could see the man sitting at his wooden desk, writing in his log, recording the day's events.

The rain pelted Annie's shoulders as she left the Porch and crossed the prison yard, approaching the brick building that housed the warden's office, the officers' quarters, and the visiting room. Inside the building, after walking down a long corridor, she heard murmurs of distant conversation. Bottle Face Buckley led the women to a small room with a series of stalls divided by partitions. It was the closest Annie had ever been to the outside, a kind of limbo between worlds. She waited with Bridget Smith, Lizzie, and Minnie, who were all in good spirits.

Peering through the wire screen that separated the stalls from the reception room, Annie saw women wearing fashionable mutton-sleeve taffeta dresses and feathered hats. Others dressed more modestly, in shawls and woolen skirts. There were men too, both young and old. The visitors sat on benches, looking solemn and talking in an undertone. Annie's pulse quickened.

Which woman is Winifred Sweet?

The reception room smelled of wet wool. Annie tugged at the collar of her dress, sweat running down her back. Watching the inmates whispering to their loved ones through the screen, she ached for her siblings. What were Maggie, Kate, and Mary doing now? Had they stayed in school? Did Thomas still have nightmares, or had he grown out of them? She couldn't allow herself to focus on the time that had passed with no letters and no money sent home.

"Time's up!" a uniformed guard shouted at one of the men. Annie watched his face crumple as he said goodbye to a young boy, perhaps his grandson.

Bessie had told her each inmate had fifteen minutes to speak to their visitor. Annie watched a red-haired girl, dressed in her Sunday best, get into a lover's quarrel with a male convict behind the screen, her voice rising behind her cupped hand, her mouth pressed against the wire. The clank of iron doors reverberated and echoed down the corridor. Annie took a deep breath in and let it out. She looked around the room, where about a third of the female convicts were gathered. But Emma wasn't among them.

Where is she?

The iron doors swung open, and a blonde in her late twenties entered the room, her hair sleek and puffy beneath her hat, her face attractive and plump, her blue eyes sharp. Behind her, a bespectacled man in a wool suit followed. Annie knew this woman was Winifred Sweet and her companion the physician. Miss Sweet had overdressed, wearing a fur stole across her shoulders. Even the most stylish Irish domestics and shopgirls couldn't afford such fine clothing. Heart thumping, Annie looked around the room one last time for Emma.

The guard shouted, "Bridget O'Brien for inmate number 13475!"

Annie stepped forward into an empty partition, its walls narrow, approaching the wire mesh that separated her from the journalist. It had been so long since she'd spoken to anyone outside of prison. She feared her tongue would stick to the roof of her mouth. But she needed to do this, for Emma. Annie forced a smile.

"Hello, Cousin Bridget. Thank you for visiting."

Winifred pursed her lips. "Your letter intrigued me." Then she dropped her voice to a whisper. "Where is Miss O'Sullivan? Her *uncle* is here to verify her condition."

Annie's heart thudded. Emma still hadn't arrived.

"I—I don't know."

She turned around, praying to find Emma somewhere in the room. To her horror, Captain Gilcrest approached, along with the prison doctor, Dr. Stanley. His eyes bored into Annie's and her heart sank into her stomach. Their plan had been foiled.

"Miss Winifred Sweet." He walked up to the wire partition, and Annie stepped aside. "Do you never tire of your muck-raking?"

Winifred Sweet smiled. "Captain Gilcrest. It's always such a pleasure to see you."

"I'm afraid you've arrived on account of a vulgar rumor."

Captain Gilcrest's mouth twitched as he spoke. He glared at Annie. "It holds no truth."

Winifred pulled a pencil from her purse, then wet her lips. "I have it on good authority that a female prisoner is with child. And that a former guard, a Mr. Corcoran, is the father."

Captain Gilcrest shook his head. "Absolute lies."

"Then you won't object to Dr. Walton Harvey examining the prisoner?" Winifred smirked. "The public deserves to know whether or not the rumors are true."

Gilcrest's face remained impassive. "There is no need. My esteemed colleague Dr. Stanley has already examined the woman. He shall refute these baseless accusations."

Annie gasped.

The beady-eyed Dr. Stanley stepped forward, a smug look on his face. "Miss Sweet, I have examined inmate 14055. She is afflicted with hysteria."

"No!" Annie cried. "He's lying!"

Captain Gilcrest spun around, all traces of the kindhearted man she'd once thought him to be erased. "Hold your tongue, girl."

The doctor stroked his beard. "The young woman was treated with an injection of turpentine. She will be confined to her cell for a prescription of bed rest."

Trembling with rage, Annie gripped the wire separating her from Winifred.

"Emma is no hysteric. She was raped." She pointed at Captain Gilcrest. "And *he* knows it! He was there!"

Gilcrest clenched his jaw. Then, with a quick nod, he summoned two prison guards, who moved quickly toward them.

Annie looked at Winifred. "Help me! You must believe—"

But the guards grabbed her roughly by the elbows, yanking her away. Annie twisted and turned, fighting to break free.

Captain Gilcrest gave her an icy look. Then he growled his orders.

"Take her to the dungeon."

PART THREE

———◆◆———

Involuntary servitude is prohibited except to punish
crime.   —California Constitution, 1974

Irish lace still survives.
                    —*The Irish Times,* May 19, 2018

21

Judy

San Francisco, 1972

didn't get to read the name of the woman who died." I sigh, frustrated at myself for arriving late to my appointment. "And my next visit to the Marin History Museum isn't until Wednesday."

Seth cocks his head. "You're really invested in finding out what happened to this Irish convict?"

It's half past six o'clock, but Seth and I have been chatting in the staff room at Glass Photo since we closed up the shop.

I nod. "I truly believe she's innocent of her crime."

Seth frowns. "Wait . . . why?"

"Because there was an affidavit tucked behind her Bertillon card." I wince. "Seth, I'm so sorry, I might have . . . removed her card from the mug book."

Seth gives me a compassionate look.

"Judy, I bought that thing for five dollars. It's okay. And

also, half of those cards are coming loose. What did the affidavit say?"

I'm so relieved he isn't angry at me. "It was testimony given by a Swedish servant after Annie's arrest saying a guy named Albert gave Annie the ring she was accused of stealing."

"Who was he?"

"Her mistress's nephew. He was already engaged to someone else."

Seth whistles. "Tough break."

The look of shock and betrayal in Annie's eyes will haunt me forever—I need to know what happened to her.

I shake my head. "Annie was only twenty, with her whole life still ahead of her. What if she died in prison?"

Seth's eyes crinkle at the corners as he smiles. "Judy, you have your whole life ahead of you too. I love that you care about what happened to this girl in the mug book, but don't forget about yourself, okay?"

I laugh. "I won't."

"Good," he says. "You're a natural with the customers. People are drawn to your energy. It's a joy to see you come out of your shell. Keep up the good work."

My cheeks warm with the compliment.

"Thanks," I say, feeling shy. "For taking a chance on me."

Seth pulls on his coat. "Do you need anything before I go?"

I shake my head. "No, I'm good."

"The San Francisco Art Institute would be lucky to have you."

My heart thumps at the thought of being accepted. "Thank you. I really appreciate your letter of recommendation."

"When you have your first gallery show"—Seth pauses in

the doorway—"because you *will*, I'll be there. And I'll bring my partner, Gary. He'd love to meet you."

"Really? I would love that."

"Maybe you'll join us at the flea market in Alameda sometime?" Seth winks. "You might find a mug book of your own. It's a treasure hunt!"

I laugh. "That sounds fantastic."

After saying good night to Seth, I settle in at the folding table in the staff room where I usually eat lunch. With Tony, I let my camera collect dust in the back of my closet. And for what? He never told me I couldn't take photographs, but he made me feel as though my dreams didn't matter. After every argument, I left feeling like there was something wrong with me. He belittled me to the point where I didn't want to put my art out into the world to be judged.

Now I'm doing exactly that, but I'm not afraid anymore. I've chosen twelve photographs to submit with my graduate student application. They include Hope's portrait; the SRO residents in their small rooms at the Knox and the Milner; my color portraits of local café and barbershop owners on Sixth Street, including a man carrying a whole pig to his butcher shop; Kevin on his cherry-red motorcycle in front of the Stud; my neighbor Vanessa and her son; a homeless man blowing a curl of cigarette smoke into the air; and the cop on horseback, sneering at the protestors gathered in front of the I-Hotel.

I'm proud of them all. They show ordinary working-class people who call South of Market home. They show activists fighting police brutality. With Seth gone, the quiet inside the shop feels oppressive, so I turn on the small television, allowing the background noise to keep me company. My UC Berkeley transcripts and letters of recommendation are already inside a large manila envelope, with my artist's statement on top.

I plan to send identical envelopes to the California College of the Arts and San Francisco State, but the San Francisco Art Institute is my first choice. Taking one last look at my printed photographs, I can only hope my work is good enough. I think of my older work—symmetrical lawns in front of Sacramento homes, the clean, austere lines of government buildings. I was concerned with formal issues like framing, symmetry, and negative space.

Not that I no longer pay attention to those things, but Annie's mug shot inspired me to focus on street photography. Redevelopment has caused so much devastation already, and I'm proud to document the people who remain. South of Market may not be a well-known tourist destination like Fisherman's Wharf, but that doesn't mean it doesn't matter.

Sliding my prints into the manila envelope, I take a deep breath. I've put forth my best effort. These pictures represent hours of work, of walking the neighborhood, of striking up conversations with strangers and learning their stories.

The TV picture crackles and then comes back into focus.

"A serial rapist has struck again, and Sacramento residents are terrified."

A newscaster with a grim look on her face speaks into her microphone.

The camera cuts to a young woman, a student on the University of California, Davis campus. She wipes tears from her eyes.

"A lot of us are really, really scared. When I'm at home, I

don't unlock the door anymore. My sister sleeps in my parents' bedroom."

I shudder as the camera cuts back to the newscaster.

"The rapist has attacked multiple women in their suburban Sacramento homes while their husbands were away. But he's grown bolder. He is now assaulting women while their husbands are at home, holding men and women hostage at gunpoint . . ."

I quickly shut the TV off. My heart thuds, even though I know the door to the shop is locked. Tony was paranoid about the serial rapist. Our neighbors stopped letting their kids walk anywhere alone. And everyone around us was gripped by the same fear: *Could we be next?* I didn't want Tony keeping a gun in the house, but he was adamant he needed one for protection. Finally, I relented.

Rubbing the goose bumps on my arms, I decide to leave.

One thing I don't like about South of Market at this time of the evening is that it's pretty quiet. The shops are closed, the gay clubs haven't opened yet, and no one is outside. Also, the city hasn't fixed the broken streetlights. Why should they, when they're planning to tear the whole place down?

I lock Glass Photo behind me, then I tug on the shop doors to make sure they're shut. In my leather portfolio case, I have the thick envelope containing my graduate school application, plus my rolls of film negatives. All the hard work I've done in the past month is here with me, and I'll feel safer having my negatives at home. Once I've mailed my application, I'll reward myself with a glass of wine. Even if I don't get into any of the schools I'm applying to, I'll have put myself out there, which is something to be proud of.

The heavy marine layer chills me to my bones, the fog hanging low and thick over the neighborhood. Passing brick warehouses with dark windows, I feel a little skittish. A man digs through a trash can across the street, bottles clinking as he rummages around. He mutters to himself, but he seems harmless. I remind myself it's not that late—only seven o'clock—and I'll probably see more people the closer I get to Folsom.

I have the unnerving sensation that someone is following me. But every time I turn around, the street is dark and there's no one there. Walking along Howard Street past hotels with laundry flapping from fire escapes, I think of the boarding-houses and rooming houses that once stood here, of the hundreds of immigrants killed in the 1906 earthquake. Out of nowhere, I imagine their screams, the floors collapsing upon one another in a crash of timber.

Walking faster, I focus on getting to the mailbox on the corner of Seventh and Folsom. But now I'm feeling a sense of panic, as if the dark windows of the surrounding apartments are eyes, looking at me. I turn left on Russ, a narrow alley with cobbled bricks between its clapboard buildings. Instantly, I regret my decision. It's spooky here.

I scan the street for any sign of life, but there's only a chain-link fence topped with barbed wire, and a series of metal roll doors with NO PARKING painted across them in block letters. Up ahead, there's a warehouse with broken windows that looks completely vacant. Suddenly, I hear a noise. My whole body goes ice-cold. Before I can turn around, someone grabs me from behind, clamping a hand over my mouth.

I want to scream, but I can't. My heart hammers in my

chest. Twisting and kicking my legs, I try to break free. My brain can't comprehend what's happening. But I know I'm being dragged behind a dumpster by the vacant building. There's no hope that anyone is inside. My throat constricts with panic as I hear a switchblade flick open.

I'm going to die.

"You shouldn't be walking alone."

The man's voice is deep and gruff and my blood freezes in my veins. He presses the tip of his knife into my back. I smell the stench of piss and rot, of putrefaction, and I look down at wet patches on the cement behind the dumpster and discarded chicken bones.

"Turn around slowly and give me your bag."

I'm too afraid to speak. To think.

"Do it now!"

Then it registers that he wants my leather bag. *My portfolio. My negatives. My graduate school application.* Hot tears press against my eyelids. Slowly, I force myself to turn around, my heart pounding. I don't want this man to stab me or to slit my throat. What if he's the serial rapist? My stomach lurches when I see him.

He's tall and muscular, dressed all in black, wearing a ski mask. Through the gap in the fabric, I can see he's white—maybe in his late twenties or his thirties. His eyes are blue. I memorize these details, even though I might not be alive to share them. His hand grips the knife, which he points now at my chest. I'm so scared, I think I might pee my pants.

"Please," I whisper. "Don't hurt me."

He lunges for my bag and I scream. When he grabs it, he

slams me against the dumpster. My forehead hits the metal with a loud smack. When I touch my hairline, my fingers come away wet with blood. My heart is slamming against my chest. *What if he wants more than the bag?* The smell of decaying fruit and decomposing flesh, maybe an animal carcass, is overpowering. This man is going to rape me. Then he's going to kill me. My mom is going to find out I was murdered in a San Francisco alleyway. I raise my arms to protect my face.

This is it. I'm going to die.

But he takes the bag and runs. I let out a relieved sob.

———◆—◆———

AT THE POLICE STATION on Bryant Street, I grip the foam cup of coffee, holding on to it like a security blanket. The cut on my forehead has been swabbed and bandaged. I should be relieved that I don't need stitches, but I'd feel safer staying at the hospital for a few hours than going back to my empty apartment. The young male officer questioning me, Officer Martinez, has kind brown eyes. The older one, Officer Jones, is all business. He looks at me, his expression serious, as if I'm the one who has done something wrong.

"Describe the assailant one more time."

I swallow, his blue eyes flashing in my mind. "He was about five foot eleven. In his thirties. White. He had a muscular build. Blue eyes. His voice was deep . . ."

"What color hair did he have?"

My lip trembles. "He was wearing a mask that covered his head. I couldn't see it."

Officer Martinez hands me a tissue. "Take your time."

I let out a shaky breath. "Do you think he's the serial rapist who has been on the news?"

Officer Jones shakes his head. "With the evidence we've collected across state police departments, your attack doesn't fit his pattern."

Officer Martinez gives me an encouraging nod.

"Tell us what was stolen."

Again I explain what was inside my leather portfolio—my graduate school application, my negatives. Tears spill down my cheeks as I think of everything I've lost, even though I'm grateful to be alive. Without my negatives, I can't print any of the photographs I took. I can't apply to the San Francisco Art Institute, California College of the Arts, or San Francisco State. My photographs are gone, forever. All my work, destroyed.

"No valuables?" Officer Jones frowns.

I shake my head. "I didn't have my camera on me."

I should be relieved, because I can't afford to replace my camera, but losing all my photographs is worse. I didn't make copies. Now I wish I had left my negatives at the studio.

Officer Jones taps his lip. "The guy sounds like a junkie. With any luck, he dumped your portfolio once he realized there was nothing inside he could sell."

My muscles tense. "He didn't sound like a junkie. He was coherent."

"Even so." Officer Jones rubs his jaw. "He could have thought you had cash in your bag. Maybe he thought you were about to make a big bank deposit."

It was plausible. Other small-business owners had been targeted on their way to the bank before. But the way the attacker told me I *shouldn't be walking alone . . .* I shudder at the memory. It was as if he was threatening me.

Officer Martinez frowns. "Do you think he targeted you specifically?"

My stomach knots. "What do you mean?"

"Is there anyone who would want to hurt you?"

I shiver at the thought.

"I—I don't think so. But he told me I shouldn't be walking alone."

Both officers look at each other, an unspoken message passing between them. I remind myself I'm not the suspect here. I'm the victim.

Officer Martinez nods. "And you're sure the assailant had a knife?"

"Yes. It was a switchblade. It had a black handle."

Officer Jones clears his throat. "Are you single or married?"

"Single. Actually, married. My husband and I are separated. Well, not officially."

I'm so shaken, I can't think straight.

The officers look at each other again, and then back at me. Officer Jones speaks slowly.

"Where is your husband now?"

"In Sacramento."

His brow furrows. "What's your husband's name?"

"Tony Morelli."

I watch Officer Jones write the name down.

Officer Martinez leans forward. "How long ago did you separate?"

"Um, a few weeks ago?"

Officer Jones is now looking at me like he doesn't trust me. "Is the San Francisco address you gave us your family home?"

I'm starting to get flustered.

"No. It's my rental."

The older officer frowns. "*You* moved out? This isn't a safe neighborhood for a young woman like you to live alone."

I grit my teeth. "I've never had a problem until tonight."

He squares his shoulders. "Do you want us to call your husband?"

"No." I turn to Officer Martinez, whom I feel I have better connection with. "Please don't."

Officer Martinez nods. "We won't contact him unless it's relevant to our investigation."

Officer Jones shakes his head. "I would want to know if my wife was attacked. When was the last time you saw your husband?"

I burn with shame, remembering how I slept with Tony. There's no way in hell I'm telling the officers about that. I try to keep my expression neutral.

"I saw him about a week ago."

"Where was this?" Officer Jones crosses his arms.

"Here, at my apartment on Natoma Street."

"How did he act when you saw him?"

"He was angry." I take a deep breath, omitting what I can while still giving a version of the truth. "Tony wanted me to come home. I told him I wasn't ready."

Officer Jones frowns again. "Are you sure you're telling us everything?"

Once again, I don't feel like I'm being treated as the victim in this situation. I was assaulted, and I feel like the police don't believe me. But what reason do they have not to trust me? Do they think I was "asking for trouble" because I was walking alone at night? I'm exhausted. All the adrenaline has left my body, and I'm angry and emotional.

"*Yes*. I was the one who was robbed. Can I go now?"

Officer Martinez nods.

"We'll contact you as soon as we have any leads."

The creases around Officer Jones's mouth deepen. "We'll file your police report and send it to the district attorney for review."

I swallow. "What happens next?"

"If we catch this guy, you'll be required to testify at trial. A prosecutor from the DA's office will be assigned to you."

Officer Martinez gives me a sympathetic look.

"Is there anyone you'd like us to call?"

I shake my head, wishing I had someone to walk me home. There's no one.

22

Annie

San Quentin, 1890

A guard marched Annie through the rain, toward the in-corrigibles' cells in the basement of the old hospital building, which was built at an angle across the yard. He shoved her through the doorway, then dragged her downstairs to the dark, cold cellblock, the *dungeon*. She swallowed as she passed cells that were narrow like coffins, with precious little light and low ceilings. He pushed Annie into a barren chamber, no chair, no mattress on the floor.

She shivered, her hair wet from the rain. "Am I to be given bedding?"

"You'll sleep in your clothes."

Annie felt a jolt of panic. "When will I get out?"

The guard spat. "When the captain sees fit."

He slammed and locked the iron door, leaving Annie in darkness. The cell was cold and as quiet as a mausoleum. San Quentin's damp and foggy climate had molded the old stone walls. In the distance, someone was coughing, and the rough voices of male convicts carried from the prison yard. Even in November, they preferred to be outdoors for their Sunday exercise. Annie smelled the stink of piss and excrement from a bucket in the corner and gagged, covering her mouth. Then she sank to the ground, hugged herself for warmth, and began to cry.

She thought of Emma and felt sick with worry. Had Emma decided against speaking with Winifred Sweet? Or had Dr. Stanley taken her away? The hospital encircled the women's courtyard, sitting above the Porch, washrooms, kitchen, and mess hall. Annie had never been inside, but she'd heard it was sterile and frightening, and she shivered at the memory of Dr. Stanley. Annie let out a sob. By attempting to tell Winifred Sweet the truth, she'd only made a mess of things. *What if Emma was punished?* Annie couldn't bear the thought of her friend, pregnant and alone, at the mercy of the cruel guards and dishonest doctor. She cried until her body shook. Finally, exhausted, she slipped into sleep.

———•◆•———

IN THE MORNING, Annie pulled herself up off the cold, hard ground, aching with discomfort. The tips of her fingers were numb. She rubbed her hands together and blew on them for warmth, noticing black mold where the cracks in the dungeon walls met the ceiling. A guard swung her cell door open, setting down a heel of bread and a tin cup of water on the dirty floor. Then he slammed the iron door shut again.

Annie's stomach rumbled. She brushed off the bread and ate it slowly. Closing her eyes, she imagined Mary's chicken potpie, with buttery, flaky crust, celery, peas, carrots, onions, and shredded chicken. Truth be told, in her time as a domestic, she had never eaten better. When she opened her eyes, they adjusted to the dim light in her cramped cell. It had no window and was more claustrophobic than her cell in the women's ward.

With nothing to occupy her, Annie stared at the ceiling, mentally practicing stitches of Irish crochet lace as had become her habit. She held up both her hands, imagining the thread in her left and a crochet hook in her right. Annie made a slip knot to start, and then made ten chains. She did a little slip stitch into the first chain, creating a central ring. Moving her right hand, she counted her crochet stitches all the way around: *one, two, three, four, five, six, seven, eight* . . .

As she was going along, she eased the stitches she'd already made over the chain, just as Emma had taught her. She needed twenty-four, making room for sixteen more. When the loop had become thicker, Annie found her very first double crochet, popped her hook under the first top two loops, and made a slip stitch to close her circle. This would be the center of her flower. She counted three crochet stitches, then secured the chain to her inner circle, forming the first of her six flower petals. This would become a beautiful daisy.

Annie created motif after motif—roses, shamrocks, grapevines—then joined them together with crocheted bars. She trusted herself to complete more difficult patterns. Even in the cold, her hands had grown nimble. When she and Emma left prison, together they would sew collars and cuffs, bodices, dresses, and coats. This vision was her life raft. Annie let her mind wander, delighting in creating new motifs, bold County

Cork–style flowers and delicate filigree, which originated in County Monaghan. A double calyx, forming a whorl that encompassed the petals of her flowers, to form a protective layer around the bud.

Hours passed, then days. Sometimes Annie talked to herself, just to hear someone talking. She jumped up and down when she needed to move, or walked in circles, humming the tunes of songs she could remember. Thomas Moore's poem set to the melody of "Aisling an Óigfhear" came to mind. She sang fragments of the sad lyric.

"'Tis the last rose of summer, / Left blooming alone; / All her lovely companions / Are faded and gone."

At night, visions of lace danced behind her eyelids. In her mind, Annie worked sprays of flowers and leaves over a cord foundation. By adjusting the padding cord's tightness or looseness, she could curve leaves in any direction, giving life to her flowers. She slept on and off, the cold gray walls of the dungeon cell slightly brighter in the wan morning light. Her muscles ached, and her chest rattled with a cough. Annie wiped her runny nose with the sleeve of her dress, no longer caring for any sense of decorum.

"Go sleep thou with them; / Thus kindly I scatter / Thy leaves o'er the bed / Where thy mates of the garden / Lie scentless and dead."

Images of County Mayo swam in her head—stone cottages covered in ivy; ruins left over from the famine; the horses and carts on market day; women in shawls, their feet bare, their buckets empty. She saw her mother on her death bed, her hands clasped over her chest, her face white, her lips blue. She fingered the ringlets in Kathleen's red hair, laughed with Patrick, taught Maggie how to light the fire. She remembered things she'd forgotten, Joseph stepping on a rusty nail, screaming as it went straight through his foot. She'd wrapped the wound with a clean rag to stop the bleeding. Her brother had wailed, believing he'd lose his leg.

Time stretched and compressed again. Annie remembered the rains—there had been two years of cold and wet weather. The harvest was meager; the villagers were hungry, angry, and unable to pay their rent. There had been fiery meetings, which her father attended, with speeches and talk of a land league. She remembered now the evictions that had frightened her so much—police officers climbing onto the thatched roofs of her neighbors' homes, forcing them out by smashing windows and doors. *"You owe three years' rent!"*

She remembered the McGrath family home, its roof caved in, the whole family standing outside amid the rubble. The O'Halloran girls, four sisters who'd bravely thrown cans of boiling water on the police when they approached. Battering rams made their way down the dirt roads, horse-drawn carts dragging the heavy load. Then the wooden logs were unloaded and used to smash down walls and doorways, the sod and stone crumbling to dust. Neighbors stuffed their windows with bushes to keep the police away. But the raids continued, year after year.

Mr. McGrath got two months in prison for fighting off the police. His wife died right afterward, evicted from her home, her heart broken. Annie sobbed, thinking of her family. *What if they were evicted?* She hadn't sent money home in months. The English who owned the land squeezed every penny out of the Irish farmers who worked it. And yet the greedy bastards would rather destroy the very property they came to claim than let the Irish live there. Her village was one of poor tenant farmers. There was no future in County Mayo for her sisters and brothers. What would become of them all?

"When true hearts lie withered, / And fond ones are flown, / Oh! who would inhabit / This bleak world alone?"

She was alone, all alone, lying in her own filth. Her anger toward Albert burned hot in her chest. He'd deceived her. Why had she accepted the ring? Why had she believed he thought of her as anything more than a maid? Delirious with hunger, cold, and solitude, Annie tossed and turned on the hard floor. She chewed her dirty fingernails down to the quick. Albert had ruined her life. And she hated him for it.

But picking at the past, like meat from a bone, wouldn't change a thing. Did Mr. McGrath whine at the injustice of his fate? No, he fought with everything he had. Yes, she was in prison because of Albert. And she'd changed because of it. Become harder, flinty, strong like steel. No matter what Captain Gilcrest or Warden McComb tried to take from Annie, she wouldn't relinquish it. This time, she had failed to expose the truth to Winifred Sweet. But she would not fail again.

At the beginning of the eighth day, when the iron door to her cell creaked open, Annie glared at the prison guard, feeling feral, like a rat in its den.

"Where's my bread?"

He wrinkled his nose. "Get up. You stink."

Annie stood, her joints aching.

The guard nodded. "Go on."

She rubbed her eyes. "I can leave?"

"Stop asking questions."

Moving one foot in front of the other, Annie stumbled

down the narrow corridor, then blinked as she emerged into the blinding sunlight.

———•••———

"WASH UP, THEN report to work duty."

The matron grimaced, unable to hide her disgust at the state of Annie's appearance. Within the confines of the Porch, and the women's ward washroom, Annie embraced the luxury of plumbing, which the dungeon lacked. Stripping out of her dress, she washed beneath her arms, washed her face, her hair, between her legs. She didn't mind the cold, salty water, pumped from the bay, the leaking toilets, the foul smells, or the rats that scurried by.

She changed into a clean striped prison uniform, wrung the water from her wet hair, and walked across the prison yard, blinking in the sunlight. To her left, she saw the hunched forms of men digging in the dirt between the old cellblocks, in Crazy Alley. Perhaps the prisoner Margaret Kerrigan, who'd slashed the face of the pretty blond widow, truly had pretended to be insane. Being outside the dungeon walls was preferable to being locked in.

Annie joined the line of female convicts awaiting their work. She looked for Emma among the group.

"You're out," Maud whispered, smiling. "I suppose a week ain't so bad. We worried you'd be in the dungeon for a fortnight."

"Where's Emma?" Annie shivered. "What happened?"

"She's poorly." Maud frowned. "No work duty today."

Annie cast her eyes at the ground and remained silent while

Matron Kane read out inmate numbers and work assignments. Once she and Maud had been sent on their way toward the tailor shop, she fell into step beside her friend, resuming their conversation.

"Did Emma lose her courage?"

"No." Maud clenched her jaw. "She meant to meet you, but Dr. Stanley took her to the hospital and examined her."

Annie shuddered. "And?"

"He knows she's with child. They all know. But he told her she has a hernia, and it's on account of her hysteria she thinks she's pregnant."

"Lies!" Annie dug her nails into her palms. "This is the warden's doing."

Some of the women convicts turned around to stare at her, and Annie clenched her teeth so she wouldn't be tempted to raise her voice again. She couldn't return to the dungeon. Being in solitary had done her head in. She dropped her voice to a whisper.

"And Bessie and May? Did Gilcrest punish them?"

Maud gave Annie a small smile. "He still doesn't know how we mailed the letter. You alone took the fall."

Annie's shoulders slumped with relief. Her friends were safe—for now. Though she shook with chills from her lingering cold and her wet hair, she felt better talking to Maud. It had been so long since she had spoken to another person. Walking toward the tailor shop, Annie noticed how the female prisoners communicated by gestures and facial expressions. She had missed this secret language, their camaraderie. And the sewing she'd once dreaded would be a welcome distraction after days of having nothing to occupy her time.

———◆—◆———

SATIATED BY A meal of hearty stew and bread, Annie returned to her cell in the Porch. It no longer looked like a cell, but like a cheery room with a proper bed, a comfortable chair, and a mat on the floor. *Five more months.* She could endure the rest of her time in prison. And then, once she was out, she would find work and a room to rent and wait for Bessie and Emma. A sense of calm came over her, knowing their freedom was near. They would survive.

After the final bell, Annie stood at the bars of her cell door while Matron Kane counted the prisoners during lockup. When the matron had retreated to her room at the end of the hall, Annie called out softly in the darkness.

"Emma? Are you there?"

She needed to hear her friend's voice. Annie had so many unanswered questions.

"You're . . . back. I was so . . . worried."

Annie sucked in her breath. "Em, you sound awful."

Emma's breathing was labored. "Me waters broke too soon. I'm bleedin'."

Annie brought her fingers to her lips. "When did they break?"

"This morning."

Emma cried out like a wounded animal, and Annie flinched. She'd heard that cry before, when her mother had birthed each of her younger siblings. A shiver ran down her spine. Why hadn't Emma been taken to the hospital? Annie's mother had died when she was thirty-nine, with a baby born still, whom she named Aoife. Though Emma was younger, her life was in danger still. Panic hit Annie like a wave.

"You need a doctor."

"It hurts." Emma's scream tore through the air as she endured another contraction. Annie felt sick with dread. She gripped the bars of her cell, yelling.

"Help! We need a doctor!"

"No . . . not Dr. Stanley."

Emma couldn't do this alone. Would Matron Kane allow another prisoner to help? Julia Ryan had borne three sons. Annie didn't have the experience of the Irish handywomen in her rural village, but she knew what was needed—clean rags, hot water, the leaves of the daisylike flower feverfew, boiled into tea to ease the pain.

"Matron Kane!" Annie screamed. "Emma's baby is coming."

The other inmates roused to attention, banging on their cell doors and calling for the matron. Their voices rose in a panicked chorus. Annie reached through the bars of her cell and stretched her fingers as far as they could go.

"Emma, I'm right here. Can you reach my hand?"

"I'm too tired, Annie."

Annie's lip quivered. "You have to breathe."

Emma screamed again. "I can't."

Annie clenched her hand into a fist, wishing she could do something. Emma needed someone to guide the baby and then the placenta out.

The matron blanched as she stopped before Emma's cell. No matter what lies the warden tried to spin, the truth was staring her in the face.

"She needs chloroform." Annie spoke firmly. "Can't you see she's in labor?"

"I can help," Julia Ryan called from her cell down the corridor. "I pulled my sister's babies out the womb, each one of them alive."

"Please." Annie looked into the matron's eyes. "Let Julia help. She isn't violent and has never been. She's in here because she loves her sons so much, she lied for them!"

The matron shook her head. "I can't let an inmate assist her."

Hot tears pressed against Annie's eyelids. "Have you no humanity? She's in pain!"

Emma let out another scream.

Matron Kane grimaced. "I'll get Dr. Stanley now."

Annie took a deep breath.

"It's all right," she told Emma. She tried to hide the quaver in her voice. "He'll bring you chloroform on a handkerchief. You'll be grand, like the queen of England."

"There's so . . . much blood."

The defeat in Emma's voice frightened her.

"Help is coming."

She swallowed the hard lump in her throat, knowing the wee soul would be lost, small enough to fit in Emma's cupped hands. These tragedies happened. But they happened by the warmth of a hearth, in the company of wise village women, not behind stone prison walls.

Emma moaned.

"I'm so cold."

"Hush now," Annie said, a quiver of fear shooting through her. She could hear Emma's teeth chattering. Fever was dangerous. She remembered her mother's sweaty forehead, her violent shivering, and how hot she was to the touch.

"You need water. We'll get it when the matron returns."

"Forget water . . . let's have poitín."

"Whiskey? We will, Emma. When we get out, we'll drink all the whiskey you like."

"And go dancin' at the fair?"

Annie blinked back tears. Emma was talking nonsense, but she would play along until help arrived.

"We'll dance until our feet are sore."

"The wildflowers . . . so pretty."

Annie remembered country fairs in Mayo and the surrounding fields of wildflowers—the stalks of purple heather, the white bursts of oxeye daisies, the delicate wood anemones, the yellow buttercups and blue speedwells.

"Will you pick them, Em?"

"No. Let them . . . grow."

"Emma." Annie reached again for Emma's hand. "Can you hear me?"

Minutes passed with no response. Annie's breath came shallow and fast. She gripped the bars of her cell and screamed.

"Where is the doctor? We need him now!"

"Did the baby come?"

"What's happened?"

Annie ignored the shouts of the other prisoners. She reached beneath her pillow and grabbed her mother's rosary, praying for her friend. *Let her live, God. Please, let her live.* Tears streamed down her cheeks. Emma had brought Annie the comfort and solace of her rosary beads. It was an act of kindness she would never forget. *Please. Please.*

Finally the matron appeared with Dr. Stanley beside her. Annie rushed to the door of her jail cell. "She needs to be taken to hospital."

The matron unlocked Emma's cell, and Dr. Stanley entered. "There's no light in here," he muttered.

Dr. Stanley dragged Emma into the corridor beneath the gas lamps, holding her under her arms. Emma's beautiful face was drained of color, her eyes vacant, her mouth slack. Her golden hair was matted against her pale forehead. She looked like Annie's mother had on her deathbed, her nightdress soaked with blood.

Annie screamed. "Do something!"

Taking Emma's wrist in his hand, Dr. Stanley bent down.

Annie's heart wrenched. "Does she have a pulse?"

Dr. Stanley didn't answer. Instead, he and the matron left Emma in the hallway while they went to alert the guards.

Annie sobbed, looking at Emma's delicate hands limp at her sides.

"Please, Emma. Stay with me."

But Emma didn't move. Her chest didn't rise and fall. She looked as if she were turning to stone. Annie screamed until her throat was raw. She screamed when the guards picked Emma up and took her away. In the time the prison doctor could have done something to save her friend, he chose not to. She sank to her knees and keened. To die without receiving the last rites of the church was an awful fate. And Emma hadn't needed to die at all.

Warden McComb's problem had solved itself. Annie was struck with the knowledge that this was his intention all along. He and Corcoran had murdered Emma.

———◆◆———

23

Judy

San Francisco, 1972

"Why didn't you call me?" Mark sits across the kitchen table from me, his eyes filled with concern.

Heat rushes to my cheeks. "I didn't want to bother you. It was late."

Mark shakes his head. "It was just after you closed up the shop." He gives me a meaningful look. "Even if it's late, you can always call me, okay?"

I nod. "Okay."

This is the first time Mark has seen my apartment, and I invited him over because I'm still so shaken by what happened, I don't want to be alone. But the dingy furniture and small galley kitchen don't seem to faze him. Mark stands up, walks over to the kettle, and pours me another cup of Earl Grey tea. He sets it down in front of me. "Look, I get it. I live on my own too. But that doesn't mean you have to be alone, Judy."

Even though I feel close with Mark because of the things we've experienced together, the I-Hotel protest, the TOOR meetings, there's so much he doesn't know about me. And it's time for that to change. "Mark," I say, meeting his eyes. "There's something you should know."

"Oh?" He pauses.

"I'm married."

He nods. "I never wanted to pry. But when we first met in the library, I saw that you were wearing a gold wedding band."

I'm surprised he remembers. But then again, Mark notices details.

"We're in the process of separating," I say, looking down at my tea. "But Tony, my husband . . . he isn't making it easy."

Mark leans forward. "Separating was your decision?"

I cross my arms. "Yes."

I've only been on my own in San Francisco for about a month now, but I feel different from the person I used to be. Suddenly, I want to tell Mark everything about my past. And so I do. He listens, never interrupting me. I open up to him about Tony's drinking, about my years of feeling lost and without focus, even about how I dreamed of becoming a mother but couldn't have children. Before I know it, I'm crying. Mortified, I look up at the ceiling and blink.

"I'm so sorry."

Mark reaches across the table and puts a steady hand on mine.

"Don't apologize. Didn't I tell you? You're brave. It took guts to leave everything you knew and to come here."

I wipe my eyes. "Getting robbed last night really scared me. Maybe that cop was right and living on my own is too dangerous."

Mark shakes his head. "What happened to you is horrible. But you have to see the good in people. I know you do, because I've seen your photographs."

He's right. I've watched Helen, the owner of Helen's Diner, give out free coffee to the homeless when it's cold outside. When kids are roller-skating in the narrow streets, the elders watch out for them, reminding drivers to slow down. South of Market is a thriving community. But my stomach sinks when I remember my stolen portfolio.

"Those photographs are gone forever."

Mark smiles. "Hey. Guess what didn't get stolen."

"What?"

"Your talent. No one can take that away from you."

I smile. "Thanks, Mark. But I won't be able to come up with new photographs in time for my graduate school application deadlines."

"You can ask for an extension." Mark takes a sip of his tea. "You have a police report. It's not like you're saying the dog ate your homework."

I laugh. Mark starts laughing with me, and suddenly everything doesn't feel so horrible anymore. Things feel possible to figure out.

"Maybe I need a dog," I say. "A big one."

Mark raises an eyebrow. "Want to go to the pound?"

"Another day. Today I need your help in the library."

———◆◆———

"OKAY," MARK SAYS, handing me a few film rolls for the microfilm machine. "Here are issues of *The San Francisco Examiner* from 1890. You said Winifred Sweet was one of their female journalists, right?"

"Right."

"And here are 1890 issues of the *Daily Alta California*."

"Thank you so much."

I crack my knuckles, eager to find the article I started reading in the Jesse Brown Cook scrapbook at the UC Berkeley Bancroft Library. Now that I know Winifred Sweet was a stunt reporter, like Nellie Bly, I figure if something salacious happened in prison, she would be the first to report on it. Winifred couldn't easily pose as a prison inmate in the way Nellie had feigned insanity to gain access to the Women's Lunatic Asylum on Blackwell's Island, but I hope Winifred at least spoke candidly with the incarcerated women.

"I'll meet you back here in an hour," Mark says, checking his watch. "I'm going to grab some food. Do you want anything?"

"No, thanks."

Mark has already done enough by helping me on his day off. Besides, I'm too anxious to have much of an appetite right now.

I load the microfilm into the machine and manually turn the newspaper pages. It takes me a while before I find anything written by Winifred. But then I see a headline.

A SAN QUENTIN SCANDAL

San Quentin is scandalized again. A story comes to the effect that Emma O'Sullivan, a convict from San

Francisco, is about to become a mother, although she has been in the penitentiary for two years. The report makes it out that in June of this year, "Fat Jack" Kiley, a convict serving fifty years, formed a close acquaintance with David Corcoran, a prison guard, while working as a trustee in the guards' quarters.

It is said that same month, they secured a key to the female ward and forced themselves upon two of the female convicts, Maud Manner and Emma O'Sullivan. A third female convict stated she defended herself with a crochet needle, stabbing her attacker, Corcoran, in the hand. The women claim they are not safe under McComb's management, and that Captain Gilcrest is aware David Corcoran is the father of Emma O'Sullivan's child.

Captain Gilcrest assured this reporter such rumors are false, and that Corcoran was let go from his post earlier this year. Mind you, this dismissal was due to Corcoran's involvement in an opium-smuggling scandal, which Captain Gilcrest was loath to bring up again. But under Warden McComb's orders, Gilcrest refused to allow a reputable San Francisco doctor, Walton Harvey, to examine Miss O'Sullivan, insisting the prison physician, Dr. Stanley, had examined her instead. Dr. Stanley made the following statement: "I have examined inmate 14055. She is afflicted with hysteria." McComb has successfully swept another scandal under the rug.

I suck in my breath, feeling sick to my stomach. Two female inmates were raped, and a third fended off her attacker with a crochet needle? The corruption at San Quentin Prison extended to the highest levels of management.

My jaw drops at the realization that Fat Jack is the very same convict whose name was written in the San Quentin Prison register I looked through at UC Berkeley. He was sentenced to fifty years for rape, and then he raped a woman *again*, this time a female inmate. But in spite of this heinous crime, the prison authorities recommended his sentence be commuted. Why? It's unfathomable.

Then I remember the name Dr. Stanley, and his declaration, in the very same 1890 prison register, that dozens of Chinese inmates were insane. They were denied their freedom and sent back to China, despite the fact that they had served the duration of their prison sentences. Dr. Stanley was likely just as corrupt as the warden. He declared Emma to be hysterical instead of pregnant, but his diagnosis couldn't be trusted.

Continuing to scroll through the microfilm, I look for any mention of Emma O'Sullivan's pregnancy, and the prison management's knowledge of it. Finally, when I switch to a new roll, I find an article printed in the *Daily Alta California.*

A REPORTER AND A PHYSICIAN

The Examiner attempts to spread a nasty scandal.

Warden John McComb was mad as a wet hen. A prominent official at San Quentin Penitentiary remarked that the warden's anger was on account of an attempt made by a reporter at *The Examiner* to spread a scandal that the enemies of Warden McComb started a few months ago, which came to naught on an investigation. The story was peddled to the press by an anonymous letter, alleging that one of the female prisoners, Emma O'Sullivan, was in a delicate condition, in consequence of a guard and a trustee surreptitiously entering the women's ward.

The Examiner was particularly zealous in trying to expose the alleged immorality of McComb. A reporter from that paper was sent to the prison, accompanied by a Dr. Harvey, and requested that Captain Gilcrest allow them to ascertain the truth or falseness of the statement. Dr. Stanley, at that time, stated that the scandal was without foundation as far as the woman was concerned. *The Examiner,* and its disreputable female journalist, Miss Winifred Sweet, will need to peddle their falsehoods elsewhere.

As I read the contrasting articles, my muscles tense. Had the imprisoned women written an anonymous letter to Winifred Sweet, asking for help? I'm inclined to believe this, rather than that Emma's pregnancy was a rumor started by enemies of Warden McComb. And I know where to find the truth of the matter—by going back to the primary source.

———◆———

"THANK YOU FOR seeing me again."

I smile at Miriam, the researcher at the Marin History

Museum. She nods. "Of course! I'm so sorry your last visit was cut short."

She hands me a pair of latex gloves and then returns with the newspaper article I requested last time, "Dead to the World," written by Winifred Sweet. I feel a shiver of anticipation, now that I finally have the complete piece. Thanking Miriam, I eagerly turn to the article. I can't stop thinking about Emma O'Sullivan and the horrible implications of what transpired when she was meant to be protected. With no prenatal care available to her in prison, she was at risk. What happened to her and her baby?

I slip on the latex gloves and unfold the newspaper, looking at a full page covering the female inmates of San Quentin prison and featuring their portraits. I skip past the inmates I've seen before, Ada, Mary, May, and Maud, and look at the illustrations of those who are new to me. There's a beautiful girl named Bessie Barclay, who was arrested for dressing as a boy and who worked as a cowhand, an elevator boy, and on a railroad crew. She's young, only twenty, and it breaks my heart to see her adventurous spirit crushed.

I see a fifty-two-year-old woman named Julia Ryan, whose name I remember from the prison register, serving twelve years for perjury. Her request for a commutation was denied, and in her sketch, her eyes are kind beneath her wrinkled forehead. Another woman, Bridget Smith, is drawn with gray hair and a pinched expression. I doubt either of these older ladies would have had much life left to live after their releases. It's a sobering thought.

There are inmates who were arrested for grand larceny,

burglary, and robbery: Rosanna Core, Lizzie Ross, and Nellie Osborn. They have shifty looks about them, none staring directly ahead. Margarita Grinilla, a Mexican woman serving time for murder, is drawn with a hard look on her face, one curl swooping over her left eye, as if she's daring the viewer to confront her. Seeing the article continues, I turn the page.

There's an illustration of two young women, heads bowed toward each other, crocheting in the women's ward courtyard on a bench beneath a tree. There are stairs on either side, leading down to the enclosed area. I gasp, a burn of excitement rippling in my chest as I read the caption: *Two friendly Irish convicts, Emma O'Sullivan and Annie Gilmurray, working on a piece of crochet lace.* Annie and Emma are sitting side by side.

"They were friends," I murmur.

Tears prick my eyes. I can't imagine the bravery and resilience it must have taken Annie to survive a year behind bars and to watch something so horrible happen to Emma. Had she used her crochet needle to fend off Corcoran? Now that I've seen this sketch, it makes sense that Annie would be the anonymous inmate with a crochet hook. My stomach feels sick with the knowledge that she was in danger of being raped by a prison guard.

"Did you find what you were looking for?" Miriam asks, returning.

I nod. "Yes. This was extremely helpful."

I hand Miriam the newspaper to let her know that I'm finished with it. Miriam smiles. "Good. Let me bring you the San Quentin Prison register of female inmates received since 1889, which you requested last time."

"Thank you. Can I see the turnkey's log again?"

"Of course." Miriam smiles.

I wait anxiously while she's getting the materials, thinking of all the female convicts I've read about. One of them did not survive. Though it's terrible for any woman to have died behind bars, I couldn't bear to learn if this was Annie's fate.

"Here you go," Miriam says, setting down the heavy volumes of the prison register and the turnkey's log in front of me. "Take your time."

Gently opening the worn leather cover, I flip through the tissue-thin pages of the turnkey's log until I've reached the month of November. I can picture the cold, dreary weather and the bleak, dark days. Then my hand stills.

Wednesday, November 12th,

Inmate 14055, Emma O'Sullivan, was buried in the prison graveyard this morning, no friends, family, or Catholic charity coming to claim the body. She died of sepsis. Dr. Stanley was unable to staunch the bleeding. The rains delayed digging the grave, but now she is laid to rest.

I cover my trembling mouth, unable to stop hot tears from spilling down my cheeks. Emma was pregnant and she died alone, in prison. Her headstone would be a redwood marker on a lonely hillside, inscribed with only her prison number. Miriam told me about the San Quentin grave markers, abandoned and forgotten now, jutting among the brambles and weeds. My heart breaks for Emma, and for Annie, who lost her friend.

But there's something else, a darker truth, nagging at the

back of my mind. Then it comes to me, the words from Winifred Sweet's article.

> The report makes it out that in June of this year, "Fat
> Jack" Kiley, a convict serving fifty years, formed a close
> acquaintance with David Corcoran, a prison guard, while
> working as a trustee in the guards' quarters.
>
> It is said that same month, they secured a key to
> the female ward and forced themselves upon two of
> the female convicts.

If Emma became pregnant in June, then by November, she
would have been about five months along. Here the turnkey's
log states that Emma died of sepsis and that the doctor was
unable to staunch her bleeding. Clenching my eyes shut, I try
to repress my worst, most painful memory, but it floats to the
surface.

I remember the solemn expression on my gynecologist's
face when she told me she couldn't find a heartbeat. How I sat
there, in my paper gown, stunned. I was fifteen weeks along,
and at my twelve-week visit, my baby's heartbeat had been
healthy and strong. Yet somehow, it had vanished sometime in
the weeks in between.

I felt like the universe was playing a cruel joke on me.

When my doctor sent me home to wait for the bleeding to
begin, I was in numbed shock. I loved my baby, I *wanted* this
baby, and Tony was so excited to become a father. We had already painted the baby's bedroom a sunny yellow. But when
my bleeding began, I couldn't deny what was happening. As I
shook with sobs, I didn't think it was possible to grieve so

deeply for someone I'd never met. But that someone was my child.

My grief morphed into terror when, hours later, my bleeding grew heavier and the pain in my uterus became unbearable. It had started out like my monthly cramps, dull and pulsing, but soon grew sharp and overwhelming. Feverish, my legs slick with blood, I started to lose consciousness. Suddenly, I was freezing cold, even though Tony told me I was burning up. And then everything went black. It was only afterward that I learned Tony had rushed me to the emergency room, where a surgeon saved my life. He told me I could have died of sepsis if I'd remained at home.

Opening my eyes, I wipe away my tears. I remember the hypnotist, Mary Martin, having her prison sentence commuted on account of her tumor. The newsprint appears in my mind.

Such an operation, to be successful, demands the services of skilled surgeons and subsequent care that this institution cannot provide for female patients.

Emma O'Sullivan was not afforded the same lifesaving care given to Mary Martin. The institution, San Quentin State Prison, did not want her to receive this care. She died from an untreated miscarriage—I feel certain.

After my own miscarriage, the doctor warned me I might never be able to have children. His words felt like a knife to my heart, even though I was grateful to be alive, and for the surgical procedure and the blood transfusion that saved me. If Tony hadn't taken me to the hospital, I would have bled to death.

But Emma could have been bleeding, alone in her cell for

hours, with no one there to help. The warden did not send a recommendation to the governor that her sentence be commuted. He did not move her somewhere safe, before she lost her baby. Clearly a pregnancy as the result of being raped by a prison guard was not a scandal he wanted exposed, and his corruption cost a woman her life.

24

Annie

San Quentin, 1890

Emma was buried on Wednesday, after a day of torrential rain. The matron wouldn't allow Annie or any of the other female convicts attend her burial. Unlike the male trustees, the women were never allowed outside the prison walls, even to pay their respects to one of their own. Misery moved into the corridors of the women's ward like an unwanted guest, the air heavy with their collective grief. Even Mary Von didn't spit her usual insults and barrage of curses. Emma's death had sobered them all.

Annie had cried herself dry. Her body ached, her will to fight gone. Her shoulders were bruised from throwing herself against the walls of her cell, her throat raw from screaming. No amount of pounding on the iron door changed the fact that her vibrant, beautiful friend was gone. Emma's stunning lace creations would never be sold in a shop, and her feet would never dance another Irish jig. Her future—their future—had been stolen.

The women watched from the Porch as Emma's wooden coffin was carried by horse and buggy down the dirt road leading to the prison cemetery. There was no funeral procession. Emma's family, if they were notified, never came to claim her body. Instead of being given a proper headstone in a Catholic cemetery, or sent home to Ireland, Emma was laid to rest in a numbered grave overlooking the bay, where hundreds of crude redwood markers dotted the grassy hillside. They bore the prison numbers of the forgotten dead.

Annie felt hollow inside. She ought to have washed Emma's body, to have laid a cloth and ribbons across her, to have sat beside her while Emma lay in repose in the home of a loved one. But there would be no Irish wake, no visitors coming and going, no covered mirrors and stopped clocks, no food and drink. How dare Emma be denied the right of tears and laughter in her memory. Of family gathered around at midnight to say the rosary. If Emma's family had truly disowned her, then Annie herself would light the candles at Emma's head and feet, would place her shoes at the foot of the bed for her to walk safely through purgatory.

Yet she had done none of those things.

In the days that followed Emma's burial, the convict women didn't laugh or even talk to one another. They knew they were being watched by the guards, the captain, and the warden— the same men who'd allowed Emma to die, her secret buried with her. The female inmates were nervous as they congregated awaiting their assignments, their eyes darting back and forth across the yard. Annie forced herself shut, like the flowers that closed up at night. She wouldn't speak. She wouldn't think. She would simply endure.

On Sundays, rather than working on her lace, which reminded her of Emma, she went to chapel with the other convict women. The chaplain berated them.

"Your hearts have been hardened and lost in sin. While the pure mother's influence has no equal, you have poisoned the souls of your children by your corrupt examples. A woman, though born virtuous, will prey upon all mankind once fallen. Gone are your virtues of piety and purity. You are the vilest of your sex, depraved, unchaste . . ."

If Annie didn't inhabit her mind, she could make it through the motions of each day. She tried not to think of Emma, of her kindness and warmth. Instead, she focused her attention on sewing for the male convicts. Her machine in the tailor shop was clean and well oiled. With one hand she turned the wheel, and with the other, she guided her material through. The clacking sound was a distraction from her thoughts. As soon as she finished one piece, she started another.

The days passed by in a blur of muted grays. It rained for the remainder of November, the prison wet, cold, and silent. Without Emma, Annie's world would never hold color again.

———•◆•———

SIX WEEKS AFTER Emma was laid to rest, Annie looked up to see Maud coming toward her, marching across the women's courtyard. Annie had skipped chapel that morning. At home in Ireland, prayers would be offered for the deceased at Mass, and their graves would be decorated with wreaths of holly and ivy, as it was nearly Christmas. But Annie was unable to visit Emma's grave, to pay her respects.

Instead, she'd picked up her crochet hook and thread. Though a hard lump rose in her throat every time she started a new motif, Emma would have wanted Annie to continue her lace making. If she sat quietly, she could hear Emma's voice, teaching her every movement: *Chain, double crochet, slip stitch, treble crochet, cluster, picot, Clones knot . . .*

Annie chained her leaf to a flower, sliding her hook under two stitch loops. It was a clear December day, the air crisp and cold.

"That's pretty." Maud nodded at the piece.

Annie swallowed. "Thanks."

Maud glanced across the courtyard at the matron, who'd been monitoring them closely. No doubt Captain Gilcrest and Warden McComb dreaded the prospect of Winifred Sweet's return. But Annie was too tired to send another letter. It would make no difference.

"Turn around," Maud whispered. "With your back to the matron. I have something."

Annie did as she was told, and Maud did the same. From the sleeve of her prison uniform, Maud pulled out a folded page of newspaper.

"How did you get this?" Annie dropped her voice.

"Paid Julia. Her son smuggled it in." Maud swallowed hard. "I heard Fat Jack got pardoned by the governor. I need you to tell me if it's true."

Annie carefully unfolded the paper. "You want me to read it?"

Maud nodded. "I never learned."

Annie could feel the matron's eyes boring into her back.

Her muscles tensed. She didn't want to be sent back to solitary in the dungeon.

"Pick up my lace. Act like I'm showing you a stitch."

Maud held Annie's flower motif toward her, and Annie began to read.

"'Governor Waterman granted the commutation of the sentence of James Kiley, alias Fat Jack, from fifty to fifteen years. He was convicted of rape.'"

Maud shuddered.

Annie clenched her jaw. "I'm sorry, Maud. He wasn't pardoned, but . . . Do you want me to keep reading?"

She nodded. "Read the whole thing."

Annie swallowed. "'The governor says, "In granting this commutation, I do so as an incentive for good conduct. In a moment of great danger to himself, he bravely stepped between the warden of the prison, John McComb, and the murderous weapon of a convict."'"

Her stomach knotted.

"'Since that time, he has remained in confinement undergoing his sentence. His former employers, who are known among the very best of the businessmen of the state, will again give him steady employment.'"

Annie gripped the edges of the paper so hard, it crumpled.

"Feckin' bastards. All of them!"

The anger that had been simmering beneath the surface of her skin began to draw to a boil. "He's vile. He deserves the rope, not freedom."

Maud gritted her teeth.

"There ain't no justice for girls like us, Annie." She shook her head. "Fat Jack has nearly served his fifteen years. He'll soon be free, and Corcoran will become a police officer in San Francisco."

Annie's mouth felt sour. "How do you know?"

"Miller and Wilson were talkin.' Corcoran meets them in a booth at the Bella Union on their days off. He's been tellin' anyone who'll listen that Chief Crowley will give him a job."

Picturing Corcoran with the other two guards, jovial in their late-night revelry at one of the Barbary Coast's notorious melodeons, Annie shook her head.

"Corcoran is a criminal. Why would the chief want him?"

Maud looked at Annie like she was as green as the day she stepped off the boat.

"The police are rotten. They'll take him on the raid squad."

Annie's heart seized. Corcoran couldn't be given a position of power. He would only use it to hurt more vulnerable women. The San Francisco police were cruel in their endless raids of Chinatown, arresting men in droves for games of chance, and the women who entertained them. She envisioned Corcoran with a badge and a baton, hungry with lust and thirsty for blood.

"He can't become an officer."

"He can. And he will. Some of the men in blue are worse than those in stripes."

Annie clenched her fists. "I hate them all."

Out of the corner of her eye, Annie saw Matron Kane approaching, her heavy dark skirt swishing against the ground. Quickly, Annie crumpled up the newspaper and pushed it up the sleeve of her prison uniform. She took her lace from Maud.

"And that's how you do a slip stitch."

Maud smiled. "Thanks for showin' me."

Without another word, Annie walked away. Governor Waterman had commuted Fat Jack's sentence. A man's life saved was worth more than the lives of two women—the mother Fat Jack raped and murdered, and Maud, a girl of only seventeen. The men of San Quentin were allowed every opportunity for forgiveness, while women bore the stain of their crimes like permanent ink. Both Fat Jack and Corcoran were to be given a clean slate. But Maud was still here, and Emma was dead.

All day long, sewing in the tailor shop, lining up for meals, waiting for the toilets, Annie thought of Corcoran. Lying on her mattress at night, she stared at the ceiling, turning over the situation in her mind. *Who can help?* If the San Francisco police force was as corrupt as the management at San Quentin, then there would be no reason to deny Corcoran a job. Men in power all looked out for one another, for they belonged to the same club. She didn't know of anyone who could make David Corcoran's life miserable.

Annie thought of her siblings in Ireland. In four months' time she would be released from prison, and she needed to keep her hands clean so she could pay their passage to America and then provide them with a place to live. She couldn't risk any criminal act that would get her sent back to San Quentin. But what kind of future would her sisters and brothers have in America if people like David Corcoran were officers of the law?

She had come to this country to make something of her life, to set down roots. And Emma had done the same. Emma O'Sullivan was a talented lace maker, a beautiful soul, and only twenty-five years old. She deserved to be known by more than her prison number, burned into a wooden marker on a desolate hillside. She deserved to be alive. Annie shivered, the clarity of her idea startling her.

———•◦•———

"Bessie." Annie stirred her spoon in her tin soup bowl. "Have you ever been inside any of the melodeons in the rough quarter of town by the county jail?"

Bessie raised an eyebrow. "Well, naturally."

In her days as a domestic, Annie had never ventured into the crime-ridden streets of the Barbary Coast, filled with pickpockets, grog shops, opium dens, and saloons. But she would need to know her way around the neighborhood.

"Can you tell me about them?"

Bessie rubbed her jaw. "Sure. There's the Olympic, the Pacific, the Adelphi, the Bella Union, Gilbert's Melodeon. These are men's clubs." She grinned. "Course, I was dressed like a boy when I went to see shows. I've seen Lotta Crabtree, Maggie Brewer, Eddie Foy."

In her ride in the police buggy, Annie remembered seeing the theater marquees—the crescent moon in front of the Hippodrome, a statue of a busty woman sitting atop it, beckoning men inside its Moorish entrance. The Bella Union was next door, on Kearny, in a building with a beautiful facade, its name written in electric globe lights.

"The Living Flea, the Red Rooster, and Bottle Koenig's are where you'll find the best dancing," Bessie said, winking. "You've got pianos, fiddles, clarinets. They're in cellars, with a bar on one end and a platform for the musicians at the other."

"What do the women in saloons wear?"

"Some wear simple dresses. Other establishments require evening gowns. The girls who work there must socialize with the patrons and must remain on or near the dance floor."

Annie nodded. "And how dangerous are the streets?"

Bessie grimaced. "I've seen a woman get her face slashed by a man she was with, after they got into a heated quarrel at the Campfire saloon. I've seen men drugged, stabbed, shot. You've got to keep your wits about you."

Annie had heard the stories. Blocks of saloons and deadfalls where men were shanghaied and shipped away to foreign lands. "Cribs" where workingwomen who were paid pennies had only a few years left of their young lives before they succumbed to disease and despair. Men stabbed, men robbed, women providing every service a man might desire.

But life in prison had hardened her. She was no longer the green lass from County Mayo who feared the big city. She'd lived alongside murderers and pickpockets. She'd learned what it took to survive under harsh conditions.

"Tell me about the Bella Union." Annie looked at Bessie. "What's it like inside?"

"Some call it a notorious dive, but it's a fine theater. You'll find merchants, bankers, men from respectable families, lumberjacks, and sailors alike." Bessie laughed. "One night, I saw a rounder hit an Englishman in the eye with a potato."

Annie laughed. "Now, I would pay to see that!"

Bessie smiled. "He wouldn't stop griping about how he was the son of Sir Robert Peel. Not one of us cared a whit."

They paused their conversation as the matron walked past

their table in the mess hall. Then Bessie leaned close to Annie so she could keep talking.

"The owner is a showman who drives a team of black Shetland ponies harnessed to a gaudy dog cart."

Annie's eyes widened. "Truly?"

Bessie slurped her soup. "You'll see things you won't believe. The pretty waiter girls are meant to dance and drink with their customers, and then to appear in the ensemble or the chorus of the show." She grinned. "One girl was sitting in the lap of a lumberjack in his box, and she missed her stage cue. But when the stage manager came to get her, the lumberjack fired his gun at the ceiling and told the stage manager she'd stay right where she was."

"There are private boxes?"

Bessie nodded. "They surround the stage, like little pigeonholes. During the interlude, the dancers go in to sell drinks. Champagne, wine, whiskey. Men's conduct isn't questioned behind their private curtains, so long as they buy liquor."

Annie shuddered. She could picture Corcoran stroking his red mustache and pulling a pretty dancer into his lap, a glass of wine—no—a bottle of whiskey in his hand.

Bessie lowered her voice. "The shows are bawdy. I've seen big names like Ella La Rue and Pauline Markham." She winked. "She's quite a dancer."

"Tell me, Bessie." Annie scratched her wrist with her nail. "What do the waiter girls wear? The ones who visit the private boxes to sell liquor."

Bessie frowned, a crease forming between her brows. "Why are you askin', Annie?"

Annie shrugged. "I'm only curious."

Bessie laughed. "You didn't get out much as a domestic, did you?"

Annie smiled and shook her head. "Not at all."

"They wear black silk stockings, for the men to stuff bank notes into, frilly bloomers, chemises or shirtwaists. Or sometimes only a corset."

"So, they're undressed?"

"Like I said, the Bella Union is a men's club."

Nodding, Annie tried to envision it all: waiter girls selling companionship and liquor, the dancers onstage with ponies, the orchestra playing in the pit. But mostly, she pictured herself in black silk stockings, rouge painting her lips, and the look on David Corcoran's face when he realized—too late—what it was she had come for.

———◆◆———

25

Judy

San Francisco, 1972

At work, I've told Seth everything I've learned: how Emma died, how deeply corrupt San Quentin State Prison was, how Annie and Emma were friends. I'm pacing back and forth, outraged by an injustice that happened more than eighty years ago. Seth has been listening to me talk about my visit to the Marin History Museum for at least twenty minutes.

Seth shakes his head. "It's heartbreaking, what happened."

"Miriam, the docent, told me that prisoners weren't even buried by name. Their graves are redwood markers with only their prison numbers."

"Another way to dehumanize them, even in death."

I think of Annie and how devastated she must have been to lose her friend.

"The truth was buried," I say, clenching my teeth. "Literally."

We stand together in the drying room, looking at a series of documentary-style wedding portraits shot in black and white. The images of the happy couple are in stark contrast to my emotions, which are heavy today. But Seth is glad we've attracted some high-end wedding photographers as clients, in addition to portrait and fine-art photographers.

He gestures at the prints. "You've really brought the magic out of this reel. Well done."

"Thanks." I smile. "I learned from the best."

"Film is both an art and a science. A print can only be as good as the negative it's derived from, but you've rendered these beautifully."

My face falls as I think of my lost negatives—my data, the information source for all my images. I can spend all day running temperature, pH, and color-balance checks here at Glass Photo, carefully replacing the chemicals for processing other people's photographs so they come out perfectly, but it won't bring back my own.

My shoulders slump. "I never should have taken my negatives from the shop."

Seth notices my mood.

"Oh, Judy, I'm so sorry about what happened." He rubs his forehead. "I feel responsible. I shouldn't have let you lock up the shop alone."

"It's not your fault." I sigh. "Besides, I wasn't robbed outside the shop. I was on Russ Street, walking toward the mailbox on Folsom."

"Do the police have any leads?"

I shake my head. "They think it was a random attack, that my portfolio looked like a cash bag for a bank deposit."

Seth grimaces. "Please let me know if you need any time off."

"No." I force a smile. "I'm okay, really."

Processing rolls of negatives in the darkroom is a welcome distraction from my thoughts. Everything is worse when I'm home alone, panic tightening my chest until I feel like I can't breathe. I've been obsessively checking the lock on my door and unable to sleep because I'm scared someone will climb the fire escape and wedge open my window. Sometimes, for no reason, I smell the scent of rotting garbage and want to cry.

When I get home, I heat up some soup on the stove, wondering what I can do to distract myself from the fear that I'll be attacked again. I ran into my neighbor Vanessa in our lobby, and though I was ashamed, I told her that the beautiful portrait I took of her and her son was stolen. Vanessa gave me a hug and urged me to knock on her door if I need anything. She told me she'd bake a casserole tomorrow night and that I should come over for dinner and a bottle of wine. I'm so grateful to have a friend in the building.

The phone rings and I jump. Every noise seems to startle me these days. But it could be the police with an update. I pick up the receiver.

"Hello? This is Judy."

"Judy." Tony's voice comes through the phone. "I heard you got robbed. Are you okay?"

I frown. "How did you hear that?"

"The police brought me in for questioning. I told them I'd do anything I could to help." He pauses. "Why didn't you call me? I would have come right away."

"You were shouting at me when you left."

Tony doesn't sound remorseful. "Well, I set the record

straight and told them I thought everything was good between us, because you jumped my bones."

I press my palm against my forehead, my cheeks burning. Now there's no way Officer Jones will take me seriously. Can I get in trouble for withholding information? But regrettable sex with my estranged husband is no one's business but my own.

"Tony, I don't need your help."

"It's not safe for you to be living there alone." Tony's voice is firm. "That must have been so scary, Judy, to be robbed by a guy holding a knife."

I blink back tears, smelling the stench of the dumpster, my chest constricting with panic at the memory. Tony continues his rant, working himself up. "If I was with you, something like that never would've happened. I would have kicked his sorry ass!"

"It's fine. I'm fine."

His voice turns remorseful, pleading. "Judy, you aren't safe there. Please, let me take you home. Or at the very least, I'll spend the night."

My bottom lip quivers. I would feel much safer with Tony lying next to me, his strong chest rising and falling as he slept, ready to spring into action if anyone tried to break into the apartment. All he's ever wanted is to protect me from the world.

"Tony, I—I don't know."

He groans. "Judy, you can't be out on the streets taking photographs of old men in their hotel rooms and faggots on motorbikes. It's not safe."

"Tony—" But my protest is cut short and my blood runs

cold. I didn't describe any of my stolen photographs to the police. And yet somehow, Tony has seen them.

———•••———

I SIT BENEATH the fluorescent lights of the interview room at the Bryant Street police station, feeling claustrophobic in the windowless rectangular space. My nerves are frayed, and I have so many unanswered questions.

When Officer Jones called and asked me to come down to the station this morning, he wouldn't tell me why. Now that I'm here, my palms are sweaty and my mouth is dry.

"Would you like some water?"

Officer Martinez looks at me with kind eyes, and I'm grateful to see him.

"Yes, please."

He returns with a glass of tepid water, and I gulp it down.

Officer Jones steeples his fingers.

"Mrs. Morelli. We decided to pay your husband a visit."

I nod, biting the inside of my cheek. I haven't told them yet that I think Tony has seen my photographs.

"We found your portfolio in the gutter on Langton Street."

My mouth falls open. "Was anything inside?"

Officer Martinez smiles. "Everything. Your photographs, your graduate school application, your film cannisters."

I press my palm to my chest. "That's wonderful."

But Officer Jones doesn't seem to share this feeling. He frowns. "Are you familiar with inchoate offenses, Mrs. Morelli?"

I shake my head.

He locks eyes with me. "It's the crime of preparing for another crime. Conspiracy, attempt, bribery, and solicitation."

"Solicitation?"

Officer Martinez clears his throat. "Solicitation is offering money to someone with the specific intent of requesting that person to commit a crime."

I shiver, rubbing my arms. "Okay?"

Officer Jones is solemn. "Judy, we think your husband paid someone to rob you."

My blood runs cold. I think of the blue-eyed man and how he slammed me against the dumpster wall. Tony has never hurt me before.

I shake my head. "But my photographs are worthless to Tony."

Officer Martinez raises an eyebrow. "Were you scared?"

"Of course I was scared."

"He meant to scare you," Officer Jones says. "So that you'll come home to him."

I press my tongue hard against the roof of my mouth, willing myself not to cry.

"He called me again, asking me to come home."

Officer Jones rubs his stubbly jaw. He looks sheepish, his demeanor changed since our last interview. Instead of siding with Tony, he's seeing things from my perspective.

He clears his throat.

"Tony made several inconsistent statements in his police interview. At first, he said you told him where you worked, and then he retracted that, saying he'd never heard of Glass Photo."

Officer Martinez nods. "We think he had you followed."

I shudder. "Why do you think so?"

"We asked him if you willingly gave him your new address. He said he found it in the phone book by looking for a phone number that matched the one he had." Martinez shakes his head. "This just isn't plausible."

I rub the goose bumps on my arms.

"So, you're saying Tony hired someone to find me, to follow me, to find out where I lived and worked, and then to rob me?"

Staring at the ceiling, I blink hard, and then I look at Officer Jones.

"Tony called last night and told me I shouldn't be taking pictures of old men in their hotel rooms and . . ." I don't want to repeat Tony's hateful slur. "Gay men."

I shake my head. "But the thing is, I never described my stolen photographs to you. I think that Tony has seen them."

Officer Jones widens his eyes. "This is helpful information." He taps the table in front of him. "Tony could have received your portfolio before dumping it. That's probably when he paid the robber—after the act was complete."

"It's a felony offense," Officer Martinez adds. "Because the robbery *was* in fact committed. If your husband is guilty, he'll be charged not just with solicitation, but with the crime of armed robbery itself."

"But," I say, licking my dry lips, "do you have any evidence?"

"No." Officer Jones is blunt. "Unfortunately not."

"We'll find your attacker." Officer Martinez looks confident. "And when we do, we'll get him to confess everything."

I rub my temples, overwhelmed by what the officers are telling me. What if they never find this guy? What if he's left the state?

"I don't know," I say.

Officer Jones leans forward.

"We need to collect enough evidence to arrest your husband. Then a prosecutor from the district attorney's office will be assigned to your case when it goes to trial."

My stomach lurches. I've never been to court before, other than being called in for jury duty. I look down at my shaking hands.

"I—I don't know what to do."

"Listen," Officer Jones says, his tone softening. "If Tony calls again, write down everything he says. Or better yet, record it. And then call us immediately."

I'm so nervous. I don't want to go to trial.

"Do I need a lawyer?"

Officer Martinez shrugs. "It can't hurt. The criminal justice system can be intimidating for victims, especially if you'll have to testify at your husband's trial."

I nod. "Okay."

Leaving the police station, I rummage in my purse and pull out Sandra's business card. I'm so glad that through Mark, I met some young lawyers involved with TOOR. From a pay phone on the street corner, I dial the number on the card.

"Sandra McFadden, San Francisco Neighborhood Legal Assistance Foundation."

"Hi," I say, biting my lip. "You may not remember me, but my name is Judy. We met at the Milner Hotel, at a TOOR meeting."

There's a pause on the line.

"I'm Mark's friend," I continue. "The photographer."

"Oh, right," Sandra says, a smile in her voice. "I remember you. How can I help?"

Shame settles around my shoulders. But then I remind myself I am not responsible for Tony's actions.

"Well." I take a deep breath. "I'm in need of a lawyer."

———◆———

A DAY LATER, I'm sitting in the South of Market office of the San Francisco Neighborhood Legal Assistance Foundation. In front of me is Ellen Trimble, a graduate of Stanford Law School, her framed diploma on the wall. Sandra assured me Ellen could help me, even though I'm worried I can't pay for her legal services.

Ellen sits up straight, looking at ease in her white button-down shirt.

"Judy, welcome."

I smile. "Thank you for seeing me so quickly."

"Of course," she says, folding her hands. "Tell me everything."

Her graying hair is cut short, and she wears a pair of gold hoop earrings. I look at the poster on the wall behind Ellen's desk. It's an illustration of four women, all different races, standing together on the street in front of San Francisco's Victorian homes. In blue letters at the top it reads: FREE LEGAL AID TO POOR WOMEN IN SF.

Squinting, I look at the series of words encircling the

women, printed in white inside a red border. CHILD CUSTODY.
MARITAL VIOLENCE. DISCRIMINATION. LESBIAN RIGHTS.

"I don't know if I belong here," I say, feeling uncomfortable.
"But like Sandra told you, my husband, Tony, hasn't reacted
well to our separation."

Ellen nods. "Go on."

I swallow. "I'm not a victim of marital violence. And we
don't have kids. But I left him and got my own apartment here
in San Francisco."

She frowns. "How long have you been separated?"

"About a month," I say. "But two weeks ago, he came by my
apartment, and I didn't give him the address. The police think
he had me followed."

Ellen steeples her fingers. "That's harassment. And
stalking."

I shake my head.

"But . . . this is so embarrassing. You see, I slept with
him. I don't know why. I guess I was lonely. Even after he
showed up when I didn't want him to, I sent him mixed mes-
sages."

Her stern expression doesn't change.

"Do you want to remain married to this man?"

I think back to when I first arrived in San Francisco, how
devastated I was, how I wished Tony and I would be celebrating our wedding anniversary together this month. Then it
occurs to me. Our wedding anniversary is today—June thirti-
eth. I forgot about it until now. But I no longer feel as heartbroken. The man I fell in love with isn't good for me.

"No." I feel a weight lift off my shoulders. "I don't."

"Okay, then." Ellen smiles. "I fought hard to make no-fault divorce the law here in California. You don't have to prove any wrongdoing by your spouse in order to divorce him."

"Well," I say, grimacing. "He's done plenty of things wrong. Right now, he's the main suspect in a criminal investigation. I was robbed . . ."

My lip trembles and Ellen hands me a tissue.

"Thanks." I dab at my eyes. "The police think Tony paid someone to rob me at knifepoint, to scare me into coming back to him."

Ellen's eyes widen and then narrow again.

"Judy, this is serious."

"I know," I say, blowing my nose in the tissue. "Part of me doesn't want to believe it's true. How could he do something like that?"

"Because he wants to maintain a sense of control over you," she says, giving me a sympathetic look. Ellen leans forward. "Is he critical? Manipulative? I see he has no problem violating your boundaries."

I think of Tony's hurled insults and how many times he's belittled me.

"Yes."

"His behavior constitutes emotional abuse," Ellen says, unblinking. "And I want to represent you in your legal case against him. I'll take you on as a client pro bono."

Driving across the Golden Gate Bridge after leaving Ellen's office, I feel as if I'm finally listening to my conscience. I've decided to proceed with my divorce. Even though it won't be easy, I know it's the right thing to do. I think of Annie, a young woman falsely convicted and wrongfully imprisoned, who endured unimaginable hardship. If she could survive a year in San Quentin, then I can survive the end of my marriage to Tony.

There's one more task to complete on my list for the day— return to the Marin History Museum. I was so emotional after learning how Emma had died, I left my museum appointment early and sat sobbing in the front seat of my Volkswagen Beetle for a good twenty minutes.

Miriam is understanding when I approach her desk inside the Boyd Gate House. She recognizes me by now, and she's able to squeeze me in for a short research visit. I'm seated at a small table in the back, where Miriam brings me the San Quentin Prison register of female prisoners received since 1889.

Opening the worn leather cover, I hold my breath. The cursive writing is elegant, each line of text meticulously noting the arrival and departure of San Quentin's female inmates.

And then my breath hitches. I place my blue-gloved hand atop the book, breathing a sigh of relief. There's an entire page filled with names of female prisoners, but I only care about one: Annie Gilmurray, received April 19, 1890, and discharged April 20, 1891.

The truth is bittersweet. Annie did not get the justice she deserved. Her sentence was not commuted, nor was she given a retrial. I should have figured as much, with Greta's witness statement given in Swedish and no official police interpreter present. It must have taken Greta incredible courage to go to the police, when her employer could have had her fired. But sadly, Greta's affidavit was not enough to make a difference in Annie's case.

I find comfort in knowing that Annie left San Quentin Prison alive. But her life would have been forever affected by this experience. What became of her after her release?

26

Annie

San Quentin, 1891

Time passed in a slow drip. The bitter winds of January gave way to February's gentle breezes, carrying plum blossoms and the scent of spring. Annie watched the flowers in the prison garden come back to life, their buds unfurling with new petals. In this new year, 1891, her grief had hardened, like a stone that sat heavily beneath her sternum. The mental fog she'd been wading through for months began to dissipate, and her purpose became clear: spend two more months behind bars, and then hunt Corcoran down.

Annie did not sleep at night. Instead, she stared at the ceiling, making patterns and shapes out of the water stains. One resembled an elephant, another a skull. She saw the ghost of Emma's outline, lying bloodied in the corridor, even in the darkness. If Annie shut her eyes, she feared she would succumb to melancholy and grief, which would pull her down into its dark depths. Instead, she nursed her anger until it burned hot like a flame.

On a chilly Sunday morning in March while she sat making lace, Annie observed Bessie move about the women's courtyard. Bessie didn't take the small, delicate steps of a refined lady constricted by her whalebone corset; instead, she walked with swagger, swinging her arms and taking long strides. Annie watched how Bessie led with her shoulders. She would have to unlearn everything she'd been taught in order to gain entrance where she wanted to go.

In her year at San Quentin, Annie's fellow inmates had become her teachers. Bessie's confidence, Maud's cunning, May's resourcefulness—she would need each of these qualities to survive. Even Mary Von's nastiness could come in handy. But she could not think of Emma's kindness without feeling as though the pain in her chest might suffocate her.

When April arrived, and with it, clear blue skies and warm days, Annie was ready. A year behind these walls had changed her—her innocence gone, her spirit hardened. She was no longer the young maid full of hope. Asking Winifred Sweet for help had not brought Emma justice. Annie would need to seek it herself. And this time, she would use more than a pen.

On her final day as inmate number 13475, she hugged May, Bessie, and Maud goodbye. Though there was little hope of another life for the older convicts like Julia or Bridget, Annie believed Bessie would roam the western mountains and plains again, her spirit fierce and free. Perhaps May and George would marry and start a family. And Maud, who'd been a pickpocket since childhood, would find her way. She was wily, but she had a soft side.

"Don't forget us," Bessie said, waving as a guard walked

Annie away from the Porch. "And don't you dare come back here."

Annie smiled. "I won't. I promise."

With her back turned, she felt her throat tighten, listening as the women clapped and cheered for her. Perhaps she'd never see them again. This chapter of her life was now closed. But she would never forget them. Together, they had endured something awful. In a holding room near the visitors' area, she received her carpetbag containing her dresses and her sisters' letters, along with the five dollars every convict was allotted upon their release.

The money she'd saved so diligently while working for Mrs. Whittier was gone. She had suspected as much; her employer was spiteful. And yet, seeing her empty coin purse brought on a wave of panic. The prison guard, a man named Jenkins, led her down the corridor, through the visitors' area, and then through the gate leading to the world outside. He tipped his cap.

"You're free to go."

Annie stood rooted to the ground, blinking in the April sunlight. To be allowed to do as she pleased, no longer under the watchful eyes of the guards, the captain, or the matron, felt strange. Then the gate clanged shut behind her, San Quentin releasing her from its clutches. And so, she walked down the narrow dirt road, past a cluster of cottages adorned with gingerbread trim and climbing vines that sat overlooking the San Francisco Bay.

She descended the wooden stairs leading to the ferry dock, where a steamboat waited to take her to San Francisco. But there would be no going back to the life she left behind. Without Emma, she had no future, no friend in the world who could understand what she had been through, what she had suffered. Nora, Ellen, and Kathleen felt like figments of her imagination, or characters she'd once read about in a book.

When the boat deposited her at the ferry depot, Annie felt overwhelmed by the sounds—hoofbeats, cable-car operators shouting—and the multitudes of people. Here, at the foot of Market Street, horse carriages clattered over cobblestones, zigzagging between cable-car tracks. Clutching her bag, Annie lifted her skirts and crossed the width of East Street, which curved along the water's edge. Ship masts bobbed in the harbor beyond.

She'd forgotten it all—the gulls cawing, the smell of horse dung, the clang of cable-car bells, the newsboys chanting. Market Street was a busy thoroughfare, lined with the finest hotels west of New York and with fashionable shops, their striped awnings and window paint boasting dentists, booksellers, carpets, cigars, and patent agencies. Annie passed women dressed in silk, wearing fashionable mutton-sleeve dresses and large feathered hats. Now they looked to her like a foreign species. Why had she wanted to become such a woman?

Turning left onto First Street, Annie spotted the Selby Shot Tower up ahead. Two hundred feet tall and made of brick, it was the most prominent structure south of the Slot. She knew of Irishmen who worked inside the shot factory, heating lead until it was molten, pouring it through a strainer until perfect round bullets hardened and cooled. Clenching her jaw, she thought of Corcoran, of the bullet she wished would find him.

The street narrowed and darkened, and when Annie reached Natoma, in the shadow of the grand hotels, wooden rowhouses crowded together, their backs nearly touching as well as their sides. She was south of the Slot now, among the horse stables, narrow alleys, machine shops, and breweries. Laundry flapped on lines strung between slanted homes with gabled roofs, and children in tattered clothes ran amuck, shoeless.

By the time she reached the corner of Third and Mission, Annie was sweating. But she'd finally spotted a sign in a shop window: LODGERS, INQUIRE WITHIN. In this run-down building, she hoped to go unnoticed. Boarding with a family would require too much intimacy—meals around a table, questions into her past. Pushing open the door to the shop, she stepped inside, looking around at the wares, dry goods, onions, potatoes, whole chickens.

A woman at the register brushed a strand of frizzy hair away from her face, her cheeks flushed, her expression harried.

Annie cleared her throat. "Good day, ma'am. Are ye the landlady?"

"Aye. Mary O'Farrell. Can I help you?"

"Yes, please. I'd like a room."

Mary O'Farrell, a plump Irishwoman in perhaps her mid-thirties, looked her up and down.

Annie straightened her back. She wore her calico day dress, which had been laundered so it was clean, and she carried nothing but a single bag.

Mary O'Farrell frowned. "Are ye new to the city?"

"Yes. I've just arrived by train. From Boston."

Poor Irish girls arrived in San Francisco every day. They

settled here, south of Market Street, where half of all residents were foreign-born and families crowded ten to a flat. Annie jutted out her chin, daring this woman to question her further.

Mary nodded. "I've only a hallway room left. It doesn't get much light."

"That's all right."

"Rent is one dollar a week. The toilet is at the end of the hall."

Mary unlocked the door to a small, dark room with a battered wooden bedstead, a single chair, and a lamp with a foul-smelling wick. There was no wardrobe—only a row of nails tacked into the wall for hanging clothes. A washstand with a pitcher and a cracked bowl stood in the corner, beneath a dirty window sealed shut. But Annie didn't intend to stay here long.

"It'll do." She reached into her coin purse.

Mary O'Farrell frowned. "Your name?"

"Bridget O'Neill." Annie placed a silver dollar in Mary's palm, her false name rolling easily off her tongue. "I'll pay for the week."

———◆———

IN THE WORKINGMAN'S quarter, Annie learned how to become invisible. At a secondhand shop, she sold her best Sunday dress along with her velvet hat and kid gloves, which she'd once loved. Because she feared she would run into Ellen, Nora, or Kathleen and also feared they may have read about her arrest in the newspapers, she avoided the area around Saint Patrick's Church.

When she walked the neighborhood, Annie stuck to back alleys, where rats ran wild behind the freight depots and railway sheds and factory chimneys belched smoke into the air. She walked Third Street all the way to the waterfront, where piers reached out to the scows and schooners bringing in bricks and cement, lumber to be milled, grain for the South End warehouses, and hay for the horses. At the edge of Mission Creek, she discovered "Dumpville," where men lived in shanties and sifted through refuse for anything of value—cans, cloth, bottles, utensils. It was a lawless area, blood polluting the waters from Butchertown to the south.

Annie no longer relied on Mrs. Whittier's home for her meals, her parlor, and her bed. She dined in cheap restaurants on Shipley Street and sipped whiskey in saloons. Among the undertakers and lead works, street urchins scurried about, picking up bits of junk. Annie learned how to pocket things unnoticed—a derby cap, a coat left aboard a trolley, a shirt from a clothesline. Before long, she had an entire men's outfit, complete with trousers and boots.

A week after her arrival, Annie tucked her tangled hair inside a flat cap and smudged her cheeks with dirt. She looked at her reflection in the cloudy mirror above her cracked basin and saw a hollow-cheeked young laborer with wiry muscles and flinty eyes. No one in Mrs. O'Farrell's boardinghouse paid any attention to her comings and goings. As Bridget, she was just another forgettable Irish face. She slipped out of her room and into the darkness, walking north until she crossed Market Street.

On Kearny Street, Annie kept her head down, walking with long, purposeful strides and swinging her arms. In Chinatown, houses of prostitution and dives lined every squalid alley, and immigrants crammed into tenements. Taking a deep breath, she kept going, past opium dens, brothels, and gambling houses, her body tense and ready. But Bessie had been right. It was easy to move about the city dressed as a boy. Nobody spared her a second glance.

She recalled every bit of information she'd stored away:

Corcoran meets them in a booth at the Bella Union.
The Living Flea, the Red Rooster, and Bottle Koenig's are
*   where you'll find the best dancing.*
Now, she's a bit o' raspberry.

But Annie didn't take Corcoran as the type to go dancing. He would be looking for a *bit o' raspberry*, a pretty girl to sate his needs. Turning left onto Jackson Street, Annie ventured toward Dupont. in search of the infamous bordellos she'd only heard about.

First, she passed the Living Flea, where a wooden sign hung, an insect lying in a bed of flowers. A few doors down at the Red Rooster, a cast-iron rooster painted brilliant scarlet held a red light burning in its beak. Piano notes carried from inside the bordellos while girls called from their upstairs windows, "Only fifty cents for a French girl, gents!"

Annie couldn't spend the few dollars she had left to gain entrance—it was far too risky. Instead, she waited in the shadows, watching the comings and goings of the men who entered. Some dressed in suits and some in bib overalls, but none had Corcoran's height or his red hair. Tired and frustrated, she returned to her boardinghouse.

The next night, Annie tried again, this time lingering outside the Olympic, the Pacific, the Adelphi, and Gilbert's

Melodeon. Crowding the narrow streets were throngs of drunken men, some dressed in top hats with diamond stick pins, others in bowler hats and dirty trousers. Annie thought she spotted Corcoran, but she hadn't. Anytime she felt a pair of eyes lingering on her, she snorted and spat on the ground, wiping her mouth with the back of her hand. She could not show weakness or fear. It would get her killed.

After eleven nights in San Francisco, Annie waited outside the Bella Union Theater, her hands in her trouser pockets. She was beginning to worry she would never find him. Below the theater marquee, a sign boasted the words:

PLAIN TALK AND BEAUTIFUL GIRLS!
REALLY BEAUTIFUL GIRLS! LOVELY TRESSES!
LOVELY LIPS! BUXOM FORMS!

She clenched her jaw. Her money was dwindling. She'd sold her last good dress and paid admission last night to both the Adelphi and the Olympic, searching the crowd of revelers for the face that haunted her dreams. He wasn't among them. Annie had bought one beer, and then another, sipping from her glass while stewing in her frustration.

Now, on all sides of her, men laughed and shoved one another, raucous with drink and excitement. They bumped shoulders and sang bawdy songs. The Barbary Coast was a men's playground, where girls dressed in silk posed like mannequins in bordello windows, winking at potential customers. Annie shifted her weight from foot to foot. It was nearly midnight, and she was tired. But then she gasped, a sharp intake of breath.

There he was. Corcoran stood with a group of men, only a

few yards from her, where he and his friends had paused to gather outside the Bella Union Theater. He wasn't in uniform, but the sharp planes of his face were unmistakable, his red hair slick with pomade, the ends of his mustache waxed. Annie's stomach felt oily with fear. Then Corcoran threw back his head and laughed, like he hadn't a care in the world.

Her skin felt clammy. She remembered the look on his face when he shoved her against the stone wall of her prison cell— Emma's rapist, Emma's killer. Seething with anger, she steeled herself. Suddenly, the theater doors swung open, and cheers rose from the crowd. Annie kept her eyes firmly on Corcoran as she followed the men inside.

Head down, she paid the fifty cents admission, then walked through a large barroom with crystal chandeliers hanging overhead into the theater itself, a domed auditorium with globe lights sparkling on the ceiling, curtained boxes circling the balcony. Annie hung back while Corcoran and his friends ascended the stairs, then entered a private box on the right.

The orchestra began to play, and men reeking of sweat and alcohol filed into the cheap seats on the mezzanine floor. With her hat pulled low, Annie stuck close to a pair of teenage boys dressed in workmen's clothes, who took their seats to the left of the stage. She couldn't quite catch her breath. Now that she'd seen Corcoran, every fiber of her being was on alert. The lights dimmed, and the velvet curtain lifted. Annie waited, her heart pounding.

After the first few musical numbers, the pretty girls who'd taken the stage emerged into the audience carrying bottles of claret, whiskey, and champagne. They had performed so poorly, it became apparent that they weren't hired for their vocal talents. Annie noted their bloomers and chemises, their black stockings, their corsets, rouged lips, and kohl-rimmed eyes. She stood from her seat, following one of the pretty waiter girls up the stairs in the direction of Corcoran's booth. Her pulse thrummed. The waitress, a petite blonde, reached for the velvet curtain, pulling it aside. But the men behind the curtain weren't Corcoran and his friends.

Annie's stomach twisted. Continuing to climb the stairs, she searched for him. Up ahead, a stage manager gripped the wrist of a petite brunette, hissing at her, his teeth bared.

"If you want to get paid, make them drink like fish."

The girl nodded, her bottles clinking.

His face was red and sweaty. "Do whatever it takes to make the sale. We don't allow stingy customers at the Bella Union. Understand?"

"Yes," she whispered.

The stage manager released the girl's wrist, and Annie watched as she transformed her features, like putting on a mask. She pinched her cheeks, then pulled aside the heavy curtain of the private box to her right, a smile playing at her lips.

"Good evening, gents. May I interest you in a bottle of claret?"

Behind the curtain, Corcoran slumped lazily in his seat, his shirt unbuttoned, his legs splayed. Annie sucked in her breath. Her chest tightened.

Corcoran smiled like a snake.

"Well, aren't you a jammy bit o' jam. Come here, sit on my lap."

The girl hesitated, but only for a moment. Smiling, she sat down. Instantly, Corcoran's hands moved to her buttocks and squeezed. She flinched.

"Now, now," she said, her voice like honey. "Not until you've bought something."

Heart pounding ever harder, Annie feared she'd lingered too long. Turning around so her back was to Corcoran, she strained to catch snippets of his conversation.

"You lost, boy?"

A man with bloodshot eyes leered at her. He was muscular and bearded and had a pistol tucked into his waistband. Fearing her feminine voice would betray her, Annie shook her head, then darted past him. She pushed through the crowd of men milling about and quickly exited the theater, gulping in the cool night air. But she would come back here, every night if she had to, until she found Corcoran again.

———◆•—

"Good evening, gents! Are you ready for a grand old time? We are the melodeon for the people, with a program that's enough to make a blind man see. Our girls are the loveliest in the world—no back numbers here!"

Annie flattened herself against the wall. It had taken her another week to formulate her plan. And tonight, she snuck backstage, found a dark corner among the ropes and pulleys, then shed her coat and trousers like a snake shedding its skin. It was warm inside the theater, but she shivered in her bloomers and chemise. Her corset was French, the finest she could afford, purchased back when she thought such garments would be an essential part of her wedding trousseau, so she could unwrap herself like a gift for Albert.

And tonight she wore it for Corcoran. Laughter and jeers rose from the audience at regular intervals. Annie listened to the comedian onstage, creeping forward until she saw Corcoran's face in the crowd. Tonight he had arrived without his friends. But he wasn't in a private booth. She would need to think on her feet, to find a way to get him alone.

Heart hammering, she waited until the curtain fell, watching as the waiter girls appeared backstage, fragrant with cigarette smoke and perfume. Annie stood as still as a statue, praying no one would notice her. There were close to twenty girls, and in the shadows, she moved unseen. Turning toward the dressing room, Annie was aware of every breath passing through her. A stagehand in suspenders looked at her, his brow furrowed.

"You're new."

"Yes," she said, trying to force the Irish from her voice. "I am."

He nodded at her. "Go on, then. Get your liquor."

She went in the direction he had pointed. The bottles were lined in rows along the wall of the dressing room. Annie bent down and grabbed two, avoiding her reflection in the mirrors surrounding the room. There was no time now for hesitation. She trembled as she took her place in the queue of dancers. When she stepped out into the bright lights of the mezzanine, she searched for Corcoran. Then she spotted him, making his way toward the stairs.

The bottle necks sweated in her palms. She wanted to run but forced herself to smile, hips swaying as she walked.

"Miss, I'll take a bottle of—"

Annie ignored the man who'd spoken. The minutes were ticking past. She could see the back of Corcoran's head, his broad shoulders. Two men had exited their private booth, leaving the curtain open. Annie's pulse pounded in her temples as she climbed the stairs. She was nearly to Corcoran now. She breathed in through her nose, feeling the air fill her lungs, then set her bottles down. Reaching out, she grabbed Corcoran's hand.

He spun around, his eyes glassy. Her stomach clenched, every instinct telling her to run. Annie fought the urge to scream. She forced a smile.

"Care for a drink, handsome?"

He leered at her. "Well, aren't you pretty."

For a moment she feared he would recognize her. But he did not. She was a chorus girl, a waiter girl, here to please him. She nodded at the vacant box.

"Let's have some privacy."

He laughed. "You're a bold little tart, aren't you?"

Annie bent over so he could see the swell of her breasts while she retrieved her bottles of whiskey and claret. He followed her into the private box. She looked at him, at his red hair and thin lips, his mustache, his forearms flexing beneath his rolled sleeves. She watched a bead of perspiration roll down his neck into the collar of his shirt. She gave him a coy smile.

"Shut the curtain."

Corcoran did as he was told, shrouding them in darkness, the noises of the theater muffled. Annie had ten minutes, perhaps fifteen at the most, until the men who had paid for the private booth would return. She fought to keep her voice calm, holding up the bottle of wine.

"May I interest you in some claret?"

Corcoran licked his lips. "No, I know exactly what I want."

Annie pushed him backward before he could accost her, and he fell into the velvet chair, startled. She sat down in his lap, her legs splayed on either side of him, her breath hot on his cheek. He was disoriented, unaccustomed to a woman being so forward.

Her heart ticked like a bomb.

"A dollar for a shot of whiskey, and you can have whatever you like."

27

Judy

San Francisco, 1972

'I 've just spoken to the district attorney," Ellen says, hanging up the phone. "We'll get your belongings out of police evidence."

I try to suppress my hopes because I don't want to be disappointed. But it's been a week since Ellen agreed to take on my case, and she's already making progress.

"When can we get them?"

"Today." Ellen smiles. "Your bag is still booked so it can be dusted for prints. But you're authorized to pick up your photographs, negatives, and paperwork."

"Oh, that's great," I say, a weight lifting from my shoulders. "You don't know what this means to me."

She winks. "No client of mine is going to miss their graduate school application deadline because of needless red tape."

I shake Ellen's hand, clasping it in mine. "Thank you so much. I appreciate you and all that you're doing for me."

Ellen squeezes my hand. "You're stronger than you know.

You're capable of anything you put your mind to, Judy. And Tony isn't going to hold you back anymore."

At the police station, I show the clerk my driver's license and she gives me back all twelve of my prints, my transcripts and letters of recommendation, and the canisters containing my film negatives. My eyes well with tears as I inspect my photographs and paperwork. Nothing has been damaged, and I still have time to mail in my graduate application to the San Francisco Art Institute and the three other schools.

Leaving the police station on Bryant Street, I feel lighter. Ellen has spoken with me about filing a restraining order against Tony. It hurts, thinking about pushing him out of my life with such authority, but I refuse to be under his thumb any longer. Ellen has helped me see that Tony's jealousy and paranoia, his constant criticism of me, and his thwarting of my professional goals are warning signs of emotional abuse.

She's warned me that if Tony contests the divorce, then we will go to court. I don't want Tony's money, but Ellen says I should fight for my share of our assets. And then there's the issue of Tony's potential arrest—Officer Jones and Officer Martinez told me to buy a tape recorder, and so I have. I'm ready to use it if Tony calls me again. I've practiced what I'll say to him, to coax out a confession. My grief has hardened into anger, but still, I'm so nervous. In the meantime, I've been carrying the recorder around with me to interview local business owners.

I walk the length of Bryant and then turn left on Seventh, thinking about Klockars Blacksmith on Folsom, and Schrader Iron Works on Harrison, both businesses that are more than seventy years old. The owners told me about how they share their tools and skills with the community, and of their admiration for people who work with their hands. There's so much pride here among the skilled laborers who live and work in South of Market.

By the time I reach Natoma Street, my legs are tired, and I can barely climb the steps up to my apartment. Inside, I check the answering machine, but there are no voicemails. Taking out a notepad and a pen, I hit play on my tape recorder so I can transcribe my interviews.

Already, I can imagine my photographs of these blue-collar workers in a gallery, with their interviews giving context to their pictures.

"We're not sure what the future is going to hold. We still sell nails by the pound."

"I'm a sculptor, and I've lived south of Market Street for fifteen years. Now the construction of the Yerba Buena Center means I have to move."

"The way things are going, it's all downhill. The cost of living will become astronomical."

"I like working with my hands and I love being by the water. Here, south of Market Street, this is the backbone of the city."

I think about the photograph I took yesterday of Becky Johnson, a short-haired woman in denim overalls and a tank top, sanding a sailboat down at the waterfront. I like the phrase she used in our interview, *the backbone of the city*. It encapsulates how the industry south of Market Street powers San Francisco's five-star hotels and restaurants. This neighborhood may not be glamourous, but it's essential.

The telephone rings, and I pause the cassette tape. My stomach twists. Tony could be calling me. With shaking hands, I eject the tape and carefully insert a blank one. The phone is still ringing. No, no—what if he hangs up? Quickly, I rush to the kitchen and pick up the receiver, setting down my tape recorder on the counter.

"Hello?"

"Judy . . . it's Tony."

My stomach lurches. It's the moment I've both been waiting for and dreading. Taking a deep breath, I recite the lines I've practiced.

"Why are you calling?"

He sighs. "I just want to say sorry."

Without hesitating, I press record and hold the cassette recorder close to the receiver. I'm so nervous, it's hard to make my voice sound natural.

"Sorry for what, Tony?"

His voice breaks. "I never meant for you to get hurt."

I swallow the lump in my throat. "The police think you paid the man who robbed me. They say you wanted me to be scared so I'd come home. Is that true?"

My heart is thudding. Tony never admits his mistakes.

"Judy . . ."

"I understand," I say, forcing the accusation from my voice. "I mean, I know you miss me. I know it hasn't been easy."

Tony's breath shudders.

"I'm so, so sorry."

He hasn't admitted anything. I try to remember the woman I was when I still loved him. I need to become her again, to get a confession.

"Babe," I say, softening my tone. "I don't want to go to the police. The officers, they don't know you like I know you." I sniffle. "Just tell *me* the truth, please?"

Tony sighs. "He wasn't supposed to be rough."

"You mean the guy you hired? He wasn't supposed to be rough? He had a knife, Tony. I was really scared. He slammed me up against a dumpster."

"Asshole," Tony growls. "Fucking idiot."

I feel cold all the way to my core. Tony is angrier with the man he paid than he is with himself. And he had the audacity to call me afterward, to ask if I was okay.

"Why did you do it?"

My heart is beating so fast, I brace myself against the kitchen counter.

He sighs. "I just wanted to scare you a little. All right? I miss you so much. I thought if somebody made you want to leave . . ."

"Then I'd come back to you."

Tony grumbles. "It was a stupid idea, okay? I was drunk."

My shoulders slump. "You're drinking again."

His voice rises. "I'm lost without you! I slipped up."

I speak slowly and clearly. "Tony, who did you pay to rob me? The police are looking for him. They want to arrest him, not you, okay?"

"Judyyyy." Tony draws out my name in a singsong voice.

"Don't worry about him. He's just a guy I know. He'll never bother you again."

"How do you know that?"

"Because he drove all the way to Mexico. The cops will never find him."

I nod. "Congratulations, Tony. You've just admitted to solicitation. You asked someone to commit a crime, and he committed it."

He scoffs. "Whatever. It's your word against mine, sweetheart."

I smirk. "Actually, I've recorded this conversation."

Tony sucks in his breath. "You bitch!"

His words hit me like a gut punch, but after this, Tony won't be able to insult me anymore. I have the power to have him locked behind bars.

"Listen," I say, "I don't have to share this evidence with the police. But I've already hired a lawyer, and you will agree to a restraining order and a divorce."

"Judy, I don't think—"

"I don't care what you think," I say, my voice flat. "You don't make decisions for me anymore. You can go to jail or never come within one hundred yards of me again. You decide."

———— • ————

BY THE TIME I meet Mark at the library, I've made peace with the fact that Tony will no longer be a part of my life. Still, I grieve for the person I was and for the loving marriage I'd hoped to have. For a while, Tony and I really cared about each other. My mother will be devastated when she finds out I'm divorcing Tony and choosing to live on my own in San Francisco. But it's 1972, the women's rights movement is swelling like a tidal wave, and I'm not going to be married to a felon.

Mark smiles when I approach his desk, looking dapper in a collared shirt.

"You can't stay away, can you?"

I laugh. "Why would I want to?"

He blushes and rubs a hand through his messy hair.

"What can I help you find today?"

"Well." I smile. "First of all, I have news."

He raises a dark eyebrow. "Oh yeah?"

"The lawyer who's helping me, she got my portfolio back." I grin. "I can still apply to the MFA program at the San Francisco Art Institute."

Mark throws up his arms. "Judy, that's great!"

He comes around the side of his desk and wraps me in a hug, smelling like clean laundry and spicy aftershave. "I'm so proud of you."

I lean into Mark, grateful for our friendship. "Thanks."

Thinking back to our very first meeting, I remember how lost I felt showing up here at the San Francisco Main Library, grieving my separation, and giving Mark a few details about Annie's mug shot. I remember apologizing for my messy handwriting—Tony made me feel like I had to apologize for everything—and how Mark told me I'd found an interesting story in Annie. Now I'm close to discovering how her story ends.

As for my own, I still need to decide whether I'll turn the recording of Tony over to the police. I want him out of my life, but that doesn't mean I want him suffering in jail. If anything, he needs therapy for his problems and his drinking. But I also don't want him to hurt other women the way he's hurt me, and maybe he deserves his consequences. I will never fold his laundry again, wash his dirty dinner dishes, or cook him another meal. Instead, I will pursue the things I find intellectually and creatively stimulating.

While Mark is helping me look for newspaper articles mentioning San Quentin in the year of Annie's release, 1891, I'm downstairs, where I thank the reference librarian who has set me up with several volumes of *Langley's San Francisco Directory* from the 1890s. Each one is four inches thick, a combined Yellow Pages and White Pages of its time. When I open the front cover, I'm fascinated by advertisements for chimney sweeps and boarding schools. In the table of contents, there's an alphabetical register of names, followed by local businesses.

This directory, its pages stained as brown as a coffee filter, shows San Francisco's working-class roots. It's filled with lamplighters, gas fitters, longshoremen, cooks, dressmakers, and glassblowers. There are so many Irish last names—Ahern, Fitzgerald, Flanagan, Fogarty—with occupations like blacksmiths, laborers, peddlers, sailmakers, engravers, saleswomen, bartenders, wharf builders, marble polishers, butchers, upholsterers, and shoemakers.

Knowing they lived and worked south of Market Street makes me feel proud of my neighborhood. It's time to make my little apartment really feel like home. I can go antiquing with Seth and his partner for furniture and decorations. I can invite Vanessa over for a bottle of wine. I can ask Michael for interior design advice, and I can meet up with his friends who are

passionate about historic preservation. I can visit Hope, Nathan, and Ken in their SRO hotels, bring them groceries or
buy them coffee, and make sure they're okay. I can even re-
create a smaller version of my vegetable garden, planting tomatoes in window boxes.

When I reach the letter *G* in the Langley directory, my
stomach sinks. Trailing my finger down the page, I find a
Gilmartin, Bridget, and *Gilmour, Rose,* but no *Gilmurray, Annie.*
I set the 1891 directory aside and pick up the year 1892. Again,
I find nothing. The 1893 and 1894 directories don't have Annie's name listed either. I even check the *K* section for "Kilmur-
ray" but only find a few men. Suddenly, an image comes to
mind—the newspaper illustration of Annie sitting next to
Emma, working on a piece of Irish crochet lace.

Turning to the business section of the 1895 directory, I
hold my breath. There are bankers, benevolent societies, and
barbers, even a California society for the suppression of vice.
But I'm not looking for jewelers or junk dealers. I'm looking
for lace makers. And then I see it—*Emma's Lace. Proprietress,
A. O'Reilly. 2981 Adeline St. Berkeley.*

I gasp.

Returning the directories to the librarian, I ask for a current issue of the Yellow Pages, my heart hammering. But I try
to quell my excitement. The business name Emma's Lace could
simply be a coincidence. A. O'Reilly might not be Annie at all.
The lace business probably closed in the eighty-year span between then and now. And, even if it *were* Annie's business, too
much time has passed. She would be 102 years old.

"Sorry," the librarian says, shaking her head. "I couldn't
find a copy of the Yellow Pages. Someone may have taken it."

"That's all right," I say. "Thanks for looking."

I make my way back upstairs to tell Mark about my discovery. I'm sure I can easily find another copy of the phone book in a pay-phone booth or at a local business. When I locate Mark, he's in the back room with the microform readers, an article already pulled up on the screen.

"Hey," I say, smiling at him. "What did you find?"

He pushes his hair out of his eyes. "Nothing about Annie, yet. But, this article mentions a former San Quentin Prison guard, dismissed for smuggling opium."

"Oh," I say. "That sounds like it could be interesting."

Taking a seat in front of the machine, I scoot closer. My eyes dart to the article, and I suck in my breath, recognizing the name of the prison guard as Emma's rapist. Covering my mouth, I can't believe my eyes. It looks like poetic justice was served.

FOUL PLAY SUSPECTED AT THE BELLA UNION: DAVID CORCORAN POISONED

———◆◆———

28

Annie

Berkeley, 1891

The ferry docked in Oakland, the choppy waters of the San Francisco Bay shrouded in fog. Annie disembarked, and then she walked the short distance to the railroad depot, carrying her carpetbag. She had two dollars left to her name, enough for a week or so in a boardinghouse. But among her possessions were her crochet hook and a spool of cotton thread, her most powerful tools. Emma's words rang clear in Annie's mind.

I'd sell my lace to the fine ladies of San Francisco.

Emma's young life had been taken from her. But Annie had survived San Quentin, and she would honor her friend's memory. In Berkeley, she got off the streetcar at the Shattuck Avenue station. Downtown comprised a small cluster of buildings, a bank, a hotel, a boardinghouse, a general store. The air was warmer here, the May breeze pleasant.

Annie had heard land was cheap and plentiful in Berkeley, where undeveloped tracts of farms, fields, frog ponds, orchards, and dirt roads spread for miles beneath a clear, blue sky. Walking up the unpaved road, she looked at the rolling hills, the shady oaks, the eucalyptus and the bay laurel trees. It felt as if she were a continent away from San Francisco.

Though her Bertillon photograph had likely made it into mug books throughout the state by now, Annie would not give the police a reason to search for her. She had been careful. And she would continue to be wary and cautious for the remainder of her life. In her hand, she gripped a copy of the morning paper, *The San Francisco Call.*

Sitting down on a bench in front of the general store, Annie unfolded the newspaper and took in a sharp breath. Finally, the article had been printed. She began to read.

FOUL PLAY SUSPECTED AT THE BELLA UNION: DAVID CORCORAN POISONED

May 10th, 1891

Coroner McMullen last night conducted an inquest on the remains of David Corcoran, a former San Quentin Penitentiary guard, who early in the morning of May 4th, began to convulse at the Bella Union Theater. Dr. Henry W. Wagner, a physician who attended to Corcoran before his death, and chemist Crackborn, who analyzed the contents of Corcoran's stomach, testified that his death in the hours following resulted from morphine poisoning.

Crackborn, who is a chemist and druggist, said the analysis showed morphine had been found in the stomach. Before death, Corcoran showed signs of slow and labored breathing, and highly constricted pupils. It is believed he ingested the morphine while drinking whiskey at the popular Bella Union melodeon at 805 Kearny Street.

Samuel Tetlow, proprietor of the Bella Union Theater, was the first witness called. Of the eighteen "pretty waiter girls" employed by Tetlow, not a one recalled serving Corcoran his two fingers of whiskey. Tetlow himself did not witness what occurred within the privacy of the curtained booth where Corcoran was found. Two businessmen, Arnold Jenkins and Winston Jones, had paid for the booth, and received quite a shock when they returned from intermission to find it occupied. They alerted Tetlow, who called the police.

Witnesses Jenkins and Jones have been cleared of any wrongdoing. It is apparent these gentlemen do not know David Corcoran and did not arrange his poisoning. Witness Samuel Watson, a guard at San Quentin Penitentiary and a friend of the deceased, stated he and David Corcoran had been drinking together at the Dew Drop Saloon on Broadway in the hours prior. C. Pieri, who conducts the Dew Drop, where Corcoran drank a coffee punch at eleven o'clock at night, prepared the drink with a teaspoon of sugar, two fingers of rum, and black coffee. Pieri said he saw Corcoran put nothing in the cup, and that he seemed cheerful.

Watson concluded that the deceased intended to become a member of the San Francisco Police Department, and that he had "pull" with the police chief. A week before his death, Corcoran bought a new suit of clothes and seemed very pleased with them. He did not appear like a man who contemplated suicide.

George K. Nagel, a police officer, was the next witness called. He was going up Kearny Street and was called into Samuel Tetlow's establishment, where Corcoran was in violent spasms. The jury in bringing in a verdict gave the following statement: "We, the jury, find that the deceased came to his death on May 4th, from the effects of poison either administered by himself or by parties unknown to us."

Annie shut the newspaper and set it down beside her on the bench. She heaved a sigh. No one suspected her. It would be safe to remain in Berkeley. Yet her hands were shaking. She clenched them tightly in her lap, trying to calm her nerves. She could still feel the small amber glass vial, how cold and hard it was pressed against her sternum.

Morphine had been easy to obtain. She'd gone to several pharmacies around San Francisco, complaining of a persistent cough, insomnia, or the pain of her monthly cramps. The chemists were helpful, eager to prescribe the drug. In her rented room at Mary O'Farrell's, Annie crushed the pills until they were as fine as sugar grains, enough for a lethal dose.

She remembered her fright that night—the blood pulsing in her veins, every minute passing with the knowledge that the gentlemen who'd vacated their private booth would soon return. Corcoran had paid for a shot of whiskey. Lust glittered in his eyes as he slipped a crumpled dollar bill into the top of her silk stocking. She'd observed the girls on the balcony of the

Red Rooster long enough to know how to slowly roll it down, how to pull it off.

——— •◆• ———

CLOSE YOUR EYES, she'd whispered, tying the black stocking tightly around Corcoran's head, blindfolding him. *Allow me to serve you.*

He'd laughed, leaning back, his hands clasped behind his neck.

I like the sound of that.

Her heart thudded as she poured his whiskey. Could he see what she was doing? She didn't have time to deliberate. Annie dipped her finger in the alcohol, then traced his lips with her fingertip, wetting them. He sucked her finger into his mouth and she shuddered, every instinct imploring her to release it. Then he reached down and rubbed his cock.

You little tease.

Annie removed her finger from his mouth. Now was the time, when he was blind and distracted with desire. She pulled the morphine vial from beneath her corset, uncorked it, and poured its contents into his whiskey glass, watching as the powder dissolved—odorless. Her pulse hammered. She allowed him to run his hands up and down her thighs as she shoved the empty vial back inside her bodice. Then she removed his blindfold.

Drink up, handsome.

Corcoran grinned, assured of himself and his place in the world. He believed he could take exactly what he wanted, with no repercussions. Annie held her breath, watching as he accepted the whiskey glass, smiling as he drank the poison down in a single gulp. He wiped his mouth with the back of his hand. Then he grabbed her buttocks and pulled her roughly into his lap. He licked his lips.

I'm going to ride you raw.

Annie held his gaze. *The last time you tried, I choked you with a length of padding cord, and then I stabbed you with my crochet needle.*

Corcoran's face contorted, his lascivious grin falling away. His eyes narrowed, then widened, as he recognized her, the pallid, malnourished San Quentin inmate now a confident, kohl-eyed, rouged woman before him. Annie picked up his right hand and traced the moon-shaped scar in the webbing by his thumb.

See? You still bear the mark.

He bared his teeth.

You . . . nasty, miserable bitch.

He lunged for her then, but when he brought his hands to her throat, his grip slackened. He began to sweat, appearing confused, his eyes wide with panic. Annie knew morphine was ten times more powerful than opium, that it was hailed as a miracle drug, but in large quantities it had the power to kill. She watched as Corcoran's pupils constricted to pinpoints.

He struggled to stay upright, his breath labored and shallow. She removed his hands from her throat, and they fell limply at his sides. He slumped in his seat, his head lolled to the right. His breath sounded wet and heavy.

I can't . . . breathe. What's happening . . . to me?

Annie whispered in his ear.

Morphine poisoning. You'll never harm another woman again.

Nearly ten minutes had passed since they'd entered the curtained booth, but Annie needed to know Corcoran's fate was sealed. Intermission hadn't yet ended; she could hear theater patrons talking and bottles clinking. Annie watched his body fold in half as he fell from his chair to the floor. Bending down, she looked into his drugged eyes.

Feeling drowsy?

His lips had taken on a bluish tint. Annie picked up his limp, clammy hand and looked at his fingertips. They were drained of color, like the fingers of a corpse.

She whispered in his ear.

Your death won't be painless. You'll spasm with seizures.

Corcoran seemed as though he wanted to speak, but his tongue wouldn't cooperate. He began to shake violently. Annie grabbed him by the hair, lifting his head off the floor and forcing him to look at her.

This is for Emma. Now, go to hell.

Releasing him, she watched his jaw smack against the ground. Then she slipped out of the private booth, shutting the curtain behind her.

———◆◆———

PUSHING THE MEMORY of Corcoran away, Annie picked up her bag. Up the dirt road, she could see a few hotels with horses out front. As she walked in that direction, she recalled a sermon Father Peter had given at Saint Patrick's Church.

Repay no one evil for evil, but give thought to do what is honorable in the sight of all.

Perhaps Corcoran had been mistreated as a child, unloved,

or cast aside. And yet, she hadn't found it in her heart to forgive him. Was it honorable to have ensured this man would never harm another woman? In her mind, it was.

———◆———

INSIDE HER SMALL room at the Acheson Hotel on the corner of Shattuck and University, Annie listened to the horses as they stomped and whinnied, tied to their hitching posts below. She removed her belongings from her carpetbag—her calico dress, her crochet needle, and her lace, along with all the letters her sisters had mailed.

Her chest tightened as she looked at the pile of worn envelopes. Today she would write to them. She would tell them she had changed employers, and there would be no further explanation. It hurt, so very much, to conceal a year of her life from those she loved. But Annie would make good on her promise. She did not intend to become a returned Yank, sailing home to the Emerald Isle. Instead, she would bring her siblings here, one by one.

Reaching into the depths of her bag, Annie retrieved the lace cuffs Emma had been working on before she died. They were ethereal—as delicate as fairy wings. The contents of Emma's prison cell had been turned over to the warden. But Annie had asked one last favor of May. And May's beau, George, had stayed true to his word, smuggling the cuffs out of Warden McComb's office and into Annie's hands.

Now, though her friend was gone, she had a piece of her to keep. Annie pressed Emma's lace cuffs against her face, remembering the whisper of her friend's last breath.

Let them grow.

She hoped Emma's soul was at peace, her spirit walking among the wildflowers of County Mayo. Annie would bloom where the winds had blown her. On these distant shores, she would set down roots. Her past would not define her, though it had altered her forever. Yet here, in this rural town, she could envision her future: a wooden gabled house on a sleepy patch of farmland, her lace creations in the windows of a shop, facing the wide, curved street.

Sitting by the hotel window, Annie looked out across the bay at Mount Tamalpais. She could smell the brine, even though she was several blocks from the Berkeley pier. How strange that she could still see this very same green mountain, serving as a reminder of her year in San Quentin. It was comforting in a way, a silent witness to her sorrow.

She picked up her thread and her crochet needle. Her fingers moved deftly, transforming the fine cotton thread, as thin as a strand of hair, into motifs of delicate roses, shamrocks, and leafy vines—with nothing more than her crochet hook and her memories. The rhythm came to her now as easy as breathing.

When she first arrived in America with nothing more than a dream, she never intended to make lace as a means of survival. She was naïve, hopeful, lured by the promise of fool's gold. Albert—she thought he would be her salvation. But instead of bettering her station in life, she fell to the very depths of hell.

Perhaps a different word, a different choice, and none of it would have come to pass. Could she have changed her fate? Annie held Emma's face tight in her memory, the original lace maker. Her dear friend. Cruel mouths branded them cruel names: irredeemable, wanton, incorrigible. But they were beautiful in their resilience, wild roses refusing to be trampled.

God would decide if Annie was innocent or guilty, whether what she did was murder or justice. She hoped he would understand, that she did what she had to do. She thought of them all, Bessie, Maud, May, and Emma, women lost and forgotten behind San Quentin's walls. She heard their voices, their tears, and their laughter, even now.

Though she would never again speak of that time, she knew an unbreakable thread still connected them. Like Irish lace, their stories were forever entwined.

———◆◆———

29

Judy
Berkeley, 1972

'm buzzing with anticipation as I drive across the Bay Bridge to Berkeley. It only takes me twenty minutes, and by the time I park on Adeline Street, next to a Mission Revival–style building with a facade that mimics the curve of the road, I'm hopeful. Yesterday, I looked through a current issue of the Yellow Pages, and I found a business listing for Emma's Lace, its address similar to the one I found in the 1895 copy of Langley's directory.

I park and step out of my car. This is a quaint business district, made up of antiques stores, a candy shop, and a delicatessen. Across the street, vendors sell clothing, jewelry, and incense from their flea market stalls in a parking lot. I take a deep breath. Emma's Lace is housed within a clapboard building from the turn of the century, with lace wedding dresses on display in the bay windows. I take a moment to admire them, their scalloped sleeves and long trains intricately crocheted. Then I push the door open, my heart hammering.

A red-haired woman in her mid-thirties looks up from behind the counter and smiles. "Hi! Welcome to Emma's Lace. My name is Alice. Can I help you?"

There's lace everywhere—lace wedding dresses and veils, lace gloves, lace collars, lace cuffs, bins of vintage lace trim. There's also every kind of lace-making tool available: wooden bobbins; bone, abalone, and rosewood crochet hooks; needle pins. I walk over to one of the bins and pick up a delicate lace cuff. It's as light as air, the fine mesh crocheted with motifs of shamrocks and tiny three-tiered roses. I drape it over my hand, envisioning how beautiful it would look on a dress sleeve. Then I realize I haven't prepared what I'm going to say. Instead, I smile, avoiding Alice's question.

"This is gorgeous."

She grins. "It is, isn't it? That piece is antique."

I nod, my stomach full of butterflies. "Are you the shop owner?"

"I am now." She gestures toward a gold picture frame sitting atop a table by the entrance. "This business was started by my grandmother Anne."

"Oh," I say, sucking in my breath.

"She died ten years ago," Alice replies, her eyes sad. "But she lived a full life. I'm honored to carry on her legacy."

I approach the table, looking at Anne's photograph, and I bring my fingers to my lips. I can see traces of Annie Gilmurray in this woman's face, her long white hair hanging over her shoulder, a constellation of wrinkles framing her bright blue eyes. She looks content, but there's a fierceness in her piercing blue gaze that's unmistakable.

I would recognize those eyes anywhere. My throat tightens

as I see the newspaper article in a silver frame, propped up next to Annie's picture. It's her obituary.

ANNE O'REILLY:
THE LEGACY OF BERKELEY'S LACE MAKER

Anne O'Reilly, who emigrated from Ireland, and later paid passage for all nine of her younger siblings to join her in America, was the beloved founder of Emma's Lace. She died on June 17th at Alta Bates Hospital of heart failure. She was 92.

Anne was born in Ballycroy, County Mayo, and had described her childhood as impoverished, where she lived in a rural mud-walled hut and learned how to hand sew her own dresses from flour sacks at a young age. Then as a teenager, she met Emma O'Sullivan at a country fair, who taught her the traditional art of Irish crochet lace.

"She was so patient," Anne told *Creative Needle Magazine* in an interview. "She would have me practice my stitches again and again. When I emigrated to America, Emma stayed in Ireland. But we wrote to one another regularly, and she remained one of my dearest friends."

Unfortunately, Emma's young life was claimed by tuberculosis. Grieving, Anne quit her position as a maid for a wealthy family, and spent six months crocheting collars, cuffs, christening gowns, and bridal veils to raise the money she needed to rent a storefront in Berkeley. It was a risky move for a young woman in 1891, but

Anne had an entrepreneurial spirit. She sold her lace creations by word of mouth while living in a boarding-house.

A year later, Anne met her future husband, Sean O'Reilly, a laborer. They married in 1892 and had three children. Anne's original storefront on Adeline Street, Emma's Lace, opened in 1895, in a shop so narrow, you could practically touch both walls with outstretched arms. But Anne didn't need much. Accustomed to the frugality of her youth, she had become enormously resourceful. No piece of thread was ever wasted.

By 1896, Anne expanded her shop when the build-ing next door became available. Her business had become successful, and she needed more space. Irish crochet lace was experiencing a renaissance, its popu-larity peaking in Paris, London, Rome, New York, and San Francisco. In 1897, *The Delineator* magazine noted that Irish crochet laces "have returned to vogue after a long period of retirement."

Anne trained her children and her husband in the art of Irish lace, so she could keep up with the demand for gowns, blouses, and coats, which were fashionable among the Parisian elite. But soon, she also hired em-ployees. After the 1906 earthquake, Berkeley's popula-tion swelled with thousands of refugees arriving from San Francisco. In the newly thriving streetcar suburb, Emma's Lace found itself stationed along the electric streetcar route, its windows visible to passengers riding to and from Oakland and San Francisco.

Jane Ahern, Mrs. O'Reilly's daughter, said her mother

was a patient teacher. "She was never cross with us. She had a way of making her children feel special."

"She loved learning new skills," her son Patrick O'Reilly said. "She collected, designed, taught, and wrote about historic forms of Irish crochet lace."

"I miss her," said her son William. "She had a way of bringing people together."

Emma's Lace became an influential center in the textile community. Trends would come and go, but Anne stayed true to her specialty, the traditional art of Irish Clones lace. She taught classes in the story of Irish crochet and the technique she learned from Emma, a unique interpretation with its own distinct character.

"I believe," Anne said in her interview with *Creative Needle Magazine*, "that one of the peculiarities of Irish lace is it comes to life by the hands of its maker. It can be knotted into shapes so various and extraordinary that to examine each motif becomes a study not only of lace, but of people."

Anne O'Reilly is survived by her children, William O'Reilly of Oakland, Patrick O'Reilly of Berkeley, and Jane Ahern of Berkeley, and her seven grandchildren.

I turn my back to Alice so she won't see me cry. What strength and resolve it must have taken Annie to earn enough money to start her business from nothing.

"Feel free to look around," Alice says.

Nodding, I venture deeper into the store, a treasure trove of lace collars, handkerchiefs, stoles, bodices, veils, fingerless gloves, bonnets, wild roses, masks, and wedding gowns.

I understand now that Annie had a beautiful life. Knowing her husband was a laborer, I believe she married for love, not money or status. From the way her children spoke about her, it's apparent they were very close. And to think she brought every one of her nine siblings over to America. That in itself signified an incredible feat. I imagine Annie's home in Berkeley, filled with siblings and cousins and nieces and nephews, children and grandchildren.

But I'm most fascinated by the way she rewrote her story, changing the facts about Emma while keeping a core truth— her love for her friend. Did Annie's husband ever know about her time in San Quentin? Maybe that part of her life was too painful to reveal. I look over at Alice, humming happily behind the counter, and I decide not to tell her why I'm here. Annie's secrets are hers alone. It is not my place to reveal them.

I choose a piece of vintage lace to purchase. It's an Irish collar with large leaf and flower trim, the thread so fine and the mesh so intricate, I can't believe it was made by human hands. It has lightly raised motifs, roses and lilies.

"I'd like to buy this," I say, placing it gently on the counter.

Alice smiles, her eyes shining. "You chose well. That was made by my grandmother."

"Oh," I say, taken aback. "Are you sure you want to sell it?"

She nods. "My family and I have so many examples of her best work. Many of her lace pieces are framed on the wall at my dad's house."

"That's lovely."

Alice smiles. "My dad took over the family business before me. His sister, my aunt Jane, became a doctor. Grandma Anne saved up so Jane could go to medical school. She was the first in our family to go to college."

My eyes well with tears. Annie, a maid who'd come from a mud-walled hut in rural Ireland, had sent her daughter to medical school in America.

I look at Alice, hoping she can feel the integrity of my words.

"Your grandmother was an incredible woman."

BACK AT MY apartment in San Francisco, I take one last look through the mug book Seth lent to me. Tomorrow, I'll give the book back to him. I don't need Annie's photograph anymore. I've seen her as a ninety-year-old woman, a mother, a grandmother, a successful business owner, beloved among the community. Holding the piece of Annie's crochet lace that I bought today, I feel a connection to her, able to touch the art she made with her very own hands.

Maybe discovering Annie's mug shot was fate. Or maybe it was my own agency—being brave enough to move alone to San Francisco, to interview for a job I wanted, to separate from my husband. I think of Annie's words, written in her obituary.

. . . to examine each motif becomes a study not only of lace, but of people.

Annie's story of resilience is a testament to the power of the human spirit. She made me look inward, study myself, and see what I'm truly capable of. Like Irish lace, my imperfections are what make me unique, what make me beautiful. I don't know what my future holds, but I know that if I have even a sliver of Annie's courage, then I will be lucky.

EPILOGUE

———◆———

▬▬▬▬

PHOTOGRAPHER JUDY MORELLI DOCUMENTED
THE CHANGING FACE OF SOMA

By Kristin Barnes, *San Francisco Chronicle*, 2015

In 1972, Judy Morelli was a 25-year-old aspiring photographer, recently separated from her first husband. One afternoon, Judy photographed Hope Carson in her room at the Hotel Rex. She didn't know it then, but that portrait would be the first of 80 to form her picture book, *Backbone of the City*, which spans the years 1972 to 1982, before anyone called South of Market "SOMA."

"I was new to the city and alone, but I became interested in the redevelopment of my neighborhood, which I credit largely to my husband, Mark, who was actively involved in TOOR at the time (Tenants and Owners in Opposition to Redevelopment)," says Morelli, now 68, who has been priced out of San Francisco's South of

Market neighborhood and currently lives with her husband, Mark Chen, 70, in Berkeley.

When she moved into her flat on Natoma Street in 1972, rent was $150 a month, and Judy had taken a photo-processing job at Glass Photo on Sixth Street, so she could access the darkroom. The owner, Seth Glass, became her mentor, encouraging her to develop her own photographs and to define her style. When he showed Judy an antique mug book he'd bought at a flea market, she was captivated by an 1890 mug shot of a young Irish immigrant.

"Annie Gilmurray's portrait inspired me to take Hope's portrait. I wanted to show the humanity of the people living south of Market Street, a working-class neighborhood that has served the city for generations. Hope, like many, was seen as expendable. In my time living on Natoma Street, I watched as my neighbors were pushed out by redevelopment."

The project Judy started in the 1970s, photographing the last of the elderly residents in their SRO hotels, the emerging gay community, the blacksmiths, machinists, casket makers, and lunch counter operators, would become *Backbone of the City*, and also her master's degree thesis at the San Francisco Art Institute. But it wasn't until decades after the Moscone Center and the Yerba Buena Center were completed that people truly began to take notice of her work.

"When the South of Market neighborhood looked unrecognizable, full of soaring glass skyscrapers with names like 'Millennium Tower' that no one could afford, suddenly my photographs drew a lot of interest," Judy says.

The tower, a 58-story $350 million skyscraper with multimillion-dollar condo units, was completed in 2009 and is now mired in scandal, literally, as it is sinking and leaning to the side. But Morelli's moving photographs of SOMA, the way that it once was, offer a retrospective moment for a city undergoing yet another sea change with today's tech boom.

"San Francisco is about big business," Judy says. "But we need to redistribute wealth to create affordable housing, or we'll lose the diversity and art that make San Francisco great."

In 2009, Morelli was offered a book deal for her series of South of Market photographs. Next came a show at the San Francisco Museum of Modern Art, followed by another show at the De Young Museum. Both museums bought prints. She currently has a permanent exhibit at Nova Gallery in the Dogpatch.

"It took many years for my work documenting South of Market to be recognized," Judy says with a smile. "But in the meantime, I raised a beautiful daughter, my miracle baby, and taught photography."

Judy Morelli is being humble. She also received a National Endowment for the Arts grant, became a Getty scholar, published new books of photography, and is recognized both nationally and internationally. At the Chen home in Berkeley, her photographs spanning the decades adorn the walls.

For our interview, Judy sits barefoot on her

mid-century modern sofa. She's effortlessly cool, relaxed, and chic. Her husband, Mark, drapes his arm around her shoulders.

"Judy has always been ahead of the curve. The way she sees the world made me fall in love with her. She's not slowing down anytime soon."

ACKNOWLEDGMENTS

———◆◆———

Thank you to my phenomenal literary agent, Jenny Bent, who changed my life with our first phone call back in 2015. I'll never forget the joy and excitement I experienced that day, and I feel lucky to call myself one of your clients. My gratitude extends to everyone at the Bent Agency.

To my editor, Cassidy Sachs: it is such a joy to work with you. Thank you for believing in this book, the strong women at its center, and for illuminating the stories of those pushed to society's margins. You have shaped this story into something beautiful, and I could talk and laugh with you over Zoom for hours.

I'm also grateful to my former editor, Stephanie Kelly, and to the entire team at Dutton, who gave me the green light to begin writing this book back in 2021, believing its themes were timely.

Thank you to Emily Mahon, who designed my gorgeous book cover, as well as Christopher Lin, Sarah Oberrender, and the Dutton art team. To Diamond Bridges in marketing, thank you for your enthusiasm and your tireless efforts promoting *The Incorrigibles.*

When I came up with the idea for this book, it was in response to California's housing crisis, which continues to impact the lives of millions. Decades after San Francisco bulldozed thousands of homes in the name of redevelopment, many Bay Area working families still struggle to meet their basic needs.

The following books were indispensable to my research: *City for Sale: The Transformation of San Francisco* by Chester Hartman, *The Irish Bridget: Irish Immigrant Women in Domestic Service in America, 1840-1930* by Margaret Lynch-Brennan, *Painted Ladies Revisited: San Francisco's Resplendent Victorians Inside and Out* by Elizabeth Pomada and Michael Larsen, *San Quentin Inside the Walls* by Nancy Ann Nichols, *South of Market* by Janet Delaney, and *No Vacancy: Urban Renewal and the Elderly* by Ira Nowinski. The August 1926 edition of the *South of Market Journal* was also a great source of inspiration. I included direct quotes in the novel from the article "Memories of the Past" written by George W. Paterson.

I was heavily pregnant with my second child while researching *The Incorrigibles,* and I am so grateful to everyone who helped me.

To Heather Powell, collections manager at the Marin History Museum, thank you for allowing me to look through both the turnkey's log and the complete register of San Quentin Prison inmates from 1889. I loved seeing the names of the female prisoners I had researched. To Jeff Craemer, curator of the San Quentin Prison Museum, thank you for taking the time to show me around and to share stories behind the prison artifacts with me. While it was fascinating to see so many objects used by the male inmates, I would love to see a larger exhibit featuring the women of San Quentin State Prison.

Several occurrences in the novel are based on real historical events and figures. For the sake of the story, I have taken creative liberty with both the timeline and the characters. Mary Von, Mary Martin, Ada Werner, Maud Manner, May Johnson, and Jean "Bessie" Barclay are all based on real people. Mary Von attempted to murder the prison matron in 1888, and Mary Martin purportedly hypnotized Ada Werner in 1895, willing her to set fire to her prison cell. Bessie Barclay was imprisoned in San Quentin in 1909, not 1890, but I found her too compelling not to include in my novel.

Emma O'Sullivan is inspired by Emma Williams, who was rumored to be impregnated by convicted rapist James "Fat Jack" Kiley, whose sentence was commuted by the governor from fifty to fifteen years.

The websites https://cdcr.ca.gov (California Department of Corrections and Rehabilitation) and https://cdnc.ucr.edu (California Digital Newspaper Collection) allowed me to piece together details of these women's lives, shaping the events that took place in *The Incorrigibles*.

Thank you to the University of California, Berkeley, Bancroft Library for allowing me to access the Jesse Brown Cook scrapbooks and the San Quentin Prison records from 1885 to 1892.

To the employees of Lacis Museum of Lace and Textiles in Berkeley, you have such a special store. Thank you for allowing me to look through examples of 1800s Irish crochet lace and for providing workshops with Màire Treanor to keep the art of Irish Clones lace alive.

Thank you to California Genealogical Society member and volunteer Pam Brett for your valuable insight into how my character Judy might have researched before the advent of the internet. And to Sarah Brett McIntire, nonprofit affordable housing developer (and my BFF since seventh grade!), thank you for helping those in need and for being an incredible friend.

Finally, to my family. Will, I wish the Bay Area were an affordable place to live on a writer's salary. Thank you for supporting us. I know it's not easy. Hazel—you amaze me every day. Baby Willie, you bring me more joy than I ever could have imagined. Maple, you're the craziest dog we've ever had, but we love you anyway.

Mom, thank you for letting me research your side of the family, so I could use the name of your great-grandfather, Henry Gilmurray, who was born in Ireland at the start of the potato famine. Carolyn, you are the best sistow and I'm so happy you moved back to the Bay.

To the readers, librarians, booksellers, bloggers, BookTokkers, and literary community, thank you from the bottom of my heart. I love meeting you, talking to you, and getting emails from you. Your support means the world to me.

ABOUT THE AUTHOR

Meredith Jaeger is the *USA Today* bestselling author of *The Dressmaker's Dowry, Boardwalk Summer,* and *The Pilot's Daughter.* Meredith was born and raised in Berkeley, California, and holds a BA in modern literature from the University of California, Santa Cruz. She lives outside San Francisco with her husband and their two children.